Falling

An LA Love Story

Book One

L.M. SKYE

Content Warning

This book contains adult themes and depictions of drug and alcohol addiction, which may be distressing for some readers. Please approach the content with care. If you or someone you know is struggling with addiction, consider reaching out to a professional or a support network for help.

www.fallinglalovestory.com

Print Edition ISBN: 979-8-218-53615-2

Cover Design by Cole Gordon

For those who have loved another with their whole heart.

Chapter One

The doorbell rings, and I know it's him. I take a deep breath and inspect myself in the mirror one last time. *Relax, relax, relax,* I tell myself as I make my way down the stairs. I take another deep breath, trying to steady my racing heart and the fluttering in my stomach.

James Hunter, my illicit crush, who also happens to be my boss, is here to pick me up for our first date.

My hand quivers as I reach for the doorknob. "Hi," he says, greeting me with his irresistible smile when I open the door.

"Hi…" I manage to respond before my mind goes blank.

He runs his fingers through his lush, wavy brown hair and waits for me to continue.

"Oh, come in!" I react, failing to match his cool demeanor.

"You look beautiful," he says, stepping inside and taking a long look at me. It took me forever to decide what to wear, but I chose a slinky, cream-colored Tom Ford mini because it highlights my tan from lying out by the pool and contrasts nicely with my chocolate-brown hair.

"Thanks," I say, admiring how effortlessly hot he looks in jeans, T-shirt, and a leather jacket.

"Um, do you want a drink before we go?"

"Sure," he says, maintaining my gaze. I lead him through the long hallway that stretches through the house to the kitchen and the adjacent den. My brother Max and his girl-friend Michelle are on the couch watching a movie.

"Yo, what's up, man!" Max sits up to greet James.

"Hey, what's up!" James says, approaching him for a fist bump. He greets Michelle and pauses to inspect Max's braced leg propped up on the ottoman. "How ya' feeling, man?" He gives Max a concerned look.

Max used to DJ at Light, James's nightclub, until a knee injury from playing basketball forced him to quit two months ago. His misfortune became my lucky break, landing me a DJ gig at the club.

I walk toward the bar and announce that I'm making drinks.

"Fuck, that's one hot man," Michelle whispers in my ear as she joins me behind the bar. I shake my head, cheeks burning, and shush her under my breath. "So, tonight's the big night, huh?" she continues in a whisper.

I meet her ice-blue eyes, unable to contain my smile. "Yes, and you have no idea how badly I need *this*," I say, pouring two vodka shots and handing her one. She smiles, and we clink glasses, taking them down in a gulp. I look over at James and Max, talking and laughing.

"I swear, Annie, if I didn't love your brother so much, I would be all over *that*," Michelle says, looking toward James with a naughty smile. I know she's joking, and we both giggle.

"Here, help me with these," I say, handing her two freshly poured vodka sodas. "Your *boyfriend* must be thirsty," I tease her.

I hand James a drink and sit on the armrest of his chair. The room feels like a sauna, so I get up and slide open the pocket doors leading to the backyard and the pool. The cool breeze is refreshing, and I sigh with relief.

"So, who knew my little sister would be killing it as your new resident DJ," Max says.

I shoot him a look, cringing inside.

"Yeah, she's pretty good," James answers, looking at me, grinning. "Thanks for sending her my way."

I shake my head, hiding my embarrassment behind a smile. When I return to my place on the armrest, James places his hand on my knee, and a rush courses through me as his fingers brush against my bare skin.

"Don't be humble, Annie," Max says, sipping his drink, "You should be proud; you learned from the best!"

"Ha-ha," I respond dryly, rolling my eyes, and they all laugh. Max loves to remind me that his DJ lessons paid off handsomely for me with a coveted Friday night gig at one of LA's hottest nightclubs. Who knew one night of filling in for my brother and playing my favorite music would lead to snagging the best DJ gig in town… and now, a date with the club's sexy owner.

The four of us continue to chat and drink our cocktails. I made mine extra strong, hoping the damn butterflies that have been torturing me all day will stop.

"We have an eight o'clock reservation," James says, looking at his watch and then at me.

"Oh, okay, we should get going," I respond, standing up.

"Have fun, you two!" Michelle says with a teasing hint in her voice after we say our goodbyes and walk out of the den.

"We'll catch your set next Friday night, Annie!" Max adds.

The clicking of my heels sounds extra loud in the quiet hallway as James and I walk in silence. I grab my Goyard tote with my laptop and headphones for my DJ set later tonight from the foyer table as we head out the door.

We hit the streets of Beverly Hills in James's sleek, black Porsche 911. It's a perfect April night, with a gentle breeze swaying the tall palm trees lining the streets. Despite the heavy Friday night traffic, there's a punch of excitement in the air as laughter and chatter mingle with thumping music beats from passing cars, creating a palpable buzz.

The butterflies in my stomach finally settle as the vodka has done its trick. "Your brother's a cool guy," James says, cutting through the silence.

"Yeah, he's the best," I say, glad for small talk.

"Does he live at home too?"

I look over at James, imagining him thinking we're pathetic for still living at our parents' house. "No," I say, "Max lives in the pool house!" I giggle at how silly that sounds, but the pool house is nicer than most starter homes in LA and standard housing for most young adults in Beverly Hills.

"And I'm just staying there until I graduate… I'll probably move in with my sister in Brentwood… or get my own place." I shrug.

"Oh, don't get me wrong, I think it's cool. You seem close with your family… It must be nice," he trails off, turning his attention back to the road.

I glance over at him, my eyes darting from his chiseled profile to his confident grip on the steering wheel. The damn fluttering in my belly returns as flashbacks from the past two months of our non-stop flirting and intense sexual tension come flooding back.

James looks over at me, "What are you thinking about?" His lips curl into a cute smile.

"Um, nothing!" I respond, cheeks burning as I look down at my dress, smoothing my hands over the silky fabric. He slides his hand over to mine, giving me a little squeeze.

"Did I mention how beautiful you look tonight?" His remark sends a tingle throughout my body, lighting me up inside.

"Yes… but you can tell me again," I flirt back, meeting his eyes.

He laughs, interlocking his fingers with mine. I sink back into my seat, smiling at the ease of our familiar, flirty banter, our first date unfolding as we speed into the night.

WE PULL UP TO MADEO, AND A CREW OF PAPARAZZI PERK UP across the street from the chic Italian bistro, aiming their lenses in anticipation. I giggle at how disappointed they'll be when they realize we're not their target A-list celebrities from whom they can profit.

The valet opens my door and then greets James by name. Inside, the host greets him in the same familiar manner and leads us through the lively, warmly lit restaurant packed with stylish patrons.

"Enjoy your dinner," the host smiles as we settle into a cozy corner booth, the perfect spot to people-watch.

I scan the room and notice a few famous faces at nearby tables—some of them are regulars at Light.

When it's time to order, James selects a vintage bottle of wine and an array of decadent Italian dishes. We ease into conversation, only pausing when the food arrives and when the server stops by to refresh our wine.

"I've been waiting a long time for this, Annie," James says, locking his intense brown eyes with mine.

"You have?"

"Yes, couldn't you tell?" He takes my hand, and his touch sends an electric rush through my body again. I smile, delighted that I can finally bask in his affection out in the open.

"I've been waiting for this moment since the first time I saw you. You came into the club, and you were wearing a little black dress that was off the shoulder... wasn't it your birthday?"

My smile widens, nodding because that's how I remember our first encounter, too.

"Your hair was loose like this..." he says, playing with the ends of my hair, "And your smile lit up the room. I asked around who you were, and when I found out you were Max's little sister, I knew I was in trouble."

I nudge him, feigning offense. "Trouble?!"

He throws his head back and laughs. "I don't know... I consider your brother a friend, and I didn't want it to be weird if I asked you out."

"I don't think that was the only reason it would've been weird if you asked me out..." We look at each other, and I know he knows what I'm talking about.

"Warm chocolate cake and berries," the server interrupts, placing a gorgeous dessert in front of us. We've been talking and laughing for almost two hours.

James and I admire the dish, and he scoops a piece of cake and brings the spoon to my lips. The cake's sweetness and the berries' tartness create a perfect symphony of flavors. I savor the bite as he takes one himself.

"You have a bit of chocolate here..." he says, narrowing his eyes on my lips while gently rubbing my bottom lip with his thumb. My cheeks flush, and I fidget in my seat, breaking eye contact. James leans closer to me, softly grabbing my chin. I shift my gaze to his mouth—he pulls me in like a magnet.

I close my eyes and surrender to the moment, finally knowing what his lips feel like on mine after weeks of wondering.

It's better than I imagined.

James rests his hand on my knee as we kiss. His fingers slowly make their way up my thigh and linger under the hem of my dress. My heart races as I pull him in closer. I don't care that we're at Madeo; everyone else in the room disappears as we remain lip-locked.

"Mmmm," he says under his breath as we slowly pull apart. Our eyes meet, and he reaches for my hand under the table. The server appears before us and asks how we're doing. We straighten up, and James drapes his arm around my shoulder and requests the check while I bite my lip, relishing the sweetness of our first kiss.

IT'S AFTER TEN AS WE SPEED TOWARD LIGHT ON THE SUNSET strip. I'm already late for my set, which goes from ten to midnight.

"Finn is going to be *so* pissed," I say, referring to DJ Adam Finn, who spins before me from eight to ten.

"Nah, Finn's cool," James says, squeezing my knee. "I'll tell him it was my fault."

Within minutes, we pull into the club's parking lot to find the usual crowd of chic party girls in sexy little dresses and handsome industry types exuding quiet luxury vibes. Everyone's chatting and laughing, waiting in line to get in. Light is the hottest nightclub in Hollywood since opening four months ago and the hardest to get into.

James and his business partner and best friend, Oliver Roy, have created a stylish nightclub with a relaxed atmosphere that caters to A-list celebrities, cool social media influencers, and industry moguls. The décor is sexy and warm, with dark wood, rich leather furniture, and gorgeous indoor palm trees that give the place an exotic and uniquely LA aesthetic. The guest list is tight, and the small club is always at capacity.

"Whoa," James says as he surveys the growing line, shaking his head. "This is fucking nuts!"

We drive past the crowd and pull into the valet line around the back of the club. The valet shakes James's hand and greets me with a friendly smile when I step out of the car. James holds my hand as we walk past the VIP line, saying hello to people along the way. Rob, the head of security, greets us at the door and reports that it's "bananas inside."

When we enter the moodily lit, intimate VIP room, we're met with more beautiful people and loud, pulsating beats bouncing off the walls. Along the way, James stops to greet friends and a few regulars, flashing his gorgeous smile and welcoming them.

As I hold onto his hand, weaving through the crowd, I notice some stares, mainly from the cocktail servers and a few of the regular party girls who flirt with James relentlessly. I used to watch these girls from afar, throwing themselves at him, thinking they were so pathetic. I never imagined I'd be caught under his spell, too.

"Finally! DJ Annie Preston in the house!" Oliver says, greeting me with a hug and James with the kind of handshake that dudes give each other, accompanied by a shoulder bump.

"What's up, man," James says over the music.

"I didn't think you guys were making it tonight," Oliver says, leaning into us with a teasing smile. Oliver stands slightly shorter than James. His beachy blond hair and green eyes contrast James's darker, brooding look, but they perfectly complement each other's style and personality. Their charm, confidence, and business savvy make them a force to be reckoned with.

"This is a sick crowd!" James responds, changing the subject.

"Yeah, craziest night so far," Oliver says, turning to me with a playful wink, "I think they're all here to see Annie."

"Oh, I'm *so* sure!" I laugh, turning toward the DJ booth, eager to start my set. James grabs my arm, halting me mid-step, and pulls me in, kissing me on the lips.

"I'll come by in a bit," he smiles.

I nod, and then it hits me, *Holy shit. We've gone public.*

Chapter Two

Cell phone cameras flash in the crowd, capturing selfies and cute group shots of friends while a hint of marijuana smoke lingers in the air, mixing with laughter and bits of conversations under the thumping beats of the hip-hop song I'm playing.

I look up from my laptop after cuing my next track and feel the rush emanating from the dance floor as bodies sway closely together under a kaleidoscope of lights to the signature sounds of my set. It's moments like these that make me glad to have badgered Max into giving me DJ lessons. I never imagined that those evenings after dinner, spending hours in the pool house with him would lead to some of the most fun nights of my life. I also never imagined that Max would ask James to let me take over his DJ gig when he got injured.

Despite my hesitation, nerves, and crippling self-doubt, I agreed to a one-time gig after Max assured me that I was ready to do a full set on my own. He was very convincing and guaranteed it would be "a piece of cake."

He was right, and I'm glad that the first night went so well that James asked me immediately after my set to fill Max's spot indefinitely. The gigs are a blast and the perfect way to let off steam from my stressful last semester at UCLA. They've also been a much-needed respite from all the drama surrounding my recent breakup with my ex, Joe.

As I turn my attention back to my laptop to select the next tracks, I look down at my phone and see a couple of missed texts from my sister, Angela:

> I'm at Darren's having drinks. Joe's here with Ruby Kirk. We're all heading to Light soon. I just wanted to give you a heads-up.

My mood instantly dips as I reply:

> He knows I'm here tonight! He's coming with her to piss me off!

Angela texts back:

> Well, he's got a surprise coming to him!

Joe and I broke up three weeks ago, and everything is still raw and complicated.

I take down the rest of my drink, hoping to ease the building anxiety in my chest and scan the dance floor and the surrounding tables. I spot James working and charming the crowd. He's an amazing host and the secret sauce for the club's success. His knack for making people feel special is part of his charm—I've experienced this firsthand.

James looks at me from across the room through the flashing club lights, and we make eye contact. He gives me a smile and a nod, and I casually wave back. My stomach tightens, remembering that Joe, who has no idea I'm now dating James, will be here any minute.

I cue my last track and spot Angela, Darren, Joe, and Ruby Kirk—the blonde, voluptuous starlet Joe is dating to torture me. I watch them take over my VIP table, which I was planning to share with my sister and our friends tonight before I knew Joe would be joining.

I take a deep breath and fumble with my laptop as I wrap up my set. I can't wait to get out of the booth and *the fuck* out of the club.

DJ Marcus is preparing to take over for the night's closing set. He's cuing his first track to come on after my last song ends. "You rocked it tonight, Annie," he says, hugging me. Marcus is one of LA's star DJs and another reason Light is the hottest place to be on Friday nights.

I hug him back and thank him before grabbing my Goyard with my DJ gear, ready to make my escape. As I step down from the booth, I feel a hand grab my arm from behind.

"You were great," James whispers in my ear. I turn around, relieved to see him and pull him in for a deep kiss.

As James and I pull apart, I feel a tap on my shoulder. I turn around, and Angela stands before me, looking hot as ever in a sexy little black dress. We hug, and she whispers in my ear, "PDA much?"

"You know my sister—Angela…" I say, turning to James, ignoring her comment.

"Of course, how are you?" He greets her with a hug. "Are you alright over there? Annie told me you guys were coming, so order whatever you want. It's on the house," he says, glancing at the corner table, from which I can see Joe staring at us.

"Cool, thanks, James!" she says. "Do you guys want to join us for a drink?"

"We were just leaving," I respond, glancing over at the table again, feeling Joe's stare burn a hole through me.

"Oh. Okay," Angela says, pulling me in for another hug. "You look great, have fun!" she whispers in my ear.

James catches me staring at her as she walks away. "Do you want to stay?" he asks.

"No, I want to leave," I say, taking his hand.

James stops to chat with a few people as we make our way through the crowd in the VIP room toward the exit. When we step outside, he gets caught up in a conversation with Blake Houston, a popular movie director, Hollywood playboy, and one of Light's most regular VIPs. James chats with Blake as he smokes on the patio while going on and on about his new movie. I smile and nod, pretending to listen because I couldn't care less.

From the corner of my eye, I see someone approaching. My heart drops when I realize it's Joe. I move away from James and Blake to avoid an embarrassing confrontation because when Joe drinks and parties, he gets nasty, and I'm afraid he's coming out to make a scene.

Joe is surprisingly calm when he reaches me. His blue eyes are bloodshot, and his dark blond hair is adorably messy. He's in head-to-toe black, and I hate to admit that he looks good despite the fucked-up state he's in.

"You weren't going to say hi?" he says, taking his hands out of his pockets and pulling out a pack of cigarettes. His voice is raspy like he's been chain-smoking. He puts a cigarette to his lips and lights it while staring into my eyes.

I hold his gaze, tensing up. "You have some nerve showing up here after what you did last time," I respond, trying to remain steady.

Joe takes a long drag from his cigarette. "Come on, Ace. You won't answer my calls or texts. How else am I supposed to talk to you?" he says without breaking eye contact.

I scoff at his answer and his audacity for using his loving nickname for me at a time when there's anything but love between us.

"I guess it's because you're with *him* now..." He looks away, glancing toward James.

"And you're with Ruby Kirk, so...?" I snap back.

He breaks into a sly grin and takes another drag. "She's just a friend," he shrugs. His smugness infuriates me.

I look over at James, and he's shaking Blake's hand. He walks toward us and doesn't say anything to Joe, blankly staring at him. Joe takes another drag from his cigarette and ignores him. The tension is thick, and my stomach is in knots. I turn to James and say, "Let's go." He takes my hand and starts to pull me away, but I can't resist looking back at Joe, still smoking and staring at me.

"It's cool, Annie, we'll talk later!" he yells as I keep walking. I squeeze James's hand, and he squeezes back. We get into his car and drive in silence for a few minutes.

"How about a drink at my place?" he asks when we hit the first red light. I nod, and we speed down Sunset and up toward the hills.

Chapter Three

We pass through a stately gate and into the curved driveway of a gorgeous, Spanish-style villa high in the hills over Sunset Boulevard. The ride was quiet. The encounter with Joe rattled me, and I can't get him out of my head.

James leads me into his sexy bachelor pad, which is every bit like him. The house is sparsely decorated with rich leather furniture and warm wood accents. The main living room has floor-to-ceiling glass pocket doors that open to the pool and the backyard.

We step outside, and I gasp, admiring the sweeping views of Los Angeles as Hollywood twinkles and buzzes below us. The one bad thing about living in the Beverly Hills flats is that we don't have these views!

James takes off his jacket, revealing toned arms and broad shoulders outlined under his crisp, white, cotton tee. "I hope I didn't cause any trouble for you tonight...." he says.

I look at him and shake my head. "No, why would you say that?"

"I noticed how tense you got when he showed up—you looked upset. I should've told the door guys not to let him in after what he did last time..." his voice trails off. "I didn't want to make things worse.... But... if you don't want him back, just say the word," he says, with an assuring nod.

I move closer to him, "I don't want any more drama..." I say, putting my head on his chest as he wraps his arms around me. "Besides, that's all over, and it's fine," I sigh.

James pulls me in tighter and meets my lips for a slow, deep kiss. "You want to see the rest of the house?"

I nod, and he leads me back inside.

James holds my hand as we walk through the house. He shows me the gorgeous chef's kitchen, a cozy den with a giant flat-screen, his office, and a sitting room with glass walls and a skylight that makes the room feel like it is suspended over the hill, floating above the city. I'm getting to *know* him and falling for him harder than I expected. We make our way upstairs, and the tour ends in his bedroom—a minimal but sleek suite with another magnificent view of Hollywood.

We barely enter the room before he pins me against a wall and kisses me hard. My hands move under his shirt, meeting warm skin and firm abs. He kisses my neck and gently bites my earlobes while his hands linger on my hips. He's hard as he presses into me. The anticipation of this moment has been building between us for the past two months, and I can't wait any longer.

James unzips my dress and guides me to his bed, barely letting go of my lips. The little silk dress falls to the floor around my feet, and I'm now in his arms in only a lacy La Perla lingerie set I bought for this moment.

He gently pushes me onto his bed and climbs on top of me. He's slow and sweet, kissing my neck and my lips, moving his hands over my breasts and my belly. I pull his T-shirt over his head, and he unsnaps my bra, taking my nipples full in his mouth, one at a time, sucking them gently. I'm wet and throbbing for him.

I bite my lips and unbuckle his belt—I *need* him. He slips

out of his pants, and we're finally skin-to-skin as he continues to kiss me slow and deep. I squirm as his fingers push past my panties and slide inside of me.

"I want you," I whisper.

He slips off my panties, and I part my legs further, pulling him into me. He positions himself between my thighs and enters me, full and hard. My breath hitches as he pushes inside me. He's rough then slow, rough then slow, building a perfect steady rhythm. I wrap my legs around him tight as he sinks deeper and deeper inside me. He buries his head in the crook of my neck and scoops me underneath him with strong arms—our curves and crevices locking into each other.

He maneuvers my body on top of his, underneath him, and alongside him for long, delicious stretches. Our lips meet face-to-face again, and he presses deeper into me. I arch my hips and climax, free-falling without a net. He cums inside me because I tell him to—the words come out of my mouth hastily, but it's fine because I'm on the pill. The weight of his body, heavy on mine, feels so *fucking* good. I close my eyes and savor the feeling. He's still inside me, and I don't want him to pull out.

Our breath steadies as we slowly uncoil. He kisses me with gentle tenderness, our foreheads lightly brushing as we hold each other close.

I wake up pretzeled with James under the sheets. We have morning sex, and it's even better than last night—any awkwardness between us is gone. Instead, we're comfortable in each other's arms, affectionately kissing and caressing each other. It feels like we're long-time lovers, back to our usual banter, and he says things to make me laugh and feel comfortable.

I love how relaxed I feel in his arms, and I'm surprised

how easy it is to be with him after recently breaking up with Joe, who I was with for five years. I feel like I've really moved on.

You're in denial—a voice immediately retorts in my head. I shake it off and focus on the fact that I'm in bed with James Hunter, and it's even better than I imagined.

"I'm starving!" James announces while stretching his arms above his head, yawning big. "You hungry?" His eyes meet mine. I nod enthusiastically. "Alright, breakfast coming right up!" he says, kissing my lips before bouncing out of bed.

Downstairs, I watch him closely as he moves effortlessly in the sun-drenched kitchen—making espresso and frying bacon —his hair is still messy from sex, and a satisfied grin still lingers on his lips. "Wow, this looks amazing," I say, looking down at the plate he places before me.

"I've been told I make a good breakfast," he says with a teasing look in his eye.

"Oh, really?" I say, taking his bait, "I'm sure you have…"

He laughs, settles onto the stool next to mine at the gorgeous marble-top kitchen island, and kisses me on the cheek. I'm starving, so I dig into the eggs, bacon, and arugula salad, enjoying each bite.

We talk and laugh over breakfast, recounting last night at the club, never running out of things to say. We're interrupted when James's phone rings, and he excuses himself, disappearing into his office.

Hmmm, where is my phone? I pause, looking toward the living room. I make my way over and locate my purse on the couch, digging for my phone and discovering six missed calls and several texts from Joe:

> Where are you?

> We need to talk!

His last text is time-stamped at six a.m.

I sink into the couch, Joe's anger staring back at me. *Should I text him back? What would I say?* I consider my options, hoping for a peaceful resolution, but I know it's an unlikely outcome considering how fractured things are between us.

My heart races at the thought of a conversation with Joe because talks with him are never easy, and I know he'll lose his shit when I tell him there's no chance of us getting back together.

"Annie?!" I hear James from the kitchen. I sigh, turning off my phone and stuffing it back in my purse, pushing thoughts about Joe out of my head again.

LATER THAT AFTERNOON, JAMES AND I LAY BY HIS POOL, making out and soaking in the hot afternoon sun. We smoke a joint, listen to music, and drink a bottle of chilled rosé to cool off. I'm glad for this oasis in the Hollywood Hills where I don't have to deal with the nightmare of the past few weeks.

"Do you have plans tonight?" James asks as we lay on a lounge chair, stoned and spent from a long, deliciously lazy day. I rest my head on his chest, entwining my legs with his, and close my eyes as I take in the sound of his voice and the scent of his skin.

"No..."

"Good. How about a second date?"

I look up at him to meet his eyes. "Ooh, a second date already? You move pretty fast, Mr. Hunter," I flirt back.

"Are you kidding me? I think we have some major

catching up to do," he says, flashing me his sexy smile, which makes it hard to resist a kiss.

"Well, what do you have in mind?"

He closes his eyes and scrunches his face to think. "Mmm, I'm craving lobster, maybe prawns, perhaps a few refreshing cocktails…" My appetite awakens at the thought. "Mr. Chow?" he says, opening his eyes.

I nod, smiling. Mr. Chow is one of my favorite restaurants, and I appreciate his suggestion because I've mentioned how much I love it.

"Is that a plan then?"

"Yes, that sounds perfect," I say.

"What's wrong?" he asks, noticing my fading smile.

I look down at what I'm wearing—one of his T-shirts and a pair of his boxers—and realize I have nothing to wear.

"Maybe I should go home and change first."

He shakes his head and looks at me, saying, "No, you're not going home. That'll take forever. Just wear what you wore last night."

I cringe at the thought of wearing a *walk-of-shame* outfit at a place like Mr. Chow. "Maybe we should go somewhere else?" I say, trying to avoid a fashion faux pas at one of LA's chicest restaurants.

"No, I'm taking you to a nice dinner at Mr. Chow and…" He trails off, and his eyes light up. "Oh! Fuck! I have something for you to wear!"

He smiles big, which deepens my confusion, "What?"

"Oh," he says again, "Fucking perfect!" He stands up and holds out his hand, "Come with me." I have no idea what's going on, but I follow him anyway through the house and up the stairs.

James leads me to a cozy bedroom, which is minimally decorated like the rest of the house. He opens the door to a walk-in closet, where I find a rack of women's clothes in the middle of the otherwise empty space. The rack contains a row of dresses, a couple of pairs of jeans, and a few jackets. I'm confused, momentarily imagining that they belong to an ex or maybe some current girlfriend I don't know about.

"Whose are these?" I ask, afraid to hear the answer.

"My sister's," he says, smiling. "I told you, she's a stylist. She keeps things here sometimes. Take a look!"

I'm relieved as I look through the rack of designer clothes. "Great stuff," I say, admiring the gorgeous dresses that happen to be my size. "Are you saying I can wear something from here?"

"Of course! I don't think Lauren remembers this stuff—it's been here forever."

I grab a lacy Dolce & Gabbana black dress and hold it to my body. He nods in approval.

"Are you sure she won't mind?"

"I'm sure. Lauren won't care," he affirms.

Last night, over dinner, James told me a little about his family. He mentioned that he has a twin sister who is a stylist. That's all I know about her, but from the selection of clothes on the rack, I can tell she has incredible taste.

I try to imagine a beautiful female version of James as I stare at him. "What?" he reacts to my gaze.

"I want to see what this twin sister of yours looks like!"

He laughs and thinks for a second. "You want to see pictures?"

"Yes! And, since you say it's cool, I'm going to borrow this one tonight," I say, holding up the black lace mini-dress.

"Great choice," he smiles.

We emerge from the closet, and he pulls out a box from a dresser drawer, spreads a few pictures on the bed, and hands me one. "Back in the day before cell phones, this is how we captured memories..." he says dryly. I give him a look and a playful shove. James loves to tease me about our ten-year age gap, which always makes him sound like he's way older than thirty-two. "This is Lauren," he says, laughing at my reaction.

I take the photo and admire the stunning girl with high cheekbones, deep brown eyes, and a beautiful smile. She's definitely the female version of James. "We're fraternal, and she's older by five minutes," he says.

I love looking at the pictures: James and Lauren as kids on the beach, a good-looking young couple in a vintage BMW convertible that appear to be his parents, and a teenage James wearing a Lakers jersey courtside at a game. "These are great!" I beam, enjoying the peek into his past.

"These are my parents—Julia and Rick," he says, pointing at the smiling couple in the convertible.

"Good looking couple," I comment.

"Yeah, those were the happier days..." he trails off, staring at the photo.

"Are they still together?" I hope that I'm not prying.

"HA. No!" he chuckles. "They were *not* good together. They split up when Lauren and I were ten. I have no idea how they even lasted that long!"

I bite my lower lip, regretting my question, but my curiosity gets the best of me. "What happened?"

James turns his attention back to the photos, scooping them together and tucking them back in the box. "Let's just say Dad was a workaholic. We never saw him. And Mom... she found other gentlemen to help her feel less alone..."

"I'm sorry, James," I whisper, reaching for his hand.

"It's all good!" he says, shaking his head, seemingly unaffected. "It all worked out fine. After the divorce, my mom moved to New York with Lauren, and I stayed with my dad." He shrugs off the story, but the sadness in his eyes is undeniable. "What sucked was being so far from my sister, but she's always been a city girl, and that just wasn't my vibe. But we saw each other a couple times a year and made it work," he adds.

The thought of living three thousand miles away from Angela and Max guts me, and my heart breaks for James and his twin having to grow up apart from each other on opposite coasts.

"Lauren and I bought this house together," he says as his expression brightens, looking around the room. "She only comes out here for business, though. New York is more her scene. You'll really like her, and she'll love you," he says, meeting my eyes.

"She sounds lovely, and I can't wait to meet her," I respond.

"So, you feel better about the clothing situation?"

I nod and thank him.

"Thank Lauren! This is her room, so there's also a bunch of girly stuff in the bathroom. Feel free to get ready here if you like," he says.

"Okay," I say, pulling him in for a kiss.

Chapter Four

I shower and slip into the borrowed Dolce, which fits perfectly. I wear my hair loose and parted down the middle and do a simple cat-eye and nude lips.

Downstairs, the pocket doors are wide open, and a soft breeze blows through the house. I find James drinking a beer and smoking a cigarette by the pool in the same spot we spent most of the day. The view is breathtaking, as lights from the houses in the surrounding hills twinkle against the night sky.

"I'm ready," I say, approaching him.

He turns around and smiles. "Wow," he says, coming close.

"Wow, yourself," I reply, admiring how handsome he looks in a slim, black suit and tie he wears so well.

He grabs me by the waist and kisses me. "You look great," he says, pulling me in close.

A few minutes later, we're zooming down the winding hill in his Porsche into the heart of Hollywood.

We pull into Camden Drive and into Mr. Chow's valet line. James takes me by the hand and leads me inside. The hostess looks up, surprised. "Hi, James!" she greets him with wide eyes.

"Hey, Kim," he replies.

"It's so good to see you," she says, emerging from behind the podium to hug him. I pick up on their comfortable embrace, which leaves me with a sting of jealousy.

"This is Annie," he says, introducing me.

"We've met," she says, finally deeming me with attention. I know Kim because I've been coming here for years.

"Gosh, I've been so busy I didn't realize you were coming in tonight!" She looks flustered, returning to the computer behind the podium. "Yup, here you are!" she says, looking up at us.

"It's cool…" James shrugs. "Is my usual table available?"

Kim calls another host over and confirms that it is. "It's great to see you," she says, smiling at him while ignoring me. *Oh, they've definitely fucked,* I conclude.

"You too," he says as we follow the host to a private area in the back.

The restaurant hums with its usual crowd of cool locals, celebrities, and industry types. I make a mental note to ask James about Kim later, when suddenly, I feel a hand grab my arm as I walk past a table. I look down, startled.

"Annie?" Darren Torres, my brother's best friend and a fixture in my life since childhood, stares back at me. He stands up, cracking a smile through his perfectly groomed stubble, which lights up his handsome face.

"Oh, hi!" I react, a bit shaken. James and the host stop to watch our exchange.

"Sorry," Darren says, meeting my eyes. "I looked up and saw you walking by—I'm surprised to see you!" he says, reaching to hug me.

I relax in the warmth of his embrace. Darren is like a

second older brother; he's been inseparable from Max and Joe since we were kids.

We pull apart, and he notices James. "Oh," Darren says, and I catch the moment it registers that we're together. "What's up, James?" Darren says, extending his hand. Daren used to be a promoter at Light and has known James longer than I have. He introduced Max to James, which is how Max got the DJ gig at the club.

Darren's demeanor suddenly cools toward James, and I'm sure it has to do with all the shit Joe talks about him.

"Look who's here," Darren says, motioning to his dinner companion.

"Hi, Annie," his glamorous mother, Sharon, flashes me a bright smile as she stands up.

"Sharon! It's so great to see you. How's Dallas?"

"Fabulous as ever!" she beams. "We'd love to have you on the ranch sometime; you must come to visit!" Sharon's been a long-time friend of my parents, so I've also known her since childhood. Our exchange is brief, but it feels like an eternity. "Take care, darling, see you soon!" she says before we part.

Seeing Darren reminds me of Joe, and a hint of guilt for ignoring his texts flashes through me. I've been trying to get over our breakup, but Joe's presence haunts me no matter what I do or where I go.

When James and I settle at our table, I notice Darren glance at us a few times, curious and probably keeping tabs to share with Joe later. James notices, too, and asks if I want to go somewhere else. I assure him I'm fine—I won't let Darren spoil our second date. Nevertheless, James and I have a lovely meal, and when I see Darren and his mother leave, I finally relax.

Sometime during the dessert course, James gets a text from Oliver. "Hmm, there's a situation at Light. I need to get over there," he says, putting his phone down. We take one last bite of our mixed berry tart and head to the club.

As we enter Light, the familiar scene of LA's most fabulous people dancing, drinking, and having a great time under flashing neon lights unfolds before us. Music beats pulsate from the walls, along with chatter and laughter from the crowd.

We make our way through the more intimate scene in the VIP room, stopping every few steps to exchange greetings with familiar faces. James grips my hand, leading me through a locked door and up a narrow flight of stairs to his office.

There, we find a more exclusive and subdued party: Oliver and Ben Kaufman, James's other best friend, and four leggy models lounging around a sleek, marble coffee table. There's a mound of coke on a plate in the center, a few rolled-up bills, and a credit card scattered about.

"What the fuck?" James says, surveying the scene.

"Look at you, *fucking sharp*!" Oliver says, getting up to greet James with a hug.

"This is the *situation* you wanted me here for? You fucker!" James says, breaking into a smile. Ben greets us with a wave while the models stare at us indifferently—they look totally high.

"Grab a seat," Ben says, motioning for us to get closer. The girls shoot me looks and say nothing while they pass around a pack of cigarettes, each taking one and lighting up.

James grabs a chair and pulls me onto his lap. "You guys look good together," Oliver says, taking a cigarette while narrowing his eyes on us.

"We do, don't we?" James says, looking at me, grinning.

Oliver turns to me, "Annie, in all seriousness, this guy right here…" he takes a drag from his cigarette and exhales while pointing at James, "This guy right here is the real fucking deal

—a stand-up motherfucker, a no bullshit type of guy…" he takes another long drag. "And, it's none of my business, but whatever is going on here, I approve!" he emphatically states after blowing out a cloud of smoke while waving a dangling cigarette between two pointed fingers at us.

I giggle as James laughs and tells Oliver to shut up and cut him a line. "You want one?" James asks, looking at me. I hesitate, staring at the mound of white powder. I've never had a problem indulging in a bit of coke now and then, but after the chaos it wreaked on my relationship with Joe, I've developed an aversion to it.

"Annie?" Oliver waits for my answer as everyone's eyes laser in on me. "C'mon, I'll cut you a little one," he insists, kneeling over the mound on the table, meticulously dividing it into powdery white lines with a black credit card. He tightens a rolled-up hundred-dollar bill between his fingers and offers it to me. James gives me a gentle nudge, and I succumb, kneeling on the floor. The carpet fibers dig into my knees as I lean over the coke and inhale the line, tasting the bitter, metallic tang as the harsh powder sears through my nostrils. I pass the bill to James, watching as he mirrors my actions; his expression lights up as the drug takes effect.

I sit back as a rush washes over me, my heart rate soaring and my mood instantly elevating. Oliver, Ben, and the models each do a line, and within minutes, the girls are dancing to the music DJ Finn is spinning downstairs, the bass pumping through the speakers in the office. Oliver opens a bottle of champagne, the cork flying across the room, and soon we're all laughing, talking, and indulging in more coke. The night feels electric, our conversations blending with the music and the fizz of the champagne.

Later, Ben rolls a joint, and we pass it around. The smoke forms a hazy cloud in the room, taking the edge off the high.

"I want to go home," James whispers in my ear, balancing me on his lap, his fingers gently stroking my leg. We're alone in the office—Oliver and Ben are on the balcony with the girls, smoking and talking loudly. The music from downstairs reverberates through the floor and the walls—I'm so high that it feels like it's pumping through me.

"Okay," I nod, pulling him in for a kiss.

The ride to his house is a blur from my hazy weed, cocaine, and champagne high. We kiss at every red light, and James's hand sits on my thigh the whole way.

As soon as we enter his house, he pins me against the door, and our hands are all over each other. We make our way up to his bedroom, and what remains of the night unfolds in foggy vignettes: The taste of his lips, the sensation of his tongue—wet and warm—between my legs, and the delicious feeling of him rocking inside of me.

Chapter Five

I wake up alone in bed, my head pounding. I orient myself in James's bedroom and stumble into the bathroom, seeing double. I turn on the shower—cold—and get in, trying to revive myself from an unbearable hangover. When I get out, I feel better. I brush my teeth, put on one of James's T-shirts and a pair of boxers, and head downstairs.

It's hot and bright outside, the sun almost blinding me. I find James sprawled out on a lounge chair by the pool, wearing trunks and sunglasses. He looks over at me as I walk toward him. "Finally!" he says, "I've been waiting for you to come down all morning." There's a beer bottle and a joint on the table next to him.

"Why didn't you wake me?" I squeeze in with him on the lounge chair.

"I had to make some calls, and you looked so peaceful…" he says, kissing me. I rest my head on his chest; everything is spinning. "You feeling okay?" he asks with a little laugh. I nod, hoping the waves of nausea will stop. "You need some of this," he says, reaching for the joint on the table. He lights it and takes a long drag, then exhales, covering us in a cloud of smoke. I take the joint from him and do the same. I know a little weed will do the trick.

I relax, sinking into the comfort of his strong arms. I'm stoned immediately, and my stomach settles. I close my eyes, and the first thing that pops into my head is Joe's texts from yesterday:

> Where are you?

> We need to talk.

> I know you're with him to piss me off, Annie.

James's phone rings, pulling me out of my thoughts. "I have to take this," he mouths, untangling his limbs from mine. He takes the phone inside the house, and I'm left alone on the lounge chair.

My thoughts drift back to Joe and that horrible Friday night three weeks ago when we broke up. The memory remains clear and haunting.

It started like any other night. I had a few drinks with Angela, Max, Michelle, Darren, and Joe—our usual crew, at my house. I had a DJ gig at Light that night, and we were all planning to go together. I was nervous as usual, partly because I feared bombing my set and mostly because I knew I'd see James. By then, we had developed a flirty yet innocent connection. He'd pop into the booth during my set, have a drink with me, and joke around and flirt for a bit. I looked forward to those few hours of escape from watching Joe get drunk and do coke all night. His constant partying was destroying our relationship.

Joe noticed the attention James gave me at the club, and it pissed him off. He accused me of having an affair with him— which wasn't true. His paranoid accusations were the catalyst of most of our fights, and I always ended up in tears, defending myself. We'd scream and fight and then have incredible make-up sex that kept the passion between us going. No matter how nasty things got between us, the passion and love we had for each other always won. How could it not? We've known each other since we were kids. He was my best friend, my first love—I lost my virginity to him!

On this particular Friday night, Joe made a pit stop at Club 16 before meeting up with us again at Light. I knew he was going there to score blow from Patrick, a promoter and well-known dealer. I was mad at Joe for ditching us, but my mood lifted when I arrived at Light and saw James. *Oh, the butterflies!* He came into the DJ booth as I started my set and greeted me with a hug. He had been drinking and was extra affectionate.

I clearly remember the moment when James leaned into my ear, "I have to tell you something," he whispered, "That dress—*Wow*," he said.

I was wearing a sexy little Gucci dress with thin straps that showed a lot of skin. I smiled and poked him in the stomach. "I'm trying to work here!" I giggled, returning my attention to my laptop to cue the next tracks.

"You drive me crazy, Annie..." he said, brushing a lock of hair from my face. I pushed his hand away to stop him from getting closer.

"You're being very distracting," I said, whispering in his ear, fighting the urge to kiss him. I didn't want him to leave, but he was drunker than usual, and I didn't want our innocent flirting to turn into something else.

"Alright... You're actually very distracting to me!" he said. I realized then that something was *definitely* happening between us.

"See you later, Annie," he said, kissing me on the cheek before stepping down from the booth and disappearing into the crowd.

At that moment, I had no idea that Joe had arrived at Light and had been watching James and me in the booth.

When I finished my set, I found Joe in the VIP room with our friends—he was cold, passive-aggressive, and being a total dick. I assumed he was just moody from the coke, as he often was, so I tried to ignore him. I sat next to him, had a few drinks, and chatted with everyone at our table, barely exchanging words with him.

Suddenly, and out of nowhere, Joe got up from the table and walked over to where James was standing across the room. My stomach dropped as I watched Joe approach him. The room went silent in my head, and as if in slow motion, I watched Joe whisper something in James's ear. James tensed up and pushed him. I scrambled to my feet and rushed toward them, hoping to stop whatever the hell was happening. But it was too late.

They started shoving each other, and two bouncers jumped in immediately. One of them grabbed Joe, and the other grabbed James. They were yelling, calling each other names, threatening each other. I pushed through the crowd that had formed around them, mortified at what was unfolding. I grabbed onto Joe's shirt while Rob, the security guard, dragged him out the back door. He fought the whole way, cursing at Rob.

Darren intervened, attempting to calm him. When we were finally outside, he had Joe by one arm, and Rob had him by the other.

"I'M GONNA FUCK YOU UP NEXT TIME YOU COME NEAR MY GIRL, ASSHOLE!" Joe kept yelling toward the club as Rob and Darren finally got him to the curb. The crowd outside stared at us.

"Calm the fuck down, Joe!" Darren kept repeating. Joe pushed Darren aside and stormed off.

"What the fuck is wrong with you?!" I yelled, going after Joe.

"Annie, go inside; I'll take care of this," Darren urged, attempting to hold me back. Despite his efforts, Joe didn't stop, and neither did I. I persisted in calling for Joe to stop as I trailed him from the VIP entrance at the back of the club to the front.

"What the fuck is your problem, Joe?! You started this— talk to me!" I kept yelling at him. But he ignored me, arms crossed, in angry silence. I barely noticed when Darren's car pulled up to the curb before us. He got out and grabbed Joe by the arm, trying to coax him into the passenger seat.

"Get in the car, Joe," he said repeatedly. Joe stopped resisting and got in, still staring at me with rage in his eyes.

"She needs to get in the car too! GET IN THE FUCKING CAR, ANNIE!" Joe demanded.

"No, I'm not going anywhere with you. You're out of control. You're acting crazy. I don't even know who you are right now!" I snapped back, matching his tone.

"Get in the fucking car, Annie!" Joe yelled again.

"No, go back inside, Annie," Daren said calmly. "I'll take care of this."

I stood frozen on the sidewalk, torn between going and staying. I watched Darren get back into the driver's seat. "If you don't get in the car right now," Joe yelled, leaning out from the window, "We're done. It's over!"

I kept shaking my head. "I'm not going anywhere with you like this!" I said as tears spilled over.

As Darren's car slowly pulled away from the curb, Joe looked right at me and yelled out, "NOW I KNOW WHY YOU DRESS LIKE A WHORE WHEN YOU COME HERE!"

Darren hit the gas, and they were gone. I was left in the middle of Sunset Boulevard—stunned. I turned around and noticed the line of people waiting to enter the club staring at me.

Angela, Max, and Michelle appeared—they heard everything. Angela hugged me, and I unraveled, crying angry, embarrassed tears as my five-year relationship with the love of my life came to an end.

The memory of that night still brings a knot to my throat, usually followed by a flood of tears. I take a deep breath and push it out of my mind, refusing to have a breakdown at James's house. I never imagined that my relationship with Joe would end over a bar brawl, a screaming match on Sunset Boulevard, and the *wow* dress that turned into the *whore* dress.

Chapter Six

It's hard to concentrate or think about anything but James. I spend the next two weeks with my head in the clouds, and he's the reason.

We've been on a few more dates—dinner, movies, and jazz night at the Hollywood Bowl—and everything has been perfect. I've been spending nights at his house regularly, and the sex keeps getting better and better. Our bond is also getting stronger—we love the same music and films, and we never run out of things to talk about.

Joe has stopped calling and texting me, and I'm convinced this is one of our smoothest breakups. We've had our share of being on and off for the past couple of years, but I've somehow managed to come out unscathed this time, and I know it's because James has provided newfound comfort and safety after the instability of the past few months.

I park in the circular driveway of my house and bounce out of the car. Despite the meager effort I've put into school lately, I feel good about the brutal Art History exam I just took. I find Angela on her laptop sitting at the island in the kitchen, glowing in the afternoon sun pouring in through the big picture windows.

"Hey, what are you doing here?" I ask, pleasantly surprised to see her.

She greets me with a smile as her big brown eyes meet mine. "I thought we could hang out and look at some potential spaces for the shop." She turns away from her laptop to give me her full attention.

Angela is eighteen months older than me, and besides being my big sister, she's also my best friend. She recently moved into her first apartment in Brentwood but she's never there, preferring to spend most of her time here, at our childhood home. I, on the other hand, am in no rush to move out; I'm perfectly content to live with our parents, who are barely ever home, while I finish school.

Angela and I have talked about opening a boutique since we were shopping-obsessed teenagers. Now that we're older and have access to a generous trust fund from our grandparents, we're ready to make it happen.

"Cool. Are you finding anything good?" I put my bag down, heading straight to the fridge for something to drink.

"Not yet, but I have a long list of leads from Aunt Gia that we can start with," she says, returning her eyes to the screen. I grab a Diet Coke and notice her expression change. Her brow furrows as she concentrates on something on the screen.

"What?" I ask, getting closer to read over her shoulder.

"Oh, nothing," she says, trying to close the laptop, but I stop her. She's looking at an LA nightlife website. I read the headline:

Sweet Sixteen: Hollywood hotspot, Club 16, was the place to be last night as Promoter Patrick Upton celebrated his thirtieth birthday with a few of his closest friends and young Hollywood elite.

I skim over the article and my stomach sinks when I see a picture of Joe holding Ruby Kirk's hand as they entered the club. The photo caption reads:

Spotted: It girl, Ruby Kirk, looking cozy with

rumored new boyfriend, Music Producer Joe Montgomery, as they make their way into the bash.

I plop on the stool next to Angela's feeling like the wind was knocked out of me. "I think I'm going to be sick," I say without exaggerating.

"Annie…" Angela turns to me, giving me a look.

"Boyfriend?" I shake my head. "It's been like a month!"

"This is bullshit, Annie. It's a stupid article, and you know very well that ninety-nine percent of this is pure PR! Her publicist probably sold these photos and this story…"

I tune Angela out as I read the article and dissect the photo and caption again. I'm awash in jealousy, resentment, and anger. My reaction is confusing because I shouldn't care what Joe is up to or who he's dating.

"I thought she was just a one-night stand, a fling!" I say, trying to understand my feelings. "I've known James longer than he's known her, and I wouldn't call him my *boyfriend* yet."

"Well, *she's* not calling Joe her boyfriend, this stupid article is!" Angela reminds me. I hate that I'm so upset.

"Well, according to you, her publicist had something to do with this, and I know Joe's mom's PR agency reps her, so there must be some truth to it." I take a deep breath, realizing I'm lashing out at Angela.

"What's up!" Max walks into the kitchen, brimming with energy. His brown eyes sparkle, and his handsome face lights up, smiling at us.

"Hey…" Angela says, giving him a look, "You're chipper."

"Am I ever!" he says, planting a playful kiss on her cheek and then on mine. I look at him, annoyed at his cheery demeanor. He opens the fridge and pulls out a Coke. "Notice anything different?" He stands before us, wearing a gray hoodie, jeans, and sneakers.

"Oh! The brace is gone!" Angela says.

"Yeah! Finally got rid of the fucking thing—the doctor says I'm good as new!" he says, flexing his knee.

I turn my attention back to the article, still obsessing.

"What's wrong with *you?*" Max says, fixing his eyes on me. I'm too annoyed to talk, so I respond with a shrug. He comes closer and peeks over my shoulder at the screen. "Oh..." he says.

"Are they *together?*" The question makes it out of my lips, barely above a whisper. He sighs and takes a seat on a stool across from us.

"I don't know, Annie. Why do you care? I thought you guys were over." He hits the nail on the head and a raw nerve all at once. I shoot him a look and dismiss his comment.

"Did you go to this party last night?" I inquire, hoping to get the scoop. He takes a swig of his Coke and looks annoyed.

"No, you know how I feel about Patrick... I was invited, but I didn't go. I had dinner with them before the party, though," he says before taking another swig.

My ears perk up. "Dinner with Joe and this *girl?*" I can't even say her name. He nods but doesn't elaborate.

"Come on, Max," Angela chimes in.

"What?!" he says, laughing, making us work for the tea. Max is twenty-five, and as the oldest, he still loves torturing Angela and me, much like he did when we were kids. "What do you want to know?"

Suddenly, I'm not sure I want to know anything at all. I've worked so hard to let Joe go, to accept that we're over and that we should move on with our lives. So many things are broken between us right now, but the love and happy memories linger, proving the hardest to erase from my heart and mind.

Angela and Max stare at me, waiting for my response.

"I just want to know how serious they are... how did this happen so fast?" The words tumble out of my mouth without much thought.

Max looks at me and shrugs. "I have no idea. All I know is that they looked like they were having a good time together."

I'm utterly annoyed at his response and shoot him a look. *"Having a good time together?"*

"Don't you have a boyfriend too? Am I missing something?" He looks at me, confused.

I'm done with the conversation, feeling called out and embarrassed. "I gotta go. I don't care anymore," I say, getting up hastily, grabbing my bag, and storming out of the kitchen.

"Annie, come back!" Angela yells out after me.

I ignore her, still simmering from Max's comment, as I make my way to my room. I hate that Max is right. Why the fuck should I care about Joe when things have been so blissful with James?

Chapter Seven

"Hi, baby," James says, pulling me in by the waist and greeting me with a deep, lingering kiss. "Come in."

I step into his house, and the aroma of fresh herbs and sizzling garlic welcomes me. "More cooking?" I comment, trailing him into the kitchen.

"Oh, it's just a couple of steaks and some veggies," he says, returning to the stove. He's casually dressed in Adidas sweatpants and a T-shirt, looking so damn sexy. We haven't seen each other since my gig at Light a few nights ago because I've been busy writing papers and trying to catch up on schoolwork.

"Wine?" He holds up a bottle of red and pours me a glass before I answer. I can't keep my eyes off his toned arms and strong hands. "Cheers," he says, handing me the glass and flashing a smile. "I hope you're hungry because this is almost done." He turns down the heat on the stove and comes closer to kiss me. I notice a trace of salt and wine on his lips, which tastes delicious.

"I can't believe you're leaving me tomorrow," I blurt out what I've been thinking all day. James is going to New York to meet with friends who want to open a nightclub. He's advising them on the deal and considering investing.

"It's just a few days, baby," he says, leaning against the kitchen island. He picks up a half-smoked joint from an ashtray and lights it.

"I know… I feel like we haven't seen each other in a while, and you're leaving now…" I realize how clingy I sound and regret saying anything, so I stop short and take a long sip of my wine.

"Aww, are you gonna miss me?" he asks with a smirk, lifting my chin with his index finger. I'm embarrassed and drop my gaze. "I'm gonna miss *you*," he says, taking a short drag from the joint. He pulls my chin toward him, stopping before our lips touch, and blows a thin line of smoke into my mouth. I close my eyes, and our lips lock for a smoky kiss.

The wine starts to kick in, and it mixes with the marijuana in my lungs, making me feel heady. He parts my legs with his knee and wedges himself between my legs—I feel his erection as he presses into me. We kiss, and I slip my hands under his shirt, running my fingers over the smooth definition of his abs. He pulls away from my lips, "Fuck it, we can eat later," he says, stepping away to turn off the stove.

I catch my breath and bite my lips, eager for more of his touch. He returns and picks me up by my hips as I wrap my legs around him. We kiss as he carries me to the living room, where we fall onto the couch. The pocket doors are open, and a warm breeze blows through the house. I'm stoned, all of my senses on overdrive as I pull off his shirt, and he unzips my denim cutoffs, sliding them down my legs.

The couch's narrowness limits us, forcing us to move closer and tighter into each other. As we continue to kiss, James unbuttons my top and takes off my bra—his lips are warm and wet as he sucks my nipples while he maneuvers me to straddle him.

The feeling is sharp and full as I sink into him. I arch my

back until he's all the way inside me, filling me up *so good*. A delicious tension builds between us as we move and press into each other. He flips me over and takes me from behind, rocking into me, encircling his arms around my waist. "You feel so fucking good," he whispers breathlessly into my ear. I push back into him and move my body just so until we climax. We fall back onto the couch, spent and buzzing from our orgasms.

"How about some dinner?" he murmurs softly, his arms still wrapped around me, neither of us wanting to let go.

"Mmhmm," I nod, smiling.

Our night unfolds with savory steaks for dinner, a delicious bottle of wine, and lots of laughter and conversation. We make love once more before drifting off into the most perfect sleep.

Chapter Eight

"Call me when you land," I tell James as he jumps out of my Range Rover at the departure curb at LAX.

"Will do," he says, grabbing his duffle bag from the back seat. He dips back into the passenger side for one more kiss. "Thanks for the ride," he says, releasing my lips.

I smile and give him a wave as he disappears into the crowd of early-morning travelers at the American Airlines gate.

I drive home in a daze with a silly grin spread across my lips, daydreaming about our fun last night. We didn't sleep much, and now I'm hungover and barely functioning. I'm also sore but in a really good way.

When I get home, I crash, sleeping through the alarm I set for my two p.m. English Lit class. When I wake up, it's late and already dark outside. I check my phone and see a few texts from Angela inviting me to come out back to an impromptu gathering. I'm disappointed that there are no texts from James.

It's Friday night, and I have my usual gig at Light from ten to midnight, but it's only eight, so I have time to get ready and join the party outside. I shower and put on a nude-colored, figure-hugging dress and tall, strappy Louboutin heels. I realize that I'm going to be on my feet for two hours, but they're so sexy and worth the pain. I style my hair in a sleek bun and complete my look with understated pink lips and smokey eyes.

The music and chatter from outside grow increasingly louder, so I peek out the window to survey the scene. People are mingling around the pool and lounging about in the back-yard. The door to Max's pool house is open, and people flow in and out, red cups and beer bottles in hand. This is an all too familiar scene—whenever our parents go out of town, Max throws a party. Luckily, they're cool with it as long as the main house stays intact.

Downstairs, a subtle, earthy scent of marijuana greets me as I make my way through the house toward the backyard. When I step outside, I'm immersed in laughter and conver-sation mixed with the thumping beats of the rap song booming from the patio speakers. I look around, recognizing familiar faces and acquaintances—mostly Max's friends. I greet a few of them, then freeze when my eyes land on Joe talking to Darren. They see me, too, and it's too late to turn around.

"Hey, Annie!" Michelle cuts through my direct view of them, approaching me with open arms. Her jet-black hair falls loose around her delicate face and pouty glossed lips. "I'm so glad to see you! I feel like it's been forever!" she says.

"I know, I've been busy with school and…"

"Your hot new boyfriend?" she interjects, cutting me off.

"I guess," I shrug, unsure how to answer. I feel Joe staring at me, and Michelle senses my uneasiness.

"Are you okay?"

"Why is he here?" I ask. She gives me a look and I realize it's a stupid question—Joe is *always* here. He's been coming to my house and hanging out with my brother since we were kids. It used to be awesome that my boyfriend was my brother's best friend and always at my house, but now, it's a total nightmare.

"Oh, God, is *she* here?" I ask, wide-eyed, looking over Michelle's shoulder, expecting to see Ruby Kirk.

"No," Michelle says, shaking her head, knowing exactly who I'm talking about. I'm relieved, but now I have to bite the bullet and say hi to everyone, including Joe because it will be awkward if I don't. "You don't have to talk to him," Michelle says, as if reading my mind.

"Thanks," I say, smiling at her. "I'll be alright." I barely take two steps before I hear Angela's voice calling out to me.

"Hey! There you are!" she says, stepping out of the pool house. She's carrying two red cups and holds one up for me. I have no choice but to get closer to the group.

"Hey," I say, walking past Darren and Joe.

"What's up, Annie!" Darren greets me, but Joe doesn't say a word. The last time I saw Darren was at Mr. Chow, and I haven't seen Joe since the night of my first date with James when I saw him on the smoking patio at Light. He started texting me again yesterday, but I never responded.

I give Darren a weak hello and join Angela at the patio table. "That's a hot dress," she says. "I *totally* have to borrow it." I can tell she's tipsy, so I start drinking to catch up. "Are you alright?" She gives me the same concerned look I just got from Michelle. I begin to answer but stop mid-sentence, noticing Joe approaching us.

"Can I talk to you for a minute?" he asks, looking directly at me. Angela waits for my reaction, and I give her a nod. She gets up from the table, and Joe takes her seat. He fidgets with the drink in his hand, avoiding my gaze. He looks handsome in his button-down chambray shirt, as it brings out the blue in his eyes. My heart races, and I feel unprepared to talk with him right now.

"Um, I'm sorry about what happened," he says, finally meeting my eyes.

"What part?" I ask. There are so many awful things that have happened between us.

He maintains my gaze and continues, "I know it's been a while, and I should've apologized sooner—for the fight, for the way I acted at Light… I was out of control, and I'm sorry."

We're both silent—I don't know what to say.

"I'm also sorry for what I said to you… I was an asshole, and I was out of line… I didn't mean it; I think you always look perfect."

I'm speechless, unsure how to respond. We stare at each other as I gather my thoughts. "Yeah, it was fucked up. You practically called me a whore," I finally say, dropping my eyes from his before I crack. I take a sip of my drink for courage.

"Why can't we get past this? I've been trying to talk to you for weeks. Why do you think I went to Light the other night? Why won't you talk to me, Annie?" His tone grows increasingly annoyed.

"You broke up with me, remember?" A wave of anger rises from the pit of my stomach. "And why the hell would I talk to you when you show up to my gig with another girl?!"

He rolls his eyes, "We had a fight, and you never gave me a chance to explain… And now you're *dating* that fucking guy? *Is that for real?*" He's deflecting, and I hate that we're about to have another fight.

"Everything you thought I was doing with him while we were together was in your head. You didn't trust me. The only reason I moved on—and yes, started dating him—was because *you* ended things—*you* made it very clear we were done. Remember?!" My voice cracks at the last word. I swallow the knot in my throat and stand up. "I have to go," I say, refusing to continue before things escalate. He grabs my hand, and I pull it back, turning away.

I weave through the guests, avoiding eye contact to hide the fact that I'm on the verge of losing it, biting my quivering lower lip and fighting back tears. Once back inside the house, I exhale and gather my things before heading to Light.

MY SULLEN MOOD STARKLY CONTRASTS WITH THE UPBEAT RAP, pop, and hip-hop soundtrack I've crafted for my set. The vibrant flashing lights and the euphoric energy pulsating from the dance floor highlight the disconnect between my internal gloom and the party atmosphere, making me feel even more out of place.

Shaken by the talk with Joe and uneasy because James is away, my imagination gets the best of me. Scenarios of James undoubtedly talking and flirting with women in New York run wild in my head. I know he has a big group of friends out there, having only moved back to LA from New York six months ago, and I know it will be a non-stop party with them.

I consider texting him, but the thought of coming across as clingy again stops me. I relax by telling myself that a bit of space and distance is healthy and good for us.

Being at Light without him feels strange, and I realize that DJing isn't as much fun when he's not around. After my set, Oliver convinces me to stay for a drink, tempting me with a shot of tequila. I oblige, eager to delay returning home to the backyard party and possibly another unpleasant run-in with Joe.

At two in the morning, forced to call it a night after last call, I return home to find that Max's small get-together from earlier has turned into quite the house party.

There's music coming from the pool house, clashing with the song booming through the patio speakers. People are sprawled out on the grass and gathered around the fire pit. The patio table by the pool is littered with red cups and bottles.

I scan the scene, and the smell of weed is thick in the air.

My eyes land on Angela, sitting on Darren's lap, and I know it's about that time when they're both drunk enough to sneak off together. After all these years, they refuse to admit they have feelings for each other even though it's obvious. I approach them, and they greet me with big, happy, drunk smiles.

"Sis! You're back!" Angela extends her arms out for a hug as she teeters on Darren's lap.

"Get in here, sis, group hug!" Darren says, extending his arms out as well. They make me laugh, and I give in as we collide into an awkward triple embrace.

"I need a drink," I announce once I'm released from their grip.

"Inside," Angela says, pointing to the pool house.

The door is wide open, and when I step in, I find Joe surrounded by a group of people. He's loud and animated, making them laugh. As usual, he's the life of the party. They're gathered around the kitchen island, and as I step closer, I spot a plate of coke and a few rolled-up bills, and my stomach drops. Joe sees me and stops mid-sentence.

"Hey, Annie!" Patrick, Joe's club promoter friend and drug dealer, greets me as everyone's eyes turn to me. I hate that he's here and wonder *why the fuck* Max let him in. I give him a weak hello and pour myself a drink from the makeshift bar on the kitchen table. "You want a line?" Patrick offers, cutting the coke on the plate with a credit card.

"No thanks," I reply flatly. "I'm just grabbing a drink." Seeing Joe with Patrick infuriates me. Their "friendship" caused many of our blowups because Joe turns into an obnoxious coke fiend whenever Patrick is around.

I step back outside, and Angela and Darren are gone. Max and Michelle are talking and laughing with a group around the fire pit, and I'm in no mood to join them. Knowing that Joe is getting high breaks my heart. I take my drink and head up to my room, ready for the night to end.

Chapter Nine

There's a soft *tap, tap, tap* at my door, which makes me sit up abruptly in bed. I was about to doze off after pounding the stiff drink I made downstairs. The door cracks open, and a sliver of light seeps in. "Annie… Can I come in?" It's Joe's voice, but I can only see his silhouette in the darkness.

He steps into my room and closes the door before I can answer. "What are you doing here?" I ask. He moves closer but stops at the foot of my bed.

"Can I lay down here for a little while?" His ballsy request makes me laugh.

"What? No!"

"Please, Annie… I just took a Xanax… I don't want to bother you. I just need to lay down."

I don't know what to say. He steps into a bit of light coming in through the window, and I can finally see his tired face and glassy eyes.

"Joe, you should go home… maybe call Ruby Kirk," I say, unable to resist the petty jab. He ignores me and sits on the edge of my bed.

"Why are you doing this? I gave you space, I apologized… Why are you treating me like a stranger?"

It's almost three in the morning, and I don't want to talk, let alone fight. "Why are *you* doing this? You're making this so much harder, Joe," I say, utterly annoyed. He sighs and drops his head in his hands.

"I know… I'm so fucked up." He looks at me, and we make eye contact now that we're closer, and I can see him clearer.

The distant chatter of people outside and the sound of cars driving off cuts through the silence. The music from the party has stopped, and the voices begin to fade.

"Please, Ace, let me stay," his tone begs, "I don't want to go to another party, I don't want to do more coke… I promise I'll just sleep—I don't want to make things worse."

He's got me cornered, playing to my sympathy and soft side. Imagined scenarios of him getting fucked-up with Patrick and his scumbag friends at some shithole in Hollywood flash through my mind. My heartbeat quickens as a wave of panic rises in my chest, imagining the potential worst-case scenarios that could result from such a situation.

Joe wins, and I scoot over to make room for him on the bed. He kicks off his shoes and lays beside me, stretching his arm under my head. "Thanks, Ace," he whispers.

I sigh, instinctively wrapping a protective arm around him. I realize how fucked up yet normal this is for our complicated relationship. Despite the hurt, anger, and resentment, there is so much history and love between us.

I slide my hand over his chest, and his heart beats wildly beneath my palm. Flashbacks of all the times we've broken up and made up during our five years together come rushing back, and my heart tightens at the realization that this time, something feels different.

James has made this breakup easier for me, and I wonder

if it's been easier for Joe, too. Maybe he's relieved that we're over so he can do drugs and party in peace without me constantly worrying and questioning him. Perhaps we're both ready for a fresh start?

I swallow the knot forming in my throat, accepting that we really are over. I have loved Joe so much for as long as I can remember, but it's true; he feels like a stranger right now.

"Annie?" he whispers, cutting through my racing thoughts.

"Uh, huh…"

"I really am sorry…"

I nod, conceding. "I know, Joe…" I whisper back.

———

THE NEXT MORNING, I WAKE UP WITH JOE'S ARMS WRAPPED around me. He's still in a deep Xanax slumber, barely flinching as I release myself from his grip. I reach for my phone on my nightstand, and a sense of dread comes over me when I realize that James still hasn't called or texted.

I hear voices outside, prompting me to get out of bed and peek out the window. Below, I discover the party's aftermath: beer bottles littering the grass and patio table and red cups floating in the pool. Angela and Darren are already up and about, talking and laughing as they collect the trash into big bags.

"Come back here," Joe says in a raspy whisper. He squints his eyes open and pats the bed on the spot I just got up from. I contemplate getting back in but quickly come to my senses.

"No," I shake my head, "I'm going downstairs to help clean up." Joe opens his eyes wider and stares at me.

"Come on, don't tell me last night wasn't nice…" He's smiling and trying to pull me back in, but I fight it. "Best sleep I've had in a long time…" he pauses, softening his tone, "I miss waking up next to you, Annie."

"I can't..." I say, reminding myself we're not together anymore and why it should stay that way. "You can stay and sleep longer if you want; I'm going downstairs." I turn to my closet, grab the first casual dress I see, and then disappear into the bathroom.

How the fuck did last night happen? I splash cold water on my face, trying to calm my shallow breathing and racing heart.

I'm mad at myself for letting Joe back in—even though *nothing* happened! I can't believe that we fell back into our usual pattern where we fight and ignore each other, and then he says something that pulls at my heartstrings, only to make his way back in.

"Please, Ace, let me stay." His tired, broken expression from last night comes rushing back.

How could I not let him stay?

I take a deep breath, trying to hold it together because I refuse to fall apart like I usually do when I remember that he's become a full-blown addict. I remind myself that his volatile behavior and his drug use is out of control and there's nothing I can do anymore to help him.

"It's time to move on, Annie," I whisper to my reflection in the mirror. It takes everything in me, but I manage to freshen up and get dressed, prepared to bury my feelings back inside. When I emerge from the bathroom with renewed strength to face Joe, he's no longer in bed, and the door is wide open.

I go downstairs, glad to see that Max kept everything under control and that the house remained intact. Outside, a blazing sun greets me, and I find Angela and Darren in the pool. Joe is sprawled on a lounge chair, barefoot and wearing the clothes he slept in. He's smoking a joint and wearing sunglasses. Even though I can't see his eyes, I feel them on me as I walk toward the pool and sit on the edge to put my legs in.

Angela swims to me and gives me a look. Her brown eyes twinkle in the sun, full of questions. *What happened?* she mouths, trying to be discreet. I shake my head and mouth back, *nothing*.

"Yo, D! You want this?" Joe says, holding up the joint and offering it to Darren as he gets out of the pool. Darren accepts and takes a few hits while chitchatting and laughing with Joe. The pungent scent gets stronger as it wafts toward me.

"Damn, you guys are loud!" Max says, swinging open the pool house door, shirtless and yawning. He rubs his eyes and sits on the lounge chair beside Joe's.

Darren takes another drag from the joint and hands it to Max. "Good morning to you too, sunshine," he says, blowing out a cloud of smoke. Max grins and takes it. "I'm fucking starving!" Darren says, rubbing his stomach, "You guys want to go out for brunch?" Going anywhere right now feels daunting.

"There are steaks in the fridge; let's just throw them on the grill," Max says while blowing out a cloud of smoke, returning the joint to Joe.

"Done! Let's do this," Darren says, looking directly at Angela. They exchange smiles, and she offers to help him get the steaks. The two disappear into the house while Max heads back into the pool house, telling us to get him and Michelle when the steaks are done.

Joe and I are left alone. "You want the rest of this?" he says, offering me the joint. I'm hungover and don't want to make things between us any more awkward, so I take it from him and smoke what's left. Pretty soon, I'm happy-stoned, and he's saying silly things to make me laugh, and the weirdness between us is gone.

By late afternoon, a few people from last night's party return for grilling and drinking. As day turns into night, I become increasingly drunk and irate because I haven't heard from James since he left for New York. *His silence is killing me!*

Against my better judgment, I call him and leave an angry voicemail sometime around eight. "Hey, it's me..." I say while trying to control the slur in my tone. "I just wanted to tell you that it's fucked up that you haven't called me even though you promised you would when you landed. I have no idea if you're okay or what the fuck is going on, but… I hope you're having *fun.* Oh, yeah… don't call me back!"

I turn my phone off and pour myself another drink.

Chapter Ten

"Hey, sweetie! Are you hungry? I made pasta." My dad greets me with a big smile as I enter the kitchen. He's an excellent cook and loves to make home-cooked meals whenever he has free time.

Dr. Will Preston is a very busy man, splitting his time between his cardiology practice in Beverly Hills and as Chief Cardiac Surgeon at Cedars-Sinai. Time off for him is rare, so catching him at home tonight is a treat.

I peek at the bowl of lemony pasta he's placed on the kitchen island. "Pull up a seat!" he says, serving me a plate. I pull up a stool and ask for a glass of wine, glancing at the open bottle on the counter. "Of course," he says, pouring me a glass. His deep brown eyes and strong brows narrow in on me. "Is everything okay, sweetheart?"

I shrug and stare at my plate—I don't want to get into it. It's been two days since I left James the angry voicemail, and all I got back from him was a short text that said we should talk when he gets back. I've been trying to play it cool, but the uncertainty of what's happening between us is *killing* me.

My dad pours himself more wine and sits across from me. "Is everything okay with Joe?"

I look up at him, shocked, realizing he has no idea what's happening in my life. "Dad, Joe and I broke up two months ago!"

"Oh, really?" he says, genuinely surprised.

"Mmm, it smells good in here!" my mom says, entering the kitchen with a bright smile. She's casually chic in slim jeans and a T-shirt, an understated contrast to her exotic Italian and Portuguese features. She heads straight to my dad and kisses him on the cheek. "Hi, honey!" she says, approaching me for a hug.

"Erica, did you know Annie and Joe broke up?" my dad says, his voice concerned.

"Yeah…" she responds, looking at me with an exaggerated frown. She grabs the bottle of wine and pours herself a glass.

"I'm always the last to know!" he says.

My parents have watched Joe grow up along with Max, Angela, and me. My mom and Joe's dad have known each other since law school and started an entertainment law firm together when I was a kid. Because of their business partnership, Max, Angela, and I became friends with Joe. He'd come to our house with his parents for play dates, which led to a close friendship with Max and Darren, who've been friends since elementary school. Joe is an only child, so he spent most of his childhood running around with Max and Darren, whom he's always considered his older brothers.

When I was little, Joe was just one of my brother's obnoxious friends, but my feelings for him blossomed when we became teenagers. He was my first crush, my first kiss, and the person to whom I lost my virginity. We've been bonded since childhood, and he's been a part of my family since. My parents love Joe like he's one of their own, which is why my dad seems to be taking the news of our breakup so hard.

"Are you doing okay?" my mom asks, pulling up a stool next to my dad's and giving me a worried look.

"I'm fine, and you guys are freaking me out," I respond,

becoming increasingly uncomfortable as they both stare at me, waiting for more details.

"Honey, we just want to make sure that you're alright, that's all," she says.

"Thanks, but I'm fine and don't want to talk about it." I sigh, taking a sip of my wine.

The doorbell rings, and we look at each other.

"Are we expecting someone?" My dad turns to my mom. She shakes her head, shrugging, and he leaves to answer the door. I look down at my food, but all this talk about Joe has made me lose my appetite.

I hear voices approaching the kitchen, and when my dad returns, I'm shocked to see who's with him. "Annie, you have a guest," he says. I sit up straight, butterflies coming alive in my belly as James stands before me.

"Hi," I say, stunned.

He gives me a tight smile and a nod. "Hey," he says.

"Um, hello…" my mom says, looking at him and then at me, waiting for an introduction.

"Hi." He flashes her *that* smile, extending his hand, "I'm James."

I snap out of shock and introduce him. "This is James…" I say, flustered, "He owns Light, you know, the club I DJ at?" I know I sound like an idiot, but they don't seem to notice as they greet each other and make small talk about the club.

James looks cute in dark jeans and a vintage concert tee. His hair's messy under a Yankees baseball cap, and he's grown some significant stubble.

"Would you like to join us?" my dad asks, motioning to the pasta and wine. James thanks him but declines.

"I just want to talk to Annie for a minute," he says, looking at me. "Is that okay?" His eyes lock with mine. I nod and tell him we can go outside.

"Nice to meet you," he says to my parents as he follows me out of the kitchen.

We step out into the cool night, and I'm suddenly nervous and shy around him. "What are you doing here?" I ask, turning to him. He puts his hands in his pockets and stares at me.

"I wanted to see you." We're silent for a moment.

"I thought you were coming back tomorrow."

He shrugs and steps closer. "I flew back early. Sorry if this is a bad time; I should've called first…" He crosses his arms, gazing intensely at me.

"No, it's alright… do you want to sit?" I turn toward the patio table, and he grabs my arm.

"Actually, why don't we go for a drive?"

Without hesitating, I accept.

We walk back into the kitchen, and my parents are chatting and eating. "I'm going out for a bit," I say, breezing past them and grabbing my phone from the counter.

"Sure, honey, have fun," my mom says.

James wishes them a good night as I lead him out of the kitchen. At the foyer, he tells me he's going to wait outside. I run upstairs, grab my purse from my room, and bounce back down in a flash. In the driveway, James is leaning against his Porsche, looking at his phone.

"Ready?" he says as I step out the door.

***

WE DRIVE TOWARD HOLLYWOOD IN SILENCE. MY STOMACH IS in knots because this is *not* how I expected our reunion to go.

"So, why the angry message?" James speaks up, looking over at me. I recoil inside, recalling my drunk dial.

"I'm sorry about that," I say, realizing how stupid I acted. I look over at him, and his eyes are on the road. "You didn't call me, and I didn't know what to think…I thought you were ghosting me," I admit.

He seems upset, and I can't stand it. "I'm sorry, James…"

I reach for his arm. He doesn't react, and I sense there's more to his chilly demeanor. I stare out the window, we're on Sunset and almost at his house. "So, is there a reason why you didn't call me? Did you need a break or something?" I ask, annoyed that he still hasn't apologized or explained himself.

"I didn't mean to ignore you. I was out there on business; I was busy," he says without looking at me. He makes a left on Selma Avenue, which takes us up the hill to his house. We drive the rest of the way in silence, and I'm on the brink of either yelling at him for being an asshole or breaking down in tears because I hate what's happening between us.

Within minutes, we pull up to his gate and into the driveway that circles to the front of his house. He turns off the engine and says, "Let's go inside."

I follow him into the house and notice his luggage in the foyer. "You want a drink?" he asks. I follow him with my eyes as he heads to the control panel on the wall to open the pocket doors in the living room. The fresh air is a relief, and some of the pressure begins to lift.

"I'll make the drinks," I offer, turning toward the bar. "Scotch?" I ask. He nods and gives me a hint of a smile. I make his on the rocks, just as he likes it, and pour myself a vodka soda, a stiff one because I need it.

I hand him the drink and raise my glass to his. "Welcome home," I say. He smiles and clinks his glass to mine, taking a sip.

"My head's been pounding all day; I'm going to roll a joint," he says.

I follow him to the living room and join him on the couch. He pulls his weed stash and rolling papers from an antique mahogany box on the coffee table. I sip my drink; the chill between us is palpable, and the silence is deafening. I'm relieved when he reaches for the remote to turn on some music.

"So, how was your week?" he asks as he selects fresh green

buds from a glass container holding some of the finest strains of marijuana in Los Angeles. The sweet, earthy smell fills the room as he puts a few buds in a grinder.

"Um, my week was fine… I went to a few classes… I played my set on Friday night…"

He concentrates as he places rolling papers on the table and begins sprinkling the finely ground weed into a thick, straight line down the middle. He looks over at me and nods. "How was it?"

"Packed as usual…" I respond.

He gives me an approving nod and turns his attention back to the joint. "Did your friends go with you?" He carefully rolls the joint, then brings it to his lips to lick the edges to seal it.

"No, I went alone," I say, suddenly feeling like our conversation is more of an interrogation.

"Really?" His expression turns surprised as he rolls the joint carefully between his fingers and then examines his work up close. "Now, that's a fine-looking joint!" he says, breaking into a full smile and holding it up proudly. I look at him, and it's clear *something's up*. "Now, let's spark this baby," he says, reaching for the lighter in the box. "Do you want to light it?" he offers, and I shake my head. He shrugs, taking a couple of quick drags to get the weed burning and then a long drag, which he holds in his lungs for a few seconds. He blows out a cloud of smoke, exhaling loudly. The smell is sweet and pungent.

He hands me the joint and watches me closely as I take a drag. I can only hold the smoke in for a second because it burns, and I don't want to cough up a lung. I hand it back to him as I exhale.

"And ah, what about Saturday?" His questions continue as he takes another long drag.

"Saturday?" I'm confused, already feeling the weed go

straight to my head. "What do you mean, *Saturday?*" I'm drawing a blank.

He blows out another cloud of smoke and passes back the joint. "Wasn't there a party at your house?"

I take another drag and think back for a second as flashes from the night of Max's pool party come into focus. I freeze for a moment, remembering that Joe slept in my bed after I got back from my gig, and wonder if James knows. I hand him the joint and he takes one last drag and puts it out after I pass on it. He looks at me, waiting for an answer.

"Yeah, Max had people over on Saturday for a barbecue… wait, did I tell you about that?" I'm stoned and very confused as paranoia sets in—*does he know about Friday night?* James leans back on the couch and sips on his Scotch.

"I don't understand what you're doing." I sigh, frustration prickling my chest.

"I'm not doing anything. I'm just asking you about your week…" he says nonchalantly. He takes a long look at me and continues, "I was curious about Saturday because you seemed to be having a lot of fun with your ex-boyfriend in all those pictures Darren posted."

"What?!" I'm taken aback. "Are you kidding?" I say, trying to keep my thoughts straight despite my marijuana haze.

"If you worked it out with him… you should probably tell me, Annie," he says, taking down the rest of his drink. He gets up from the couch to make another one.

"James!" I get up after him. "Is this a joke? I have no idea what you saw or what you're talking about, and it's fucked up for you to imply whatever the hell you're implying!" I'm starting to fume.

"Forget it," he says in a dismissive tone.

I'm pissed off, and I don't want to drop it, but at the same time, I'm scared that I've done something wrong and am too stoned to remember.

I pull out my phone to look through Darren's posts to see

what James is talking about. I scroll through his photos from the last few days and see a few from the barbeque on Saturday. I stop at the shot of Joe and me—his arms are wrapped around my waist, I'm wearing my new red bikini, and he's trying to push me into the pool. We're both smiling big, and we look... happy. It was a brief moment I forgot existed, let alone aware that it had been captured and posted online. I, unlike the rest of my generation, barely use social media.

I stare at the post—I'm clearly drunk and stoned off my ass in the photo since that's exactly how I spent the entire weekend, ironically because I was so upset that James had pretty much ghosted me the minute he landed in New York.

"Nothing happened! I was with my friends, and we were having fun, that's all... And Joe apologized, I'm just trying to move on..." My cheeks burn with embarrassment as tears pool in my eyes, threatening to expose my vulnerability. *I have to get out.*

"You know what, fuck this," I say, storming toward the door. It's dark when I step outside, and I suddenly remember that I don't have my car. *FUCK.*

James follows me. "Annie, come back inside..." He stands in the doorway for a few seconds, then comes closer, reaching for my arm.

"Did you bring me over here to interrogate me?" I ask as tears finally break. I cup my face with my hands, wishing I hadn't come to his house.

"I'm sorry, forget about it. Come back inside." He wraps an arm around my waist, coaxing me toward the door.

I hesitate, still stunned by his implications and awash with inexplicable guilt.

"I'm not with him anymore; I'm with you..." I say, barely above a whisper.

He lifts my chin with his finger, but looking him in the eye is hard. "Come on... let's go back inside..."

I'm stoned, and I don't want to fight.

James wipes a tear from my cheek, and I compose myself, allowing him to pull me toward the door.

Inside, he leads me by the hand to the couch. "How about some water?" he offers, walking toward the kitchen. I catch my breath, hastily wiping my cheeks. *Gawd, I must look like shit right now.*

"Here..." he says, returning with a glass of water. I take a sip, and the cold drink calms the storm of emotions inside. James sits next to me and reaches for his drink, an awkward silence wedging between us.

"I assumed you had made up with him... you both looked pretty cozy..." he finally speaks up.

My chest tightens as I meet his eyes, full of scrutiny and doubt. "It wasn't like that," I whisper. James takes a sip of his drink, still maintaining my gaze. "But I can see why you thought that..." I inch closer to him, desperate to bridge the distance between us. "I told you—it's over with him," I insist.

He doesn't answer, and the storm awakens in the pit of my stomach. "If you don't believe me, you should probably take me home..." I say, hastily getting up from the couch.

"No. I don't want you to go," he says, reaching for my hand.

"Okay, then why are you doing this?!"

James pulls me onto his lap, looking me directly in the eye, "I don't like games, Annie. I need to make sure you're not fucking with me..." His tone softens as he lets down his guard.

I shake my head, trailing my fingers down his cheek. "I'm not fucking with you, James... I only want to be with you."

He responds with a hint of his sexy smile, and the tightness in my chest loosens. "I'm sorry if I was a dick... I don't want to fight," he says, gently lifting my chin, our lips meeting for a deep kiss. I throw my arms around his neck, surrendering.

We continue to kiss with full lips and tongue. He climbs on top of me, gently biting my earlobes and covering my neck with kisses. He's hard, and I'm already wet. When we finally come up for air, he leads me up the stairs to his bedroom.

Our kisses turn feverish as we fall into his bed while peeling clothes off each other. "I missed you so much," I breathlessly whisper as he licks my nipples. I squirm, my back arching and my breasts swelling in response.

He takes my lips again, full and deep, while moving his hand between my legs. His fingers trace me *there*, then slip inside of me. "I missed you too, baby," he whispers in my ear as I part my legs, desperate to feel him inside of me.

It hurts so *good* when he enters me full, in one thrust. Our fingers lock as our bodies move in perfect rhythm as he fucks me hard with just the right amount of tenderness. We've been dating for a little over a month and having lots of sex, but this time, it's different—we're making love.

Chapter Eleven

I leave James's house in the morning in his Range Rover —he's not ready to let me drive his Porsche yet. I have to be in class at ten, and he's too tired to drive me. I get home with enough time for a quick shower, throw on some clothes, and grab an apple as I bolt out the door. I curse LA traffic all the way to campus in Westwood but make it in time for class.

The day moves slowly and feels endless, and I can hardly concentrate on anything my professors say because my thoughts are still on last night. I replay the fight with James and can't believe how angry he was. I've never seen him like that before— accusatory, jealous.

Darren's post, the catalyst of our fight, flashes through my mind, and I'm immediately drawn to revisit it on my phone. I smile, scrolling through the snippets of time captured in the photos: Max, shirtless and wearing sunglasses at the grill, Angela and Michelle giving kissy faces and peace signs to the camera, a selfie of Darren with the crew, and the last shot— Joe and I looking close and flirty right before he threw me into the pool.

The sweet memory turns sour when I recall how angry I

was at James for seemingly abandoning me. My thoughts drift to Joe and how helpless he looked standing at the foot of my bed and how nice it felt to fall asleep next to him again. I stop that train of thought, hastily closing the app. I can't go there again—Joe and I are over.

By three p.m., I've sat through three classes, ready to return to James. I text him a few times but he doesn't answer. I worry that he's still pissed from last night, but I can't imagine why he would be after the amazing sex and intimacy we shared.

I decide to call him because I have his car and want to return it, but mostly because I want to see him again and maybe indulge in some afternoon sex.

"Hello," he answers in a groggy voice.

"Are you sleeping?"

James is not one to sleep the day away; he's usually up early and getting ready to head to the club by now for his usual afternoon meeting with Oliver and their staff.

"Ughhh... I don't feel well," he says in a mumble.

"What's wrong?" His tone is concerning.

"I don't know, my head's pounding... I feel like shit," he says.

"Okay, I'm coming over right now," I tell him, quickly hanging up.

<hr>

"James?" I call out, walking through the kitchen and living room. I head upstairs and find him in bed just as I left him this morning. "Babe..." I reach down to touch him. His skin is warm and clammy. "James..." I nudge him—he's deep in sleep. "James," I repeat, and he squirms and moans softly. "What's wrong?" He doesn't look well.

"I feel like shit," he says, barely opening his eyes. I pick up a prescription bottle on the nightstand— it's Vicodin.

"Did you take this?"

He stirs and grimaces.

"What's wrong? What do you feel?"

"Sharp pain," he says, touching his stomach. It's clear something's wrong.

"You have a fever," I say, touching his forehead, "I think we should go to the ER."

"No, no," he protests. "I don't have to go to the hospital." He tries to sit up, but I can see on his face that he's not well. "I'll be fine," he says, getting up to go to the bathroom.

As soon as he closes the door, I hear him throw up. I go to the bathroom door, "James, are you okay? I think we should go to the hospital… My dad always says that a fever, pain, and vomiting indicate something's wrong." I don't want to freak him out, but I can't ignore what my dad has told us for years.

He emerges from the bathroom, looking pale and still clutching his stomach. "Okay…" he reluctantly agrees. "Yeah, something's not right."

James moves slowly and shivers uncontrollably as I help him get dressed. He leans on me, his arm around my shoulder, for support as we make it down the stairs and into his car. I'm scared, but I'm doing my best to remain calm.

I speed down the hill in his Range Rover, down to Sunset, and head toward Cedars-Sinai on Beverly. I look over at him —eyes closed, pain spread across his face. "We're almost there," I reassure him.

At Cedars, I bring the car to a screeching halt, barely missing the curb at the valet line. An attentive valet peers into the passenger window, his eyes scanning James. "Do you need a wheelchair?" he asks, darting his eyes between us.

"No. I can walk," James responds, sitting up, grimacing.

"I think we'll be okay." I give the kind young man a tight smile as I hand him the keys and help James out of the passenger seat. He puts his arm around my shoulder, and I help him into the ER, almost limping.

"I need to sit down," James says, suddenly stopping. He's hunched over and sinks into the nearest empty seat among the other patients and their caregivers in the ER lobby.

"I'll be right back," I say, leaving him to find help. Waiting rooms are absolute hell, and even though we're at a posh hospital like Cedars, it's no different. I know we will be waiting for a while, so I tell the nurse who my dad is and that James needs to be seen immediately. Nepotism works like magic in this town.

Almost immediately, a nurse appears with a wheelchair, calling James's name. It's unsettling to see him like this—vulnerable, weak, and in pain. The nurse takes us into a small room, "Take off your clothes and put this on," she instructs him, handing him a hospital gown. I can tell this is his first time in a hospital. His expression alternates between pain and absolute annoyance.

"Let me help you," I say, grabbing the gown from him and closing the door when the nurse steps out.

"This is so fucked up, Annie," he says, sitting on the edge of the bed, shaking his head. "I feel like I'm gonna die!" There's fear in his voice, and I try to calm him.

"Don't worry, everything's going to be fine," I assure him while helping him remove his shirt. He grimaces as he lifts his arms.

"Do I have to wear that thing?" he says, looking at the gown with disgust.

"Yes, just put it on. It's fine."

His skin is still hot and clammy. He looks boyish and cute sitting in his boxers and socks. I help him with the gown, and he lies on the bed. "I gotta get more Vicodin or morphine for this, Annie," he says, "Where the fuck is the doctor?!" I fold his clothes and put them on a chair in the corner.

"Soon," I assure him.

The door opens, and the doctor finally appears with a nurse close behind. "What seems to be the problem?" he asks as the nurse types away on the portable computer, taking notes. James explains his symptoms, and then the doctor examines him, listening to his heart and lungs. He feels around his body, pressing on his abdomen. James jumps and lets out a loud "OWW!" which startles me.

"Hmm," the doctor says, furrowing his brow. "Based on your symptoms and from what I'm feeling here, I believe it's your appendix." James and I look at each other, and there's panic in his eyes. "We'll run some tests and do an ultrasound to make sure, but it'll probably have to come out," he says matter-of-factly.

"What… when?" James asks, confused.

"Well, as soon as possible," the doctor replies. "If the tests come back positive, it will have to be immediately. Don't worry, it's pretty common, but it can be very dangerous if we ignore it. It can rupture inside of you."

James looks stunned as the doctor instructs the nurse on what tests to run before leaving the room. I grab James's hand and say, "You're going to be fine, and this is common. You heard him."

"I know," he says, "I just don't understand how this happened. I never get sick, and I've never had surgery before."

I understand him completely; I would be freaking out too.

EVERYTHING THAT FOLLOWS HAPPENS FAST. A NURSE DRAWS HIS blood, and then another one comes around to take James away in the gurney to get the ultrasound. I wait for him, and thirty minutes feels like hours. When he returns, we wait for a long, uncomfortable time until the doctor finally returns to confirm that the appendix has to come out *NOW*.

Two nurses join us in the tight space with forms for James to sign and details about the surgery. James is quiet as he listens to them while looking over the papers. He reluctantly signs the consent forms and hands them back to the nurse. He looks up at me when we're alone again, "Annie, if anything happens to me, please call my parents and Lauren. Their numbers are in my phone… my code is seven, eight, two, one… Call Oliver, call my lawyer…" I place my hand over his mouth to halt his emotional spiral.

"Nothing is going to happen to you! You're freaking out, and that's normal. Trust me, you are going to be fine!" I say in my most convincing tone.

He closes his eyes and takes a deep breath. "Yeah. You're right. I'm sorry." I lean over and kiss him on the forehead.

"It will be over before you know it, and when you come out, I'll be right here waiting for you."

"Thank you," he says. "I'm so glad you're here." We're suddenly interrupted by the two nurses who are back to take James to the operating room.

I walk beside his bed as he's wheeled from the room down sterile, harshly lit hallways to the OR, holding his hand the whole way.

We finally reach two big double doors. "I'm sorry, but you can't go beyond this point," the nurse says softly. "The waiting room is through that door," she points across the hall. "When the procedure is over, Doctor Hughes will talk to you."

I nod, though fear grows in my chest, finally overtaking me. I look down at James—he's frozen, looking up at the ceiling.

"Hey," I say, trailing my fingers down his cheek. His eyes dart to meet mine. "Everything's going to be fine…" I whisper, leaning down to kiss him on the forehead.

He nods.

"I love you…" The words tumble out of my mouth. It's the first time I've said them to him, and there's no taking them back.

"I love you too," he says, his expression softening.

The nurse wheels him through the double doors, and they're gone.

Alone in the stark, silent hallway, the reality of what's happened finally hits me. The dam keeping my emotions at bay finally breaks, releasing a deluge of tears. I can't believe James is about to have surgery and that we just professed our love for each other for the first time outside of the OR at Cedars-Sinai. Never in my wildest dreams did I think it would happen this way.

I sink into one of the plush couches in the tastefully decorated waiting room. I'm glad there's no one else here to witness my tearful breakdown.

James's phone startles me when it rings in my purse. Oliver's name pops up on the screen. I answer it, unable to hold back tears as I explain what's happened. He tells me he's on his way, and I pull myself together enough to assure him that James will be fine and that I'm just freaking out. I convince him to go to the club and not make a big deal because James would hate all this fuss over him. He agrees, and I tell him I'll call him as soon as the surgery is over.

I call Angela next and tell her everything, breaking down again. She's having dinner in Malibu and offers to drop everything to be with me. "No, it's fine," I insist as I calm down. "The nurse said the procedure would only take about an hour. I'll be fine. I'll call you later," I say before hanging up.

Exhaustion overtakes me, so I curl up into a ball on the couch in the waiting room. I'm physically and emotionally drained and doze off.

I have no idea how long I've been out, but I'm awakened by a nurse tapping me on the shoulder. I open my eyes, disoriented and half asleep, but sit up quickly. "Mr. Hunter is out of the OR," she says softly. I look around the room, and it all comes back to me.

"How is he?"

"He's good. Everything went as expected. Doctor Hughes will be out soon to tell you more."

"Great. Can I see him?"

"Yes, wait here for the doctor, and then you'll be able to see him."

My stomach is in knots as I pace the room. At last, the tall, silver-haired man appears, greeting me with a smile. "Everything went well, just as expected. I removed the appendix, and I don't expect any complications. He'll be admitted tonight and stay twenty-four to forty-eight hours for observation. He's resting comfortably and coming out of the anesthesia."

I'm still stunned, and all I can say is, "Okay, thank you."

"The nurse will be back to take you to see him, okay?" He gives me a warm smile. "He's going to be fine, don't worry." I nod as he disappears through the doors.

Within minutes, the kind nurse returns to escort me to the recovery area. This time, the walk is less terrifying. I avoid looking at the other post-op patients lying in beds separated by curtains. The calm atmosphere, cloaked in soft lighting and silence, relaxes my nervous system. Occasionally, the quiet is broken by the beeping of machines and hushed voices.

"Okay," the nurse whispers. "I'll give you a few minutes to see him. He might be out of it, but that's normal. I'll return to take him to his room, and you can meet us there."

She pulls open the curtain, and I see James lying there. A thin tube is in his nose, and an IV is in his arm while monitors and machines beep softly around him. I turn to the nurse and ask about the tube. "It's just oxygen to help him be more comfortable," she explains, noticing the worry in my eyes. "He's doing great; he's going to be fine," she reassures me before leaving.

I walk over to him and gently touch his hand. He stirs, moaning softly. "It's me," I whisper, "It's Annie."

James barely opens his eyes but manages to squeeze my hand. "You're going to be fine," I say, trying to comfort him.

He moans softly again and tries to remove the tube from his nose. "No, don't do that; it's oxygen," I say, pulling down his hand.

"I feel like I got hit by a truck... did I get hit by a truck?" he mumbles, but I understand him clearly.

"*No*, silly," I stifle a giggle. "It was your appendix, remember?" He stirs again. His eyes remain closed, and he doesn't say anything else. "It's okay, everything is fine. You're going to be better soon," I assure him. He doesn't respond, dozing back to sleep.

A few minutes later, the nurse returns, peeling back the curtains. "Okay," she says, "The room is ready, so we'll take him up. It's on the fourth floor, so you can go up and wait in the sitting area. I'll get you when he's settled."

"I can't go up with him now?"

"No, honey," her tone softens. "Give us some time to get him settled; it won't be too long. Did you eat anything? Why don't you grab a snack or a coffee in the cafeteria? It's on the first floor," she says. It's almost ten p.m. I haven't eaten anything since lunch, but I have zero appetite.

"Okay," I say reluctantly as she checks James's vitals. I bend down and kiss him on the forehead. "I'll be here when you wake up," I say before slipping out of the curtained space to let the nurse do her job.

***

Angela shows up at the hospital even though I told her not to come. She finds me in the waiting area on the fourth floor, and she's carrying a take-out bag from Nobu. I'm glad she ignored my wishes because I'm *so* happy to see her.

She hugs me, and it's the first time I've felt better since this ordeal began. We're alone in the waiting room, and I dig into my favorite sushi rolls, realizing I'm starving. I fill her in on everything, and she listens, reassuring me that James will be fine.

"It's an appendix; nobody needs that thing, Annie," she says in her typical, dry humor, which makes me laugh. "Did you know that Marilyn Monroe had her appendix removed at this very hospital too?" She sounds proud, knowing such random trivia. "Don't forget to tell James that; it'll make him feel better," she says.

"Oh, I'm *so* sure it will," I say, and we laugh.

"It's getting late. Are you really spending the night here?"

"Of course. I'm not leaving him here alone. He just had surgery!"

"Yeah, I know. You should've at least called Dad. I'm sure he would've hooked James up with one of those *luxe* suites on the eighth floor."

I give her a look and shake my head. "No, he'll be fine right here, Angela."

The nurse finally shows up and tells me James is all set in his room and resting comfortably. "You can go in whenever you're ready," she says.

"Do you want me to go in with you?" Angela's voice quivers, and there's reluctance in her eyes. I know how much she hates hospitals—probably more than I do.

"It's okay," I say, "He's sleeping, and I'll be fine." We get up, and I give her a tight squeeze. "Thanks for coming, sis."

"Of course," she says. We say goodbye as she heads toward the elevators, and I head down the hall to James's room.

Chapter Twelve

I spend an uncomfortable night on a recliner chair next to James's hospital bed. It's impossible to sleep when the nurse comes in every few hours to check his vitals, turning on the harsh overhead fluorescent lights and making all kinds of noise.

James wakes up a couple of times, but he's so pumped with painkillers that he's mostly out of it.

At six a.m., there's a shift change, and the morning nurse arrives, bright and chipper, to check on him. When James wakes up this time, he's lucid and more like himself, though still groggy. He tells the nurse he's in pain, but only after she asks him. She checks his temperature and blood pressure, recording everything on the computer.

"Everything looks good," she announces before leaving the room to get him more painkillers.

"I'm so glad you're okay," I say, looking at him closely. His hair is a cute mess of waves, and his eyes look tired, but he manages to give me a small smile as he reaches for my hand.

"You didn't have to stay all night," he says.

"Of course I did. I wasn't going to leave you." I run my fingers through his hair, and he closes his eyes, sighing deeply.

"This is probably the craziest shit that's ever happened to me," he says flatly. "Thank you for being here."

I think about what we said to each other yesterday, and I wonder if he remembers. I want to tell him again that I love him *so badly*, but I get scared and keep my mouth shut.

"Can I go home now?" James asks the nurse when she reenters the room. She laughs, shaking her head.

"Not yet, Mr. Hunter. You had surgery less than twenty-four hours ago! We have to make sure you're as good as new before you leave here."

She's still smiling as she hangs up the fresh IV drip, carefully connecting it to the thin tube in his arm. "Right now, all you have to do is rest. This will help you relax and ease the pain," she says with a kind smile. James looks annoyed and restless.

"Thank you," I say as she exits the room. I try to stifle a yawn, but it escapes from me.

"Annie, go home. You should get some rest." James says, reaching for my hand. "I'm going to be fine, really."

I don't want to leave him, but I have class in a few hours and my usual gig at the club later tonight. I reluctantly agree to go home. "Please promise that you'll call me as soon as the doctor comes by," I say, looking into his eyes. He nods, pulling me in for a kiss.

"I promise," he agrees.

I'M IN MY CLOSET TRYING TO PICK A DRESS FOR MY GIG tonight. I feel like a zombie from lack of sleep and the stress of the last twenty-four hours. I'm cozy in my cashmere robe and would do anything to crawl back in bed and stay in for the rest of the night. But I have to suck it up and pick something to wear because I have to be playing my first song at the club in two hours.

I finally decide on a simple black slip dress—it's sexy, effortless, and the best I can come up with now. I sit on the edge of my bed, lacing my new Sergio Rossi heels that I picked up this afternoon on Rodeo Drive. I had to indulge in much-needed retail therapy after class to get my mind off things.

My energy level continues to dip, so I call Max to see if he has anything to help pick me up.

"Hey, what are you doing?" I ask when he answers the phone.

"Chillin'. Where are you?"

"I'm at the house. I have a gig tonight and feel like shit. Do you have anything to pick me up?"

"What, like a Red Bull?" he deadpans.

"Max!" My reaction makes him laugh.

"What do you want? Coke?"

I hesitate because I always feel like a hypocrite doing blow after giving Joe so much shit for it.

"What else? Got any Adderall?"

"Yeah, come down," he says.

We hang up, and I complete my look with my usual cat-eye and swipe shiny lip gloss across my lips for the finishing touch.

The door to the pool house is wide open, and I find Max on the couch rolling a joint.

"Where are *you* going tonight?" I give him a once-over, admiring his look. He's freshly showered, shaved, and looking sharp in a black button-down shirt and black pants.

"Darren's and then Sixteen," he says, barely taking his eyes off the joint he's assembling.

I join him on the well-worn leather couch, sighing heavily.

"What's wrong?" he says, looking over at me.

I shrug, unsure of where to start. "James is in the hospital."

"Oh yeah, Ang told me." His expression turns concerned. "How is he?"

"Fine. We spoke a few hours ago—he can go home tomorrow," I say, grateful for the good news. James was in good spirits over the phone. Oliver and Ben were with him, so I'm glad he wasn't alone all day.

"That's great," Max says, "He's going to be fine, Annie, I hope you're not worried."

"I'm not… It's just been a lot to deal with."

"I bet," he says, holding up the joint. "But this right here will make you feel better!" He hands it to me with a lighter.

"I don't want to be stoned," I shake my head, refusing it.

"Chill out; I'll make you a drink; you'll be fine."

I briefly think about it, then light the joint as Max gets up from the couch. "You want to come to D's?" he asks.

I take a long drag, hold it in for a few seconds, and then blow out the smoke. "I don't know. What are you guys doing over there?"

"The usual—have a few drinks, shoot the shit, and head to the club."

"Why the fuck are you going to *that* place?" I can't hide the disdain in my tone.

"It's an industry party—all the record labels will be there; we're just checking it out," Max says, returning with a vodka soda for me and a beer for him.

Max, Darren, and Joe are music producers who are always scouting for new talent. The first album they produced for a rap artist named Trent has been a hit since it debuted last summer, and they've been looking for their next big artist since.

I hand Max the joint and take a sip of my drink. "Ugh, I hate that place." Club 16 reminds me of coke dealer Patrick, who practically lives there.

"I know you do," Max says, putting out the joint. "But

there'll be a lot of important people there, and we have to network."

I'm stoned and glad to feel more relaxed from the few hits.

"So, do you want to come with me or not?" he asks, getting up from the couch. I still have time to kill before my set, so I agree to join him.

Within minutes, we're out the door and in his BMW, heading to Darren's condo.

***

Joe and Darren have condos at the Sierra Towers, and being here feels bittersweet. It brings back memories of when I practically lived here with Joe when we were together. It's been months since I was last here, and all those memories come flooding back as soon as I walk into the luxe high-rise in the heart of West Hollywood.

As Max and I ride the elevator up to Darren's floor in silence, a knot of anxiety forms in my stomach. Flashbacks from seeing Joe last week at the pool party that caused so much drama between James and me run through my head. I'm relieved that Joe and I cleared the air that weekend after he apologized for being a dick to me the night we broke up. We haven't talked since, and I'm grateful for the space.

"What's up!" Darren greets us at the door with a big grin and outstretched arms. Music and chatter fill the air as people mingle. I recognize some of them from the club scene— mostly music industry execs from various labels. I scan the room and notice Joe smoking on the balcony.

"Yay, you came!" I hear Angela's voice behind me. I turn to face her, and she pulls me in for a hug.

"Yeah, I can't stay long; I have to be at Light by ten."

Her smile fades as her eyes narrow on me, "How's James?" she asks.

"Better…" I exhale. "The doctor said he can go home tomorrow."

"I'm so glad to hear it!" she responds, her smile returning.

I feel Joe staring at me from the balcony, so I excuse myself from Angela to talk to him. I'm dying to know if we can keep our friendly momentum going.

Joe puts out his cigarette as I step onto the balcony. We greet each other with an awkward hug. He has a drink in his hand, and as I look at him closer, I can tell he's already had a few. Regardless, he looks handsome, as always.

"I wasn't expecting to see you here." His face lights up with a smile. The knot in my stomach from earlier loosens, releasing a swarm of butterflies. I turn away from his gaze and lean over the balcony, staring at the twinkling lights over Hollywood.

"I'm spinning tonight—I'm not staying long."

He leans over the balcony, too, mere inches away, yet our silence stretches between us like an ocean.

"I miss you, Annie," he finally says.

I glance over at him, meeting his eyes. "Joe…" I don't know what to say.

"You don't miss me? You don't think about me? You don't think about us? Last weekend was great. Can't we go back to the way it used to be?" His tone is sincere, and my heart breaks because there are so many reasons why we *can't* go back to the way it used to be.

"Don't do this," I plead. I don't want to fight, and I don't want to have this talk when we're both fucked-up at a party.

"Why not?" he stands up, squaring his shoulders.

I match his posture to face him, "You know why…"

He gives me a look, his expression hardening. "Why, because of *him*? Fuck HIM," he scoffs as his tone turns nasty. "He doesn't care about you, Annie. He's just using you. He's just like every other sleazy club owner in this town—fucking girls half his age until someone better comes along."

Heat rises in my chest. "Stop, stop…" I halt his verbal assault with my hands and turn away, refusing to let him disrespect me.

Joe reacts, grabbing me by the arm. "Okay, okay, I'm sorry…" he backpedals.

"You're an asshole," I say, shoving him off me.

My heart pounds as I step back into the party, desperate to leave. I grab my bag with my DJ gear and hastily bolt toward the door. I feign a smile when I say goodbye to Angela and Darren, refusing to let them in on what just happened.

I call an Uber when I get to the lobby and pop the Adderall on the way to Light.

Chapter Thirteen

My first thought when I wake up is my encounter with Joe on Darren's balcony last night. My head throbs, and the room spins, amplifying the queasiness in my stomach. I peer under my sheets and discover I'm still wearing the little black slip-dress.

I vaguely remember getting dropped off at home way after the club closed by James's friend, Ben. I stayed at Light after my set and had a few drinks with him and Oliver, letting off steam after the stressful last few days. I was seething when I left Darren's, and the only way to get through the night was to get shit-faced.

Heat pumps through my veins as my rage from last night awakens. *Joe is such an asshole.* I thought it would be different after we had such a nice time last weekend after we cleared the air, but I was wrong. I was a fool to believe that we could be friends.

I knew Joe was going to be at Darren's last night. I wanted to be sure that things were good between us like they had been last week. But I had no idea that our encounter would turn ugly and that we'd be back to where we started.

It's only nine a.m., and I toss and turn in bed—I'm pretty sure I'm still drunk. Joe's accusations of James and his implications that I'm some stupid girl he's using ring loudly in my head, and I can't shake the anger lodged in my chest.

I know James has a reputation for being a player. How can he not be? He's thirty-two, handsome, successful, and charming. And? *So what* if he's ten years older than me? *It doesn't mean that he's using me!*

I knew exactly what I was getting into with James. When I started going to Light when it opened, I'd see him with a different girl every time. Some were models, some were starlets, and others were random, hot party girls he'd met there. Girls threw themselves at him. I used to watch from afar as they clamored for his attention and how much he enjoyed it.

Back then, I couldn't care less. To me, he was just the hot owner of Light. It wasn't until I took over Max's DJ gigs and started spending more time at the club and got to *know* him that my crush on him developed. It was harmless—I was still in a serious relationship with Joe, after all. But it was fun to flirt with someone who gave me attention and made me feel good. It was better than what I was getting from Joe, who had suddenly become more interested in partying than being with me.

James was flirty, sweet, and affectionate with me from the start. He was brazen and didn't care that I had a boyfriend. Joe was slipping away from me, and the attention James gave me was exactly what I needed to distract me from the addiction that was taking over Joe's life and destroying our relationship.

I know Joe can't accept that we're over and that I've moved on. He put a seed of doubt in my head last night about James's intentions just to fuck with me. But I know he's wrong—what James and I have is real. I know it by the way he looks at me and the way he touches me. I know because he's genuine and less guarded around me, just as he is with Oliver and Ben, his best friends. James loves me, and I love him—we said it to each other at the hospital the other night! Even though our relationship has moved fast—I know in my heart that it's real. I'm certain that I'm not just another random girl he's fucking.

I DRAG MYSELF OUT OF BED AFTER SUFFERING THROUGH A massive hangover all morning. It only takes three Advils, a cup of coffee, and a big bottle of Gatorade, currently tucked away in my Celine tote, to do the trick.

I arrive at Cedars around two in the afternoon and find James in bed on his phone. I beam at the sight of him, and he lights up when he sees me. "Hi, baby," he says.

I get closer and look him in the eye, and the insecurity that's been gnawing away at me since last night is gone. I cup his face in my hands and give him a soft kiss on the lips. "I missed you," I say, sitting on the edge of the bed.

He smiles, "I missed you too," he says, looking into my eyes.

"How are you feeling?"

"Great! Doctor Hughes was here a little while ago and said, I'm good to go."

"Really? Well, let's go!" I say, getting up from the bed.

"I have to wait for the nurse to get back with my discharge papers—did you get my clothes?" I hold up the shopping bag with the stuff I picked up from his house on my way over and hand it to him. "Thanks… I have to get out of here, Annie; I'm literally going nuts."

"I know, babe, just a little while longer. Do you want me to help you get dressed?"

He shakes his head and carefully gets out of the bed. I

help him get steady on his feet, and he grabs the shopping bag, limping into the bathroom, holding his side.

I'm relieved this nightmare is almost over, and I can't wait to take him home.

"Oh, hello!" A nurse enters the room. Her eyes dart to me and then to the empty bed.

"He's getting dressed," I inform her.

"Ah, good! I have papers for him to sign and some care instructions. Will you be driving him home?"

"Yes," I nod.

"Fabulous!" she replies with bright eyes. My hangover can't handle her cheerfulness.

James emerges from the bathroom wearing the jeans and crisp white tee I picked up for him. He's also wearing the Yankees cap he specifically asked me to bring, and he looks scruffy and sexy.

"How are you feeling, Mr. Hunter?" the nurse asks.

"Like shit," he says, flashing her his flirty smile, which makes her giggle.

"Well, all you have to do is sign these, and you can go home."

He eases carefully onto the recliner chair I slept on the other night, making a pained expression. "Okay," he says, reaching for the papers. She hands him a clipboard with the forms and goes over prescriptions for pain medicine and a topical antibiotic for the stitches. I pay close attention to what she's saying because I know he isn't. James signs the papers and hands her back the clipboard.

"Okay, just a few things to remember…" she says, reading from another sheet, "Avoid lifting anything heavier than five pounds, no sports or strenuous activities for two weeks, and don't drive while taking prescription pain medication… Please read this carefully; there are more instructions here," she says, handing him the sheet of paper.

"Thank you," he says.

"Okay, that's it! Oh, one more thing—here are some gauze and sterile pads for you to take home. You should change the dressing on the incision site every twenty-four hours and after showering." He nods, taking the small paper bag she hands him.

"I'll be right back with a wheelchair, and you'll be on your way!"

"Um, what? I can walk," he pushes back.

"Hospital policy, Mr. Hunter," she gives him a stern look and a smile.

"Fuck these, I have better shit at home," James says, looking over the prescriptions. He pulls the shoes and socks from the shopping bag and tries putting them on, but he can't bend over because it hurts too much.

"Let me do it," I say, kneeling on the floor to put them on for him. I can tell he hates being in this state. "Babe, I'm going to be your nurse, and I'm going to take excellent care of you," I say, looking up at him.

He smiles, relaxing a bit. "Oh yeah? I can't wait for that."

I finish tying his laces and give him a hand to stand up. He looks around the room, and we stuff the papers and his other belongings into the shopping bag. The nurse returns with the wheelchair, James begrudgingly accepts it, and we finally leave the hospital.

***

WE WALK INTO JAMES'S HOUSE, AND HE LETS OUT A LOUD SIGH of relief, "Finally!" I called his housekeeper earlier to make sure the place was perfect for his arrival, and I'm happy to see that it's spotless. "Home sweet fucking home!" he says, heading straight to the control panel on the wall to open the pocket doors—his single most favorite feature of the house.

"Can I get you anything?" I ask, heading for the fridge.

My head is pounding, and I feel like I'm slipping back into my hangover.

"No, thanks," he says, sitting on the couch, immediately reaching for the mahogany box where he stashes his weed. I grab a Diet Coke and join him.

"I'm going to roll the fattest joint, smoke it, take a shower, take two Oxys, and then I'm going to fuck the hell out of you!" he says excitedly.

"Ha!" I laugh out loud. He's clearly joking since he's already wincing in pain from making himself laugh. "Babe, no strenuous activities for two weeks, remember?" I say, nuzzling his cheek.

He smiles and says, "Yeah, we'll see about that." He gets to work rolling the joint, then we smoke it and share the Diet Coke. I fill him in on last night at the club but leave out the part about going to Darren's condo.

James's phone rings—it's Oliver. He smiles big and laughs at whatever Ollie is saying. "Naw, there's no way I'm going anywhere tonight, dude," he says into the phone. "But if you want to grab some Mastro's and come through, you are welcome… Cool, man, I'll see you soon," he says, hanging up. James turns to me and tells me Oliver is coming over with dinner, and I'm glad to hear it because I'm starving.

"I'm jumping in the shower," he says, slowly getting up from the couch. "You want to join me?" He gives me a naughty look, holding out his hand.

I shake my head, "You're being a bad patient!" I tease him.

"You're being a bad nurse; where's my sponge bath?!" he says, laughing.

"I owe you one, babe," I say, too stoned to move.

"Alright, I'm gonna remember that!" he says, heading up the stairs. I can't stop smiling because I'm happy he's acting like himself again, and we're back to being silly and playful.

I stretch out on the couch, dazedly staring out into palm

trees swaying in the backyard. Joe's voice rings through my ears, crashing my mood. *"He doesn't care about you, Annie. He's just using you."*

I shake my head, refusing to let the seed of doubt he planted bloom into insecurity. Joe was trying to hurt me. He doesn't know what he's talking about, nor will he ever understand that my relationship with James is, in fact, real.

———

OLIVER SHOWS UP LATER WITH STEAKS FROM MASTRO'S, A bottle of wine, and a fresh supply of weed from the dispensary. The three of us enjoy an alfresco dinner by the pool as dusk turns to night over Hollywood.

We spend the next few hours enjoying a lighthearted conversation with Oliver and sharing much-needed laughs over the latest gossip from Light.

Oliver doesn't stay long because it's Saturday night, and he has to be at Light for the weekend madness. He and James talk business while I clean up and put away the leftovers.

When Oliver leaves, James and I share a glass of wine while enjoying the warm spring night, sprawled out on a lounge chair by the pool.

"Thanks for saving me, babe," he says out of nowhere.

"What?" I turn to face him.

"Yeah, I'm sure that if I had been alone the other day when I got sick, I would've tried to suffer through it. I would've never gone to the hospital if it weren't for you."

"Come on." I give him a look.

"No, really, the fucking thing would've probably burst inside of me if it weren't for you." He smiles and kisses me on my forehead.

I'm unsure how to answer, but I manage to say, "I'm glad you're fine and that it's all over."

It's only ten p.m., but it's been a long day, and we're

exhausted. Later that night, as we settle in bed, James wraps his arms around me and whispers in my ear, "I love you, Annie."

I smile, a steady calm washing over me, "I love you, too, James."

Chapter Fourteen

"So, is everything all set?" I ask Oliver. He's on speaker in my car as I drive to campus for another long day of classes.

"Yup, we're all good here, and don't worry, he doesn't suspect a thing."

A pleased grin spreads across my lips. It's been hard to keep my plans for James's birthday a secret, but luckily, Oliver's been a great co-conspirator.

"How did you reserve the whole VIP room for his party without him finding out?" I giggle.

"You know, this is going to sound shitty, but lucky for us, our guy's been a little *out of it* lately if you know what I mean," he says.

I do know what he means. When James got out of the hospital, he went back to working, drinking, and partying way too soon and ended up with a viral infection. He was bedridden for a week and became a cranky, miserable nightmare to be around.

"Tell me about it," I agree, "But he seemed a lot better this morning, so I'm sure he'll be back to normal in no time."

"Sounds accurate. He just sent me a string of texts and five emails!" Oliver chuckles. "Did you talk to Lauren?"

"Yes! Thanks for sending me her number. She's *in* and will be arriving on Thursday." My smile widens, becoming giddy over how seamlessly my plan is unfolding.

James turns thirty-three on Friday, and I wanted to do something special to mark the occasion, especially after everything he's been through. I thought a birthday party with his twin sister and best friends would be the perfect way to cheer him up.

"That's great; he's going to be thrilled!" Oliver exclaims.

"I know! Apparently, the last time he celebrated his birthday with Lauren was three years ago!" I shake my head, eyes still on the road.

"Great work, Annie. Hit me up if you need anything else!" he says before we hang up.

I pull into a parking spot on campus and let out a loud sigh. With graduation looming, I've been frantically trying to catch up on school. Juggling James's recovery, my classes, and planning his party has been rough. I have no idea how I've managed it all.

Alright, let's do this! I say to my reflection in the visor mirror, trying to motivate as I freshen up my lip gloss. Just a few more weeks of classes, and I can finally put this stressful part of life behind me.

After two weeks of plotting and planning, James's birthday finally arrives. He is excited about the dinner with his closest friends but has no idea Lauren will be there, nor does he know about the party at Light afterward.

As I pull into his driveway, I'm a nervous wreck—I want everything to be perfect! Approaching the door, I fidget with my hair and smooth my hands over my slinky, red, vintage Hervé Léger dress.

"Babe! I'm here!" I announce as I let myself in.

"Hey!" I hear him call out from upstairs.

I head up and find him getting ready in his bedroom. He stops in his tracks when he sees me. Naughty thoughts run through my head because he looks *sexy as hell* in a sharp, black suit that he wears so well.

"Wow," he says, approaching and pulling me in by the hips. I throw my arms around him, taking in the subtle yet intoxicating scent of leather, sandalwood, and musk from his cologne, mixing with his skin.

"Happy Birthday, handsome," I say as he embraces me, nuzzling my neck and gently biting my earlobe.

"Thanks, baby," he says as his hands linger over my curves, his body pressing into me. We haven't had sex in three weeks, and now that he's feeling better, it seems that he's *ready to go*.

He nibbles my neck, then kisses me deep on the lips. He guides me toward the bed, removing his jacket and unzipping my dress.

"James… We have to be at dinner soon!" I remind him as he pushes me into his bed to devour me in kisses.

"It's okay, I'll drive fast," he says, barely releasing my lips. I know my makeup and hair will be ruined, but I don't care. I want him badly, too.

We continue kissing with full lips and tongue. He slides his hand under my dress, tracing the inside of my thighs. My body awakens, singing at his touch. He glides his fingers up further, slipping past my panties and slide inside of me.

"Ahhh…" I exhale, relishing the warm sensation blooming between my legs. My hands tug at his belt buckle, desperate for him to make love to me. Our desire escalates as we feverishly undress each other—his shirt, my dress, and his pants land scattered on the floor.

"Mmm… you feel so good," he whispers, pushing inside of me as our limbs intertwine with each other. My breath hitches as he sinks deeper and deeper inside me while a delicious intensity builds between us.

"I love you so much…" The thought slips between my lips as a breathless declaration. I wrap myself tighter around him, savoring his skin, his scent, and his touch until the intensity finally peaks.

"Yesss…" my voice hisses. A glow of satisfaction engulfs me as he cums inside of me. I smile big, steadying my breath as my body pings and tingles under the comfort of his weight.

***

James and I arrive at his birthday dinner at Craig's fresh from orgasms and in high spirits. We got dressed in a flash after making love, and I had no choice but to refresh my makeup in the car on the way over, but the mad dash was worth it.

I clutch James's hand tightly as the hostess guides us through the packed, lively restaurant to a private room in the back.

"Finally, the man of the hour!" Oliver announces, standing up and clapping when we enter the room. All eyes turn to us as James's closest friends erupt in applause and loud cheers around the table.

James beams, greeting everyone with a wave as he walks toward Ollie for a hug. Relief washes over me as I take in the sight of everyone gathered—smiling faces, drinks in hand, and plates of appetizers adorning the table.

I glance at Lauren, wide-eyed and grinning big, waiting for James to notice her. She shifts her gaze to me, excitement lighting up her face.

James exchanges a few words with Oliver and then turns his attention to the rest of the table. He stops, and his jaw drops when he sees Lauren. "What the…?!" he mouths, going straight to her. "What are you doing here?" he says with a shocked smile.

Lauren mirrors his excitement as she leaps into his arms and wraps him in an exuberant hug. I watch him choke up as he greets his twin sister, who is also visibly moved.

James turns to me, still smiling, "Did you do this?"

I shrug coyly, and Lauren answers, "She sure did!" I'm thrilled that all my efforts paid off.

I finally meet Lauren face to face. She's as sweet and warm as she is gorgeous. She looks so much like James, especially when she smiles; they definitely have that in common.

After all the hugs and greetings, James and I finally settle in with the group at the table. We have an amazing time eating, drinking, and laughing. I'm pleased that everyone is having a great time.

As our meal draws to a close, two cakes are brought into the room, and the group bursts into a lively rendition of "Happy Birthday" while James and Lauren blow out their candles amidst laughter and joy engulfing the room. James looks relaxed and in a great mood, and I can't wait to see the look on his face when we get to Light for his surprise party.

OUR GROUP ARRIVES AT LIGHT IN SEPARATE CARS AND FINDS the usual crowd of stylish locals eagerly waiting to get in. We breeze past the line and enter through the VIP door, where Rob greets James with a hug. "Lookin' good, man!" Rob says in his usual jovial manner.

James barely managed to get out of bed while he was sick, and apart from attending a few meetings with Oliver, this marks his official return to a club night.

Rob gives me a wink, and I know he's signaled DJ Finn, who's covering for me tonight, via text that we've arrived, just as we planned. James stops a few times to greet familiar faces on our way in, and I'm happy to see him back in his element.

When we finally make it into the VIP room, right on cue, Finn gets on the mic and says, "Ladies and gentlemen, James Hunter in the house! Please join me in wishing him a happy birthday!" He sounds the air horn three times and plays a high-energy song while the cocktail servers appear with sparklers and champagne bottles to pass to all the tables. The crowd cheers, and James looks surprised yet amused by the spectacle.

"Surprise!" I say, throwing my arms around him. He's speechless, but his broad grin and sparkling eyes reflect his excitement.

"Wow!" he says, looking around the room and then back at me. I beam as he pulls me in for a kiss.

James and I circulate through the crowd, greeting his guests, whom Oliver and I personally handpicked. They include Hollywood types like film director Blake Houston, actors Jimmy Vance and Erik Cade, and rapper Malik Jones, among other A-listers. James's friends from the dinner party are mixing with his party friends and business associates, and everyone seems to be having a blast.

I become more excited when I spot Angela, Darren, Max, and Michelle at the corner table I reserved for them and dash over to greet them. "AGH!! You're here!!" I exclaim, approaching them with open arms. Max greets me with a hug, then I loop around the table, embracing everyone else.

"That was quite an entrance!" Darren says over the booming beats DJ Finn is spinning.

"Yeah, James sure looked surprised!" Angela adds. She was incredibly supportive throughout the planning process, and I can tell she's just as thrilled as I am that everything went off without a hitch.

James emerges through the crowd and the flashing lights to join us at the table, with Lauren and her boyfriend Scott in tow. Laughter and hugs ensue amidst the introductions. I'm giddy, watching our siblings meet for the first time, immediately hitting it off.

The group decides to hit the dance floor, but James and I hang back, enjoying a moment to ourselves.

"Thanks for tonight, baby," he says, putting an arm around me and leaning into my ear. "I'm not big on birthdays, but this is probably the best one I've ever had."

I smile, thrilled to hear him say it, and pull him in for a kiss as the crowd around us disappears.

When we pull apart, I turn my eyes toward the dance floor and do a double take when I spot Joe in the crowd talking to Max. A cocktail server appears at the table, blocking my view of him. She delivers another bottle of vodka and fresh mixers and talks to James.

My heart races, fearful that another bar brawl will break out. It's an unlikely scenario, yet I still grapple with the lingering trauma from that horrible night.

I look over at James, seemingly unaware that Joe is here.

Why the fuck is he here? I didn't invite him, and I can't believe he has the nerve to show up here again!

Joe hated coming to Light when we were together but continued showing up to keep tabs on me after we broke up. Lucky for him, I never banned him, and James was cool enough to move on from the night of the brawl, for my sake.

A couple of guests come to the table to greet James, and he's fully engaged, laughing and talking with them. I look back at the dance floor and see our group returning to the table, along with Joe and a striking woman, hand in hand. Since breaking up with Ruby Kirk, he's moved on to at least two model types, wasting no time enjoying the single life.

I narrow my eyes on Joe and his companion as they get closer. Everyone helps themselves to the bottle service at the table, talking around me as Joe and I lock eyes.

James finally notices him and turns to me with a blank

expression. Even though we're in the middle of a loud and lively nightclub, the tension feels uncomfortably thick.

Joe steps closer, directly approaching James while maintaining his grip on the woman's hand. She has long, silky, dark hair and a cherubic face framed by big green eyes and pouty lips. She has quite a striking presence.

Joe cracks a smile and extends a hand to James. "What's up, man? Happy birthday."

He certainly has balls.

James appears calm and unbothered and shakes his hand, thanking him. I'm sure deep inside, they want to beat the shit out of each other, but I'm grateful they're being civil right now.

Their exchange brims with tension, marked by hesitant glances and forced smiles, and I wonder if this is Joe extending an olive branch. The thought fades quickly as I recognize a subtle smirk forming on Joe's lips and a familiar glint of mischief in his eyes. It suddenly hits me that he's here to flaunt this woman to fuck with me. I know him too well for it to be anything else.

Joe's attention shifts to me, and I rise from my seat. I greet him with a brief hug, opting for the high road despite the lingering sting of his cruel words on Darren's balcony. The memory still burns in my chest, but now isn't the time or place to address it.

As we part from the embrace, I find myself face-to-face with her, her ample cleavage drawing attention in her form-fitting dress. Joe's grin widens as he introduces us, his voice close to my ear. "This is Audrey," he says, his smugness unmistakable.

I extend my hand toward her, "Nice to meet you." My words are barely audible over the thumping music. She returns the greeting with a half-hearted handshake and a smile as forced as mine. Our exchange is brief, as the club's noise makes conversation impossible. I catch a flicker of satisfaction in Joe's eyes as they turn away and disappear into the crowd.

Throughout the night, I observe Joe and Audrey from a distance. An unsettling feeling lodges in my chest, spurred by his presence and, I hate to admit, his unabashed affection toward her. While I've witnessed Joe with other women before, his interaction with Audrey seems different, even though I can't pinpoint why.

"You, okay?" James asks, leaning into my ear.

"Yes, I'm great!" I smile brightly, hoping he doesn't pick up on the unease brewing inside. I pull him in for a long, lingering kiss, determined to give him my undivided attention for the rest of the night, refusing to let Joe sour my mood.

So, I drink and return my focus to James and my friends, who surround us at our table.

Just before midnight, the cocktail servers present the gorgeous cake I picked out for James and Lauren while DJ Finn leads the crowd in a boisterous rendition of "Happy Birthday." Amidst the overflow of champagne, dancing, and celebrating, James and I slip away from the club, opting for a more intimate celebration back at his place, just the two of us.

Chapter Fifteen

James and I spend a perfect morning in bed—making love, snuggling close, and rehashing last night's festivities. We drag ourselves out of the house close to noon to have brunch with Lauren and Scott before they fly back to New York tonight.

Later that day, as I reluctantly return home to work on a paper I've procrastinated on for far too long, my stomach sinks at the sight of Darren's and Joe's cars parked in the driveway. The unease from last night resurfaces as I step into the house and quickly morphs into inexplicable anger at the thought of seeing Joe again.

I pause in the foyer, torn between going out back to where I know everyone is gathered by the pool or going upstairs to my room to get started on my paper, as planned.

My mom appears, gliding down the stairs in a chic summer dress and toting her favorite Birkin. "Annie! Sweetheart! I didn't know you were home!" she says, approaching me for a hug. I smile, squeezing her tight. I've been spending all my free time at James's house and haven't seen her or my dad in days.

"I just got here," I say as she inspects me with her big, brown eyes.

"Is everything alright?"

"Yes, everything's fine." I force a smile and change the subject. "You look nice; where are you going?" I ask, admiring her look.

"Oh, I'm helping Gia pick out some light fixtures and then meeting Daddy at The Palm for dinner."

"Oh good," I say. Gia is her younger sister and my favorite aunt. She and her hot architect husband, Aaron, are building their dream house in Bel Air, and my mom has been helping her decorate.

"Um, what's going on out back?"

"What do you think, Annie? Max and the boys! Go join them. They've been here for hours, and it sounds like they're having a great time." She puts on her sunglasses and reaches for her car keys in her bag. "See you later, honey," she says, hugging me before stepping out the door.

I FIND MAX AND ANGELA IN THE KITCHEN. SHE'S IN A BIKINI, and Max is in swim trunks. They're both busy grabbing things out of the cupboards and fridge. Through the picture window that looks out into the backyard, I see everyone sitting around the patio table. My eyes land on Joe and his new girl perched on his lap. The pocket doors in the adjoining den that lead to the yard are wide open, and music and laughter float into the kitchen.

"Hi," I blurt out. Angela and Max finally notice me.

"Sis! It's good to see you!" Angela approaches me for a welcoming hug.

"Um, you saw me last night," I reply dryly, wriggling out of her embrace. Angela is affectionate, and I love that about her, but I'm not in the mood right now.

"I know, but you haven't been home with us in a while!"

"Yeah," Max chimes in, "She dumped us for her boyfriend."

I know he's teasing me, but it's just the right nudge to push me over the edge. "What the fuck is that supposed to mean?" I snap. He gives me a surprised look.

"Um, what the fuck is wrong with *you*?"

"Why the fuck are your friends here twenty-four-seven?" I fire back, "Maybe that's why I'm never here, it's always a fucking zoo!"

"What?! Are you fucking kidding me?!" Max laughs and shoots me a dumbfounded look.

"Hey, HEY!" Angela steps between us, "Calm down, you two." Her eyes widen with surprise. "Annie, what the hell is wrong with you?"

"Nothing!" I snap at her, too. "I'm just annoyed that every time I'm here, they're here!" I say, waving my hand toward the backyard.

"You're nuts!" Max says, "If you don't like it, then fucking leave! Go back to your boyfriend's house." He grabs a few beers from the fridge and storms out of the kitchen.

Angela turns to me again, "Annie," she shakes her head, taking me by the arm, "What the hell is going on? This is so unlike you."

I pull away from her grip. "Nothing's going on! Can't I be annoyed because the one day I come home, there's no peace and quiet? I have a huge paper due on Monday, and this is what I come home to?!"

"Um, well, in case you forgot, this is our house too, and second, you don't have to hang out with us! Go to your room, use Dad's office! It's a big house; I'm sure you can find peace and quiet somewhere. And if not, there's always the library!" Angela is pissed, and I know I'm acting crazy.

I sigh, "Why is she here?"

Angela's expression softens. "Oh, I get it... Is that what's bothering you?"

"No." I instantly regret asking, having now given voice to the icky feeling of insecurity simmering inside me since meeting Joe's new girl last night.

"Yeah, it is." She pauses, choosing her words. "Annie, you have a boyfriend. A boyfriend you're attached to at the hip and basically living with! A boyfriend you've been flaunting to the world, including Joe, for weeks! Joe's moved on. You guys are over; you have to let him go and let him get on with his life."

"*Let him go? Let him get on with his life?* I'm not holding him back from anything!" Her statement irks me.

She crosses her arms, and it feels like she's looking right through me.

"That's not it, Angela," I say, trying to sound convincing. "I swear I'm over Joe, and things are great with James..."

She steps closer, pulling me in for a hug, silencing me, "I know how hard this breakup has been for you, Annie. If you don't want to see Joe, you don't have to."

"No. I'll be fine... I don't know why this is bothering me," I admit with a deep sigh. "I'm sorry for losing my shit; I think I'm PMSing or something," I say, looking her in the eye.

"It's fine," she smiles back. You don't have to join us, but it would be nice if you did," she tries to convince me.

I hesitate for a moment, looking out to the yard. *I have to face Joe again eventually.*

"Okay, I'll stay for a bit," I give in. Angela claps excitedly and immediately ropes me into helping her make a pitcher of sangria.

"What's she like?" I ask as I begin slicing strawberries on the cutting board.

"Honestly? She's nice... Sweet girl, a little spacey... but cool. I think you'll like her," she says, but I doubt it.

Angela shares more details about Audrey. I learn that she

recently moved to LA from Orange County and works as an A&R assistant at a record label. I'm not surprised to hear that her ultimate goal is to break into acting. Joe met her at an industry party at Club 16 a few weeks ago, *of course.*

I look out the window at the group sitting around the patio table. Joe says something, and everyone laughs. Audrey is still sitting on his lap with her arms looped around his neck. She plants a kiss on his cheek, and my stomach turns.

"You know, I think I'm just going to go upstairs…" I say, putting down the knife, abandoning the peach I'm slicing. Angela shoots me a disappointed look.

"Don't do this. It's not a big deal. Be a big girl, Annie," she says, nudging me with her elbow. I reluctantly pick up the knife again and continue my task.

Angela uncorks two bottles of white wine, empties them into a glass pitcher, collects our sliced fruit from the cutting board, and dumps it in. She adds OJ, Peach Schnapps, sugar, and ice, and I tease her for being such a sangria mixologist. We laugh, and it takes the edge off from the anxiety growing in the pit of my stomach. She samples her concoction and pours me a glass. I take a sip and congratulate her. The drink is crisp, cold, and sweet. I take another sip, and it goes straight to my head. "Two of these, and I'll be on my ass," I giggle.

I help Angela with a tray of glasses as she proudly carries her pitcher of sangria outside. As we approach the group at the patio table, I hide behind my sunglasses to avoid eye contact with everyone.

"Sick party last night," Darren says, greeting me.

"Yeah, it was fun," I say, squeezing him back.

"Where's the birthday boy?"

"Meetings at the club," I say as I go around greeting everyone at the table.

I get to Joe, and Audrey is still perched on his lap. "Hi," I say. They both smile and return my greeting. She's wearing a flower print dress that accentuates her full breasts. Her skin is golden tan, and her dark hair looks more auburn, shimmering in the sunlight. Joe's wearing his Ray-Ban Clubmasters and looks like the cat who swallowed the canary.

"You remember, Audrey?" he says.

"Yeah, we met last night," I answer flatly. I turn to her with my best smile, "It's good to see you again."

"We had so much fun last night; it was such a fun party," she says, pulling Joe closer to her.

I feel Joe's stare even behind his sunglasses, and the uneasiness in my stomach returns. "Try the sangria," I tell them, "It's delicious."

I spend the rest of the afternoon getting drunk on the fruity concoction, postponing my paper for yet another day. It's hard to leave the group when there's so much laughter and fun banter between us. The only downside is having to sit through Joe and Audrey's PDA, but Angela's words from earlier echo in my mind: *"You guys are over; you have to let him go and let him get on with his life."* This reminder forces me to endure their kissing and cuddling because Joe and I are *beyond* over.

The afternoon starts to wind down, and Darren lights a joint. A reggae song booms from the stereo, and Max and Michelle dance close. Audrey is finally off Joe's lap and sitting in her own chair at the patio table. Joe leaves the group, and sits on the lounge chair next to mine to hand me the joint. Our sunglasses are off, and we make eye contact for the first time today.

I take a few hits and turn to him, "I don't get you…" I say, shaking my head. I've been holding my tongue for too long, and now that I'm buzzed, there's no holding back.

Joe furrows his brow, meeting my gaze.

"You talk shit about James, but you had *no problem* showing up at his birthday party last night. What the fuck was that about?"

He scoffs, taking the joint from me, "I was only there

because Audrey was meeting up with her friends. I bumped into Max and found out about your little *private party*—I guess my invite got lost in the mail."

He's being a dick, and I'm getting heated, but I have enough self-control not to let the lava burning in my chest erupt all over him.

"I wished the guy a happy birthday, for fuck's sake." He smirks. "Didn't you appreciate that?"

I turn to him and look him directly in the eye, maintaining as much composure as possible, "I don't want to see you at Light ever again," I say, standing up and walking away.

Chapter Sixteen

A week later, on a Friday night, I leave the UCLA campus and head straight to James's house after wrapping up a long study session for English Lit. Finals begin in two weeks, marking the official countdown to graduation. There's a private event at Light tonight, so James and I are taking the night off, looking forward to a quiet evening.

I let myself in the house and find James in the kitchen. He's on the phone but hangs up when he sees me. "Hi," he says, approaching me with open arms. I collapse into his chest and hold him tight.

"Ugh, finally!" I sigh. We haven't seen each other in a few days because I've been deep in schoolwork.

"How was your study sesh?" he asks, squeezing me.

"Fine, I'm so glad to be done for now," I say, looking up at him, loosening our embrace. He smiles, and I notice that his eyes are glassy. "What have you been up to?" I ask, reading him.

He chuckles, "Nothing."

He doesn't have to explain because I can tell he's stoned. "Did you start without me?" I tease.

"Nah, Ollie and I had a few drinks after our staff meeting for the event, nothing crazy… Why don't I make you a drink? What's it gonna be?" he says, heading toward the bar.

"Something strong," I answer, plopping down on the couch. The pocket doors are open, prompting me to admire the night sky—dark and cloudy, with a faint orange hue from the city lights reflecting off the smog and coastal clouds mingling in the atmosphere.

James hands me a drink and joins me on the couch. "So, what should we toast to?" He raises his Scotch on the rocks to my glass.

"To us, of course," I grin. We clink glasses and kiss before taking a sip. I pucker my lips, "Wow!" I taste straight vodka.

"You said to make you something strong!" he says, laughing, "There's club soda in it, I promise."

I give him a look, "A splash, maybe?" I say, taking another sip. He offers to remake it, but the vodka is smooth and cold, and after a few sips, I'm okay with it. Lunch was hours ago, and the alcohol kicks in right away.

I lean back on the couch and rest my legs on his lap. He turns on the stereo with the remote, picks up a half-smoked joint from the ashtray, and lights it.

I close my eyes, enjoying the buzz from the vodka and the music wafting from the speakers. The earthy, sweet smell from the joint is tempting as James hands it to me. I take a couple of puffs as he unties the thin leather straps of my sandals. I'm already high, and the moment is perfect.

After taking a few more hits, James puts out the joint and then turns his attention to my bare legs, caressing them with a gentle touch. I'm quickly aroused and sit up to get closer to him, letting my legs dangle over his lap. I can't resist pulling him in for a slow, deep kiss.

As our kiss smolders, I reposition my body to straddle him. He grabs me firmly by the hips, and I respond, moving back and forth on his lap, creating friction. I release his lips, tracing the edge of his strong jawline, meeting slight stubble. He slips his fingers into the belt loops of my denim cut-offs as he pulls me closer into his lap, causing my knees to sink deeper into the couch.

He slips his hands under my shirt, cupping my breasts. I rub on him more, feeling him getting hard under his jeans. James takes off my shirt, then my bra, releasing my breasts into his hands. He traces my collarbone with his nose, peppering kisses down to my breasts, pausing to suck my nipples.

Our lips and tongues meet again for a deep kiss as I fidget with his belt buckle until it comes undone.

I pull his shirt off over his head, and my breasts meet the warmth of his bare chest. "Just relax," I whisper into his ear and take control. I kiss his neck as I unzip his pants and reach in—he's so hard. I get up from his lap and kneel on the floor between his legs.

He smiles slightly and says, "Oh, okay…"

"Shhhh…" I say playfully and plant soft kisses on his firm abs, making my way down past his belly button. I tug on his pants, and he inches up slightly, allowing me to pull down his boxer briefs. I lick my lips and kiss his erection, then wrap my mouth around the tip of his penis.

He exhales slowly with a quiet, "Mmmmmm."

His head falls back as he sinks into the couch—his body relaxing. I take him deeper into my mouth, moving my lips and tongue slowly, building a rhythm. I move up and down, up and down, holding onto his thigh with one hand for leverage as I wrap my other hand around his perfect cock, creating just the right amount of stimulation.

He grips my hair between his fingers, and his breath quickens. "Mmmmm," he exhales again. I continue—up and down, up and down. He's sweet and salty and slippery in my mouth. I work the tip again, and he whispers, "Yes," drawing out the *s*. I massage the base of his penis with my fingers and take him in as far as I can. He twitches a little, "Oh fuckkkk."

I keep going, determined to give him the best blowjob he's ever had. "I'm gonna cum soon," he says in a whisper. "Don't stop…"

I continue sucking and working his penis with my lips and tongue. I pick up the pace slightly—up and down, up and down… "MMMMM… AHHHH," he says as I feel him twitch and release in my mouth. I swallow a big gulp but some spills from my mouth and onto his legs. I wipe my lips with the back of my hand and catch my breath.

"Fuckkkk," he says, lifting his head and slowly sitting up. He's breathing fast and heavy. "That was… amazing," he says, looking at me, dazed from his orgasm. A smile creeps across his lips, and he shakes his head. "Baby, that was… incredible…"

I'm pleased and take a big sip from the now-watered-down vodka on the coffee table. Although semen isn't my favorite flavor, it was worth taking it in the mouth to see him so… satisfied.

"Come here," he says, pulling me up by the hand to join him on the couch. I rest my head on his chest—rising and falling as he steadies his breath. He plays with the ends of my hair, then moves his hand down my back to slip off my shorts. We kiss again as he slips his hand between my legs and fingers me. It doesn't take long until I cum too.

***

"How about a cig?" James says, breaking the silence after our delicious orgasms. The music has stopped, and I notice faint car sounds and the occasional siren below on Sunset Boulevard. I nod, and he wriggles out from under me. He stands tall, in boxer briefs before me, smiling big and flexing playfully. I laugh, and he bends down to kiss me.

"Don't go anywhere," he says, heading toward the stairs. I turn the music back on to something mellow and take the last sip of my drink.

James returns with an unlit cigarette dangling from his lips and something in his hands, and sits next to me. His hair is messy and cute. "Here," he says, handing me two small boxes. I look down at them—a pack of cigarettes and a small crimson box with gold detail around the edges. I immediately recognize that it's from Cartier.

He takes the lighter from the table and lights his cigarette.

"What is this?" I ask, giving him a look.

He blows out smoke and meets my eyes with a smile.

"An early graduation present," he says, tapping the red box.

"What?" This is so unexpected.

James takes another drag and runs his fingers through his hair. "Open it," he says. I can't contain the grin on my face. I open the box and find a sterling silver key ring engraved with my initials; there's a key attached. I'm confused and give him a look.

"A key to your heart?"

He laughs and shakes his head, "Close, it's to my front door… Your front door, too, if you want." He takes another drag from his cigarette and then puts it out. "Since you've been spending a lot of time here and we've been having so much fun together… I thought that maybe you'd like to move in with me."

"Really?" I'm surprised and delighted by his offer. "Live HERE?"

"Yeah, like, you know… move in with all your stuff… We cook, go to bed together and wake up together, do everyday stuff, you know… live together!"

"James…." I say, looking down at the key ring in my hand. A knot forms in my throat, and I don't know what to say, so I inch toward him and throw my arms around his neck.

"Is that a yes?"

"Yes," I whisper in his ear. I pull away from him to meet his eyes, "But I can't until after graduation…" The thought of moving feels overwhelming right now, and I have to conserve all my energy for finals and walking across that stage.

"Of course," he says with his sexy smile, "We have all the time in the world."

Chapter Seventeen

James

I arrive at Light to the usual pre-opening activities: Barbacks stocking bottles, the cleaning crew getting the place spotless, and the cocktail servers hanging around the booths, gossiping and giving me flirty looks when I greet them.

I find Oliver at the bar, having a beer and reviewing meeting notes with Dave, our General Manager, and Nicole, Light's publicist. "So, what's on the agenda?" I ask the group, pulling up a stool and signaling Tom, the bartender, for a beer.

"It's looking like a pretty good night," Oliver says, handing me a printed sheet of paper.

"Nice. Is every table sold out?"

"Yup," Nicole responds. "Table three is for Dennis McKay and his *entourage,*" she says with an eye roll. "Table four is for Richardson Black and his party, you know the producer of that alien show? And table six is for Russ Strong, the singing competition guy, and his people." Nicole is from the New York City club scene and is utterly unfazed by celebrity. "Do you guys want me to hold table five for you?" she asks, looking at me and Oliver. We nod—we always have a table reserved for ourselves and whatever friends show up.

"Great," she says, adding a note to her sheet. "Oh, before I forget, *The LA Times* reached out to me about doing a piece on Light, and they want to come in on one of our big nights to capture *the scene,*" she says with air quotes and another eye roll for good measure. "They also want to interview you two—pretty standard," she says, barely raising an eyebrow.

I give Oliver a look, "Fuck yeah!" I say, reaching out to give him a high five.

"Great, I'll set it up," Nicole says. "Dave, what do you have?" she says, looking over at him.

Dave fills us in on new hires and an issue with our alcohol distributor—typical operational stuff. We wrap up and break for a few minutes before calling the entire staff to start our group meeting.

The meeting lasts an hour, and afterward, Oliver and I retreat to our office upstairs to bullshit and smoke weed as we do every night.

"So, where should we have dinner tonight?" I ask, taking a hit from a freshly rolled joint.

"Dan Tana's?" Oliver answers without looking up from his phone.

"Cool, I'm down," I say, taking another hit before handing him the joint. "Dude, you've been on that phone since I got here. What's up?" Oliver finally looks up and takes a drag, grinning. I know the look on his face because he's been my best friend since we were twelve years old, and we know each other like brothers.

"Okay, what's her name?" I ask, chuckling.

"Kristen…" he says without missing a beat. "She's cool—and hot." he grins.

"Okay, here we go!" I can't help laughing. Oliver is a hopeless romantic looking for love in an unlikely place—the Hollywood nightclub scene. He falls hard and, unfortunately, gets his heart broken often. Meeting women in LA who aren't social climbing, gold-digging, or clout-chasing is not easy. "Alright, spill it, man!" I demand.

"I'm pretty sure you've seen her…" he says, leaning back in his chair, hitting the joint. "She had a small role in one of Blake's movies—she's been here a few times with him. He introduced me to her at your birthday party."

I think back to that night and draw a blank. Every night, I meet so many people at the club that it's hard to remember everyone. My birthday was especially a blur, and although I vaguely recall seeing Blake that night, I have no idea who he was with.

"I don't know, dude…" I say, taking the last hit before putting the joint out, "Kristen doesn't ring a bell."

"Well, whatever. She's gorgeous, cool, down to earth…" Oliver gets that look in his eye again. "I like her," he says.

I give him a nod, "Hey, man, if you like her, I'm sure she's great."

"Yeah, I invited her and her friend to join us for dinner tonight. Are you okay with that?"

"Sure, I can't wait to meet your future wifey," I tease him.

The old-school Italian eatery on Santa Monica Boulevard has been a long-time favorite for me and Ollie. It's close to Light and the perfect dinner spot before a long night.

The restaurant is quiet when we arrive. Oliver and I take a seat at our usual corner table. We order Peronis and a few appetizers. It's not long before the hostess leads a leggy blonde and a pretty redhead straight to our table. Oliver perks up and greets the blonde with a kiss. He introduces us, and then Kristen introduces her friend, Stephanie.

As we settle into dinner, I watch Oliver and Kristen talk and flirt closely. She's pretty in an unassuming, girl-next-door way. She has happy eyes and a nice smile. Her friend, Stephanie, is talkative, and by the looks of her thin frame and the way she pushes food around her plate, it's clear that she parties—a lot.

"You know, we've met before," Stephanie says, looking me in the eye. Her voice has a raspy edge that's kinda sexy.

"Yeah, where?" I look at her closely, trying to place her face. She seems somewhat familiar, but at the same time, she could be any of the countless girls I meet at the club every night.

Right on cue, she says, "At Light." I nod and apologize for not remembering. She gives me a flirty smile and tells me it's okay because she remembers meeting me.

After a few drinks, we're all relaxed and happy. Oliver and Kristen are rapt in conversation, and I'm left entertaining Stephanie, who says all kinds of things to hold my attention and keep the conversation going. Her train of thought is erratic, and it's hard to keep up with what she's saying. Stephanie touches my arm a few times and flirts aggressively. I'm amused by her brazen behavior and even throw a few flirty words her way for fun.

Stephanie returns from her third trip to the bathroom and leans into my ear, reaching for my hand under the table. "Here," she presses a small baggie into the palm of my hand. I know exactly what it is, and I shake my head, trying to give it back. "No," she squeezes my hand. "Come on, have a little fun," she says. I look into her big green eyes, and she gives me a wink. Oliver and Kristen are talking and laughing, and it feels like Stephanie and I are crashing their date. I look at my watch, and it's only nine—too early to return to Light. I look down at the baggie. *Fuck it.* I get up to go to the bathroom.

The coke is incredible—a clean high without a trace of jitteriness or aftertaste. I do a couple of bumps and feel great when I return to the table. The plates have been cleared, and only drinks remain.

"So, where to next?" I ask, anxious to get out into the night. The mellow vibe of Dan Tana's is no longer suitable for my coke buzz. The girls are adamant about going to The Chateau Marmont for a drink. Oliver is game for whatever as long as Kristen's happy, and I just want to get the fuck out of here. We decide to have a few drinks at The Chateau and then hit up Light around midnight when it gets lively.

A few minutes later, Oliver and Kristen leave in her car, and Stephanie rides with me to our next stop. The whole way, she doesn't stop talking.

AT THE CHATEAU, WE GRAB A TABLE OUTSIDE UNDER THE PALM and banana trees. The vibe is pleasant, and the drinks flow one after the other. Stephanie's bag of coke makes its way around the group, and it feels like time passes in hyper-lapse. I'm borderline euphoric from Stephanie's coke—it's the best blow I've had in a long time.

I pull out my phone, briefly considering calling Annie. A twinge of guilt creeps in for flirting with Stephanie, but it's all in good fun. I set my phone aside, recalling that Annie made me promise not to disturb her while she writes a paper. Besides, I'm not in the best state to talk with her right now.

At midnight, I text Dave to check how things are going at Light. Oliver and I are having too much fun with the girls, and we're not in a hurry to get back. Two hours go by in a flash, and it's closing time for all the bars and clubs in LA. Oliver and I consider our options for the rest of the night and decide to go to my house, which is just up the hill. It's the best option considering we're all fucked up, and driving around Hollywood at this hour is asking for trouble.

I pick up the tab; then we head to my house. Stephanie rides with me, and Oliver and Kristen follow behind.

"Holy shit, nice pad!" Stephanie exclaims, walking into

my house. I open the pocket doors, letting in the cool night breeze.

"Ollie, want to make drinks?" I ask while I turn on the music.

"Sick view!" Stephanie says as she returns to the living room from exploring the backyard. She sits on the couch and pulls out the baggie of coke from her purse. "Got a mirror?" she asks, looking up at me.

"You should slow down with that," I say. She's been going pretty hard all night.

"I'm fine," she says flatly.

I'm surprised how well she's holding up, considering the amount of alcohol and coke she's consumed all night—the girl is clearly a pro.

"Use one of those," I say, pointing to the books on the coffee table. She looks at her options and picks a book of photographs with a smooth, glossy cover. I sit next to her on the couch and pull out weed from my mahogany box to roll a joint. Oliver and Kristen are still at the bar, giggling and kissing and taking forever to make four drinks.

Stephanie dumps the remaining contents of her baggie on the book, and there's enough blow for us to keep going for a bit longer. "How about a bill and card?" she demands, looking up at me and batting her eyes. I chuckle, handing her a hundred-dollar bill and my credit card. "Thank you," she says sweetly.

I look at her closely as she kneels on the floor, cutting skinny lines from the mound of white powder, and catch myself getting turned on. I'm familiar with her type—I've had my share of LA party girls and know how wild and fun they are.

"Whoa, Tony Montana," Oliver says, handing me a Scotch on the rocks as Kristen puts a vodka soda on the coffee table for her friend.

Stephanie shoots Oliver a look and rolls her eyes. "Would

you like to go first?" she asks, handing him the tightly rolled bill.

"Nah, our host should go first," he says, slapping me on the shoulder before sitting on the opposite couch, pulling Kristen onto his lap.

Stephanie hands me the bill. "Pass," I say, still occupied rolling a joint.

"Kris?"

Kristen shakes her head and tells her to go first. Stephanie shrugs and does two lines, one after the other. Kristen then joins her on the floor and does two lines herself.

The hours unfold in a blur of coke lines, weed smoke, and countless cigarettes. Sometime before dawn, we get into the pool before finally calling it a night. The coke is gone, and the crash is starting to set in.

Oliver and Kristen disappear into one of my guest rooms with a freshly rolled joint, while I'm left with Stephanie—dripping wet, in her underwear and a towel in the middle of my living room.

"Can I borrow some clothes?" she says, shivering. I'm in swim trunks and dripping wet myself as I go around the house picking up ashtrays and collecting empty beer bottles. I'm wired and can't wait to take a Xanax to sleep.

"Uh, sure. Be right back," I tell her, heading up the stairs.

As I rummage through my dresser drawers, I hear Stephanie's voice behind me, "Is this your room?"

"Yup," I reply, turning around and tossing her a T-shirt. She grabs it and walks around the room, peeking into my closet and bathroom.

"I like it; it's very *you*," she says, dropping her towel and unsnapping her bra, revealing full, naked breasts before putting on my shirt. I'm well aware of her intentions, and if I were single or more fucked up, I'd go for it.

"Ah, so much better!" she says. Without missing a beat, she

slips off her panties and asks if I have sweats, "I'm freezing!" she says.

I know this girl means business, and I have to keep cool because, at this point, my current state of monogamy hangs by a thread. But Annie's face flashes through my mind, and I resolve to resist temptation.

I grab a pair of sweatpants and toss them to Stephanie before entering the bathroom. "You want something to help you sleep?" I ask.

"Sure," she answers.

I close the bathroom door, turn on the cold water in the sink, and splash my face—my ears are ringing, I'm so high. I haven't partied this hard in a while. I brush my teeth, break a Xanax in half, and take it down with a full glass of water. I emerge from the bathroom with the other half and a glass of water for Stephanie and find her in my bed under the sheets.

"What are you doing?" I try not to smile. I can't believe how aggressive she's being.

"What?" she says, giving me a flirty look while snuggling into the covers. I move closer and hand her the Xanax and the water.

"You're going to join me, right?" she says, inviting me into the bed before taking down the pill.

I sit on the edge. "Look…" I try to be careful with my words, "You're a hot girl. I'm not gonna lie, but I have a girl-friend, and this isn't going to happen."

Stephanie stares at me. Her eyes are a deep shade of green —vacant, beautiful even—smudged makeup and all. She breaks into a little smile and stares at my lips as she inches closer to me, running her fingers through my hair. "I know… Annie," she says. "My brother knows her; he's good friends with Joe." She looks me in the eye, and her comment makes me freeze.

I pull away from her touch. "What?" I try not to sound

stunned. She eases back into the pillows with a mischievous grin.

"It's all good, James; I would never say a word to anyone," she says, reaching for my hand.

My mind races as I pull away from her touch. "Who's your brother?"

"Patrick Upton," she says, "Do you know him?"

I think hard, trying to remember where I've heard the name.

"He's a promoter at Club 16," she adds.

My stomach drops as I realize who she's talking about—Patrick is Joe's friend and coke dealer and probably the supplier of Stephanie's party stash tonight. I've heard Annie talk shit about him because she can't stand him. It dawns on me that if Joe finds out about tonight, he'll tell Annie, and I'll be fucked.

"Nope, don't know him," I say, getting up from the bed. "You know what, it's cool…that pill is gonna kick in any minute now, so make yourself comfy and enjoy the bed. I'll be downstairs."

"Okay…" she says, relaxing back into the pillows with a big smile, "If you get cold or lonely, I'll be right here."

I return downstairs and take one last hit from a joint to help me sleep and pass out on the couch in the den.

Chapter Eighteen

"Hey, Annie!" My cousin, Matt, greets me at the hostess stand at his newly opened restaurant, Raleigh's, in Westwood. The place is a cozy American Bistro named after our late grandfather. It has a warm and relaxed vibe with comfort food and stiff drinks—just like he liked them. The restaurant opened a few weeks ago and Matt has been hosting friends and family dinners every Wednesday night. I arrive a little after eight and join the crew at the big communal table in the back.

"Hey, sis!" Angela greets me with a big smile. She pats the chair next to hers, inviting me to sit. I put down my purse and go around the table greeting everyone. Joe's here, and our encounter is awkward. I'm surprised to see him because he's been MIA now that he's apparently in a serious relationship with Audrey.

"Are you still mad at me?" Joe asks, looking me in the eye after my tepid hello. I can tell he's already had a few drinks.

"Yes," I reply flatly.

"Come on, Ace. You can't be mad at me forever..." he says, breaking into his cute smile that thaws the iciness I've felt toward him. "How about a truce?" he says, extending his hand.

I cross my arms, shaking my head. "You said some fucked up things to me. You don't know James, and you have no right to say anything about our relationship."

"What are you talking about?" He gives me a puzzled look, but I know he knows damn well what I mean.

"The thing you said on Darren's balcony. I haven't forgotten, you know."

"Ah. Yes, you're right. I'm sorry. I say fucked-up shit sometimes, I can't help it." He cracks a smile again, meeting my eyes. "I'm sorry, Annie, I really am," he says. His tone is sincere, and the iciness between us further melts. "Can we please move past it?" he asks, opening his arms. I give in, yet again, allowing him to pull me in for a hug. I accept his apology because it's exhausting to be mad at him. Joe pulls out a chair for me at the table, and I sit, fully aware that he still has a strong hold on me that I can't seem to shake.

Angela shoots me a look from across the table, and I give her a shrug. Joe sits next to me, chatty and curious about what I've been up to. He asks about school—he'd be graduating with me if he hadn't dropped out last year to produce Trent's album. School was never his thing, anyway. He shares that Audrey is out of town shooting for an indie film. Apparently, she quit her A&R job and is focusing on acting.

The food is served family-style, and Matt puts several bottles of wine on the table. After a few glasses, I relax and talk mainly to Joe throughout dinner. His humor further breaks the ice between us—he knows the way to my heart.

I get a text from James, and I tell him that we're about to finish dinner and that I'll be at Light soon. He tells me to invite everyone and that he'll have a table for us. Even though I told Joe I never wanted to see him at the club again, my stance has softened, and I ask him and the group if they want to come.

"Yo, what about that thing at Sixteen tonight," Joe says, turning to Darren.

"What thing?" I ask.

"Oh yeah, that's right…" Darren says, "We were going to check out a set by a new DJ we want to work with."

Max chimes in and says he wants to check out the DJ. "He goes on early, so we could roll there for a little while and then hit Light after."

I can't hide the annoyed expression on my face, and Joe notices. "Come on, Annie, you're at Light all the time—your boyfriend can wait a couple of hours for you." His tone is condescending, but he softens his expression, trying to down-play his obnoxious comment.

"Fine, I'll go for two drinks, but you know how much I hate that place," I tell him.

"Yes, I know," he says.

WE PULL UP TO THE VIP LINE AT CLUB 16, AND THE VIBE IS similar to that at Light on Wednesday nights. A crowd of skimpily dressed women and men in logo-printed shirts gather outside, waiting to enter the super scene-y nightclub. Joe insisted that I ride with him, so we arrive together.

Sixteen is loud and obnoxious. Its décor is a tongue-in-cheek throwback to the 80s, complete with mirrored walls, glass tables, and neon signs that say things like *"Pursue Pleasure"* and *"The Good Life."*

I spot Patrick at a reserved table and follow Joe as he beelines to him. The scene gives me bad flashbacks of all the nights I spent here blowing lines with Joe in the bathroom and partying with him after hours because I was afraid to leave him alone with Patrick.

"Fuck yeah, my man Joe Montgomery in the house! Let's get this party started!" Patrick says, standing up to great Joe with a hearty handshake and an animated hug. I roll my eyes because Patrick is so cheesy, and I know he kisses Joe's ass because he's one of his best customers. The rest of our party joins us at the table, and Patrick greets everyone before barking orders at the cocktail servers like he owns the place.

"Well, well, well, if it isn't *the* DJ Annie Preston gracing us with her presence!" he says when he greets me. I give him a weak smile and cringe when he leans in for a hug. "So, when can we get you in here for a set, Annie?" he says, flashing a big toothy grin. "Seriously, just say the date and the rate—money is no object!" he says, loud enough so that everyone hears him.

Our group settles into a big booth, where cocktail servers deliver a full bottle service of top-shelf vodka, tequila, and all the essential mixers.

"I can't believe you came," Angela says, leaning into my ear. I tell her I'm only staying for two drinks as I pour myself the first one.

The DJ we're here to see is pretty good, spinning fun party tracks and old-school rap. Joe and Patrick disappear, and I'm sure they're getting down to business, blowing lines somewhere. Angela tries to pull me onto the dance floor, but I'm starting to feel like it's time to go since I've reached my two-drink limit.

As I pull out my phone to text James, I feel someone sit next to me. I look up, startled to see Stephanie. "Oh my God, Annie! I was just with Joe and Patrick, and when I heard you were here, I had to find you! I have to talk to you…" she says, leaning into me, talking loudly over the music. Her breath kicks with alcohol, and from the way she's talking, I can tell she's high as a kite.

"Talk to me about what?"

"Can you wait here a minute? I have to give you something," she says. I shake my head because this is so weird, and I'm utterly confused about why she's talking to me like we're best friends, considering we've barely ever exchanged a few words.

"I was actually about to leave," I say, getting up from the booth.

"Oh! Okay, no worries. Are you parked out back? I'll walk out with you. I need to give you something, and it's in my car," she insists, rising with me.

"I have no idea what you want or what you're talking about. Can we talk another time?" I say, starting to make my way through the crowd. I feel her close behind me, and I'm bothered yet curious about what she wants to give me. I don't tell anyone that I'm leaving because I need to get out of here as soon as possible because Stephanie is freaking me out.

The fresh air is a welcome relief from the stuffiness inside. "Listen, I only need five minutes of your time," Stephanie says, stepping before me and catching her breath. Her pupils are dilated, and her lipstick looks dry and cracked around the corners of her mouth—I almost feel sorry for her.

"Fine," I give in. "I have to wait for my Uber anyway."

"Perfect," she says, "I'll be right back!"

A queasy feeling grows in my stomach, but at least I'm out in the open, and there are people everywhere if things get weird.

I watch Stephanie talk to a valet. He hands her keys and points toward the parking lot. She practically skips to her car, and I wonder if I made a mistake engaging her. I look around and spot Joe smoking on the patio with a group of people. He sees me and makes his way over.

"Leaving already?" he asks, taking a drag from his cigarette.

"Yeah, I gotta go."

"You want a ride?"

I look at my phone, realizing I never called the Uber because I was so distracted by Stephanie. "No, thanks," I say.

I watch Stephanie make her way back, and she

approaches me, holding a small shopping bag. She's out of breath but gives me a big smile when we're face to face again.

"Okay! Thanks for waiting, Annie," she says, looking me in the eye. I give Joe a look, and he continues to smoke his cigarette.

"Um, Joe, can you give us a minute?" she says, looking at him.

"No, it's fine," I say, feeling safer with him.

"Okay, then," she shrugs. "Here," she says, handing me the shopping bag.

"What is this?"

"Take it," she insists.

I reach for the bag and look inside—it's clothes. "What is this?" I repeat.

She lets out a deep sigh and says, "Those are clothes that James let me borrow when I spent the night at his house a couple of weeks ago. Look at it—a T-shirt and sweatpants— they're his. Please tell him I said thanks," she says, smiling at me.

I'm stunned as she turns on her heels and disappears into the crowd entering the club.

I pull out the T-shirt and instantly recognize the sweatpants underneath it. I feel sick to my stomach. "Is this some kind of joke? Did you have something to do with this?" I turn to Joe, seething with anger and embarrassment. I feel totally set up.

He gives me a look and puts out his cigarette. "Annie, I have no idea what this is about." I stare at him as my heart pounds and my hands shake. I look toward the club and consider going back inside to find Stephanie because she owes me an explanation.

"Fuck this, I have to go," I say, taking off with the bag in hand. My thoughts start racing, imagining vivid scenarios of James and Stephanie together. Panic grows in my chest at the thought of him cheating on me and deceiving me for weeks!

BOOM, BOOM, BOOM, my heart pounds loudly in my chest, echoing in my ears. I freeze when I make it to the curb.

Joe catches up to me and grabs me by the arm, "Stop, Annie. Where are you going?"

"Leave me alone, Joe!" I snap at him. I'm confused and humiliated, and Joe is the last person I want to talk to about the possibility that my relationship might be over.

"Let me drive you wherever you want," he says.

I look up and down Hollywood Boulevard in a frozen state. I know all I have to do is call an Uber, and I'll be on my way, but I'm still in shock. Suddenly, I don't care that Joe is here, and I let him drive me to Light.

Chapter Nineteen

The short ride from Sixteen to Light feels like torture. I press Joe for information, and he swears he knows nothing. He tries comforting me when I break down in tears over the thought of James cheating on me with Stephanie, and the imagined scenarios return with wild abandon.

I take a deep breath, tears clouding my vision as I stare out the window. Snippets of seeing them together, chatting at Light while I was spinning a few nights ago, resurface. The rage in my chest climbs up my throat, threatening to erupt. My stomach tightens, certain that *something happened* between them.

Joe pulls up to the VIP entrance, and I jump out of the car. "Do you want me to come in with you?" he asks.

"No, it's okay. Thanks for the ride."

As I close the door, I hear him say, "I'll wait for you…" As if he knows I won't be here long. I look back at him and disappear into the VIP line.

Light is twice as packed as Sixteen, and I'm having trouble getting through the crowd. James isn't in the VIP room, so I head into the main room, where he usually hangs out at one of the bars or the reserved tables near the DJ booth.

I scan the room and finally spot him standing at the main bar, talking to one of the bartenders. I feel like I'm going to be sick as I make my way to him. James sees me and lights up.

"I need to talk to you," I demand. He looks puzzled as he pulls me in for a hug, but I push him off.

"What's wrong?" His look turns concerned.

I want to scream at him and fire off accusations, but it's too loud and crowded, and I don't want to make a scene. "We need to talk," I yell over the thumping music. He asks me again what's wrong, and I have no choice but to pull him by the arm into the nearest semi-private spot—the alcove behind the bar where the cocktail servers ring up orders.

"What, Annie, what's wrong?" he asks when we're finally able to hear each other.

"Why don't *you* tell *me*?" I say, shoving the shopping bag into his chest. "Open it!"

He gives me a look, then opens the bag. "What is this?" he says, pulling out the T-shirt.

"Did you fuck Stephanie Upton?" My voice breaks as I fight back tears.

He shakes his head, "What?"

"You know, the girl you lent these clothes to when she SPENT THE NIGHT AT YOUR HOUSE? She just gave them to me and wanted me to *thank you*. What the fuck, James? Tell me everything right now!" My tone escalates as I poke him in the chest.

"Whoa," he says, backing up against the wall. "That's not what happened." He tries to grab me by the wrists, but I pull away.

"Don't touch me!"

"Annie, listen to me. I'll tell you everything right now..."

"Oh! So, it's true?" I'm shocked that he's not denying it. I don't care to hear the rest of what he says because the tears have already spilled, and my heart is breaking. Without thinking, I'm back to pushing through the crowd as I exit the club. *How could he do this to me?*

James trails behind, grabbing at my arm, but I manage to pull away every time.

I make it outside, feverishly wiping embarrassed tears from my cheeks, suddenly realizing that I'm out in the open under the dull orange streetlights, exposed to the crowd of people waiting to get into Light.

James catches up to me and takes me by the arm, but I can't shake him this time.

"Calm down, Annie. Listen to me…" he says, facing me.

I look at him blankly as imagined scenarios of him with that *slut* flood through my mind.

"*Nothing happened*," he says, stressing each syllable. "She showed up with Kristen—*Ollie's Kristen*—while I was having dinner with him. Ollie invited me for drinks with them at The Chateau, and we went back to my house afterward, and they all crashed there. I slept on the couch—*alone.* I swear, Annie, NOTHING HAPPENED. Ask Oliver, ask Kristen." He's calm, and my stomach settles with a subtle feeling that he's telling the truth. But the feeling quickly dissipates as skepticism returns because *nothing makes sense*—I still have so many questions.

"I don't believe you," I say, walking away.

"Annie, come back," he orders, following me.

"Leave me alone, James," I yell over my shoulder, "I can't talk to you right now!" I see headlights flash from a car, and it's Joe. I hurry toward his car and get in.

WE PULL INTO THE CIRCULAR DRIVEWAY AT MY HOUSE, AND JOE turns off the engine. The last hour is a blur and I'm a storm of emotions inside. I cry openly, and I don't care that Joe is probably getting a kick out of witnessing my relationship with James implode. But instead of saying *I told you so* or talking more shit about James, he puts his arm around me, then rummages through his glove compartment, looking for tissues.

"I'm sorry, Annie," he says while I lean on his shoulder, silently crying. "Honestly, Stephanie's shady as fuck, I wouldn't believe anything she says." This is the last thing I expect Joe to say.

"What?" I pause to dab my nose with a scratchy take-out napkin and look at him.

"The girl's a cokehead and a pathological liar. Trust me, I've known her for a long time—she's just like Patrick." His words are comforting, and I start to calm down.

"Why are you telling me this?"

"I don't know," he says, pulling out a pack of cigarettes. He offers me one and I take it. He puts one in his mouth, and it dangles from his lips as he lights mine. The nicotine sends a warm rush through my body, exactly what I need to relax. He lights his cigarette, takes a long drag, and leans back into his seat, blowing smoke out the window.

"*You don't know?*" I say, waiting for him to continue.

He shrugs, "I just want you to be happy," he says, taking another drag. "If he makes you happy, then I'm happy."

We continue smoking in silence, and I'm surprised at Joe's sudden, reasonable behavior. "I thought you'd be happy about this; I thought you hated him," I say.

Joe sits up and sighs, looking me in the eye. "Annie, why would I be happy that you're upset? I know I fucked things up between us, and I can't make you happy right now, so if he can… then…" he trails off.

I appreciate his words and the sweet, caring Joe I once knew peeks from under the coke and booze mess he's turned into lately. I take one last drag from my cigarette and drop it into the water bottle in the cup holder. I lean over and kiss him on the cheek. "Thank you," I say, jumping out of his car and entering the house.

I sink into my bed, numb and exhausted. I check my phone and have four missed calls and several text messages from James. The phone vibrates in my hand, and it's him again. I consider all the reasons I should and shouldn't answer. Joe's words, still fresh in my head, are the deciding factor, so I answer.

"Yes?"

"Where are you? Can I come talk to you? I don't know what happened tonight, but I swear you have it all wrong, Annie." His voice sounds desperate and pleading.

"I don't know, James… I don't understand why she had your clothes… it doesn't make sense."

"I told you everything, but I can explain it again; just tell me where you are."

I'm silent, grappling with the decision to see and hear him out. My heart sinks at the possibility that these last couple of months have all been a game—a dream! All of the happy moments, the laughs, our intense chemistry—*Was that all an illusion?*

"Annie?" He pulls me out of my thoughts. "Can I please come see you?"

The subtle possibility that he's telling the truth stirs softly in my gut. *I have to hear him out, at least.*

"I'm at home. Come if you want," I answer and hang up.

James texts me a few minutes later:

I'm outside.

I look out my window and see him leaning against his Porsche. I check myself in the mirror—flushed cheeks and puffy eyes. I don't care that I look like shit.

I go downstairs and open the door. His eyebrows are furrowed, and his lips are pressed into a hard line. We stare at each other before he tries to embrace me, but I recoil at his touch. I head back up the stairs, hear him close the front door, and then trail behind me.

In my room, he stands against the door and watches me closely. We're silent again.

"So?" I finally speak up, facing him.

"I know this looks bad, Annie," he says, sitting on my bed. I sit at my vanity, giving him my attention. Externally, I'm calm, but I'm seething inside.

"*Looks bad?* This is fucked up, James. You came here to explain, so explain," I demand.

He runs his fingers through his hair, and I observe him for any sign of deceit.

"Annie, this girl is stalking me," he says with a nervous chuckle, acknowledging how ridiculous he sounds.

"What?" I laugh, too. "Are you joking?"

"I'm not. That's the best way I can explain it. I've only met her once—at Dan Tana's—the night she showed up with Kristen when Ollie and I were having dinner. I had no idea they were coming!" His tone is defensive, but I let him talk because I need to hear the whole story. He looks down at his hands and then back at me, "We ate dinner, we had drinks. I was going to leave, but Ollie wanted me to stay to keep her entertained while he talked to Kristen."

"*Keep her entertained!?*" I laugh at his choice of words.

"Annie, I was just being his wingman, that's all."

I shake my head, searching his eyes for the truth. "So, how exactly did you *entertain* her?"

"Look, nothing happened. She had blow, we did some there, we went to The Chateau for drinks, and by then we were all fucked-up. They couldn't drive anywhere, neither could I, so we went to my place…"

"And…?"

"And nothing," he says. "We did the rest of the coke, I gave them some Xannys, and we crashed. I slept on the couch, ALONE."

"So how the fuck did she end up with your clothes?!" I'm annoyed that he hasn't explained that part yet.

"She went in the pool, her clothes were wet, and she asked to borrow dry clothes—end of story. Everyone was gone in the morning when I woke up. Ask Ollie, ask Kristen, I swear."

"Okay, and now she's *stalking* you? Yeah, right." I roll my eyes at how silly that sounds.

"You don't have to believe me, but it's true… She's been showing up at the club, hounding me to talk, offering me coke. I've rejected and ignored her. She knows you're my girlfriend. She doesn't care. Can't you see what she's trying to do?"

The snippets of watching them talking at Light return. I admit, it was brief, and I didn't see them near each other for the rest of the night.

He moves from the bed and kneels in front of me, placing his hands on my hips, and our eyes meet. "This whole thing tonight was a setup. She's psycho. She wants you to be mad and wants us to fight. She wants to get back at me for rejecting her. Can't you see? I promise, Annie, nothing happened."

There's sincerity in his voice and honesty in his eyes. I recall Joe's words from earlier, and I know that he's right—Stephanie is shady as fuck.

"I'm sorry that I didn't tell you about that night. I fucked up with that, but it wasn't a big deal." He wraps his arms around my waist, resting his head on my lap. "Please believe me," he pleads, pressing his face into my belly. The warmth of his breath cuts through the thin layer of my silk dress, and I'm immediately aroused.

"Remember when you told me that you 'didn't like games'

and that you 'don't like to be fucked with'?" I ask, referencing our fight over the picture of Joe and me in Darren's post.

He looks up at me and nods.

"Well, I don't like games either, and I don't want to be fucked with. I've been through enough with my last relationship, and I'd rather be alone than lied to and deceived again."

He nods. There's a clear understanding in his eyes. "I'm not him, Annie. What we have is different. I promise I'm not going to hurt you."

James pushes back the hem of my dress and caresses my thighs. I run my fingers through his hair—surrendering, choosing to believe him.

He meets my eyes and pulls me in for a kiss, and all the doubt and anger immediately dissolve.

"I love you," he says, releasing my lips to trail kisses down my neck and cleavage. He wedges himself between my thighs, pulling me closer to him as our lips lock again for a passionate kiss.

He moves his hands down my back to unzip my dress, causing the straps to fall off my shoulders. He cups my bare breasts with his hands and licks my nipples because he knows it's my weakness.

He stands up, bringing me up as my dress falls to the floor. We kiss and fall into my bed. I pull off his shirt, and he unbuckles his belt, slipping out of his pants as we kiss fully. He slips off my panties and makes love to me. The make-up sex is incredible.

Chapter Twenty

A week later, things are back to normal with James, but I'm still trying to recover from the stress caused by Stephanie's antics. It took a lot of apologizing and sweet gestures for me to forgive him. I've decided to leave it all in the past and move on from the drama.

We're having a special dinner with James's friends and two potential business associates tonight at Craig's. James and I arrive to a buzzing Friday night crowd, eager for a good meal, stiff drinks, and plenty of fun. The warm and casually chic dinner spot is packed with starlets, industry insiders, reality TV personalities, and other cool LA locals. We're here to meet with two British nightclub owners who want to consult with James and Oliver on a project.

At the table, Oliver is already seated with two stylish gentlemen and Kristen, whom he's now seriously dating. Ben is also here with two so-called "hot influencers."

I've heard about the Brits all week, and I'm not disappointed when I finally meet them. Thomas and Henry are both handsome forty-somethings. They're sharply dressed, charming, boisterous, and ready for a good time.

James told me they partied at Light a few weeks ago and

were so impressed with the club's concept, design, and feel that they set up a meeting with him and Oliver. They discussed the possibility of collaborating on their new night-club in London, and James is excited about working on the project.

When we started dating, he told me he lived in London in his early twenties after his dad cut him off for hitting the LA party scene too hard. He moved to New York for a few months, but his mom also cut him off for the same reason. James ended up in London, crashing with Lauren, who was studying fashion at Central Saint Martins. He slept on her couch and wandered around the city, trying to figure out his life. Eventually, he returned to New York and launched his nightlife career, which led him to move back to LA less than a year ago to open Light.

I look over at James, and he's beaming, charming the Brits, tag-teaming with Oliver, and talking business. They want to give the Brits the ultimate Hollywood experience with dinner, drinks, and partying at Light tonight.

While the Brits describe the dream club they want to build, I tune them out and chat with Ben, sitting next to me. Ben is a screenwriter and a total jokester. He cracks me up whenever I see him, and tonight is no different.

"What's so funny over there?" James says, turning his attention back to me. He puts his arm around my shoulder and looks at Ben on my other side.

"Ben's making me laugh," I say, holding back a giggle.

Ben smiles and takes a swig of his beer. I know he has a crush on me; it's been obvious since we met, and I know James sees it, too, even though it's harmless.

James smiles and plants a kiss on my temple. "Hey, did Annie tell you—she's moving in with me." Ben looks surprised, and I feel slightly embarrassed because James sounds territorial.

"Cool, when?" he asks.

"Next week, after graduation," I respond.

Ben doesn't miss a beat and raises his beer for a toast. "Mazel Tov!" he says with a laugh, and the three of us toast.

James looks pleased as he turns his attention back to Oliver and the Brits, while Kristen, sitting across from me, looks surprised after hearing our exchange. I smile at her because I know she'll tell her best friend Stephanie that her plan to come between James and me didn't work.

Thomas and Henry are engaging and hilarious. They laugh a lot and drink heavily but remain charming and composed. They've been bumping coke all night and hyped to keep the party going, so we have one final round at Craig's, then head to Light for more fun.

I ride with James, and he's in a great mood. He's excited about the club the Brits want him to help open. I'm happy to see him satisfied with how the night is going.

At Light, we find the usual crowd of beautiful people mingling about and filling the dance floor, dancing to DJ Marcus, spinning his signature mix of pop, rock, and rap tunes.

Our group settles into a reserved corner table in the main room and is immediately attended to with full bottle service and *owner-of-the-house* treatment. I'm tipsy from the two martinis I had at dinner but waste no time pouring myself a vodka and soda from the bottles before me. DJ Marcus is playing a great mix that gets the crowd going, and I'm high from all the energy around me.

I sway in my seat to the music and take a sip of my drink but nearly spit it out when I see Stephanie approaching our table. *What the fuck?* I freeze as she stands before us with a big smile and her usual smudged eyeliner, which I can't tell if it's intentional or because she's such a mess. Anger flares hot in my chest because I thought James had banned her from the club after what she did to me.

"Hey, guys!" Stephanie says as if we're all best pals. I look at her without reacting.

James shoots Oliver a look, and he answers her, "Hey, Steph, how's it going?"

"Hey, Ollie," she says, getting closer to hug him.

I turn to James, and he leans into my ear, "I'm gonna kill Rob; I told him she's not allowed here."

Kristen gets up from the table and greets Stephanie with a hug. I watch her whisper something in her ear, then discreetly usher her back into the crowd. I know James is fuming because the last thing he needs is Stephanie fucking up the night with the Brits, who are oblivious, having the time of their lives chatting up the models at the table next to us.

"Bro, I'm gonna kill Rob…" James says, leaning over me to talk to Oliver.

"I can get her out of here if you want," Oliver responds.

James shakes his head, "Naw, let her be. We don't need a scene tonight."

Kristen returns and tells us she talked with Stephanie, who promised to stay on the other side of the club for the rest of the night.

As last call approaches, our group heads to the office upstairs to keep the party going. I hang back to say hi to DJ Marcus and thank him again for pulling a double to cover my set tonight.

In the DJ booth, Marcus greets me with a hug, and we chat for a few minutes. He asks me to pick the closing songs of the night, and I happily oblige, making a careful selection, which includes one of Trent's songs for good measure. The crowd loves it, and Marcus approves, "I knew you'd pick the good shit, Annie!" he says with a wink.

As we say goodbye, I notice Stephanie staring at me from one of the tables. Despite the darkness and flashing lights, I can feel her eyes burning through me.

I stop in the ladies' room before heading to the office, and

Stephanie comes in behind me. "Hey, Annie," she says nonchalantly. I scan the bathroom, glad that there are other women here because I suddenly feel unsafe.

"What are you doing here?" I ask, calm and composed.

"What do you mean? Why wouldn't I be here?" She's smug, and her makeup looks even messier in this lighting.

"I don't have anything to say to you, Stephanie," I say, turning toward the door to leave.

"Annie… Why are you mad at *me*? It's James you should be mad at… I don't know what he told you about that night, but he was the one flirting with me the whole time. It wasn't until I told him that my brother is friends with Joe that he backed off. I wonder what would've happened if I hadn't told him…" she trails off with an obnoxious grin.

It takes everything in me to keep from lunging at her with closed fists as adrenaline pumps through my body, rushing straight to my head. I think about James and Oliver and how important tonight is for them, so I swallow my rage and leave the bathroom without taking Stephanie's bait.

I push through the crowd, fuming. When I reach the office upstairs, I find that the group has expanded to include two of the models the Brits were flirting with downstairs, and everyone is sitting around the coffee table having a great time. There's coke on the table, along with champagne flutes and cigarettes, and it's clear that the afterparty has officially begun. James is all smiles while engaged in conversation with Thomas. I'm still shaking from anger, imagining him flirting with Stephanie.

"Can I talk to you for a minute?" I lean down, whispering into James's ear. His smile fades as he follows me to the balcony.

"What's up?" he says, lighting a cigarette.

"Did you know Patrick is Stephanie's brother?"

He takes a drag from his cigarette, looking closely at me. He blows out smoke and shrugs, "Yeah."

"When did you find that out?" I press him.

"Annie, what's this about?" he looks annoyed.

"Well, Stephanie accosted me downstairs and told me that the only reason you didn't fuck her is because you found out that her brother is friends with Joe…"

He takes another drag, rolling his eyes. "This shit again? I thought we were past this! You know nothing happened. What else do you want me to say?" He runs his fingers through his hair, and the bright expression on his face from a minute ago is gone.

"Tell me the truth, would you have slept with her if you didn't know about Patrick?" My voice cracks because it breaks my heart to imagine it. Tears burn in my eyes as the feelings from our argument last week resurface, and I have to fight the urge to release them.

"That's a ridiculous question, Annie… And you already know the answer." He inches toward me, pulling me, and I stiffen. I hate that he's not answering my questions directly. "I don't give a fuck who her brother is, and I don't give a fuck about her. Nothing happened, and nothing was going to happen," he says.

"Okay," I sigh, coming back to my senses. I hate that I doubt him, and I hate that Stephanie got under my skin. The rage dissipates as James pulls me into his chest.

"Let's have a good time tonight, okay?" he says, looking into my eyes as his lips curl into a cute smile.

I nod, giving in to his request. I refuse to let Stephanie ruin my night or fuck with my relationship again.

Chapter Twenty-One

Graduation day was last week, and it's all a blur. The only thing I remember is the sea of people at the ceremony, the clusterfuck trying to find my friends and family in the gathering area after, and my anxiety over having James and Joe present.

I grappled with the idea of inviting Joe and decided to do so at the last minute. Now that we're both in serious relationships, our tension has softened. James made the best of it for my sake, and luckily, no verbal jabs or physical blows were thrown as they both stayed out of each other's way. I ended up having a lovely time—with a low-key cocktail hour hosted by my parents at our house after the ceremony, followed by dinner at Madeo with all my guests later that night.

Now that school is over, I'm enjoying living with James—officially. The moving process was smooth, considering I only brought clothes and some basics to his house. We've been practically living together for months, so things don't feel that different.

Angela and I also wasted no time getting serious about looking for the perfect space for our boutique, which we've been planning to do for so long. The goal is to find something chic and small in a prime location where we can sell pieces from our favorite designers and local undiscovered talent. So far, we've met with a few of Aunt Gia's recommended real estate brokers without any luck.

"Don't worry, sis, we'll find something! We have a few more spots to look at next week," Angela says, doing her best to remain optimistic as we wrap up another day of futile retail space hunting. I appreciate Angela's positive outlook after a particularly disappointing week of terrible listing appointments.

"Thanks for the ride," I say, hugging Angela as she drops me off at James's house. "Do you still want to come to Light for my set tonight?" I ask, getting out of her car.

"Yes, I'm down!" she says, and we plan to meet again later.

"Babe?!" I yell out, walking into the house. I peek into the kitchen and living room, looking for James. His cars are in the driveway, so I know he's home. "James?!" I call out again at the foot of the stairs, about to go up. I turn and spot him on his phone in the backyard. He's pacing back and forth, smiling big, and I wonder who he's talking to.

He's so deep in conversation that he doesn't notice me standing at the threshold of the pocket doors. He laughs and runs his fingers through his hair, unaware that I'm watching him. When he finally looks up and sees me, his smile fades, and he suddenly looks flustered. He says something into the phone, then hangs up.

"Hi," he says, approaching me as his gorgeous smile returns.

"Hi," I reply.

"I didn't hear you come in. How long have you been standing here?"

"Just a few minutes," I say as he pulls me in for a hug and a kiss. "Who were you talking to?"

"Uh, a friend," he says, releasing his grip and walking into the house. I follow him into the kitchen, where he grabs a beer from the fridge. "Do you want one?" he offers, pulling out two beers. I shake my head, so he puts one back, uncaps the one in his hand, and then takes a swig.

"So…?" I say, waiting for him to answer my question.

"Oh, yeah," he says, taking another swig from the bottle. "My friend Liz—from London—is in town. I'm meeting her for dinner later."

"Oh, dinner. With another Brit?"

He smiles and comes close, pulling me in again, meeting my eyes. "Yes, she's a friend I haven't seen in years; we're just going to catch up."

"Catch up? Okay…" I can't help the awkward pitch in my tone. I pull out of his grip and walk out of the kitchen and into the living room.

"Why are you being weird?" he asks, following me.

"Weird? I'm not being *weird.*" I drop my gaze because it feels like he's looking right through me. "I didn't say anything… If you want to have dinner with your friend, it's fine!" I sit on the couch, pulling out my phone from my purse.

"How was your day? Did you find any good spaces for the store?" he asks, sitting beside me.

I'm annoyed because it feels like he's changing the subject. I scroll through emails, fighting the urge to ask, *Who the fuck is Liz, and why are you having dinner with her?* Instead, I bite my tongue. "No, all the spaces sucked," I say, barely looking up at him.

"You'll find something, babe," he says, grabbing my hand for a kiss.

I give him a little smile and get up from the couch. "I'm super tired. I'm going to take a bath—it's been a long day," I say, walking away. He grabs my hand and pulls me back.

"Can I come?" he asks with a naughty look in his eyes. He looks so damn cute, and I can't help but smile.

"No," I answer, leaning down to kiss him on the lips.

I soak in the tub, trying to relax after a stressful day while still trying to process whatever the fuck just happened downstairs. I'm annoyed that I didn't ask James more about who this *friend* is, and I hate that I've become so insecure about our relationship lately.

Ever since the Stephanie incident at Light, I've become paranoid and mistrusting of him. I've started to wonder why James got so serious with me when he's—from all accounts—a total womanizer. I feel like, at any moment, he'll go back to his old ways and decide he doesn't want me to be the only woman in his life. I'm also aware that some residual insecurity from my relationship with Joe still lingers, making me feel crazy.

In the stillness of the bath, as thoughts run wild in my head, I become more suspicious and anxious when I remember that James didn't invite me to go with him to dinner. I close my eyes. *Don't go there, Annie,* I repeat to myself, *don't go there...*

I take deep breaths to calm down and notice the smell of marijuana wafting into the bathroom from downstairs.

I'm pruning, so I get out of the bath, and as I start toweling off, James appears in the doorway. "There you are," he says, peeking into the bathroom. I'm at the large marble vanity, and our eyes meet in the mirror that stretches across the wall. He walks toward me and wraps his arms around me from behind, kissing my neck. I want to be mad but can't— I'm weak to his touch.

"You smell good," he says, tracing my neck with the tip of his nose. Our eyes meet again in the mirror, and he cracks a little smile. I feel him, hard, pressing into me from behind. He unwraps the towel from my body and admires my naked reflection in the mirror. I'm suddenly shy and try to grab the towel back from him. "No, let me look at you..." he whispers in my ear, "You're so fucking beautiful..."

I relax and let the towel fall to the floor. "Can I help you with this?" he asks, taking my lotion from the counter.

"Sure," I respond, and he pours some on his palms, rubbing them together. He rubs lotion on my shoulders, then my breasts and my belly. He kisses my neck, and we watch each other in the mirror—I want him badly. I close my eyes and lean back into him as he continues.

His hands move gently across my breasts and my stomach and rest on my hips. My breath quickens as he moves his hand between my legs. His fingers gently trace me *there*, then slip inside of me. I bite my lips as he whispers in my ear, "You're so soft and warm… You feel so good…" He stops and brings his fingers to his lips to taste me. "You taste good too."

I turn around and kiss him, relieved that he's come up here to be with me, relieved that his words and touch have tempered my insecurity.

He kisses me slowly and deeply, and I taste my sweet saltiness on his lips. I slide my hands under his shirt, meeting firm abs, and tug at the waist of his jeans, putting my hand down his pants—he's hard, and I tell him to fuck me.

"Turn around," he whispers, and I oblige. He pulls off his T-shirt, and the sensation of his bare skin and firm chest pushing against my back further arouses me. He drops his pants and spreads my legs with his knees, pushing inside me while holding me firmly by the hips.

"Mmmm, yesss…" I gasp, relishing in the rush of pleasure blooming between my legs.

He fucks me hard as I hold on to the cold marble countertop of the vanity. I try to hold steady with my palms flat on the mirror as he thrusts into me from behind. We watch our reflection as our bodies move in perfect sync, and a delicious tension builds between us. He wraps his arms around me tight, and I respond, squeezing him inside of me. The tension peaks, and I can't hold back any longer, climaxing hard. "Ahhh," I exhale loudly.

"Mmmm," James responds as his body relaxes amid mini spasms.

We move to the bed, tingling from orgasm. The warmth of his arms around me and the cool breeze coming in through the open window is blissful, and I wish we could cancel our plans and stay in for the rest of the night, just like this.

"I have to get going, Annie," he says, stirring, untangling his limbs from mine.

"What time is your dinner?"

"Eight." He yawns and sits up on the bed. He kisses me on the lips, "It's just dinner," he says, looking me in the eye as if reading my thoughts.

"I'm not upset!" I say, trying to sound convincing.

He gets up, and I give him a playful spank on the butt as he heads toward the bathroom. I pull myself together and start getting dressed for my dinner plans as well.

Thirty minutes later, we're both ready and back downstairs, about to go our separate ways. He looks handsome, freshly showered and shaved, and looking effortlessly cool and *classic James* in jeans, a crisp tee, and a leather jacket. "So, I'll see you later?" he asks before heading out the door.

"Sure," I reply with a tight smile.

"Okay, I'll bring Liz to the club for your set, and you can meet her." He grabs me by the waist and pulls me in for a long, deep kiss goodbye.

Chapter Twenty-Two

I thought I was having dinner with Angela, but she shows up with Darren to pick me up. "I didn't know I was going to be third wheeling it on your date," I tease, getting into Darren's SUV. I still don't understand why they always hook up but refuse to be "official." However, I suspect things are evolving because they've been spending more time together and less time dating other people.

"Shut up, you're not a third wheel," Angela giggles.

We head down the hill to Sunset, toward Hollywood Boulevard, and to Katsuya for dinner. My mood dips, and Angela and Darren notice.

"You okay, Annie?" Darren asks, looking at me through the rearview mirror.

"Yeah, you're acting weird," Angela adds, turning in the passenger seat to face me.

I play it off because I don't want to talk about it. I'm not even sure why I'm upset. James and I just had amazing sex, and he said he wanted me to meet his *friend* later. I should be feeling great. "Nothing's wrong," I say, trying to fix my mood.

When we get to the restaurant, I notice how cute Darren and Angela look together. It's weird but sweet to see them so close and affectionate, especially this early in the night. Once their guards are down, they usually start flirting after a few drinks when they stop caring what other people think.

We order sake and appetizers, and my mood finally lifts. Darren's been on his phone texting. "Do you guys mind if Joe and Audrey join us?" He looks directly at me. They've become quite serious, and I've yet to spend one-on-one time with them as a couple. Even though things are civil between Joe and me right now, it's still weird to be around him and his new girlfriend.

I shoot Darren a look and shrug, "I don't care." Actually, I care a little, especially since I'm now going to be the fifth wheel on their double date.

"Okay!" Darren says, returning his attention to his phone, presumably texting Joe back.

Twenty minutes later, Joe and Audrey join us for dinner.

* * *

ANGELA POURS ANOTHER SAKE AND HOLDS MY GAZE AS SHE hands me the serving cup. I know she's checking to see how I'm handling all this *closeness* to Joe and Audrey and their unapologetic public display of affection. I give her a subtle eye roll and she returns a knowing smile.

Joe is his usual self—funny, charming, and I hate to admit it— handsome in his usual quirky, cool look. The silk flower print Saint Laurent button-down shirt he's wearing brings out the blue in his eyes and the gold tones of his dirty blond hair. His arm's been around Audrey's shoulder almost the entire time since they sat down, and she looks smitten.

I take a sip of my sake and avoid making eye contact with Joe as much as possible, but I can't help giggling at the funny story he's sharing about the time he ate a whole bit of wasabi the first time his parents took him to sushi when he was a kid. I've heard this story countless times, and I know he's telling it for Audrey, but I still get a kick out of his humor and colorful storytelling. Our eyes inevitably meet across the table, and I can't deny the pull he still has on me, even though we couldn't be farther apart after all the time that's passed and all the things that have happened between us.

* * *

IT'S ALMOST TEN WHEN WE ARRIVE AT LIGHT, AND I'M LATE for my set. I look around the club and can't find James anywhere. I ask Oliver if he's seen him, and he says he hasn't shown up yet. I get increasingly anxious after an hour goes by, and James still hasn't arrived. I resist texting him and try to relax so I can focus on my set for the next two hours.

After eleven, James finally arrives with a tall, slim woman with a stylish platinum blonde bob. From what I can tell, she's pretty and older than I expected. She also looks out of place in her minimalist little black dress among the pretty young party girls and their sexy nightclub attire.

James takes the woman to his reserved table, and I bristle as he introduces her to Oliver and Ben. I squint my eyes to get a good look at her through the darkness and flashing lights. He talks to them for a few minutes and then makes his way over to me.

"Hi, baby," he says with a kiss and a tight squeeze.

I wrap my arms around him, "Where have you been?"

"Dinner ran late," he says, getting close to my ear and talking over the music.

"Is that your friend?" I ask, glancing over at his table.

"Yes," he says, still holding me by the waist. He kisses my neck and says, "Come over when you're done."

I nod and watch him as he returns to his table. I have a full view of the club from the DJ booth, and I catch Darren and Angela sharing a kiss, which makes me giddy inside. At dinner, I extended a solid olive branch to Joe, inviting him and

Audrey to join us. I was surprised when he accepted, and now, I don't know what's worse—watching him and Audrey make out at one table or watching my boyfriend at the next table, laughing and smiling with another woman.

I try to stave off the jealousy and insecurity that overtake me as I watch James and Liz talk closely. So, I ignore them and turn my full attention back to the music I'm spinning and have a great time—playing the songs I love and dancing by myself in the DJ booth. I'm not going to let anything ruin my night.

DJ MARCUS ARRIVES TO DO THE CLOSING SET, AND I'M relieved to see him when he appears in the booth. We chat as we swap our laptops from the console, and when he finally cues up his first track at midnight, I slip out of the booth and make my way through the packed dance floor of swaying bodies to join my friends at my table.

I know I'm being petty by not going to James's table first, but I don't care. I'm annoyed that he hasn't left that woman's side since they arrived. But it doesn't take long for him to come to me, which I was waiting for.

"Hey," he says, leaning to whisper in my ear. Our eyes meet over the spinning neon lights cutting through the darkness. "Come with me," he says, reaching for my hand.

I oblige, and he leads me to his table, where Liz is chatting with Oliver. Ben is also here and currently flanked by two hot girls who have him rapt in attention. Liz is beautiful, with sharp features and bright blue eyes, and older than I imagined — she looks to be in her forties.

James introduces us, and I lean in to greet her. She shakes my hand and then gets up to hug me. "It's so wonderful to meet you, Annie," she says with a smooth British accent. "James has told me so much about you!"

I'm glad to hear it because I've been dying to know what the fuck they've been talking about all night.

"Can you join us for a drink?" She flashes me a welcoming smile. I nod and squeeze into the booth beside her while James sits on my other side. His body presses into me as he wraps an arm around my waist from behind and rests his other hand on my thigh. Oliver tells me how great my set was, and Liz echoes his compliment, adding that it was "amazing." I thank them as James squeezes my thigh.

The club is loud, and having a decent conversation is hard. So, we make small talk, and I ask her how dinner was. She tells me about their fabulous meal at Spago and how much fun she's having in LA. I learn that she's in the art industry and is in town to meet with people from The Getty. Her effortlessly cool demeanor strikes me, and my insecurity suddenly peaks as I find myself sitting next to such an elegant and worldly woman.

Ben and the girls slip out of the booth, and James and Oliver excuse themselves to chat with a group of young Hollywood VIPs sitting at the table next to us.

"So, do you DJ at other clubs?" Liz asks, trying to engage me in conversation. I imagine she's judging me as she stares at me with intensity.

"No, I just do this for fun," I respond, trying to speak over the thumping music. I lean a little closer to her, "My sister and I are in the process of opening a boutique."

"Oh, that's brilliant! You have amazing style; I'm sure it will be a smashing success," she says.

Liz and I chat for a few minutes, and I get a few details of her friendship with James out of her. She tells me they've been friends for almost a decade and met when James lived in London. They are seeing each other again after losing touch for a few years. It's clear by the tone in her voice that they were more than friends.

I watch James at the table next to us—smiling and

laughing with Brock Murray and Tony Jay, stars of a popular action movie franchise and two of the hottest Hollywood *It Boys* of the moment. The guys are accompanied by a group of typical party girls in sexy little dresses and full glam, who dance in their seats to the hip-hop mix DJ Marcus is spinning. Watching James, I wonder about him and Liz and what else I don't know about him.

I TAKE A SIP OF MY SECOND TEQUILA AND SODA, AND although I've spaced out my drinks, I'm very much buzzed. I glance at my table and see Angela and Darren talking closely, noticing that Max and Michelle have arrived. Joe and Audrey, however, are nowhere in sight. James returns to the table to check on us, and Liz tells him she's having a great time.

"I'm going back to my table," I whisper in his ear. I don't care to talk to Liz, and I'm peeved that he never mentioned her before. I hate that I'm now thoroughly jealous and inse-cure about their friendship.

"Really?" James says, leaning into my ear.

"Max and Michelle just got here, and I want to say hi," I say flatly. I know it's a weak excuse, but I can't imagine sitting with him and Liz for the rest of the night.

He looks annoyed and gives me an equally flat "Okay."

I turn to Liz and excuse myself. "It was great meeting you," I say, sliding out of the booth.

"Lovely to meet you too, Annie," she says with a bright smile. James stands at the edge of the booth and pulls me in for a kiss, and I feel Liz's eyes on us.

"I'll just be at my table," I tell him as I pull away.

When Light closes at two in the morning, I leave with my group for an afterparty. James drove Liz to her hotel an hour ago, and I regret telling him I would meet him at home. I know it was petty to not go with him, but I'm still irrationally pissed.

Max drops me off at James's house close to five in the morning, and I'm relieved to see his car in the driveway. I don't know why I feared he wouldn't be home. I feel bad for ignoring his texts earlier, and now I feel guilty for coming home so late.

Guilt quickly turns to anger when I find an empty bottle of red wine and two dirty wine glasses on the kitchen island. I try to ignore the suspicions swirling in my head and head straight toward the stairs, ready to crash.

"Annie?" James says, sitting up on the couch. I hadn't noticed him.

"Hey, sorry I woke you."

"You alright? Where have you been?" he asks, looking sleepy and cute.

"Yeah… We went to an afterparty, and it got late… I'm going to bed," I say, heading up the stairs.

"I'm coming with you," he says, getting up from the couch and trailing behind.

Once in the bedroom, I head straight to the bathroom to wash my face and peel off my dress, which reeks of cigarette smoke and alcohol.

When I emerge from the bathroom, James is in bed and already asleep. His clothes are in a pile on the floor. I grab one of his T-shirts from his dresser drawer and throw it on—I love sleeping in his soft cotton tees. I join him under the covers and try to fall asleep as a whirlwind of thoughts creates a storm in my head. Paranoia lingers as I fixate on the empty bottle of wine on the kitchen counter.

Chapter Twenty-Three

"JAMES!" I call out. No answer.

A sinking feeling grows in the pit of my stomach as flashbacks from last night return—Meeting Liz, being a total brat to James and staying out until five in the morning. I'm embarrassed over the whole thing, so I force myself out of bed before my thoughts spiral further.

I remember the empty wine bottle and wine glasses on the counter from this morning and my irrational anger returns. I peek in the dishwasher and discover the wine glasses. Like a psycho, I look in the recycling bin under the sink and find the bottle. My mind begins to wander as I imagine James and Liz sharing it.

I know my paranoia is unfounded because he was asleep on the couch when I got home—we slept in the same bed together! I know I'm being irrational, but the sinking feeling that I was a mess last night and that he's hiding something from me still lingers. So, I call James to get a sense of how bad last night *really* was.

"Hey!" he answers. His tone is cheerful, and I immediately feel better.

"Hi," I say, trying to sound normal.

"You're finally awake; how are you feeling?"

"I'm fine… I didn't feel you get up… where are you?"

"You were knocked out, so I let you sleep. I'm at the club," he says. "Is there something wrong?" He reacts to my sudden silence.

"No, no…" I bite my tongue so I don't blurt out questions about the empty wine bottle and his whereabouts with Liz after they left Light.

"Well, Dave and I are wrapping up our meeting soon. Come pick me up, and we'll go get lunch."

"Okay, I'll see you soon," I say before hanging up.

ROBERTSON BOULEVARD IS PACKED WITH THE USUAL CROWD OF shoppers, tourists, and fashionable locals. The hostess at The Ivy greets us with a smile and shows us to a corner table on the iconic patio with the white picket fence and chic market umbrellas.

"You, okay?" James asks, looking up from his menu. I nod, take a sip of water, and tell him I'm still hungover.

"Did you have fun last night?"

"Yes," I lie.

He nods and returns to his menu.

"What happened after you left Light?"

He grins and pauses, "If you're asking *what happened* after I left Light, nothing *happened*. I invited Liz to the house for a drink and then took her to her hotel."

We're both wearing sunglasses, so I can't read his eyes. "Is there something you want to ask me?" He's starting to sound annoyed.

"No.…"

"Did it bother you that I saw Liz?"

I'm not sure how to answer.

He clears his throat and leans in closer. "Annie… she's just a friend."

"Was she always *just a friend?*" I can't help asking.

"No. We dated when I lived in London… But that was a long time ago."

I fucking knew it. "Tell me more," I say.

"We dated for about two years, and… we lived together…" We're interrupted by the server who takes our order, but I've lost my appetite.

"What else do you want to know?" he asks, returning his attention to me.

"Were you in love with her?"

"Yes…" he replies without hesitating.

I want to know more about their relationship, but I don't want him to know I'm an insecure mess right now. I hate that I'm regressing to how I felt in my previous relationship, and I don't want to feel this way with him.

"Were you in love with Joe?" His question catches me off guard.

"James…" I take off my sunglasses and give him a look.

"I'm serious, Annie. The difference between your ex and *mine* is that yours is always around," he smirks. Now he's being a smartass. And *I know* I'm being a hypocrite, and this reality check is exactly what I needed to quell my insecurity.

"You're right. I'm sorry," I say and refrain from asking more questions.

I DROP JAMES BACK OFF AT LIGHT BECAUSE THEY'RE interviewing for new cocktail servers, keeping him at the club for a few more hours. I'm still in my head, replaying last night and the awkwardness between us at lunch. My phone rings, interrupting my thoughts.

"Hey! Where are you?!" It's Angela, and her tone is urgent.

"Um, I'm in Hollywood. I just dropped James off at Light; we had lunch at The Ivy."

"Oh shit, well, go back!" she says, sounding excited.

"Where… why?"

"Well, I just got a call from Aunt Gia, and she just got a message about a new listing. It's a retail spot on Robertson that's going on the market on Monday, so if we want to look at it before it goes public, we have to look at it right now!"

Aunt Gia is a savvy real estate broker, so if she wants us to look at a property urgently on a Saturday afternoon, we have to drop everything and go.

"Oh, shit!" I say, matching Angela's excitement. We've looked at dozens of retail listings all over town without any luck. I've been feeling defeated about the whole process, and if it weren't for Angela's unshakable optimism and Aunt Gia's encouragement, I would've given up on our dream to open a boutique by now.

I ARRIVE AT THE STOREFRONT ON ROBERTSON, A PRIME location just up the street from The Ivy. It is on a block with a high-end makeup boutique, a wellness shop, and a cute café, among other cool businesses. I've often walked up and down this block and always loved its good vibe.

Angela, Aunt Gia, and a tall, handsome man in a sharp, gray suit are already here. "Hey, Annie!" Aunt Gia and Angela welcome me.

I look around the space, and it's the perfect size for a small boutique. It has spacious storefront windows and a gorgeous, exposed brick back wall. I'm already digging the place's look.

Aunt Gia hugs me and introduces me to the handsome

gentleman with chocolate-brown skin and gorgeous eyes. "This is John Thompson," she says as he extends his hand.

"Nice to meet you," I say, shaking his hand. I look over at Angela, and she's lit up with excitement.

Aunt Gia is calm and graceful as ever. Her dark brown hair is parted down the middle, which she wears long and straight in an effortlessly, cool way. "We're all here, John. Can you show us around?" she asks in a gentle purr, batting her long lashes. John obliges and shows us around the space—an empty box of a room with the necessary foundations for a boutique.

The space has two drab dressing rooms, lousy lighting, outdated mirrors, and a gaudy counter with cracking pink paint. However, it has many open areas that can be transformed into whatever we want. John shows us the back of the space, and we find a nice-sized room that he says we can use as an office or for storage. Angela and I walk around, imagining a chic transformation of the place.

Angela grabs me by the arm. "I love it!" she whispers in my ear. Per Aunt Gia's advice, we're both trying to temper our excitement so we don't seem eager around the listing agent.

"Me too," I whisper back, mirroring her excitement. John takes us back to the main room and steps outside to give us time to talk.

"Well?" Aunt Gia says, looking at Angela and me with a smile.

"We love it," I say, nodding, ready to make an offer.

"It's going to need a lot of work..." she says, turning serious.

Angela and I look at each other and shrug. "Okay?" we say, utterly naive about the process of opening a boutique from the ground up.

"What do *you* think?" Angela asks her.

Aunt Gia looks around the space. "I love it, too. Yes... It

will need work, but I have a great contractor who can help. I love the location, and it's a great price. It also has the foundations of a boutique already built in. I think you should take it!" she says with certainty.

Angela and I look at each other and know we have finally found the spot for our dream boutique.

Chapter Twenty-Four

It's been a month since Angela and I signed on the dotted line to become the new retail space owners at 323 Robertson Boulevard. We've been overwhelmed with excitement and stressed over the entire process of opening a shop. Right now, we're barely at the first stage—trying to find the best contractor, interior decorator, painter, and electrician to transform the current dull space into a stylish LA boutique.

We hit the ground running as soon as we got the keys, meeting at the space daily and interviewing vendors to start the remodeling process. Unfortunately, I've been spending so much time at the space lately that I've seen less of James—ironic since we live together.

Our routine has become monotonous: I'm usually out all day, and when I get home, he's already at Light. We try to make the most of our time together, like Friday nights when I DJ and Sunday mornings when we make breakfast and lay around the house, trying to enjoy our one day off together. Otherwise, we catch up or make love in the wee hours of the morning when he gets home from the club or have coffee together before I have to meet Angela at the shop.

The last time Angela and I did anything social with our friends was two weeks ago, on the Fourth of July. Otherwise, it's been work, work, work!

We only scheduled two morning meetings today because it's Darren's birthday. He and Angela finally made it official on the Fourth when they showed up holding hands at a friend's barbecue. Since then, she's taken on her first official girlfriend task of planning his birthday party quite seriously, and she's never been happier.

The plan is to have dinner at Raleigh's, then drinks and dancing at The Tropicana, the hip poolside bar at The Roosevelt Hotel. But first, we need to get through our final meeting of the day with the contractor, who comes highly recommended by Aunt Gia and arrives promptly at eleven a.m. with his assistant.

I'm pleasantly surprised when he walks in—He's tall, handsome, and sharply dressed in a cool gray suit and loafers. He has sleek, dark blond hair and bright green eyes. His name is Ryan Ellis.

Ryan charms and impresses Angela and me during the hour-long meeting, so we hire him on the spot. Aunt Gia was right. He supports our ideas and has excellent suggestions for helping us create the shop of our dreams. He estimates the project will take six to eight weeks to complete, which gives us enough time to start buying merchandise and strategizing our marketing plan.

Angela and I leave the space at noon after our meeting, happy and relieved to have finally found our ideal contractor. We then treat ourselves to a celebratory lunch at The Ivy and facials to prepare for our big night out to celebrate Darren.

<hr>

I'M SURPRISED TO FIND JAMES AT HOME BECAUSE HE'S USUALLY at Light by now.

"Hey, babe," I greet him, happy to find him sprawled out on the couch in the den on his phone.

"Hey, babe," he echoes with a big smile.

"What are you doing here? Why aren't you at the club?" I lean down to kiss him on the lips and join him on the couch.

"We have a private event tonight. Dave's gonna handle it, so I thought we could stay in… maybe make dinner… maybe order dessert…" he continues, pulling me onto the couch and covering my neck with kisses. Spending time apart due to our conflicting schedules has been challenging, but we make up for it during moments like this, making our time together feel much more special.

"Mmmm… That sounds nice…" I say, surrendering to his affection as his hands slide under my dress, and our lips meet for a slow, deep kiss.

"But…" I pull away, "Darren's birthday party is tonight, so now that you're home, you can come with me!"

"It would be my pleasure," he says, returning to my neck to devour me with kisses.

LATER THAT EVENING, WE'RE IN JAMES'S PORSCHE, HEADING west on Sunset to Raleigh's in Westwood. It's a beautiful LA summer night. Traces of orange and pastel clouds streak against the darkening sky, creating a breathtaking backdrop to the bustling city.

I look over at James, and I can't resist running my fingers through his effortlessly sexy head of hair. He looks so handsome tonight in his signature cool, laid-back style.

At Raleigh's, we find Darren's dinner party in full swing as guests mingle in the back area at the communal table. Matt and his partner, Daniel, greet us upon arrival. "You look *so hot,*" Matt says in my ear when he hugs me. I giggle at his compliment and thank him for approving my look. I'm wearing a sexy, white, off-the-shoulder mini-dress that makes my cleavage look amazing. I've completed the look with sky-high strappy heels, loose hair, and red lips.

James and I mingle around the room, greeting Max, Angela, Michelle, and then Darren, who welcomes us with exuberant hugs. I can tell he's had a few drinks, and I'm happy to see him in such a great mood.

"I'm so glad you guys made it!" Darren says excitedly. "The bar's open, grab some drinks!" He motions toward the small bar in the private room.

I nod, glancing toward the bar, and spot Joe sitting alone, talking to the bartender. He's smiling big and, from the way the bartender laughs, is apparently cracking jokes.

Joe looks over, and we make eye contact.

"Do you want a drink?" James asks, drawing my attention back to him.

"Sure," I nod.

I start feeling jittery and uncomfortable as I brace myself for another one of their awkward encounters. I remind myself that they were cordial the last time they crossed paths, but the tension between them is always thick, and I hate being in the middle.

James and I walk to the bar, and Joe stares at us. He's got that look in his eye and that smirk on his face that tells me he's wasted. My stomach sinks at the sight of him, even though he's well put together in a fitted navy blue suit, black tee, and sneakers.

"Well, well, well, if it isn't Mr. and Mrs. Hollywood!" Joe says, in an obnoxious tone and a smug grin. James glares at him with a clenched jaw without responding. Instead, he turns to the bartender to order drinks.

I step closer to Joe to determine what version of him I'll get tonight. I'm pretty familiar with his erratic moods and unpredictable behavior after seeing him through countless benders.

"What are you doing?" I ask, unable to hide the disappointment in my voice. I thought we were in a good place, but now I'm not so sure.

He gives me a look and raises his glass, "I'm having a drink, baby!" He's loud enough for James to hear, but James ignores him. I shake my head, looking into his glassy blue eyes —He's obviously high.

"C'mon, Annie. Chill out, I'm just trying to have a good time—don't look so mad!" he says, getting up from his stool to give me a sloppy kiss on the cheek. I know he's trying to provoke James, but his attempt is futile.

James glances over at us, stoic and composed, clearly holding back from taking Joe's bait. He takes the two cocktails from the bartender and hands one to me. I'm stunned by Joe's behavior and brace myself in case they go to blows.

Joe sits back down, almost missing the stool. "Hey, what's up, man?" he says, extending his hand toward James for a fist bump. James gives him a nod and reluctantly returns his greeting. Despite his calm demeanor, I can tell he's simmering inside.

"I'm glad you could join us at our little family dinner!" Joe says with thick sarcasm, looking directly at James. It's not the first time Joe makes a sly comment intended to make James feel like an outsider. He's keenly aware of his leverage with me and uses our long history together and our mutual friendships to fuck with James and to make him feel unwelcome. James doesn't respond and instead takes my hand.

"Don't be an asshole..." I say to Joe as James pulls me away.

"Oh, come on, Annie... Relax! It's a party!" Joe calls out as James and I walk off to the other side of the room. I'm shaking inside from anger and embarrassment.

"Are you okay?" James asks as he pulls a chair out for me at the far end of the table set for Darren's dinner.

"I'm fine," I lie. I'm still seething over how rude and nasty

Joe was to us. I glance back at the bar and see Joe talking and laughing with none other than Trent, who just arrived.

If the tension between Joe and James had previously cooled, it was undoubtedly fleeting because neither is hiding how much they despise each other tonight. I can't help but wonder why Joe went from being friendly with me a few weeks ago to being a total dick tonight.

"I'm sorry about that," I say, sipping my drink and turning to James.

"Don't apologize for him…" James says, looking me in the eye, "I don't give a fuck about him and his antics. I hope you don't either."

"Of course not," I say, maintaining his gaze.

"Good, then ignore him—he doesn't exist," James says with a smile, leaning in to kiss me.

Angela comes over to tell us that she saved us seats at the other end of the table where she and Darren are sitting with the rest of the crew.

"We're going to stay here," I tell her. She looks at me and then at the other end of the table, where Joe sits next to Darren and Trent.

"Okay," she says, giving me a nod. I'm sure Angela sees how wasted Joe is and knows how volatile he gets when he's in this state.

Darren's birthday dinner goes as well as expected. Raleigh's food and atmosphere are excellent, as always, and the mood is celebratory. Even though James and I sit away from my friends, we make the most of dinner by enjoying the delicious meal and chatting with the guests near us, who are people from Darren's music world whom I've only met in passing. I do my best to ignore Joe, who glances at me throughout dinner. I can't help but notice that he barely eats and takes frequent trips to the bathroom, surely to keep blowing lines.

At the end of the meal, Angela presents Darren with a gorgeous cake, and we all sing "Happy Birthday" to him. My anger toward Joe has cooled, and now I'm happy drunk after my third cocktail. After the cake is served, the guests mingle around the room as everyone talks about our next destination.

"Are you guys coming to The Tropicana?" Angela asks, taking the empty seat next to me.

"Of course," I nod, turning my attention to her. James is engrossed in conversation with a friend of Darren's who used to host parties at Light.

Angela leans into my ear, "Did you know that Joe and Audrey broke up?"

"No," I shake my head, suddenly understanding why Joe is extra messy tonight. He's so predictable—when things get tough, he turns to booze and coke for comfort.

"I don't know the details, but I heard that Joe's been partying at Sixteen for the past few nights and hanging out mostly with Trent…"

I glance over at Joe; he seems like he's having the time of his life. Those who don't know him the way his closest friends and I do would never be able to tell how much pain he's in right now. He plays it off so well with his jokes, banter, and charming demeanor.

My mood plummets. Even though I wasn't thrilled that Joe was dating Audrey, I'm sad for him that it ended because they looked genuinely happy together. I feel bad for Joe, just like I always do—and I'm drawn to help and comfort him. But I remind myself that I can't save him—I've tried that too many times. Now, he's on his own.

Darren's birthday dinner ends, and the party continues at our next stop: The Tropicana at The Roosevelt Hotel in Hollywood. The outdoor bar has a livelier atmosphere, a chic crowd, and a great DJ. The group from dinner disperses throughout the bar and the iconic hotel. James and I stay close all night, talking, dancing, and stealing kisses. We hang out with people from our party and people James knows from the nightclub scene.

We decide to call it a night before the last call rush at two a.m., and as I'm saying goodbye to everyone, I realize that I haven't seen Joe since we left Raleigh's.

Chapter Twenty-Five

The relentless buzzing of my phone wakes me. It's been repeatedly vibrating on the nightstand, but I'm too tired to answer it. I DJ'd last night, and James and I barely got home from Light a few hours ago. The phone goes quiet, but when it starts vibrating again, I reluctantly answer it. "Hello," I say, half asleep.

"Hey, Annie…" The voice on the other end sounds like my brother.

"Max?"

"No. It's me… Joe."

I look over at James, sleeping.

"What's up?" I whisper, slowly sitting up.

"Um… I need to see you," Joe says. I'm groggy, and for a split second, I wonder if I'm dreaming. "Are you there?" he asks, waiting for me to answer.

"Yeah," I respond, getting out of the bed.

I'm naked, so I grab James's shirt from the floor and slip it on as I move to the adjacent den so I don't wake him.

"It's six in the morning, what's wrong?" I whisper. Joe is quiet, and a sense of dread comes over me. "What is it, Joe?

What's going on?" I ask, sitting on the couch, trying to be as quiet as possible.

"Can you come over? I need someone to talk to."

I can't believe what I'm hearing. "Right now?" I try to wrap my head around his request. "Can we talk later?"

"I need your help, Annie…" he says, "…I really need your help."

Joe's flat affect and monotone voice alarms me, and it's becoming more apparent that something is wrong.

"Where are you? What do you need my help for?"

"I'm at The Roosevelt, in one of the Cabana Suites," he says. "Can you come over… please?" His urgent tone rattles me. I sigh and try to formulate a coherent thought, considering it's the crack of dawn, and I'm probably still drunk.

I get up from the couch and peek at James, who is still sleeping.

"Annie?…" Joe says.

"Yeah, I'm here…" I answer and agree to see him.

I hang up with Joe and tiptoe back to the bedroom. I head straight to the bathroom to splash water on my face. *What the fuck was that about?* I wonder as I brush my teeth. I reconsider seeing Joe now that I'm awake and more clear-headed. But I can't shake the sound of his voice, and I know I have to see him.

I go to the walk-in closet as quietly as possible to get dressed. I put on a summer dress and slip on my Chanel ballet flats. James stirs in bed as I hunt for my purse in the dark bedroom cocooned in blackout curtains.

"Mmmm… what are you doing?" James says in a raspy, sleepy voice, turning toward me.

Fuck, he's not going to like this. I sigh, dreading what I'm about to tell him. "I have to go out for a bit… I'll be back soon," I whisper.

"What?" James says, now more awake. He sits up and I

move toward him, sitting on the edge of the bed. A hint of morning light filters into the bedroom from the skylight in the adjoining bathroom, and I can see the confusion on his sleepy face.

"I know this is going to sound crazy, but… I just got a call from Joe, and he doesn't sound good. He asked for my help… so I'm going to see him."

James scoffs and falls back into the pillows. "Really?… And you're going?" His tone is incredulous.

"Yeah, he's my friend… I have to…" I say, turning quiet. I know how ludicrous this sounds, and I know there are so many reasons why *I don't have to* see Joe at dawn on a Saturday morning, no matter how desperate he sounded. But I'm concerned by the tone of his voice and unable to shake the unsettling feeling in my gut.

"He said he needs my help…" I repeat. James is quiet and stares at me blankly. "He's my friend, James," I say, reaching for his hand. "I can't… ignore him." I look him in the eye.

James shrugs and says, "Okay."

"I'll be back soon… I promise," I say, kissing him on the cheek.

"Wait, where are you going?" he asks as I head toward the door.

"The Roosevelt," I answer.

* * *

It's six-thirty in the morning, and Hollywood Boulevard is deserted. The Roosevelt is only a ten-minute drive from James's house, and when I arrive, I head straight to the Cabana Suite, where Joe told me he's staying.

I knock on the door, and fear sets in for what's on the other side. Joe answers, and my heart sinks. He's pale and scruffy, and his pupils are dilated. He's wearing the same clothes from Darren's birthday party two nights ago, minus the jacket.

"You came," he says, surprised, opening the door further so I can enter. The suite is gorgeous but littered with beer bottles, plastic cups, and empty cigarette boxes strewn around the tabletops. An empty champagne bottle floats upside down in a pool of water in an ice bucket. The room feels stagnant, and there's a trace of cigarette smoke in the air.

"You said you needed my help, so I'm here," I say, quietly assessing the situation and realizing that I've walked into a drug den. "What's going on, Joe… what are you doing?" I survey the room as a knot forms in my throat. I notice the bed in the adjacent room, which looks intact; I don't think he slept at all.

"Joe…" I say, facing him. His usually piercing blue eyes look tired and dull. I shake my head and cross my arms—stunned. Tears burn in my eyes, and I hold myself tighter, trying to compose myself. "Why are you doing this?"

Joe runs his fingers through his hair and drops his gaze. He's quiet and fidgety. "I didn't think you'd come," he says, sitting on the couch.

I move to sit next to him but freeze when I spot a mound of coke and a rolled-up twenty on a glossy magazine on the coffee table. Seeing it makes my stomach turn, so I instinctively grab it and take it to the bathroom to dispose of the coke in the toilet. Joe is silent and avoids looking at me when I return. I pull up a chair and sit across from him, waiting for a reaction.

"I'm fucked up, Annie…" he says. "I'm really fucked up." He finally looks up at me. I search his face, trying to understand, but all I see is pain and exhaustion.

"I'm scared that you're going to kill yourself," I blurt out, unable to hold back tears any longer.

Joe looks down at the floor and shakes his head. "I'm not going to do that."

We're both silent—I take a deep breath and wipe my tears. "You asked me to come here... to help you... will you let me help you?"

He looks up at me and says, "I don't know what to do." He gets up from the couch, opens the sliding glass door, and steps out onto the suite's private patio. I take a moment to gather my thoughts before joining him. He looks defeated, sitting on a lounge chair with his head in his hands.

"Joe..." I try again. "I think you should go somewhere... to get help." We've had this talk many times before to no avail, but it doesn't hurt to try again.

"Do you remember when we went to Palm Springs last year to visit my grandparents?" he asks, looking up at me, masterfully changing the subject. I sit on the other lounge chair and nod—I have no idea where he's going with this. "I think about that trip a lot—it's the last trip we took together," he says as his expression softens with a smile.

I vividly remember that trip last summer. We took an impromptu drive to the desert to surprise his grandfather for his birthday. We didn't know that it would be the last time we'd see him, as he passed away a few months later. They were incredibly close, and the loss shattered Joe.

I crack a little smile, remembering how much fun we had on that trip. We talked and laughed the whole way there. We planned on going for the day but ended up staying the week-end, having wholesome fun with his grandparents, playing cards, and cooking dinner together.

We swam in their gorgeous pool during the day, and in the evening, Joe played the piano with his grandfather while his grandmother and I played chess and drank Manhattans—her favorite. When they went to bed, Joe and I stargazed the magnificent desert sky late into the night and made love into the morning.

"I remember it," I say, meeting his eyes.

"The house is for sale, you know... My grandmother is

moving back to LA; I'm thinking about buying it. Maybe it's time to get out of here and start over…. Maybe you could come with me…" he says with a smile, and I know he means it.

"What?" I shake my head.

"Yeah, we wanted that once—remember? We talked about living in the desert or on the beach—we can still do that."

I shake my head, "Joe, we talked about *retiring* there," I chuckle.

He looks me straight in the eye and says, "Yeah, I know, but we can do that now. We can retire now—we would be just fine. I can take care of us—forever." I'm speechless because I know he's spinning a fantastical story fueled by the drugs in his system.

"No, Joe… we can't do that," I say. My voice cracks, and tears spill over again.

His smile fades, and his expression turns cold. "Because of him, right?" he says, needling me.

I'm at a loss for words, shaking my head, "This has nothing to do with him," I say in disbelief, realizing that he's antagonizing me, looking for a fight—another familiar pattern between us.

"I can't believe you're still with him," he says, refusing to let it go. The shock over everything that's transpired so far slowly morphs into anger as I start to feel manipulated and roped into Joe's delusions after his drug binge.

"I didn't come here for this," I say, abruptly standing up, determined to leave. I hurry back into the suite as hot, angry tears burn my eyes. I feel like such a fool.

"Annie, stop—I'm sorry!" Joe says, grabbing my arm. I push him off and make my way to the door. "You're right—this has nothing to do with him!" he calls out. "This is all my fault… I fucked everything up… I ruined everything between us and live with regret every single day…"

I pause with my hand on the door handle. *All I have to do is open the door and walk out.*

"Please, Ace… I'm sorry about everything… I don't know what to do…" His voice is desperate, and when I turn around to face him, his eyes are brimming with tears. He looks like a shell of the Joe I grew up with and the Joe I fell in love with. My head tells me that things will never change and that we've been here before. *But my heart*—my heart tells me that I can't leave him like this… it tells me that I have to do everything in my power to help him.

I walk back to him and wrap my arms around him as he cries openly.

JOE FINALLY AGREES TO GO TO REHAB, AND I HAVE TO FIGURE out how to make it happen before he changes his mind. He's getting fidgety, pacing the room, and making me nervous. I convince him to take a cold shower while I look things up on my phone and make a few calls. I'm not getting through to any of the rehab centers in the area, and I start to feel desperate.

I call my father begrudgingly as a last resort. The conversation is hard and uncomfortable. My father is in disbelief about what I tell him and what I'm asking help for. He cares for Joe deeply, and the sadness in his voice is clear. Nevertheless, he agrees to make a few calls and tells me he'll call me back.

Joe emerges from the bathroom—shirtless and wearing the navy-blue suit pants. He's barefoot, and his hair is slicked back and wet. He disappears into the bedroom and returns, carrying a Supreme shopping bag and wearing a camo T-shirt with the recognizable red logo.

"Where did you get *that* from?" I ask, trying not to laugh— this is *so not his style.*

"It's Patrick's," he chuckles. "He forgot his new purchases here," he says, rummaging through the shopping bag, pulling out two equally vibrant, printed shirts. He shrugs, settling on the camo shirt and ripping the tags off the sleeve. Joe confirms my suspicion that Patrick was part of this mess.

"Who else was here?" I ask, unable to suppress my curiosity, certain that Stephanie was here too.

"Just some people…" he says as the phone rings, sparing him from answering my question.

It's my father informing me that he was able to make arrangements through an addiction specialist he knows at the hospital. He gives me the details on where to go and who to ask for. He managed to get Joe a spot at one of the premier rehab facilities in Malibu.

"Thanks, Dad," I say, hopeful that this is finally happening. Joe extends his hand, asking for the phone. "Hold on, Dad, Joe wants to talk to you," I say.

I hand Joe the phone, and he apologizes to my dad and thanks him for his help. He nods as my dad surely encourages him. "Yeah, thank you," Joe says again. "I promise I won't let you down, Dr. P," he says, pausing again and nodding to whatever my dad is saying. "Okay, I will…" he says before saying goodbye and handing the phone back to me.

Joe calls the front desk to let them know he's checking out and wants his bill delivered. He asks me to sign for him when it arrives because he's too cracked out to handle it himself. He's racked up a thirty-five-hundred-dollar tab in two days, and I'm sure there'll be more charges, considering the state of the room.

I make Joe search the room for any forgotten drugs or paraphernalia while I gather the debris from his bender into a pile of bottles, plastic cups, and random trash on a table. Joe stuffs his black shirt and suit jacket into the Supreme shopping bag as I survey the room one last time before we finally make our exit. As we walk through the hotel, Joe reaches to hold my hand, and I let him.

———

THE DRIVE TO MALIBU IS QUIET, BUT MY MIND RACES AS I process everything that's happened. I feel energized and focused even though I'm on three hours of sleep and pushing through my own hangover—I'm operating on pure adrenaline.

I look over at Joe, reclined in the passenger seat, arms crossed and wearing his Ray-Ban Clubmasters. He looks so still that I'm drawn to nudge him.

"I'm just closing my eyes, Annie; I didn't die," he remarks dryly. We both burst out laughing at the absurdity of his comment, and it's the lightest moment we've had all morning.

We finally arrive at the stately facility, which overlooks the ocean. It looks more like a five-star resort than a detox center.

"Wow," Joe says, admiring the surroundings as we approach the entrance. "If I had known about this place, I would've hit rock bottom sooner," he jokes.

We're welcomed by a friendly counselor and a nurse, who usher us to an office where Joe begins the admission process. After signing the appropriate consent forms and paperwork, the nurse takes Joe to the medical wing for an evaluation. "Will you wait for me?" he asks. There's not much else I can do here, but I know staying will make him feel better.

"Sure," I say and wait in the lobby.

I look at my phone and see texts from James. It's almost eleven in the morning, and I feel bad that I've been gone for so long. I step outside into the pristine manicured garden of the facility and call him. James's tone is chilly, but he also sounds concerned. I tell him what happened in as few details as possible—I'm not emotionally prepared to rehash the whole experience.

"Do what you have to do; I'll be here when you get home," he says before we hang up. I appreciate that he's being understanding.

I wait for Joe's medical evaluation to end. When he returns, it's finally time to say goodbye. He looks exhausted.

"Everything's going to be fine," I assure him.

"I know…" he says flatly. "I'm going to stay for thirty days… Please don't tell anyone besides our friends."

I nod, understanding how hard this is for him.

"I'm going to call my parents later," he adds.

"Okay," I say, reaching out to hug him.

He holds me close and whispers in my ear, "Thanks for being here, Annie… I love you…"

I hold him closer, fighting back tears. "I love you too, Joe," I answer.

I CRY THE WHOLE WAY BACK TO HOLLYWOOD. WHEN I GET home, James is in the kitchen, freshly showered, dressed, and making espresso.

"Hi," I say, standing in the entryway.

He walks toward me with open arms. "Are you okay?"

I nod, and when we pull apart, he smiles, but I notice scrutiny in his eyes. "Did everything go okay?" he asks, and I nod, feeling numb. "Good," he says without asking further questions. "Come sit, let me make you something to eat."

My head is pounding, and I'm not hungry, but I sit at the kitchen island because I feel guilty for abandoning him this morning. I try to make small talk, asking him about his morning and plans for the day while he makes me an espresso and avocado toast. He tells me he got up not too long ago and is heading out to meet Oliver for a club related something or other. I barely listen but try to make him feel like he's got my full attention. I'm still trying to process everything that happened this morning, and I can't stop thinking about Joe.

I eat half of my toast and only take a few sips of my espresso. "Thanks for breakfast, babe," I say, kissing him on the cheek. "I'm going to shower and get into bed—I'm totally drained."

He gives me an understanding look and pulls me in for a hug. "Okay," he says, "I'll try to be back in a few hours before I go to the club for the night."

"That would be great," I answer.

After my shower, I get into bed and pass out. It's after seven p.m. when I wake up, and the house is silent. I look at my phone and find texts from Angela with shop updates but nothing from James. I figure he couldn't make it back home after his meeting, and I'm sure he's at the club by now.

When I open the blackout curtains, the sun is still beaming on this July evening. I shut the curtains again because the light feels blinding to my tired eyes. I consider going downstairs to get something to eat, but I have no appetite—I only feel a dull sense of sadness. I close my eyes, and everything that happened this morning comes rushing back. I wonder how Joe is doing, and I start tearing up again.

I get back in bed and try to understand how Joe got to this dark place, but I know it was a long time coming.

Even though our circle of friends parties a lot, Joe has always pushed the line. In high school, he partied often, stayed out late, and went on benders. We started college at the same time, but he dropped out last year when he began producing Trent's album with Max and Darren, which resulted in a record deal. From then, it was all-nighters at the studio and long stretches of partying with music industry types all over Hollywood. That's when he met Patrick, and it was all downhill from there.

I knew things had taken a turn when his behavior changed —He became secretive, distant, and irritable. Keeping up with his mood swings was hell for me, but I loved him, so I put up with it. Things escalated at the end of last year when the guys finished Trent's album. That's when Joe started partying more, and our distance grew.

I reach for my phone after tossing and turning in bed, flooded with flashbacks and anxious for what's to come. It's now close to midnight, and still no calls or texts from James. I wait another hour, then give up on him coming home early. I know he's probably staying at Light until closing, so I resign to falling asleep without him.

Chapter Twenty-Six

It's been three weeks since Joe went into rehab, and I haven't heard from him since. Darren and Max were able to check in on him, and they let me know that he's doing well. I'm relieved he's getting the help he needs, but I'm still shaken by that morning at The Roosevelt Hotel.

There's a *strangeness* that has settled into my life since then. At home, James is distant—he's been going to the club earlier than usual and staying out much later, sometimes coming home at dawn. I've had to pull back from my DJ gigs and from partying with him because now that the shop's remodeling is almost complete, I have to be up early to take care of business, and it's no fun showing up hungover.

James is understanding of my new schedule and is encouraging about the shop, but the distance between us has even infiltrated our sex life. When we make love, I feel like I'm crazy for imagining distance because the sex is still incredible. However, there are long stretches between our once frequent lovemaking, and that's when the distance starts to feel real. There are moments when he becomes aloof, and I get paranoid, thinking it's deliberate, and I have no idea why.

At some point during these past strange weeks, James got

news from his father that he's getting married to his long-term girlfriend, and that they are expecting a baby. The news was a complete shock to James, who, at thirty-three, will soon have a half-sibling and a new stepmother who's only five years older than him.

James's father, Rick, lives in Laguna Beach and is a renowned real estate developer. According to James, his girlfriend Carrie is a reformed LA party girl he fell in love with after meeting at the Polo Lounge six years ago. Rick is twenty-four years older than Carrie, and at this point in his life, it was more likely that he'd become a grandfather than a father for the third time.

The wedding will take place next Saturday, coincidently the same day that Joe gets out of rehab. Max and Darren are already planning a welcome home gathering for him at my parents' house. I'm bummed that I can't make it, but also somewhat relieved that I don't have to see Joe yet—I'm still trying to get over everything that happened.

On Friday, James and I pack up his Range Rover and drive to Laguna for the wedding. It feels great to get away from LA, and I'm looking forward to taking a break from the non-stop grind at the shop. I'm also looking forward to spending time with James and hopefully repairing the distance between us.

WE ARRIVE AT OUR DESTINATION, PULLING UP TO A BEAUTIFUL beachside estate. We're welcomed at the door by Carrie, an excited, petite woman with shiny blonde hair and pretty green eyes. "Ahh! You made it!" she says, pulling James in for a hug.

"Are you kidding me? I wouldn't miss this for the world!" he beams.

She turns to me with a bright smile when they pull apart, "You must be Annie!" James puts his arm around me and formally introduces us. She pulls me in for an equally exuberant hug and tells me it's good to finally meet me. I didn't know that James had talked about me to his father or her, but it makes me feel good that he did.

A handsome older man joins us in the foyer and flashes a gorgeous, welcoming smile. "There's my boy," he says, greeting James with a hug. After their embrace, James introduces us, and he welcomes me warmly. Rick looks me in the eye when he speaks, and it's like seeing James thirty years from now. I note the resemblance—the same brooding dark eyes, great smile, and lush head of hair—except Rick's is mostly gray.

After the introductions, we move to a grand sitting room with huge windows facing the ocean. It's a bright, sunny beach day, and a slight salty breeze fills the house.

We settle into the minimalist, chic room as cocktails and light appetizers arrive, delivered by Rick's staff. Carrie seems madly in love as she excitedly talks about the wedding and the baby they're expecting. She shares that she's only fourteen weeks along, so it's no wonder she isn't showing. Rick is equally excited about the wedding and the baby; they both seem over the moon.

The house buzzes with excitement as various staff members start setting up for tomorrow's wedding. The ceremony will take place at sunset on their private beach, followed by a reception at the house. Carrie bops around, handling arrangements and graciously answering the staff's questions while James and I chat with his father.

"Hi, guys," a familiar voice greets us, and Lauren enters the room. She looks sleepy but welcomes James and me with tight hugs. "Sorry, I'm a little bit out of it. Scott and I took the first flight out of New York this morning, and we're exhausted," she says, yawning. She sinks down on the couch with a cocktail and a plate of appetizers, and we all join in a lively catch-up conversation.

A FEW HOURS LATER, EVERYONE RECONVENES IN THE GRAND sitting room for another round of cocktails. Lauren and I are in chic evening dresses, and the men are in handsome, sharp suits. After drinks, we take two chauffeured SUVs and head to the Ritz Carlton for the intimate rehearsal dinner.

I smile throughout the night, my heart swelling with genuine joy in the warm atmosphere alongside James and his family. There are multiple toasts, heartfelt speeches, lots of laughter, and good times. James and Lauren make a hilarious speech, roasting their father while also welcoming Carrie to the family. The vibe is loving and fun, and I'm thrilled to share it with James.

We're back at the house by eleven, and everyone heads for bed, anticipating the big day ahead. I'm tipsy from the cocktails at dinner and affectionate with James. The whole day has felt like one long emotional foreplay session. Watching him interact with his family, seeing him in such an intimate way, and sharing such a special occasion with him has been exhilarating.

"Let's go upstairs," I whisper in his ear as we admire the ocean and night sky from the house's magnificent wraparound deck. He pulls me in for a hug and kisses me on my forehead.

"You go up first; I'm going to have a drink with my dad and catch up."

I drop my gaze, feeling a sting of rejection.

"Hey…" he says, lifting my chin with his finger to meet my eyes. "I haven't seen him in over a year; I just want to spend some alone time with him, that's all."

I nod and tell him that it's fine. "Okay, come up when you're ready," I say, mustering a smile. He pulls me in for a lingering kiss, and I instantly feel better. But as I make my way upstairs to the bedroom, a wave of confusion overtakes me. *Am I overreacting? Am I imagining things again?*

I wait for James for as long as I can until I fall asleep. I have no idea what time he comes to bed.

IT'S FINALLY WEDDING DAY, AND GUESTS MINGLE IN THE SITTING room as Rick and Lauren make their rounds welcoming them, while Carrie gets ready somewhere in the estate before she makes her grand entrance. James introduces me to uncles, cousins, and long-time family friends. The wedding is set to be small; only about forty people are here, and everyone I meet is lovely.

The wedding coordinator announces that the ceremony is about to start, so everyone moves outside and descends a winding staircase toward the area on their private beach where the ceremony will take place. I saw Carrie's couture Chanel wedding dress earlier, and I know she's going to look incredible.

As everyone takes their places, James stands proud at the end of the aisle next to his father, serving as his best man. A harpist plays as Carrie's eight-year-old niece appears in her adorable flower girl dress down the aisle. Carrie's sister Jen appears next down the aisle and takes her place as the maid of honor.

A string quartet plays a beautiful melody announcing that the bride is on her way, and we all stand up in anticipation. Carrie appears at the top of the aisle and looks stunning as her father escorts her. Rick gets misty-eyed at the sight of her, and James beams next to him. The ceremony is brief but beautiful, ending just as the sun sets over the ocean. Everyone cheers and claps as Rick and Carrie are pronounced husband and wife and share a loving kiss.

After the ceremony, there's dinner and dancing, and everyone is jovial and tipsy. James and I are at a table with Lauren, Scott, and a few boisterous uncles, and we have a rowdy time—eating, drinking, and laughing for hours. James has been taking shots with his uncles. He handles his liquor well, but I can tell that he's drunker than usual.

The party continues late into the night, with more music, drinking, and dancing. James disappears from time to time to socialize while I also mingle.

"Hey, let's get out of here," he whispers in my ear, returning to my side and wrapping his arm around my waist. I get a rush from his touch as his lips brush past my cheek. We haven't had sex in over a week, and I'm desperate for him.

"Okay," I nod, and he grabs me by the hand, leading me out of the party and up the grand staircase to our room.

As soon as we close the bedroom door, we start kissing and undressing each other. A bright, full moon is out tonight, bathing the room in white light.

James and I fall into the bed—his touch is electrifying, and his kiss reignites my burning desire for him. I don't care that his longing for me is fueled by heavy drinking. I don't care that it will probably be different in the morning, as it's been for the past few weeks. The only thing I care about is him and I at this moment—touching, kissing, tasting each other, and making love. I savor every minute of it, glad the distance has finally lifted.

Chapter Twenty-Seven

A ngela and I are in the final stages of opening our shop. The construction crew has put up shelves, clothing racks, and merchandising units. The final steps will include paint touch-ups and adding the aesthetic details to turn it into the minimalist, chic boutique we envision. We're lucky to have Aunt Gia helping us because her impeccable taste has shaped our vision and helped us find the perfect interior design team to bring it to life.

Our contractor, Ryan, has assured us that the shop will be ready in two weeks, so our grand opening is approaching. So far, everything has gone smoothly, and the most stressful thing Angela and I are dealing with is picking a name.

We spent the last week brainstorming, hoping to capture everything we want the shop to be: cool, sexy, classic, and modern. So far, we've done the impossible and narrowed our choices to three options: Bella, after our maternal grandmother Isabelle; Moxie, because it sounds strong and cute; and Preston, our last name. We know Preston is a bit cheesy, but we like the contrast between a strong name and the softness of women's clothing.

"Ryan said we need to pick a name *today*," Angela says,

opening a box of newly arrived merchandise. We're in our storage room, excitedly unpacking the gorgeous clothes we just received from a few of our favorite designers and small local brands. It feels like Christmas morning, unboxing all the beautiful clothes we'll soon be selling.

"Yeah, totally…" I respond, admiring a sexy pink slip dress I just pulled out of a box. "Ooh, look at this one! Maybe I should wear this for our opening night party!" I turn the dress toward Angela, excited over my find.

"Annie, focus! We're *super late* picking a name, and Ryan said today is the deadline; otherwise, we'll pay triple to rush the signage!" she sighs. "Plus, we need to start marketing and social media…" Angela gives me a look—she's pretty stressed.

"Okay, okay! Yes, let's decide *today*," I say, trying to quell her escalating anxiety.

"I think we should go with *Moxie*," Angela says the name with emphasis. "It's cute, unique, and has a cool ring." I nod in agreement, but I'm not convinced it's *the one*.

"Are we sure we didn't think of everything?" I give her a skeptical look, hoping we can come up with something better.

"I don't know anymore," Angela says, throwing her hands up, exasperated. She returns to unboxing more clothes.

"Hey, ladies," Ryan appears at the door. He's what I imagine the person who coined the term *tall drink of water* wanted to convey. Today, he's wearing another impeccably tailored suit with a skinny tie and stylish pocket square. His hair is perfectly styled, and his skin is golden tan, which compliments his bright green eyes. He has my full attention.

"They just installed the last shelving unit; come check it out," he says.

Angela and I drop what we're doing and follow Ryan to the front of the shop. "What do you think?!" he says, motioning toward the beautiful glass shelves that will soon display stylish clutch bags and small accessories.

Angela and I gasp and look at each other with matching grins. "It's perfect!" I say, turning to Ryan. He looks pleased.

"Thank you so much!" Angela says, turning to the four construction workers who have been working all day to make the installations.

"Yes, you guys did an amazing job!" I add, turning to compliment the workers. The men thank us and return to gathering their tools and cleaning up the space before they leave for the day.

"So, that's the last install, next up—paint touch-ups, light fixtures, and signage!" Ryan says enthusiastically, looking at Angela and me.

"I can't believe we're almost there!" Angela says, clapping with child-like excitement.

I walk around, admiring how everything looks just like we imagined. The space is one big room with minimalist clothing racks built into the two opposing walls. Between the racks are glass display cases and sleek, clear acrylic tables for merchandising folded items. The coolest part is the exposed brick wall that commands the entire back of the room—a nice contrast to the clean aesthetic.

I rejoin Ryan and Angela, and they're discussing a possible delay with the light fixtures, which are being custom-built. "You have to make sure they're here next week. Otherwise, we're screwed!" Angela pleads to Ryan.

"I know, I know… let me try them again," he says, pulling out his phone. Angela and I look at each other, arms folded, hoping for a favorable outcome. She's right, if the light fixtures arrive in two weeks, as Ryan fears, we're *fucked*, and we'll have to delay the opening.

"Hey, this is Ryan Ellis. I'm calling about the light fixtures for three-two-three Robertson," he says in a commanding tone. Angela and I look at each other as he continues the call.

Three-Two-Three, she mouths, looking at me with wide eyes. I let the words sink in and feel them passing through my lips—

Three-Two-Three. I give Angela an affirming nod—this is it; we found the name for our shop.

ANGELA AND I ARE ELATED THAT WE FINALLY SETTLED ON A name for the shop: Three-Two-Three. It's the physical address of the building, and it conveys the vibe we've been looking for: clean, simple, and unique. We're so grateful to Ryan for inadvertently helping us find the name that we invite him for a celebratory dinner and drinks at The Ivy, our new go-to dinner spot since it's conveniently down the street.

After wrapping up for the day, the three of us stroll to The Ivy and snag one of the coveted tables on the patio. "I'm sorry I can't stay long, but it's too late to change my dinner plans," Ryan apologizes after we order martinis.

"What, you have a hot date tonight?" Angela teases him.

"Nope, I'm a single guy," he says with a big smile as he shifts his gaze in my direction.

Angela's been telling me for weeks that she thinks he's crushing on me, but I don't see it. I can't deny that there are moments—like the one just now—where I'll catch a flirty look or comment here and there. But after getting to know Ryan for the past month, I know this is all part of his charm.

"Yeah, right!" Angela laughs, giving him a playful nudge across the table. Part of Angela's charm is disarming people with her own playful, coquettish ways.

"Seriously! There's no special lady in my life—but that doesn't mean I'm not looking for one," he says with a coy grin.

We make eye contact across the table, and this time, my cheeks burn. The server appears with our martinis, and I'm grateful for the distraction so we can change the subject.

"Well, Ryan, we want to thank you for helping us name our shop," Angela beams, lifting her glass for a toast. Ryan and I do the same, and she continues, "To Ryan, the godfather we didn't know we needed for Three-Two-Three!"

We cheers, and Ryan looks equally embarrassed and tickled with the toast. "I have to say, this is my first time as a godfather to anyone or *anything*—but I like it!" he says, easing back to his charming demeanor. "I'm honored and will gladly take the credit." We laugh and continue our lively banter over ice-cold, stiff martinis.

Ryan leaves after the first round, and Angela and I stay for a second and third with dinner. "I'm telling you—he's *so* into you!" Angela continues teasing me about Ryan.

"Honestly, if James doesn't snap out of the bitchy funk he's in, I'm going to start flirting back," I answer. A heaviness settles in me as the words come out of my mouth.

Angela gives me a concerned look, "Really? I thought things were better since you got back from Laguna."

I take another sip of my drink as I try to temper the heat and the sadness rising in my chest. "Yeah, it's been fine... But I still can't believe he told me *yesterday* that he was going to Vegas for the weekend. What the fuck do you think that was about?"

I've already asked Angela this question. I texted her immediately last night after James casually told me he was going to Vegas today on an impromptu trip with two of his best friends visiting from New York. I felt so excluded, and I can't shake the feeling that *the distance* has returned.

"I told you—I don't think it's that weird, Annie. People do it all the time, '*Let's go to Vegas for the weekend!*' Did you expect him to invite you with his boys?"

I know Angela's right and remember James being sweet by saying he felt bad for leaving so abruptly. I didn't expect an invitation on his guy's trip, but it all felt so hurried and, quite frankly, inconsiderate. "Yeah, I know you're right." I shrug.

By the time we finish dinner, I'm tipsy and, in my feelings, in no mood to be alone tonight, so instead of returning to

James's house, I head to my parents' and crash in the comfort of my childhood bedroom.

***

THE NEXT MORNING, I'M IN MY PAJAMAS, HAVING OATMEAL AND an espresso at the kitchen island. The three martinis snuck up on me when I got home, and now I'm slightly hungover and trying to recover so I can head back to the shop in a few hours.

I look up from scrolling on my phone and see Joe walk past the big picture window, heading toward Max's pool house.

Oh, shit! I drop the spoon into my bowl and jump off the stool to catch up to him. This is it—I'm about to face post-rehab Joe, and I hate that I'm looking like a hot mess in pj's, messy bun, and traces of last night's makeup.

"Joe!" I yell out from the door. He turns around just before reaching the pool house. I give him a wave, and he smiles. My heart races as he approaches.

"Hey," he says, standing before me. I fidget and reach out to him for an awkward hug.

"Hi," I respond as my mind goes blank—I have no idea what to say. We look at each other in silence. "You look great," I say, finally able to formulate words. He's grown a rugged but well-kept beard, and his hair is longer and wavier than usual.

"Thanks," he says, lighting up. "What can I say? I'm a new man!" His eyes are bright and clear, and it's quite the contrast from the state he was in the last time I saw him.

"Do you want to come in for a minute?" I open the door wider, and he steps into the kitchen with me.

"Late night?" he asks, looking me over.

"Not really… Angela and I have been working non-stop… I'm just tired."

"Oh, right. I heard you found a space. Congratulations."

"Yeah, thanks…" I'm suddenly nervous and start to fuss with the flyaways in my hair, which I'm sure look unruly. I invite him to sit and offer him an espresso.

"What are you doing here?" I ask, fumbling with the bag of espresso beans. He pulls out a stool and sits—his calm demeanor unnerves me.

"Max and I are going over a few things before we go into the studio. We're starting to record Trent's new album today."

I nod as I grind the beans in the machine. "Oh, cool! Second album already?"

The first album that Joe, Max, and Darren produced for Trent is doing incredibly well for a new artist. He's got one hit song that's been getting heavy airplay on the radio and at the clubs. I always include a few of his songs in my set when I DJ, and they're always a crowd favorite.

"Yeah, I came out of rehab with a stack of new songs for Trent. You have no idea how good being sober and isolated from the world is for the creative process." Typical Joe, making light of a serious situation.

I place a freshly brewed espresso before him, and we lock eyes. *I love you, Annie.* It's the last thing he said to me when we said goodbye at the rehab facility, and it comes rushing back. I drop my gaze, blushing at the memory.

"Really? That sounds great," I say, sitting on the stool across from him. "So, was it okay?"

He takes a sip from his cup and shrugs, "I don't know… it was a shit show at first. Detoxing from all the poison in my body was no joke!" He's smiling, but I can sense the unpleasantness of the experience in his tone. "Honestly, I barely remember that part. But things got better after the second week… I'm glad I did it." He looks me in the eye. "I have you to thank for it."

I blush, uncomfortable with the credit.

"No, that was all you… You decided to go… I'm proud of you, Joe," I say.

His phone rings and the intimacy of the moment disappears. "Yeah, I'm here… I'm in the kitchen with Annie… Okay, cool…" I know it's Max on the other end.

"I'm sorry I wasn't here for your welcome home party, and I'm sorry I haven't called to check up on you," I say when he hangs up. I've been overcome with guilt for not reaching out to him.

"It's cool. I heard you were out of town… And you don't have to apologize—it's fine." He takes another sip from his cup. "When did you get so good at making espresso?" I sense he wants to change the subject, so I drop it.

Max enters the kitchen, and the energy shifts. He's chatty and excited about getting back into the studio. I hang around to hear about their plans for Trent's new album and his upcoming first tour. I still can't believe how Trent's stardom has risen since the guys met him over a year ago at a new artist showcase at a club downtown. I was lucky to be there that night and remember being blown away by Trent's confidence and presence on stage. I'm also in awe at how the guys helped shape Trent into the rising star he is today. It's incredible how much work they've put into writing songs, producing his album, and helping him shape his first tour.

I leave Max and Joe in the kitchen so I can get ready to go to the shop for another day of work. Before we part, Joe and I plan to have dinner to catch up. I'm intrigued by this new sober version of Joe—a version I haven't seen in a very long time.

Chapter Twenty-Eight

Angela and I are still unpacking clothes and overseeing the paint crew's final touch-ups at Three-Two-Three. We estimate we can start merchandising next week and have our opening party the week after. I can't believe how quickly it all came together, and I am thrilled with how everything has turned out.

"I saw Joe this morning," I blurt out as I fold tees into neat stacks. Angela stops what she's doing and gives me a wide-eyed look.

"Really? How was it?"

I've been telling Angela for days how guilty I feel about missing Joe's welcome party and that I've been purposely avoiding him because I have no idea what to say to him.

"It was fine… kinda awkward. He went to see Max and I caught him on his way to the pool house." Angela nods and waits for me to continue. "We talked for a little… He looks good…" I say, remembering how healthy and handsome he looked.

"Didn't I tell you?!" Angela reminds me. "I'm *loving* the longer hair and that scruff… Mmmm, he looks hotter than ever!" She smiles big and playfully shimmies her shoulders.

"Angela!" I throw a balled-up T-shirt at her, and we laugh.

"All jokes aside, he's looking *so* much better, and he seems a lot happier, too," she says. I agree and tell her I'm having dinner with him tonight.

THE PAINT JOB IS COMPLETE AT THE END OF THE DAY, AND THE workers are gone. Ryan comes by to inspect everything and review the final installation plans before our big opening. He tells us that the light fixtures will make it in time, after all, so we can finally set a date for our opening party in two weeks.

Angela and I are giddy at the news. We're probably more excited about the opening night party than opening the shop for business.

My FaceTime rings, and I'm surprised to see James's name pop up. I answer it immediately. "Hi, babe!" I say, smiling big. I walk over to the other side of the space for some privacy.

"Hey, how's it going?" He gives me his sexy smile that melts me.

"I'm good, how are you?"

"Pretty good… chillin' for a bit. Taking a breather…"

"From all the partying?" I ask. He looks hungover but handsome nonetheless. I wonder for a moment if he's been talking to other women out there, and I have to shake off the sudden pang of jealousy that blooms in my chest.

"You know it—Vegas, baby!" he chuckles. I ask him how his boys' trip is going, and he fills me in on their escapades— Gambling, checking out restaurants and new nightclubs. "Research," he calls it.

"*I'm so sure,*" I respond, rolling my eyes, knowing full well he's been partying non-stop.

He laughs, "What about you? Are you at the shop?"

I tell him about our progress and show him around the

nearly completed space. "Wow, it looks amazing! I'm so proud of you," he says.

"I miss you." The words stumble out of my mouth. My heart sinks as I remember how weird and distant things have been between us.

"I miss you too. I'll be home tomorrow," he says with a smile. "What are you up to tonight?"

I freeze, remembering my plans. "Um, nothing. I'll probably have dinner with Angela," I say, hoping he doesn't pick up on the shakiness in my voice.

"Okay, cool… have fun," he says before we say goodbye. There's no way I could've told him that I'm having dinner with Joe tonight. He would've flipped.

I ARRIVE AT A LITTLE SUSHI SPOT ON BEVERLY TO MEET JOE. He's already here and waiting at a table. He gets up from his seat and welcomes me with a hug. I'm glad our embrace is less awkward than the one this morning.

"Sorry I'm late," I say, taking a seat. He's relaxed and smiling.

We chat about our day as I try to contain the excitement and nerves that have suddenly come over me. I could use a sake bomb right now, but I remember that Joe isn't drinking, so when the server comes to our table, I order hot tea.

"How was the studio?" I ask.

"It was great! We laid down one track—Trent killed it—I can already tell it's going to be a great album," he says, looking me in the eye. He tells me more about Trent's album and his songwriting process in rehab. "I can't wait for you to hear these songs, Annie," he says.

When our tea and various sushi rolls arrive, I feel more relaxed. He tells me more about his rehab experience—the morning yoga and meditation classes, surfing in Malibu, and group hikes in the nearby canyons. The experience sounds more like a vacation than a detox program.

"I've been meaning to call your dad to thank him for the hookup," he says, turning serious.

"I'm sure he'd like to hear how you're doing. You know he wants the best for you... we all do," I say, holding back the impulse to reach across the table for his hand. Although Joe looks great, there's a hint of sadness in his eyes, and I imagine it's from the emotional toll this whole experience has taken on him.

The conversation turns to me, and I update him on the shop's progress. I've been telling Joe about my dream to open a boutique since we were teenagers, and he's always encouraged me to go for it.

"We're calling it Three-Two-Three, and Angela and I are having a big opening party in two weeks. I hope you can come." I can't contain my joy in sharing the news.

"I'll be there," he assures me. "What about the club? Are you still DJing?"

I shake my head. "Sometimes, but it's hard to do both... we'll see what happens when the shop opens."

Joe turns serious again. "How's James?" His question takes me by surprise because he's never *given a fuck* about how James is doing.

"Um... he's fine... He's in Vegas for the weekend with some friends," I overshare.

"I feel like I should apologize to him or something..." His response is even more shocking than his question.

"What do you mean?" I'm still confused.

"I don't know. I was a total asshole the last time I saw him at Darren's birthday, and you know... for everything else..."

I'm suddenly speechless. This is a side of Joe I never thought I'd see, but then I wonder if this is him making amends as part of his recovery—after all, isn't that one of the steps of the program?

"It's fine, Joe, I don't think it's necessary… James doesn't have a problem with you." I know I'm lying as soon as the words come out of my mouth. James hasn't softened his disdain for Joe, but I don't have the heart to tell him.

"Okay," he says with a shrug and drops it.

We continue dinner, catching up and sharing laughs as we polish off our rolls and the pot of green tea. The server clears our plates, and we order matcha ice cream for dessert.

"I have to tell you something, Annie," he says, getting noticeably fidgety. His tone is unsettling.

"Um, Okay…"

He drops his gaze and hesitates, searching for his words.

"What is it, Joe? You're freaking me out," I say, waiting for him to spit it out.

He takes a breath and looks me in the eye. "Audrey's pregnant."

The world stops. *Did I hear him correctly?*

"What?" I shake my head, trying to make sense of his words.

"Audrey's pregnant…" he repeats, "And it's mine…"

My blood drains cold. "What? I don't understand… I thought you two broke up…" My stomach turns, so I take a sip of water so I don't hurl all over the table.

"We did… it happened right before we broke up… She found out while I was in rehab. She told me last week when I got back."

The matcha ice cream arrives, and my appetite is shot. We're silent as the server places the delicate dessert bowl before us and sets the table with fresh napkins and two spoons. My heart races, and I have to fight the overwhelming urge to cry as I struggle with the gravity of his news.

When the server leaves, the awkward silence remains. "Annie, she doesn't want to keep it," he says, dropping another bomb.

"What?" is all I can muster.

"She has dreams and auditions, and she wants a career. And I… I can't be a father right now… I just got out of rehab, for fucks sake. I'm a goddamn mess!" I reach across the table and grab his hand. I gather inner strength and put my feelings aside—right now, I have to be his friend.

"I'm so sorry, Joe."

He lifts his eyes to meet mine again. "It's pretty fucking crazy, right?" he says, shaking his head in disbelief.

"So, has she made up her mind? What are you going to do?"

He shakes his head and shrugs, "We both agreed… it's for the best that she…" He doesn't finish the sentence. "It's just not a good time… the kid doesn't stand a chance!" he chuckles, attempting to appear stoic.

"If it's for the best, then you're doing the right thing." I can't think of anything more supportive to say.

He nods, "Yeah, it is, and we're both on the same page, so…. She wants to do it as soon as possible… I'm going with her on Monday."

My heart breaks. "I'm so sorry, Joe." There's not much more to say.

Our dessert remains untouched as we make our way out of the restaurant. We wait for the valets to bring our cars and try to have a casual parting exchange despite the emotional rollercoaster we both just went on. When our cars pull up, we hug goodbye.

"Annie, I'm sorry if that was too much. I wasn't sure if I was going to tell you, but… you're one of my best friends… even if shit's been fucked up between us… and… I didn't want you to find out from someone else, so…" He's nervous and rambling.

I grab his hands to pause him. "It's okay, Joe. I'm glad you told me. I'm here for you if you need anything."

I drive home in silence. The shock wears off, and the dam holding back the deluge of emotions breaks, and I start sobbing. I'm not sure if the tears are from the sadness of the whole situation or if they're from relief—which makes me feel worse.

Joe and I used to talk about having babies. I still believed it would happen when we were together at the beginning of the year. I know that things are different now, and we've both moved on, but that doesn't make the thought of him having babies with another woman any easier to accept.

Chapter Twenty-Nine

Angela and I spend long days at Three-Two-Three for the next week and a half, preparing for our big opening. We're having a party on Thursday night with our family, close friends, local magazine editors, social media influencers, and writers from LA lifestyle blogs to help us celebrate.

When the day finally arrives, Angela and I spend the morning with our two newly hired shop girls, Hillary and Kate, helping us with final merchandising touches and overseeing the flower delivery and bar setup for the party. We leave in the afternoon to get dressed and glammed and reconvene back at the shop at six to make last-minute preparations before our guests arrive at eight.

I'm a giddy ball of nerves as I do a final walk through the shop, admiring the finished project's beauty. Clothes are perfectly hung and merchandised, and the display tables are topped with neatly folded T-shirts, jeans, and accessories. The custom glass shelves displaying jewelry and handbags and the sleek lighting fixtures are the perfect finishing touches to our minimalist aesthetic.

I inspect myself in the mirror for the hundredth time.

Despite my escalating anxiety, I feel good about my look: a black minidress with a cinched waist flared skirt and a lacy, corseted bodice that hugs every curve, complemented by tall, strappy Louboutin heels. The glam team gave me sexy, wavy hair, dramatic smokey eyes, and glossy lips.

"Here, have this." Angela hands me a flute of bubbly champagne as I fidget with my hair. She looks nervous but gorgeous in a slinky silver dress, black Manolo pumps, and dramatic red lips. We have the same wavy, chocolate-brown hair, but hers is sleek and straight tonight.

"Thank you, I really need this," I say, accepting the drink.

"To Three-Two-Three!" Angela lifts her glass as we toast and sip the first of many drinks ahead.

"I think we're ready, do you?" Angela takes another sip of champagne, seeking assurance.

"Yes, everything's done. The bar and flowers look great, and Finn will be here any minute to set up." She nods, scanning the space one more time.

"Oh look, he's here!" I announce, relieved to see DJ Finn entering with a rolling equipment case. I walk over to greet him.

"Hey, Annie... *Sick place...* Congrats!" he says, admiring the shop. I thank him and show him around while we chat about the vibe and the music we want for the night.

As time inches closer to eight, our guests start to arrive. Our parents arrive first with Aunt Gia and her husband Aaron. They all just had dinner, and are in a great mood.

"You girls did an incredible job!" My mom smiles, giving Angela and me tight hugs.

"We're so proud of you both," my dad adds, admiring the shop and giving us equally warm embraces. Aunt Gia and Aaron congratulate us, and we return the sentiment, thanking her for helping us find the space and for her creative input.

"It was all you, girls. I just did my best so that you got what you wanted!" she says, getting misty-eyed as she hugs Angela and me.

DJ Finn starts his set— a signature mix of classic hip-hop and pop songs to start the party. Darren, Max, and Michelle arrive next, and Matt and Daniel show up shortly thereafter. Soon, the shop is buzzing as the rest of our guests arrive while Angela and I work the room, talking to as many people as possible.

I take a moment to catch my breath and grab a second glass of champagne at the bar when I suddenly feel a hand on my back.

"Hey, Annie."

I turn around expecting to see James, but I find *Mr. Tall Drink of Water* himself, standing before me in a sharp, slim suit and a big smile.

"Hey, Ryan!" I greet him with a hug. I'm buzzed and giddy, and the nervous energy from earlier has lifted.

"So, what do you think?!" he says, beaming proudly of his work.

"I am beyond thrilled—*we're* beyond thrilled!" I say, meeting his smile. His hard work and dedication to the once lackluster space made our dream a reality. "There is no way we could've done this without you. Thank you!" I hug him and hand him a glass of champagne to toast.

"I'm glad you're happy, Annie… and if you don't mind me saying… you look gorgeous tonight," he says, looking me in the eye as we clink our glasses. I can almost hear Angela teasing me that he's flirting with me again because he clearly is.

I thank Ryan for the compliment just as I spot James entering the shop. I watch him greet Darren and Max, then scan the room until our eyes meet. I give him a wave, and he flashes a smile as he approaches me. He looks incredibly sexy wearing black jeans, a black tee, and his favorite Saint Laurent black leather jacket.

"Hi, babe," I greet him as he pulls me in by the waist for a kiss. Ryan sips his champagne, watching us. "Ryan, this is my boyfriend, James. James, this is Ryan Ellis, our contractor."

"Hey, man, nice to meet you," James says, extending his hand. Ryan returns the greeting, and the three of us chat about the space, marveling at how great it turned out.

"I'm so proud of you, Annie. This place looks amazing," James says, turning to me when Ryan excuses himself to mingle. I throw my arms around him, beaming. He pulls me in, and we kiss again—It feels like it's just us in the room.

Angela appears, grabbing me by the elbow. "Sorry to interrupt, but I think it's time for our speech," she says with a nervous smile.

"Oh, a speech! Glad I made it in time for that!" James teases us.

"Ugh, okay." I give in, rolling my eyes.

"Do I look alright?" I ask, turning to James.

"You look gorgeous," he says, giving me another kiss. "And you look beautiful too, Ang," he says, giving my sister his flirty smile.

"Thanks, James," she answers, batting her lashes playfully while pulling me by the hand into the crowd.

I tell Finn at the DJ table that we want to say a few words, so he slowly fades the music and makes an animated announcement to the crowd, "Ladies and gentlemen, a word from our hostesses and proud owners of Three-Two-Three!"

The crowd cheers as they turn their attention to us. Finn hands Angela the mic, and my heart races, but I do my best to stay composed as all eyes in the room land on us. *Just Smile and be charming,* I repeat in my head.

"Hi, everyone!" Angela says, smiling at the crowd. "Annie and I would like to take a moment to thank you all for coming tonight and helping us celebrate the opening of Three-Two-Three!" The crowd cheers again, and my nerves settle as I make eye contact with my mom, dad, James, and so many other people that I love. "We'd like to thank a few very special people who made our dream possible," she adds before handing me the mic.

I clear my throat. "Yes, thank you all for coming. Angela and I appreciate your support… We want to give special thanks to our parents, Erica and Will, and our Aunt Gia, who helped us find this amazing space and shared her impeccable taste and knowledge with us. And… an extra special shoutout to Ryan Ellis and his team for bringing our vision to life— thank you, Ryan!" I pause and clap as the room joins in with more applause.

I hand the mic back to Angela, and as she continues her speech, I spot Joe and Audrey entering the shop, pausing behind the crowd. Joe's eyes meet mine, and he smiles. I acknowledge him with a nod, and my heart sinks as I remember our emotional dinner two weeks ago. We've texted a few times since then, and I know that Audrey terminated the pregnancy as planned. He told me that she's been feeling down, and he's been spending time with her for moral support. He also alluded to giving their relationship another chance.

Angela wraps up her speech, Finn starts the music again, and the party continues.

"I'm proud of you, babe," James says, pulling me in for another embrace. I'm high from the adrenaline rush of the night's events and enjoying his affection, which I've been missing so much lately.

"Sorry we're late," Joe says, standing before me, holding Audrey's hand.

"It's okay; thanks for coming," I reply, greeting him with a hug. He looks handsome with the scruff and longer hair slicked back and casually tucked behind his ears. I'm glad that he looks normal and healthy again.

"Congratulations, Annie. The shop looks beautiful," Audrey says, greeting me with a hug. She looks great in a silky black mini-dress and knee-high boots. If I didn't know what she's been through, I would've never guessed. She seems in good spirits, but I can't begin to imagine what she's feeling inside.

There's an awkward moment as the four of us stand looking at each other.

"What's up, James." Joe extends his hand, breaking the silence. I'm glad that James keeps his cool as he greets Joe with a handshake and Audrey with a smile. He excuses himself and leaves us to talk.

The conversation is light—mainly about the shop and random shit like the new restaurant down the street where they just had dinner. It's evident by their body language that they're back together, and Audrey looks more smitten than ever.

———

As the party winds down, guests start approaching Angela and me to say goodbye. The crowd thins until only a handful of people, including our family and closest friends, are left.

"We're going to Light for the afterparty if you want to come," I say to Joe and Audrey as we stand outside the shop while everyone lingers about. His arm is around her shoulder, and her arms encircle his waist.

"Thanks, Annie, but I don't think a nightclub is the best place for me right now," he answers with a smile. I feel like such an idiot for suggesting it.

"Yes, of course." My cheeks blush from embarrassment. I give each of them a final hug goodbye and watch as they walk hand in hand down Robertson Boulevard.

Chapter Thirty

The opening party's press coverage and influencer posts created a buzz for Three-Two-Three, making it the new "it" place to shop. Although we've only been open for a week, business is already exceeding our expectations.

I'm at the counter, taking a breather after helping several customers with their purchases. I look down at my phone, and the name Ryan Ellis is flashing on the screen. I pick it up and walk toward the dressing room area for privacy.

"Hello?"

"Hey, Annie. It's Ryan. Are you at the shop?"

"Yes," I respond. I'm surprised to hear from him.

"Cool, come outside for a second," he says.

I start to ask why, but he cuts me off. "Just for a minute, Annie, I want to show you something."

"Okay," I say, intrigued. The shop is busy with customers, but Angela, Hillary, and Kate are taking care of everyone, and I'm sure they won't miss me for a few minutes.

I step outside and find Ryan perched atop a stunning motorcycle parked at the curb. He grins at my surprised reaction. It's a sight to behold—a magnificent piece of machinery with an equally striking man seated upon it. He's dressed down from his usual three-piece suit and expensive shoes. It's just a white T-shirt, jeans, and motorcycle boots today. He's casually holding a black helmet on his lap.

My eyes widen as I approach him. "Wow," I say.

"What do you think?!" he grins proudly.

The bike is a beauty. Although I know nothing about motorcycles, I can tell that it is vintage and a Harley Davidson.

"Wow," I repeat, "It's gorgeous!" It takes me a minute to peel my eyes off the bike, and when I do, our eyes meet.

"Isn't she? I just got her."

"You did? Really?"

"Yup, I usually buy myself something nice after I complete a project I'm particularly proud of. And this is in honor of Three-Two-Three... since I'm the godfather and all," he chuckles.

"Hmm... looks like we may have overpaid you!" I tease, and we laugh.

"Come for a ride," he says.

He catches me by surprise, "Oh, I can't..."

"Come on, Annie. Take a little break. Let me take you for a ride. We'll stay close by; I promise you'll be very safe."

I look down at my silk summer dress and heels. "I'm not dressed for it."

"You're fine. We're not going racing, just a little ride," he says with a smile. I'm surprised at how persistent he's being. But I'm tempted to go—how bad could it be?

"Okay," I give in. "I have to tell Angela, though. Can you give me a second?"

His smile widens. "Of course," he nods.

"What's going on out there?" Angela cranes her neck to look over my shoulder toward the door with curious eyes.

"Ryan's here, and he just bought a vintage Harley, and I'm going for a ride with him! I'll be back in a little while."

I'm being deliberately short so she doesn't give me a hard time.

"Really?" She gives me a *you must be kidding* look. "And you're going?"

"Yes! It's just around the neighborhood. I'll be right back!" I say, turning on my heels and heading toward the door.

"Be careful, Annie!" she says as I step outside.

The bike's engine is already running, and Ryan looks pleased.

"Um…" I'm perplexed by how I'm supposed to get on the bike in my dress.

"Ever been on one of these before?" he asks.

To his surprise, I tell him I have—once. Max borrowed a friend's bike when we were in high school. He gave Angela and me rides up and down our street until our mother flipped and demanded that he return it to his friend ASAP.

"It's been a while," I add.

"Well, there's nothing to it," he says, handing me a helmet from a compartment on the back of the bike. "First, put this on, then climb on, and all you have to do is hang on." He says it like it's no big deal.

I take the helmet, suddenly regretting my decision. Ryan helps me put it on, securing it tightly and fastening the strap under my chin. He looks me in the eye with a grin. When the helmet is secure, he gives me a hand so that I can hop on.

Robertson is busy with lunch-hour traffic as people pop in and out of shops and restaurants lining the street, making me paranoid that someone will see me get on the bike with him.

I step on the footrest while he holds my hand for balance. I slowly throw one leg over the bike to straddle it while holding my dress down so I don't flash all of Robertson Boulevard. He looks back at me, amused as I struggle. When I'm finally on, he backs up into me to position himself between my thighs. The closeness between us triggers naughty thoughts.

"Okay, hold on to me like this," he says, grabbing my

thighs and pressing them tighter into him. His firm yet gentle touch feels electric on my bare skin. "And hold on to me here —tight," he says, grabbing my hands and wrapping my arms around his waist.

I do as instructed, noticing the definition of his abs and firm chest under his soft tee. He smells good, too—like fresh laundry and sunshine.

Ryan puts his helmet on and re-checks my thighs and arms to make sure I'm tightly secured around him.

"Hang on," he reminds me as he revs up the engine. The bike jerks forward, pressing me closer to him, and then we're off.

We head down Robertson and make a right on West Third. We drive a few miles until we reach Santa Monica Boulevard. Our helmets have a wireless connection, so we can talk while we ride.

"You doing alright?" he checks in on me.

"Yes!" I nod while holding on for dear life. I'm freaked out of my mind and having the time of my life! The bike is smooth, and Ryan handles it beautifully. It feels like we're floating in the air. I'm holding on so tight that I wonder if I'm hurting him. I have no idea where we're going, but I don't bother asking—I let him lead the way as I try to enjoy the ride.

We hit the beach when we get to the end of Santa Monica. "Want to grab lunch?" he asks. I don't want to spoil our fun ride, even though I told Angela I was going around the neighborhood and would be right back.

"Sure," I accept.

We ride up Ocean Avenue, and he pulls into the parking lot of a quaint beachside restaurant. He parks the bike, and we finally come to a stop. I remove my helmet, and the salty air and warm sun greet me.

"So, how was that?" he asks, getting off the bike, smiling big.

"Fucking incredible!" I'm unable to contain my excitement. He gives me a hand, helping me down. My knees are wobbly from squeezing him so tight.

We walk into the restaurant, helmets in hand. The hostess shows us to a table on the patio facing the beach, and we settle into our seats. The server arrives within minutes, and Ryan orders a dozen oysters and two beers for us.

"Isn't this better than being at work?!" He gestures toward the crashing waves before us.

"It is, except I wasn't expecting to be kidnapped," I giggle.

"Oh!" he says, clutching his chest like I just drove an arrow through his heart. His dramatics make me laugh. "Now I feel like an asshole!" he says, sinking into his seat.

"No, no! That's not what I meant!" I reach for his hand, and our fingers intertwine. "I'm glad that you kidnapped me," I say, releasing his hand abruptly. I'm the one being flirty now.

Our eyes meet, and I can't help noticing that *something* just happened between us. "Two Stellas," the server announces as he places the ice-cold glasses of beer before us.

Ryan raises his glass when the server leaves. "To afternoon kidnappings to the beach," he says with a smile.

I lift my glass, "Cheers to that."

The oysters arrive, and the beer kicks in. I'm relaxed, enjoying a pleasant afternoon buzz and a fun conversation with Ryan. Even though we saw each other almost every day while Three-Two-Three was coming together, we never had much personal time to get to know each other.

Over lunch, I learn that he's from San Francisco and has lived in LA for a decade. He tells me he has a house in Malibu, and I can only imagine how *sick* it must be, considering his impeccable taste.

"So, Annie. How serious is it with your boyfriend?" He looks me in the eye, and I'm taken aback by his directness. It's clear that Ryan is the type of man who goes after what he wants.

"Um… pretty serious. We live together." I have no idea how else to answer.

"Hmph… lucky guy," he says.

His phone buzzes on the table, interrupting the moment. He looks at it and then shows it to me—it's a text from Angela:

> Is Annie still with you?

"Oh fuck! Angela!" I freeze, remembering I told her I'd be right back even though I've been gone for over an hour.

Ryan texts her back, reading out loud his response: "Yes, your sister is with me, and she's safe. I promise I will have her back soon. We're having lunch." He puts the phone down and looks at me. "I hope I didn't piss her off. Your sister will have my head!"

I laugh at the accuracy of his statement. Angela does not fuck around. The phone buzzes again, and he reads her reply out loud, "Make sure she gets back in one piece." He laughs, "I think she's mad at me!"

I shake my head. "She'll get over it."

Ryan picks up the phone again and reads his response as he types: "Get ready because when I bring Annie back, I'm taking you for a ride." I giggle because I know he's kidding, and because there's no way in hell Angela would go for it. He flashes the phone screen at me when it buzzes again.

> Not a chance.

We laugh at Angela's response and take down our beers and the last couple of oysters because it's time to go.

The ride back to Robertson feels quick. In twenty minutes, we're back in front of Three-Two-Three. Ryan gets off the bike and then helps me climb down. He removes my helmet and looks closely at me as if he wants to say something. I flatten my hair when the helmet comes off.

"I hope I wasn't too forward today, Annie," he says, turning serious.

"No, you were fine…" I don't know what else to say.

"I just thought, since we're no longer working together and all… maybe we could hang out and get to know each other better." I blush, unable to hold his gaze.

"Ryan, I'm flattered… I think you're great, but I'm in a relationship, and…"

He cuts me off before I finish my sentence. "I know, it's all good. And I'm sorry if I was out of bounds. I just really enjoy spending time with you."

"I had fun today. Thanks for the ride—and lunch," I say, smiling at him.

He smiles back. "You're welcome. Thanks for helping me break her in." We hug goodbye before he jumps back on the bike and takes off.

I walk into the shop in a daze. I'm still high from the rush of the ride and shaken up by the last few minutes. I feel guilty for momentarily fantasizing about being with Ryan.

"Hey, Annie." A voice pulls me out of my thoughts. I look over and see Kristen. She's standing by a rack of clothes by the window where she had a direct view of what just happened outside.

"Oh, hey," I say, walking over to her, trying to act casual. She has a few dresses draped over her arm, and we greet each other with a hug. "What are you doing here?" I try, sounding pleasantly surprised to see her.

"Shopping!" she says, holding up the armful of dresses. "My sister and I are hitting all the shops on Robertson, so we had to come by. I'm sorry Oliver and I missed your opening party last week—we were visiting my parents in San Diego."

"Oh, it's okay. I'm glad you finally came in," I say, turning my attention to the blonde behind her.

"This is my sister, Ashley; she's visiting from New York; she goes to NYU," Kristen says, introducing us.

"Oh, hi. Nice to meet you." I reach out to shake her hand.

I look down at the clothes they're both holding. "You guys picked out some good stuff," I say, eyeing their selection.

Ashley steps closer to me and admires my dress. "I love what you're wearing. Do you sell that dress here?"

"Yes, we do!" I say, turning to one of the racks near us to pull out the pretty pink Rodarte summer dress I'm wearing.

"Do you mind if I try it on?" she asks, eyeing the dress.

"Not at all," I say, handing it to her.

Angela's at the counter watching our exchange. I walk the girls over to her and introduce them. Kristen and Angela haven't officially met, even though they've been at Light at the same time on multiple occasions.

Ashley disappears into one of the dressing rooms behind the counter, and Kristen turns to me. "So, who was the hottie on the bike?" Her eyes widen as a curious grin lights up her face.

"Oh, Ryan! He's a friend—our contractor, actually. He designed and built the shop…" I catch myself over-explaining. She stares at me as if unsatisfied with my answer. "He came by to drop off some documents, and he just got the bike, so he gave me a ride around the block." I shrug, stretching the truth a notch. I stop talking to keep from blabbering.

She nods, "Who knew contractors were so hot!"

"Yeah, he was *so* hot!" Ashley chimes in from inside the dressing room behind us, and we laugh. I look over at Angela, and she's smiling big. I'm sure she's dying inside at how awkward this exchange is for me.

"Well, I'm gonna try these on," Kristen says, disappearing into the other dressing room.

"Yes! I want to see them on you!" I exclaim. This is probably the longest conversation Kristen and I have had one-on-one. As soon as she disappears into the dressing room, Angela gives me a look and shakes her head as I mouth to her to *shut up.*

The girls emerge from the dressing rooms, modeling the dresses, and Angela and I *ooh and ahh* at their picks. When they finalize their selections, I ring up their significant purchase.

"So, are you DJing tonight?" Kristen asks as I hand her the shopping bag.

"I am. I go on at ten," I say, walking them to the door.

"Cool, then I'll see you there. We're having dinner with Oliver, then heading over. I think James is coming too…" she says. I freeze as the words come out of her mouth.

"I'm sure we'll be at Light in time for your set," she adds.

"Okay, great," I try to keep my cool as we hug goodbye.

I walk back to Angela at the counter, freaking out about Kristen seeing me with Ryan. *Why do I feel like I've done something wrong when I haven't?!* I'm sure Kristen won't say anything to James. But why wouldn't she? She's Stephanie's best friend, and it wasn't long ago that they were trying to sabotage my relationship. I conclude that she must've been in a good mood today because she's usually kind of a bitch.

I turn to Angela and say, "I have a feeling I'm going to be in so much trouble…."

Chapter Thirty-One

"This is my last track," DJ Finn says, smiling at me. "She's all yours!" he exclaims, doing a little dance to the rap song he always closes his set to.

I catch my breath because I barely made it in time for my set. Angela and I stayed at the shop for hours after we closed, taking inventory and reconciling sales. As new boutique owners, it's been a hell of a learning curve.

I pull out my laptop from my Goyard tote so we can make the switch at the console. As his song fades out, he says a few words to the crowd to close out his set and announces me as my first track fades in. Everyone on the dance floor cheers, and I'm officially ON.

The energy in the club feels exceptionally electric tonight, but it's not enough to get me out of my head as I wonder where James is after I'm three songs in and there's still no sign of him.

When James finally shows up halfway through my set, he's not his usual affectionate and *happy-to-see-me* self. The familiar distance from the past few weeks has returned, and my heart sinks because I hate his aloofness and the chill in our interactions.

"Are you okay?" I ask, pulling him close, trying to make eye contact through the darkness in the booth.

"Yeah, I'm fine," he shrugs. "I'm just a little high." He smiles and kisses me on my forehead.

"Where were you?" I ask, unsatisfied with his answer.

"Upstairs," he responds.

I have to cue a few more songs, and I'm getting annoyed by how short he's being.

"Who's up there with you?" I ask, returning my attention to him.

He gives me a smirk, which annoys me. "Some people."

I drop it and return to the console—he's being a dick, and it's starting to piss me off.

I feel his arms around my waist from behind. "It's just Ollie, Kristen, and her sister," he says into my ear. I flashback to earlier this afternoon at the shop and my encounter with Kristen. I wonder if she has anything to do with his icy demeanor.

"Cool," I say flatly. He kisses me on my shoulder and releases his arms from around me.

"I'll be back later," he whispers into my ear, then steps down from the DJ booth and into the crowd.

My set lasts another hour, and James doesn't return like he said he would. I kept scanning the crowd for him and the people he's with, but I never saw them. I'm relieved when DJ Marcus, the night's headliner, arrives at eleven-thirty for his midnight set. All I want to do is finish my set, find James, and tell him off for being an asshole.

Marcus distracts me with chit-chat, and when we switch spots, I sign off and announce him, causing the crowd to erupt with excitement. At exactly midnight, he takes over, and I'm free. I rush to unplug my laptop and pack up my things. My heart's racing, my hands are trembling, and I'm suddenly claustrophobic and need to get out of the booth ASAP.

Once on the dance floor, I weave through the crowd toward the door leading to the upstairs office.

I ring the buzzer at the door that conceals the staircase to the office. I feel the lock click, and the green light above the handle turns on, signaling I'm being let in. The office has a wall of security monitors that capture every corner of the club via cameras, and I know they can see me.

I make my way up the stairs, and when I reach the top, the green light above the door handle is already on. I let myself in, and my stomach drops. Kristen and Oliver are on one couch—her legs draped over his lap. James and Ashley are on the other couch—talking and laughing. There's a bottle of champagne in a bucket of ice, a mound of coke, and a couple of rolled-up bills on the table.

"Hi," I manage to say, surveying the room. Oliver and Kristen seem more excited to see me than James.

"That was a dope fucking set, Annie!" Oliver says, grinning. Kristen chimes in, agreeing. I thank them without taking my eyes off James as he cuts a line of coke on the table and snorts it. He looks up, sniffing and rubbing his nose, finally making eye contact with me.

"Yeah, that was great, baby," he says with a smile.

The office is dimly lit, and several candles are burning—the mood is almost *romantic*, except for the pounding hip-hop DJ Marcus is playing downstairs, filtering crisply through the speakers. Anger burns in the pit of my stomach as my mind races with wild speculations of what's been going on between James and Ashley.

"Come, sit," James motions for me to sit on his lap. He's on the small couch with Ashley, and she's not getting up for me. She gives me a forced smile as I join them on the couch. I can tell she doesn't want me here.

"Do you want a line?" James offers, wrapping his arm around my waist. I shake my head. I hate that I'm so uncomfortable. Even on James's lap, I sense the distance between us.

Oliver pours me a drink, and I play it cool. I don't want to give Ashley the satisfaction of knowing I'm bothered by her presence.

"Come with me for a smoke," James says, gently nudging me off his lap. We stand up, and I follow him to the small balcony that overlooks the VIP patio, the valet entrance, and out toward the Sunset strip. James lights our cigarettes while I watch him closely. The crowd below us talks and laughs loudly.

"Why are you acting like this?" I break the silence and take a drag from my cigarette.

He gives me a look and takes a drag himself. "Like what?" he says with a shrug.

I look toward the office, and Oliver, Kristen, and Ashley are dancing and laughing. I could say so much to him right now, but I hold back because it's not the right time or place.

"Forget it," I say.

James puts out his cigarette and gets closer, pulling me in by my hips. "I told you, I'm just a little high," he says, holding me tight. I know there's more to it than that, and I wish he'd tell me.

"Maybe you should stop blowing lines then," I retort. I can't even look at him; I'm so mad. When he gets this high, it reminds me of Joe, and I get anxious, reliving those terrible moments all over again.

James releases me, and our eyes meet. "I will, I promise," he says with an obnoxious smirk, making me madder.

I finish my smoke and tell him I'm going back downstairs to see if Angela and Darren have arrived. I'm lying—Angela and Darren aren't coming to Light tonight—I just need an excuse to leave the office before I get angrier and start laying it on James.

Through my escalating anger and discomfort, I'm sure that I don't want to argue with him in front of Oliver and Kristen, and especially not Ashley. I'm convinced that Kristen and Ashley told James about seeing me with Ryan today, and that's why he's being a dick. There is no other explanation for the way he's behaving.

"Are you going to come back up?" James asks, grabbing my hand to pull me back as I take a few steps toward the office.

"Yeah, I'll come back," I say, releasing myself from his grip.

Chapter Thirty-Two

James

As soon as Annie left the office, I knew she was pissed, and now I feel like an asshole. But I'm pissed too!

I didn't appreciate the little story Kristen and Ashley shared over dinner about Annie taking some joy ride on the contractor's bike. I remember meeting the guy at the opening party for her shop, and I knew there was something about him I didn't like.

The door buzzer rings, pulling me out of my thoughts, and I see Ben downstairs on the security monitor. *Finally*! I'm glad he's here, not just because he's bringing weed but because it's getting weird with Kristen's sister. She's been touchy with me all night and flirting hardcore. I need a fifth person to break up the foursome we've been since dinner.

Ben changes the vibe in the room for the better with his loud humor and infectious laugh. "You guys ready for this?" he says, showing off a freshly rolled joint.

I grab my phone—I can't resist texting Annie:

Where are you?

A few minutes go by, and no answer. I know she's mad at

me, and I don't blame her; I was a total dick. I'm in a better mood now that I've stopped doing coke and leveling out with weed. Annie isn't responding to my texts, so I go to the balcony to call her. There's no answer. I can feel Ashley watching me from inside, and I know it's time to go.

"I'm gonna split," I announce, returning to the office.

"Naw, dude, stick around," Oliver says, giving me a disappointed look.

"I have to take care of something," I say, grabbing my jacket from the couch.

Ben furrows his brow at me, "What do you gotta take care of?"

Kristen can't help herself and chimes in, "Aww, trouble in paradise, James?" I know she's been keeping tabs on Annie and me, so I'm not surprised by her bitchy comment.

"Nope, paradise is just fine," I respond.

I say my final goodbyes to the group and head downstairs to find Annie.

It's past one-thirty, and last call was just announced, so people are scrambling to the bars. I greet a few friends and look around, but I don't see her. Marcus is finishing his set, and I join him in the booth.

"What's up, man," I greet him, extending my hand. I look around the booth for Annie's things, but they're gone. I chat with Marcus for a while, then ask if he's seen her.

"Yeah, she said she was going home," he says.

I'm surprised to hear that she left the club. I thought she'd be with her sister and their friends, but I don't see them here either. I thank Marcus for the dope set and step out of the booth. Now that I know Annie's at home, I immediately head out without stopping to talk to anyone else.

I weave through Friday night Hollywood traffic, irritated at how slow everyone's driving and eager to talk to Annie. I hate the jealousy and anger gripping my chest, and I know, deep inside, that I'm probably overreacting. I'm dying to know, though—*What the fuck she was doing on that guy's bike today?*

When I arrive, the lights are off in the house, and everything's silent.

"Annie?!" I call out. She doesn't answer.

I see that the bedroom light is on from the bottom of the stairs. "Annie!" I repeat, making my way up.

As soon as I enter the bedroom, she steps out of the walk-in closet wearing a silky nightgown. She's taken off her makeup, and her hair is loose and beautifully unkempt. She takes my breath away.

"Hey," I say as our eyes meet.

"Hey," she responds.

We're quiet for a few seconds.

"Why did you leave without telling me?" I ask, stepping closer.

She gives me a look and turns to walk away from me. She's *definitely* pissed off.

I follow her to the bathroom and watch her at the vanity.

"Since when do I have to tell you where I'm going?" she asks, glancing at my reflection in the mirror. I can't help but chuckle because she's so fucking cute when she's mad.

"You don't. You can come and go as you please… you can take joy rides on motorcycles with other men…. You don't have to tell me anything, baby." I regret the words as soon as they come out of my mouth.

"Fuck you," she says, pushing me out of the doorway and shutting the bathroom door in my face.

I press my forehead to the door and exhale loudly, "Annie, c'mon." She turns on the faucet to silence me. I try the doorknob, but it's locked. "I'm sorry, babe, I know I'm being an asshole." I knock on the door to no avail.

I sit on the edge of the bed and talk to the closed bathroom door. "Annie, I'm sorry… come out here…" Exasperated, I put my head in my hands, prepared to wait her out.

The buzz I had earlier is just about gone. I consider rolling a joint to level me out more, but I'm too fucking tired.

The bathroom door swings open, and I look up.

"If you have something to ask me, why don't you just ask me?" she demands, arms folded.

I get up and take a step toward her. She's still as I get closer, looking away from my eyes as I pull her in slowly.

"I'm sorry," I whisper, burying my face in her neck. Her scent makes me immediately hard. "I'm sorry… I'm sorry…" I repeat, "I'm an asshole…" I feel her body loosen, and I hold her tighter.

"Nothing happened," she whispers.

"I know…" I release her to make eye contact. Her big brown eyes are misty, and I feel like a dick for being so cold to her earlier.

She wraps her arms around me, "Then why are you being like this?"

"Because I'm a jealous prick." I shrug. I hate to admit it, but the thought of her with another man boils my blood. I know I lost my shit earlier when Kristen blabbed about seeing her with the contractor, but now I'm just tired and in no mood for a fight. I take Annie's hand, guide her to the bed, and pull her onto my lap.

"I don't like how you get when you party too much. It brings back… bad memories…" she says softly, looking down at her hands. I know exactly what she's talking about. I'm sure the last thing she wants is to date another addict.

"Annie…" her comment upsets me, "It's not like that…" I'm irked that she would think I'm anything like him.

She's quiet, and her expression makes the anger I felt earlier turn into heaviness and guilt. I hate seeing her like this.

I'm drawn to her lips, and I pull her in by her chin for a kiss, and she lets me. "I'm gonna chill out with that—I promise," I whisper. "I'm not like him…" I can't say his name.

I taste her lips, and I want more, kissing her deeper. I

move my hand under her nightgown; she's soft and warm, and she squirms on my lap as my fingers inch closer to the spot between her legs. Her breath hitches as my fingers meet the silk of her panties. She's wet, and I'm rock hard.

"I don't want to fight anymore," she whispers as my fingers slip inside of her.

"We're not fighting…" I reply, my lips barely releasing hers.

I trail kisses down her neck, falling back into the bed with her. I pull off her nightgown and take her nipples in my mouth. I know she wants me to fuck her, but I want to taste her. I want to touch every inch of her body. No other woman has made me feel the way she does.

"James…" her tone begs. I love hearing her say my name. I remove my shirt as she tugs at my belt buckle and unzips my pants. Our foreplay doesn't last long before I'm inside her warm softness. She pulls me in, deeper and deeper like a current, and I sink, swallowed up by her skin, her lips, her hair, her scent. I'm engulfed in waves of bliss as I rock into her —I'm drowning in the ocean that is Annie, and I don't want to be saved.

Chapter Thirty-Three

I wake up with an emotional hangover from being pissed at James for being a dick to me at Light, then having the best sex we've had in a long time.

I make it to Three-Two-Three, barely functioning, and I'm glad the shop is quiet. Hillary and I opened today and she helps the few customers browsing the racks. I rest my chin on my hand, elbow firmly on the counter, daydreaming as flashbacks from last night with James and our delicious morning sex come flooding back. I close my eyes, blushing.

I flinch, startled by the vibration of my phone buzzing on the counter. Joe's name flashes on the screen.

"Hello?" I answer, coming out of my haze. Whenever he calls, I panic—I have no idea what he'll say—He's so unpredictable.

"Hey!" Joe sounds chipper on the other end.

"Hey… what's up?"

"Have you talked to Max yet?"

"No, why?"

"Oh, then you haven't heard the good news."

"What good news?"

"Trent's song just hit number one on Billboard. Number

one in the country this week, Annie! Can you fucking believe it?!" He sounds elated, and it makes me smile.

"Holy shit! That's amazing! Congrats!" Joe, Max, and Darren produced Trent's entire album, so I know how important this moment is for them. "I'm so proud of you," I say as my heart swells with joy.

"Thanks, we're celebrating with dinner at Raleigh's tonight. Can you make it?"

"Of course!" I exclaim.

As I end my call with Joe, Angela walks into the shop holding a tray of iced lattes, wearing dark sunglasses and a big smile.

"Did you hear the news?!" she beams, placing the tray on the counter.

"Joe just called me—I can't fucking believe it!" I say, shaking my head. The whole thing is so surreal. Trent! The guy I've been watching play small clubs in town for the past year now has the most popular song in the country! "Was Darren freaking out?" I ask, reaching for one of the cups.

"Ugh, so much!" Angela says, taking off her sunglasses. "He was so cute and excited—he literally cried!"

"Aww, really?!" The thought of Darren crying over the news makes my heart melt. "Have you talked to Max?"

"No, have you?" she asks, sipping her drink.

"No. We're calling him right now," I say, dialing him on FaceTime. Angela and I huddle close, waiting for him to pick up.

"Hey," he finally answers. He's shirtless, and his hair is messy as if he just woke up.

"Good morning, sunshine!" I greet him with a big smile. Angela squeezes in with me to be in frame.

"Um, did you know that your boy, Trent has THE number one song in the country right now—the song YOU GUYS freakin' produced?!"

Max cracks a smile and shrugs, "Yeah, fucking crazy,

right?" Max is super humble and weird about compliments, so I know all this attention and praise is a lot for him.

"Aren't you excited?!" I ask, emphasizing what a big deal this is.

"Of course! I think I'm in shock." His smile widens as he relaxes a notch.

"Max, we're so fucking proud of you!" Angela says, her voice cracking as she tears up.

"Thanks, sis," Max says, noticing how moved we both are. "I mean it, thank you both…" he says sincerely.

"Do Mom and Dad know?" I ask.

"Nope, I haven't seen them yet. They're probably already gone for the day."

Even though Max lives in the pool house, he rarely sees our parents due to their busy schedules.

"They're going to be so proud," I assure him.

He thanks us again for the call, and we finalize our plans to celebrate at Raleigh's tonight.

When I arrive at Raleigh's, everyone is in a great mood, chatting and mingling. Max, Darren, and Joe are beaming from the day's news. The man of the hour, Trent, joins us, and we're now in the presence of a bona fide superstar!

Joe is alone. He tells me Audrey is shooting a small part for an indie film in Canada for the next two weeks. I'm glad to hear she's moving on with her life and back to doing what she loves. I'm also happy that the animosity and awkwardness plaguing my relationship with Joe since our breakup has lifted. Rehab changed his life and saved our friendship.

We're sitting together at the long communal table among our best friends, and he has me laughing all night. Our banter feels familiar and comfortable. His humor and confidence have returned, and so has his old look—the scruff and the long hair are gone. He looks happy and healthy, and I couldn't be more relieved that he made it through such a shitty, dark time.

"The label's throwing a party for Trent at The Chateau later. Are you coming?" he asks. I tell him I was planning on swinging by before going to Light. Joe seems conflicted, and I'm reminded that a bar is not the best place for a newly sober person.

"Are you?"

"Yeah," he says, perking up, "It'll be fun."

I don't know how to broach the topic of his sobriety; I feel totally inept when it comes up. I hate being passive about it, but this is all new for me, and I have no idea how to navigate it.

When dinner wraps up, our group splits into different cars to head to Trent's party at The Chateau Marmont. Joe asks me to ride with him, and I accept.

On the way there, I text James to let him know about the plan, and to my surprise, he tells me he'll join us. The friendliness that Joe showed him at the opening party for Three-Two-Three must have eased his hostility toward him.

We walk into a lively scene at the poolside party at the famed hotel. The crowd consists of starlets, mega artists from Trent's label, and many suited industry types.

I spot our friends, and as Joe and I approach them, we come face-to-face with Patrick and Stephanie. I freeze and instinctively grab Joe's arm, wanting to lead him in the opposite direction.

"My MAN!" Patrick greets Joe excitedly, happy to run into one of his best customers. He pulls him in for an overzealous bro hug, and Joe seems shaken.

"Hey," he responds.

Patrick turns to me and gives me his smarmy smile, "And if it isn't the beautiful Annie Preston," he says, coming in for a hug. I stiffen at his touch.

"Hey, Joe," Stephanie looks up at Joe, flirting with her eyes while completely ignoring me.

I know Joe hasn't seen Patrick or his old party friends since he got out of rehab. At his counselor's suggestion, he got a new phone and changed his number to avoid temptation. I know that was hard for him, considering he works in the music industry and a good portion of Patrick's clients are musicians and execs—temptation is everywhere. I'm not surprised Patrick's here, as this is his type of party—full of people who want what he's selling.

Patrick fawns over Joe, congratulating him for Trent's song. Stephanie's overly enthusiastic and laser-focused on Joe too, and it's obvious that she's high as a fucking kite, per usual. I observe Joe trying to keep cool while making small talk with Patrick, but I can tell his mood has shifted from his earlier happy demeanor.

"So, I got a little private party going on in room sixty-four, swing by, man, everyone's coming, let's celebrate!" Patrick says, then turns to me, "I'd love for you to join us too, Annie," he adds with a wink.

"Cool, man," Joe says as he walks away. I'm still gripping his arm, in shock over the interaction. If there were ever temptation for Joe, this would be it.

Patrick and Stephanie disappear into the crowd, and Joe and I are quiet as we head toward our group.

"Are you okay?" I ask, finally releasing him. He gives me a nod and tells me that he's fine. I can only imagine how hard it must be to stay sober on nights like this.

James arrives and finds me in the crowd with my friends. He's jovial, and I'm surprised at how friendly and congratulatory he is with Joe, Darren, and Max.

"You're in a good mood," I reflect, pulling him close.

"I sure am… I got some good news today," he says, smiling ear to ear.

"Okay?" I wait for him to continue.

"Let's sit down," he says, taking my hand. *This must be serious.*

He leads me to an open table, and we sit.

"Okay, what's the news?!"

"Remember the Brits—Thomas and Henry?"

I nod.

"Ollie and I had a call with them today, and they officially made us an offer to consult with them on their new club in London. Well, they officially made *me* an offer …"

My heartbeat quickens as my mind tries to follow what he's saying.

"Ollie's going to stay back and hold down the fort, but he's going to contribute long distance." He pauses, "They're giving me full reign on concept, design, hiring. They want me to manage the team that will bring their ideas to life since they want an LA vibe for the club," he adds, beaming.

I'm stunned. "That's great…" It's all I can say. "And how are you going to do that? Are you moving to London?" My heart sinks as the words come out of my mouth.

He looks me in the eye, and his smile fades, "Not *move*, but I'll be spending some time out there—I'll be back and forth for a few months."

I don't know what to say.

"Annie…" he smiles, taking my hands. "Don't freak out—I'm not moving, and when I go out there, you can come with me. Wouldn't that be cool? Going to London for a few days every few weeks?"

"Yeah…" I finally respond, nodding. I don't want him to see how *not cool* this sounds to me. "When is this all happening?"

"Before the end of the year. I'll know more next week when I meet with them in New York."

"New York?" Another surprise.

"It's just for a few days. They want me to meet some silent partner of theirs who lives in the city… I want you to come with me." His smile turns flirty. "You can meet my mom; we can explore the city, and I can show you my favorite spots."

This sounds more like it, and I nod in agreement. "Yeah, that sounds great," I smile, easing up. He pulls me in for a kiss, but I can't shake how stunned I still feel.

<hr>

TRENT'S PARTY IS BUSTLING WITH GORGEOUS, INFLUENTIAL people mingling around the pool and dancing to the DJ's energetic soundtrack on the dance floor. There's an abundance of alcohol flowing, and everyone is having a great time. After two glasses of champagne, I've forgotten James's shocking news about London and am having a blast with him and my friends on the dance floor.

Looking around our group, I realize I haven't seen Joe in a while. I scan the crowd, but there's no sign of him. When thirty minutes pass, and he still hasn't appeared, I wonder if he's at Patrick's party.

I sneak away from the group to look for him, checking around the patio and the hotel lobby—still nothing. When I return to our group, I pull Max aside and ask him if he's seen Joe. I tell him about running into Patrick and his party in one of the rooms. "Patrick said it was room sixty-four. Can you go check if he's up there?" I ask Max, worried.

Max has been drinking since we arrived, and he's clearly wasted. "Are you fucking kidding me?!" He sounds irritated. "I'm not doing that."

I'm surprised by his response—I don't see the harm in checking on Joe.

"No, Annie, I'm not Joe's babysitter or sponsor… He's a grown man who can do whatever he wants."

"But aren't you worried that he might be with those people getting high?" Now *I'm* turning angry at how indifferent and callous he's being.

"Like I said, I'm not his babysitter. Listen, Annie, if Joe goes back to that shit, then that's on him, and you nor I can't help him. He's gonna have to figure this out on his own."

I start to say something, but he cuts me off.

"And another thing, if he's going leave us, *his friends*, his *family* on a night like this when we're celebrating something so special that we did *together*, to get high with those fucking scumbags, then fuck him! He can get high all he wants. I don't care."

I'm stunned at how heated Max is, and I don't understand why he doesn't want to help. "If you want to go up to look for him, that's all you; go right ahead," he adds, walking away.

I seethe as I look for James. I'm furious at Max for his reaction.

"I want to go," I demand when I find him.

"Right now? Did something happen?" James's confused look turns concerned. He presses about what's wrong, and I tell him Max is being an asshole.

"Can we please go?" I say, turning on my heels toward the exit—I don't wait for him to answer.

I push my way through the crowd. *I can't breathe.* I'm so angry at Max, and I'm *so* angry at Joe. I can just picture him upstairs in one of those suites that overlook Sunset, joking and laughing with those people, blowing lines, while that fucking bitch Stephanie laughs at his jokes and flirts with him shamelessly. The imagined scenario infuriates me even more.

I make it outside to the valet stand and take a deep breath. *What a fucking night.*

James catches up to me and pulls me by the arm. "What the fuck just happened, Annie?"

"I'm sorry… I just had a stupid fight with Max; it's not a big deal. I'm just drunk, and I want to leave."

He nods and pulls me in for a hug. "Okay, we'll go then."

In the car, I look at my phone to see if Joe returned the

text I sent him earlier. Still, no response. *Yup, he's definitely at that party,* I conclude.

I text him again:

UM, hello?? Where are you??

James's house is a stone's throw from The Chateau, so we're parked in his driveway within minutes.

"Are you going to tell me what happened?" James asks as we walk into the house. I head straight to the fridge for some water. I don't feel like going into details, so I repeat that I'm pissed at Max but that it's no big deal.

"Okay," he says, dropping the subject. "Let me roll you a joint; it'll make you feel better," he says.

I take down a full glass of cold water and feel calmer as I sit with James on the couch as he gathers the items for his joint. I need to vent, so I start telling him what happened.

I tell him about seeing Patrick and Stephanie—talking about her makes me angry all over again because it reminds me of the stunt she tried to pull with James. I tell him about Joe's reaction and how he disappeared for the rest of the night. I finally tell him what Max and I argued about.

James listens to me vent as he finishes rolling the joint. When I finish my story, he looks at me and shrugs, "I don't blame Max for not wanting to look for Joe. He's right; if Joe falls off the wagon, that's on him."

I stare at him blankly, pissed that he's siding with Max.

"You know what I think is going on…?" he says, leaning back on the couch to take a long look at me. "I think Joe's pulling this shit to get your attention."

"What?" I scoff at his words. "What's that supposed to mean?"

James lights the joint and gives me a calculating stare. "I think he likes getting your attention. He likes your sympathy, and he likes it when you save him."

I shake my head in disbelief. "You don't know what you're talking about."

He takes a long drag and blows out a cloud of smoke, his demeanor turning smug. "I can't believe you don't see it..." he continues. "He's manipulating you, Annie. He wants to continue being a part of your life and this is the only way he knows how."

His words are cutting, and I react, "He IS a part of my life!" My tone escalates, "I'VE KNOWN HIM SINCE I WAS TEN YEARS OLD! HE'S MY FAMILY!!" My heart races as I fume. I can't believe he's being such an asshole.

James puts down the joint, and his tone matches mine, "WHY THE FUCK DID HE CALL YOU AT SIX IN THE MORNING THAT TIME TO SAVE HIM FROM HIS THREE DAY BENDER? WHY THE FUCK DIDN'T HE CALL ONE OF HIS BOYS, HIS *BROTHERS*, TO HELP HIM? WHY THE FUCK DID HE HAVE TO CALL YOU?" His voice softens, "He wanted to get your attention, and he wanted you to save him," he reaffirms.

I'm shocked, realizing how much that incident's been gnawing at him. It's been over two months! I can't believe how much resentment he's been holding inside, which now explains the tension and distance that seeps into our relationship from time to time. I finally find my words, "Fuck you," I say, storming out of the living room toward the stairs.

Tears start rolling down my cheeks as soon as I enter our bedroom. I lock myself in the bathroom and cry hot, angry tears. *How the fuck did this night go so wrong?* I pull myself together as I take off my makeup and splash cold water on my face. I emerge from the bathroom expecting to find James, but he's not here. I take off my clothes and slip on my nightgown. I'm on autopilot as my head swims. I look out the window and see James sitting on a lounge chair facing the pool, smoking a cigarette. He's got a drink in his hand.

I have nothing to say to him right now. I get into bed and

check my phone, but there is still no text from Joe. James's words come echoing back. *"He's manipulating you. He wants your attention, and he wants you to save him."* I shake off the thought—James has no idea what Joe's battle with addiction has been like. I'm the only person who has seen him at his lowest, and it's far more complicated than he thinks.

I'm exhausted and numb, and when the thoughts finally stop, I fall asleep.

———

THE NEXT MORNING, I WAKE UP WITH JAMES SLEEPING NEXT TO me. I have no idea what time he came to bed. I get up with a sinking feeling as flashbacks from last night come flooding back, but I have to push through because I have to be at the shop in an hour.

James sleeps through my morning routine, and I don't bother waking him up to say goodbye when it's time for me to leave.

Later that day, I finally hear from Joe. He texts, apologizing for not responding to my calls or texts from last night. He tells me he left The Chateau after seeing Patrick and turned off his phone because he didn't want to deal with calls or texts from anybody. As I suspected, it was too hard for him to be near so much temptation, so he did the responsible thing and went home.

I'm relieved that Joe didn't *fall off the wagon* as Max and James suspected, but now I feel stupid for overreacting with Max and for doubting Joe. The sinking feeling from this morning returns as I think about my fight with James. I'm still angry at how nasty and insensitive he was. I'm offended that he implied that Joe is manipulating me, and I can't believe how much resentment he's been holding.

Chapter Thirty-Four

James left for New York to meet with the Brits three days ago, and it's been hard staying at his house. There's too much space and silence to fill with thoughts about the last few days and the incredible awkwardness that wedged between us. Even though we apologized to each other for the night of the blowout, a heavy distance set in, now more amplified by the physical distance between us.

I'm no longer upset that James didn't mention wanting me to go to New York with him again. I had too much pride to bring it up, and at this point, it's probably for the best that we're giving each other some space.

"Mom wants us to pick up dessert," Angela says, looking up from her phone.

"Oh, okay, sure…" I answer, snapping out of my thoughts. We're having Sunday dinner at our parents' house, where I've been crashing for the past few days because it's been too hard to be alone at James's.

I glance at the time, and we only have an hour left until we close the shop. I'm glad a few customers are browsing around, and I try to get out of my head by helping them pick out party dresses for an event. After I ring up the last sale, Angela and I tidy up and close up for the day.

"Hey, girls," our mother greets us with a bright smile as we enter the kitchen. She's chopping vegetables and greens, preparing a salad.

"Hi, Mom," I greet her with a kiss. She's her usual chic self in skinny jeans, Gucci loafers, and a silk button-down shirt.

"Looks like everyone's here," Angela says, grabbing a Diet Coke from the fridge while craning her neck to look out the picture window toward the backyard. I follow her gaze and spot Max, Michelle, and Darren sitting at the patio table and my father and Joe at the grill. I wasn't expecting to see him here.

"What's Dad making?" I ask, turning to my mom.

"Daddy's grilling! We're making steak and lobsters, rosemary potatoes, and this salad!" she says, proudly tossing its contents with silver serving spoons. I watch my father and Joe share a laugh, and it makes me smile.

"Do you need any help?" I ask since Angela is already outside, sitting on Darren's lap, looking enamored.

"Nope, I'm almost done here. Go join them; I'll be right out!" she says.

I step outside into the warm fall evening. The sun is about to set, and the sky is streaked with orange and pastel clouds.

"Hey, Annie!" Michelle greets me. I hug her and make my way around the table, greeting Darren and then Max. It took Max and me a few days to get over our fight, but we apologized and put it behind us, just like we always do.

"Hey, Dad." I wrap my arms around my father, who greets me with a kiss on the top of my head. I stand before Joe, who smiles at me, and we hug.

"How's everything coming along, Will?" My mother asks, joining us on the patio. She sets down her salad and lights the votive candles lining the center of the table.

"I'm plating everything right now, honey," my dad responds, flashing a smile.

"Great, let's eat!" she says, motioning for everyone to sit at the table.

My dad's playing his favorite jazz station, and it's the perfect complement to our relaxed and cozy meal. Joe sits next to me, and we catch up. The last time we saw each other was at The Chateau Marmont when he bailed from Trent's party.

I flash back to my fight with James and how nasty he was about Joe. *"He's manipulating you. He wants your attention, and he wants you to save him."* My blood boils remembering his words. He doesn't know anything about Joe or our relationship.

Max opens two bottles of wine for the table, and I suddenly feel bad for drinking around Joe. However, he doesn't seem to mind, and I know how much he hates it when we *don't* drink because of him.

Over dinner, we all have a great time catching up and discussing everything from current events to Trent and the new album the guys are producing for him. We laugh and talk for hours, and for once this whole week, I feel happy.

At the end of our decadent meal, my mother brings out the chocolate cake Angela and I picked up at Erewhon, and it's the perfect way to end the night. I'm tipsy from my third glass of wine and not ready for the fun to end. "Do you guys want to watch a movie or play a board game or something?" I ask, looking around the table and taking my last bite of cake.

My parents are in the kitchen, and Angela and Darren are helping clear the table. "I'm exhausted, Annie. Darren and I are going back to his place," Angela says with an apologetic look. I'm bummed because Max and Michelle also want to call it a night.

I sigh, disappointed.

"I'll hang out with you, Annie," Joe says, turning to me, "A movie sounds good. I can Uber home later," he adds, looking at Darren, who gave him a ride. I'm relieved that Joe wants to hang out because I'll probably go crazy alone, stewing in my thoughts and my simmering anger toward James.

Darren and Angela leave, and Max and Michelle retreat to the pool house. Joe and I stay behind to help finish clean up. "You guys cooked, so we'll take care of the rest," I tell my parents, insisting they drop what they're doing so Joe and I can take over. They happily oblige and wish us a good night, leaving us with tight hugs.

Joe and I are alone in the kitchen. We're silent as I rinse the dishes, and he loads the washer. The adjacent den's pocket doors to the patio are wide open, and jazz softly wafts in from the outside speakers, along with a cool breeze. After completing our task, we step back outside to gather stray items from the table.

The full moon illuminates the backyard, creating shimmering ripples in the pool. "Looks like we got everything—except this," Joe says, holding up a half-empty bottle of white wine. "Wait here a sec," he says, entering the kitchen and returning with two wine glasses. He pours the bottle's contents evenly between the glasses and hands me one. I give him a look. "Relax, Annie. This isn't the first drink I've had since rehab. I'm fine. I can have a beer or a glass of wine every once in a while. As long as I stay away from the gin and eight balls, I'll be okay," he chuckles.

I'm unsettled by his response. I had no idea he's been drinking—he always looks so put together and sober. *Maybe he's a responsible drinker now?*

"Okay, if you say so," I respond. Who am I to judge how he manages his sobriety?

"Cheers," he says, lifting his glass as I lift mine.

"Cheers," I echo.

Our eyes meet over the two flickering votive candles that remain lit, "Do you want a smoke?" he asks, pulling out a pack of cigarettes from his pocket. I nod, and he puts one in my mouth and lights it before lighting his.

"I was really worried about you the other night," I say, taking a drag.

"What night?" His eyes lock with mine.

"You know, the night at The Chateau."

He smiles and takes another drag from his cigarette. "You were?"

"Of course… I was sure you were up in that suite with Patrick and his slut sister. I was worried…."

He chuckles, "You don't have to worry about me, Annie. I know what I'm doing." He flashes a smile, and I believe him. "I appreciate that you care, but I can handle it. Haven't I proven that?" he says, reaching for my hand. Our eyes meet again, and I nod because he has.

"I've said this to you before, but… I'm sorry that I've put you in the middle of my shit. You've never deserved it," he says with sincerity in his tone, "… And it will never happen again," he promises. I squeeze his hand. The Joe who's been missing for so long is finally back.

The last candle burns out, and we're left in the dark except for the light from the kitchen and the bright moon above us. We put our cigarettes out and take down the rest of the wine.

"Let's go inside," he says, getting up from the table and picking up the glasses and the empty wine bottle. I follow him into the kitchen and lock up.

"Do you still want to hang out and watch a movie?" I ask, turning off the stereo and some lights.

He leans against the kitchen island and looks at me, "Only if you want me to."

I nod. "Let's go upstairs."

Joe doesn't say anything as he follows me through the dark, quiet house and up the stairs to my bedroom.

He closes the door behind him as I take off my earrings at my vanity. "Have you been staying here?" he asks, surveying the room. My Louis Vuitton duffle is sitting on my bed with clothes spilling out.

"Yeah," I shrug and move the bag to the floor. He doesn't ask any more questions, and I don't volunteer more information.

"Do you want to pick the movie?" I hand him the remote, and he sits on my bed.

"Sure," he says.

I don't know what's come over me, but I'm feeling impulsive after the wine and the hours of laughing and flirty banter over dinner.

I kick off my Chanel ballet flats and join Joe on my bed. He follows my cue, stretching out and getting comfortable. My heart races as we lean back on the pillows, our shoulders brushing lightly. He scrolls through our movie options, the soft glow of the TV casting flickering shadows across the room. I turn off my bedside lamp, leaving us in dim light.

I put my head on his shoulder.

"I miss this," he says, sliding his arm under my head.

I spread my fingers across his chest—his heartbeat feels as fast as mine.

He pulls me closer, his touch warm against my skin, and I tilt my head to meet his gaze. Our eyes lock, his intense stare penetrating mine. As he inches closer, anticipation builds, and our lips finally touch. The intensity of his kiss clashes with the alarm bells ringing in my head, warning me of all the reasons this shouldn't be happening.

Joe kisses me deeper, and I don't resist. His hands caress my body and rest on my belly.

I kiss him back with equal intensity.

He climbs on top of me, nibbling my neck as I trail my fingers down his firm back.

We kiss again with awakened passion as his fingers move further down, making their way under my dress. He releases my lips and dots kisses along my neckline, leading to my cleavage. His lips brush past my nipples, creating an explosion of goosebumps on my skin as every nerve in my body comes alive.

Joe unzips my dress from behind, slipping it off me. He unsnaps my bra and licks my nipples, taking them fully in his mouth and sucking them gently.

The alarm bells go silent—my mind is completely blank.

My yearning for him intensifies as he pushes his fingers past my panties, slipping inside of me, causing a rush of pleasure to surge directly to that spot. Every inch of me aches and throbs for him.

"I've missed you so much," he whispers in my ear as I unbuckle his belt, meeting his desire. We continue undressing each other until we're skin to skin. I'm desperate for him as we continue kissing, my longing for him escalating until he finally enters me.

"Ahhhh," I sigh, releasing my breath as the intensity of his erection fills me deeper and deeper with each thrust. He encircles my waist, gripping me in his strong arms, pulling me closer into him as he buries his head in the crook of my neck, sinking deeper inside of me.

Our bodies move in perfect rhythm as pleasure builds slowly and deliciously between us. He rocks into me hard, he rocks into me slowly, we kiss, we roll around in my bed, and I get on top of him, gasping at how good he feels inside me as he grabs me firmly by the hips, pulling me down, deeper and deeper into him.

He pushes me back on the bed and climbs on top of me again. Each time he enters me, the delicious pleasure builds a little more. *This feels so good… this feels like home.*

We rub noses between kisses and lock fingers as we make love. All the days and nights we've been apart and all the things we've said and done to each other dissolve, no longer mattering.

The light of the TV flickers in the background, and our

eyes meet from time to time in the blurry darkness of the room. I hold his face in my hands, kissing him deep as he pushes harder and faster into me until he cums. The friction, the warmth of his release, and the overwhelming emotions cresting within me peak into a delicious orgasm.

Joe collapses on top of me; we're both out of breath as our bodies tingle in unison. My mind is swimming with thoughts again—the blankness is gone. I run my fingers through his hair as he rests his head on my breasts, steadying his breath.

Chapter Thirty-Five

M y room is flooded with sunlight. Joe is still sleeping, and our limbs are entangled with each other. He hasn't let go of me all night.

OH FUCK.

The gravity of what happened sets in.

I slowly climb out from under Joe's arms and legs, unraveling myself from the sheets. He squirms but doesn't wake up. I slip into my bathroom, and dread washes over me, hitting me like a bucket of ice water.

What have I done?

I stare at myself in the mirror. Flashbacks from last night return full force, and I try fighting them off as guilt engulfs me.

My heart drums loudly in my tightening chest, squeezing the air out of me.

I feel like I'm going to be sick, so I get in the shower to keep myself from having a full-blown panic attack.

So, what? I fucked my ex-boyfriend. Big deal! I try to reason with myself, but it only brings a fleeting sense of relief.

I stand still under the rushing water as anger builds. I'm angry at James for being such an asshole, for being so passive-aggressive and cold. The last fight we had was brutal—he was so hurtful! I blame James for what happened last night, though I'm acutely aware that I'm grasping for any excuse to alleviate the overwhelming guilt consuming me.

I bet he's talking to women in New York—hell, he probably already fucked someone!

I become paranoid at the thought and know I'm being a complete hypocrite. I'm a mess of emotions, and I don't feel any better when I get out of the shower. I towel dry my hair and throw on my cashmere robe. I step back into the bedroom, where Joe is still sleeping soundly.

THE LUST AND BUZZ FROM LAST NIGHT HAS WORN OFF, AND JOE and I are pretending like nothing happened as I drive him home on my way to Three-Two-Three. The first few minutes after he woke up were awkward. He did his best to ease the weirdness by cracking jokes and making me laugh. I appreciate that he's treating this whole situation as lightly as I am, even though I'm a fucking mess inside. I have no regrets about what happened, and I've convinced myself there is no harm in what occurred. *Joe and I are adults who have history and a very deep bond, and we expressed that to each other last night in a physical way.* I cringe at my own bullshit.

"You're home," I say, turning to Joe in the passenger seat. He's wearing his favorite Ray-Bans and a smile as he looks over at me. His hair is still messy from sleep, and I refrain from reaching over to tame it.

"Thanks for the ride," he says, reaching for my hand. I'm still as he brings it to his lips for a kiss.

"You're welcome," I respond, barely above a whisper.

"See 'ya later, Ace," he says, jumping out of my car.

I nod as he closes the door and watch him enter the building.

Now that I'm alone, I can no longer push away thoughts of James and the tornado of emotions churning inside. It's past ten a.m., and I think about what he might be doing in New York as his afternoon is just starting.

"Ugh," I sigh, realizing what a mess our relationship is and how I've made it worse by sleeping with Joe in a moment of weakness. *He can never find out*, I vow to myself. It's a secret I will take to my grave.

I pull up to my reserved spot behind the shop and am relieved to see Angela's car.

Hillary is setting fresh flowers around the shop and tidying up the clothing racks. "Hey, Annie!" she greets me.

"Hey, Hill," I respond, stepping closer to admire the tea roses she's arranging. "These are beautiful."

"Aren't they? Ang just brought them," she says proudly, showing off her arrangement.

"Oh, cool, is she in the office?"

Hillary nods as I make my way to the back of the shop.

I find Angela at her desk, typing away on the computer.

"Hey," I say, closing the door behind me and pulling up a chair to face her. She glances at me with barely a greeting, her eyes remaining focused on the screen.

"I have to tell you something." My heart starts thumping as I gather the words in my head.

"Uh, okay…" she shifts her eyes toward me while still typing.

"Something happened last night…"

She pauses, giving me her full attention, waiting for me to continue.

"I had sex with Joe," I blurt out.

Angela's eyes widen and her jaw drops. "WHAT!? Tell. Me. Everything," she demands.

Chapter Thirty-Six

Joe

I can't stop thinking about last night. I tried distracting myself with my phone and the TV, but my thoughts kept wandering back to Annie's bedroom and our incredible time together. I'm turned on just thinking about it.

I make several attempts to text Audrey to check in, but I can't get myself to do it. I feel so fucking guilty.

I know how much she loves me—she tells me all the time. And I love her too, but I realized sometime after the pregnancy was over that I was not *in love* with her. This became clearer when we started seeing each other again. The truth is, I never saw a future with Audrey, and I *definitely* never saw us having a kid together.

I look at my phone, and my last text exchange with Audrey stares back at me. She's returning from her movie shoot later today, so I'll wait to talk to her then.

I'm glad that the guys and I have a studio session with Trent this afternoon—I'm getting restless and having the worst craving for a drink, especially after having that glass of wine last night. The old me would've been on my third drink by now, and the anxiety I'm feeling would be history. I'm trying hard to stop smoking weed as well, but it's the best of what I consider the lesser of all evils.

Fuck it. I decide to roll a joint.

My phone pings, and it's Darren texting me to ask if I want to ride with him to the studio. Darren lives two floors below me in the Sierra Towers, so we're always hanging out at each other's condos or driving to places together since we're usually going to the same spots.

Twenty minutes later, I'm stoned as Darren and I head toward Hollywood to the recording studio.

"What time did you get home last night?" Darren asks, turning to me. My attention is on the beats we're listening to, but his question takes me back to Annie's bedroom and all the things we did last night, which I've been daydreaming about all morning.

"Uh, I didn't go home last night."

He looks over at me, eyebrows raised. "Where did you go?"

"Um, I didn't go anywhere… I slept with Annie last night."

"WAIT. What was that?!" Darren turns down the volume on the music. *"You slept at Annie's?"*

"No. You heard me."

Darren is momentarily shocked at my revelation, "I knew that was going to happen. I knew it was only a matter of time," he says, shaking his head; *I told you so.*

I smile, remembering all the pep talks and encouragement Darren has given me since Annie and I broke up. I've been a wreck since losing her—consumed by guilt, shame, and regret. I've tried to move on and let her go, but it's been so fucking hard when we're still so good together. I'm aware that I've been in denial over our breakup and the fact that she's with that asshole now.

But after last night, who knows?

Chapter Thirty-Seven

After divulging my deep, dark secret to Angela, I feel so much better, like a massive weight has been lifted. Except that the weight returns every time I get a flashback from last night: *Joe's hand under my dress, his lips and tongue kissing me deep.*

These thoughts make it hard for me to focus on front-of-the-house tasks, such as talking to customers and making sales, so I remain in the office most of the day, doing mindless work like unpacking boxes and folding clothes.

As I fold T-shirts, I reflect on my conversation with Angela, which helped relieve some guilt because she thinks it was Joe who finagled the whole situation. She assured me that his intentions were *obvious* the minute he volunteered to stay back when everyone else called it a night. I have a hard time accepting her theory because I was there! I'm the one who suggested we watch a movie in my room; we could've done that in the den.

Oh hell, what does it matter anyway? What's done is done. I try to focus on her advice: *"Just admit that you both wanted it and move on, Annie."*

I'm pulled out of my thoughts when my phone rings. James's name flashes on the screen. My stomach drops as I debate whether to answer or not.

"Hello?" I give in.

"Hey…" His voice makes me smile, but I freeze, worried I'll say the wrong thing as paranoia creeps in.

"How are you?" he asks. There are loud noises in the background—cars honking, a faint siren wailing in the distance.

"I'm good, what about you—where are you?"

"I'm in a cab on my way to dinner."

Hearing his voice makes me emotional. I sincerely miss him and want to cry, heartbroken by how things have been between us.

"I've been thinking about you all day," he says.

"You have?"

"Yeah, I feel bad about what happened before I left. I know I was an asshole…. I'm sorry."

I swallow hard. *Why the fuck didn't he call me yesterday to tell me this?*

"I'm sorry too…" I sink into the couch. We're quiet—I only hear city sounds on his end. "I miss you," I whisper, and I swear I can hear him smile.

"I miss you too, baby," he says, and now I'm smiling too. "I wanted you to come with me, Annie." His admission brings tears to my eyes. I was hurt when he made final plans to go to New York without me after he invited me to join him.

"I thought you changed your mind about that," I respond.

"No, that was just me being a dick…." he pauses, "Why don't you come out here?"

"What?"

"Yeah… Let me make it up to you." I picture him smiling again.

"Okay," I respond without giving it a second thought. I try to remain steady as waves of conflicting emotions take over.

"Great, I'll make the arrangements. It'll be fun," he says before we hang up.

An hour later, I receive my flight information from Heather, Light's Executive Assistant. I'll be arriving at JFK airport after six tomorrow evening.

Chapter Thirty-Eight

Joe

Being in the studio is exactly what I need to distract myself from thinking about how I cheated on my girlfriend with my ex-girlfriend, whom I'm still in love with.

The guys and I have been in the zone with Trent for hours —laying tracks, listening to playbacks and making adjustments to make the songs perfect. It feels great to finally record the songs I wrote in rehab. As much as I resisted the absolute hell of getting clean, at least I got some songs out of it, and I have to admit, it's the best shit I've written in a long time.

Darren rolls another joint—there's just something about making and listening to music high! Even though I've given up the hard stuff, there's no way I'm giving up weed.

We get hyped over the last song that Trent laid down, and we all agree it'll be his next hit. The song is called "Home," a love song cloaked in cocky bravado and raw rap. It captures everything I felt when Annie and I broke up, and Trent kills it with his smooth style and brash delivery.

I get a text from Audrey. It's past seven, and her flight has just landed. I hesitate to respond as guilt gnaws at me from within, but I know it's time to face her. I just have to be chill and normal—there's no way she'll ever find out about last night.

My thoughts suddenly return to Annie's bedroom—*her soft skin, the curves of her hips, and her full breasts.* The guilt in my chest intensifies.

> Come to the studio.

I finally text Audrey back.

We're about to wrap up our recording session, and it'll be good to see her with the guys around to distract me from the shitstorm of nerves brewing inside.

AUDREY ARRIVES THIRTY MINUTES LATER, STRAIGHT FROM LAX. She looks so fucking hot in her tiny denim cut-offs, cowboy boots, and black crop top. Her hair is long and loose, and her bright green eyes trap me when we make eye contact.

She smiles her cute, shy smile when she greets the guys with a hug. This isn't the first time Audrey has joined us at a recording session—the guys love it when she joins us, and I'm glad she's a chill girl who can hang with my friends.

I greet her with a kiss and pull her onto my lap. Her skin is soft, and I take in her familiar, sweet, vanilla scent.

"How did it go?" I ask, meeting her eyes.

"Amazing. I'm really happy with the part. I think you're going to like it," she beams.

"I know I will. I'm proud of you," I say, pulling her in for a kiss as the nerves from earlier finally settle.

The vibe in the studio feels like a party as we listen back to the tracks, shoot the shit, and smoke more weed. Audrey is her usual bubbly self once she relaxes after taking a few hits from the joint. She's funny and flirty and lights up the room with her charm.

When we finally wrap for the night, our group splits and everyone goes their separate ways.

"You want to go somewhere?" Audrey asks as we reach her car.

"Want to come to my place?" I suggest, grabbing her by the waist and pinning her against her car. I can't resist leaning in for a kiss.

I haven't been able to get last night's sex out of my mind all day, and now I'm high and horny. All I want is to take her home and fuck her. We jump into her car and head to my place. I finally stop thinking about Annie.

Chapter Thirty-Nine

I land in New York City on Tuesday evening. James sends a driver to pick me up at JFK, and after a wild ride, zigzagging through city traffic, I arrive at The Bowery Hotel, where James is staying. A bellman approaches me at the entrance of the chic downtown hotel and takes my luggage to the front desk. I tell the staff member at the desk that I'm here to see James Hunter, and he rings him up to tell him I've arrived. Within minutes, I'm escorted to the penthouse suite.

My heart pounds and guilt uncomfortably settles in the pit of my stomach as the elevator ascends until it finally pings and stops on the fourteenth floor. "I'll take it from here," I tell the bellman, taking my Louis Vuitton carry-on and leaving him with a tip. My thoughts race as I mentally prepare to see James.

Flashbacks from my night with Joe flood back without warning—*the weight of his body on mine, his mouth trailing kisses from my neck to my belly.* I shake my head—*This has to stop!*

I take a deep breath at the door of the penthouse suite and knock.

James opens the door with his gorgeous smile, and I immediately burst into tears. The pressure of the last few days—hell, *the last few hours*—finally hits a breaking point.

"Aww, babe," he says, scooping me in his arms. I'm overcome with joy, relief, anger, guilt. "Annie, why are you crying?" He holds me tight while I break down.

I catch my breath and finally face him, "I just missed you so much," I say, wiping away tears. I'm being partially honest, there are so many reasons why I'm crying. James kisses my forehead and wipes the tears from my cheeks.

"I missed you too," he says, pulling me in for a kiss.

I start to relax as James shows me around the gorgeous suite, which features a living room, kitchen, dining area, balcony, and floor-to-ceiling windows overlooking The Bowery. We end up in the bedroom, where he pulls me in for another kiss.

The sun has just set, and the natural light in the room is fading. We undress each other between kisses and make love, making up for the horrible last few days together we had back in LA.

JAMES AND I LAY IN BED POST-ORGASM. WE HOLD EACH OTHER, talking in the dark. He tells me about his trip and gets excited recounting his meeting with the Brits. The contract is signed and sealed—he's officially been hired as the creative director and lead consultant for the Brit's new London nightclub.

I'm stunned as he shares the news—I can't believe this is happening so fast.

"So, when are you going to London?" I ask.

"In a few weeks… early November sometime. They want to open the club as soon as possible—early next year… Spring at the latest."

November is about six weeks away, so I have time to get used to the idea.

"Don't worry, Annie…" he says as if reading my mind, pulling me tighter into his chest, "I'm not moving there—I'll be gone a few weeks at a time, and you can come with me whenever you want—it'll be great!"

I nod, trying to muster up excitement. I remember his story about living in London a decade ago and falling in love with Liz. I get irrationally jealous and push the thought out of my mind. *I'm the biggest hypocrite ever.*

A few hours later, James and I are in a chauffeured car heading to Balthazar to have dinner with the Brits. The city is alive with overstimulating sights and sounds: beeping horns, people everywhere, sirens blaring. James is on the phone with Oliver, talking business about Light.

I stare out the window as my mind wanders and the intrusive thoughts return—*Joe's fingers interlocked with mine as we made love, his arms wrapped around me when I woke up yesterday morning.*

I take a deep breath and pull out my phone to distract myself. The weight of my actions feels like a boulder on my chest.

I look over at James, laughing at whatever Ollie is saying, and I want to cry again. *I'm a horrible person!*

It happened, I can't change the past, and James will never find out. I repeat the mantra in my head that I return to every time I have a flashback of that night. I feel awful for leaving LA so abruptly. *Should I have talked to Joe about our night?* My mind is a mess, and I can't wait to get to dinner to distract myself from my spiraling thoughts.

JAMES AND I SLEEP WELL INTO THE AFTERNOON THE NEXT DAY after an incredible night in the city. We had dinner with the Brits, partied with Lauren, Scott, and James's New York friends, and didn't return to the hotel until five in the morning.

So, we recover in his suite for the rest of the day, ordering room service and having lots of make-up sex.

The next few days in the city are a bit more subdued. James and I explore the East Village, Soho, and the West Village. He takes me to his favorite restaurants and bars—I love seeing the city through his eyes.

On Saturday, James has a final meeting with the Brits and their silent partner before they head back to London, so I spend the day uptown with Lauren. We have a lovely time at the spa, then lunch, and end up at Bergdorf Goodman to shop for something cute to wear to dinner with their mother, whom I'll be meeting for the first time tonight.

As I wait for the salesperson to bring me the Jimmy Choos and Manolo Blahniks I want to try on, I get a text from Joe:

How's New York?

I stare at my phone as my stomach knots. The guilt returns, crashing into me like a wave, and I irrationally feel *caught*. I look over at Lauren, talking to a salesperson as she works through the mountain of shoes she's trying on.

Fuck, he knows I'm here. I don't know why I'm freaking out. I don't owe Joe an explanation of my whereabouts, yet I can't shake the guilt. I analyze his text—three words and a question mark loaded with anger and passive aggression.

I wait a few minutes to respond:

It was a last-minute trip. There are obviously some problems in my relationship right now, but we're working on them. I'm sorry if I got you involved. You're one of my best friends, and I hope we're still okay.

It's the best I can come up with, and I know that it's a bull-shit response.

I feel guilty because I initiated our illicit encounter, even though Angela assured me it was mutual. I know I gave Joe all the signs and signals, and the opportunity was his for the taking. *I invited him to Netflix and chill, for fucks sake!*

Joe has been so respectful of me and our friendship since he got out of rehab. All the bitchy jabs and subtle digs he used to throw at me have stopped. He's been nothing but a gentleman and a good friend. That's why I was furious at James for accusing Joe of manipulating me and playing with my emotions. He doesn't know Joe like I do, and his assumptions couldn't be farther from the truth.

I regret sending Joe such a weak text. It sounded so cold and dismissive, and I worry that I said too much. He takes his time responding, and it feels like an eternity.

Have fun.

He finally replies, and I'm crushed.

"Annie? Which one?" Lauren looks at me, showing off a gorgeous sandal on one foot and a sexy pump on the other. She snaps me out of my thoughts.

"Oh!" I muster excitement, "Um, they're both cute!"

"Yeah, so hard to decide," she says, inspecting herself in the mirror. "Ugh, okay, I'll take them both," she tells the salesperson, whose eyes light up as her pile of purchases stacks up.

The shoes I wanted to try on were brought over a while ago, but I've lost interest in shopping. My thoughts are back in LA, wondering how badly I've damaged my friendship with Joe.

"You, okay?" James looks over, narrowing his eyes on me. We're in a cab, heading to dinner with his mother at Jean-Georges.

"Yeah, I'm fine." I smile and reach for his hand across the backseat.

"Are you sure? You've been quiet all night," he says, squeezing my hand. He's right; my mind has been all over the place since Joe's text, and it's been a struggle to remain present.

I shake my head, assuring him that there's nothing wrong.

"If you're freaking out about London, don't." He cracks a smile, looking me in the eye.

"I'm not…" I say, trying to perk up.

"I mean it, Annie. The London project is only a few months, and I want you to come with me as often as possible." He brings my hand to his lips for a kiss.

"I would love that," I respond.

***

THE NEXT DAY, ON OUR FLIGHT BACK TO LA, JAMES NAPS beside me in the plush first-class cabin seats while I gaze out the window at the billowing clusters of clouds fading into the horizon. My thoughts drift back to the decadent meal and delightful evening we shared with his mother, Julia. She was as cool and lovely as I had imagined and welcomed me with open arms. A smile spreads across my face as I recall her sweet compliments and how she mentioned having heard "so much" about me.

The happy memories are fleeting, as the anxiety I woke up with this morning returns like a current, flooding me with flashbacks of my night with Joe. I glance over at James, still sound asleep, as paranoia and fear grip my chest at the thought of him finding out. I have to fight back tears as guilt tears me up inside. *He can never find out.*

I think about Joe and the absolute mess I've gotten myself into with him, and I feel like a terrible person as his *have fun* text flashes through my mind. I pull out my phone to delete our entire text history; it's too risky for it to exist.

Dreading the return to reality at home, I numb the pain with my second vodka soda, contemplating a third—anything to silence these thoughts.

TWO HOURS LATER, WE FINALLY LAND IN LA. THE BUZZ FROM my in-flight cocktails has morphed into a dull headache, and all I want to do is climb into bed and never come out.

James and I maneuver through the thick crowd of travelers at LAX, which is no easy feat for me. Luckily, he has a driver waiting to take us to my parents' house to pick up my car. I remain quiet the entire ride, my stomach in knots as dread about what might happen next takes over.

"ANYONE HOME?!" I call out as soon as James and I step into the foyer. My echo greets me—there's no one here. "I'm just going to grab my keys," I say, turning toward the stairs, "I'll be down in a sec!"

More torturous flashbacks of *that* night return when I enter my bedroom. Joe's and my sex sheets are still a crumpled mess on the bed, and it all becomes real again. *Too real.* Without hesitating, I strip the bed of the sheets and pillowcases, clearing away the evidence. *If only it were that easy to strip my conscience.*

I leave everything in one big pile on the bed and hope the housekeeper comes by soon and takes care of it. I grab my keys from the dresser and look around the room for anything I might be leaving behind. I do the same in the bathroom and pause when I spot the toothbrush Joe used the morning after on the sink. I grab it and throw it in the trash. *I need to get out of here.*

"Let's go," I say, returning to James in the foyer.

"What's wrong?" he asks, giving me a look.

"Nothing!" I affirm with a smile, hoping that I seem composed despite the nerves rattling me inside.

As James and I step outside to pack our luggage into my car, Darren's car pulls up, and my heart starts pounding, fearing that Joe is with him.

I don't want to look up to see who's in the car; I just want to leave. But I have no choice—they've seen us, and we've seen them. We can't leave without saying hello.

Darren's car stops, and Angela emerges from the passenger side. "You're back!" she says, approaching me with outstretched arms. "I missed you!" she says, squeezing me tight.

Darren trails behind her, and the four of us chat in the driveway. The knots in my stomach ease up as relief washes over me, grateful that my feared scenario didn't occur.

"So, how was your trip?" Angela asks, turning to me as Darren and James chat.

"It was good..." I shrug, throwing in a few details to appease her curiosity.

"We're going to Catch for dinner later. Do you guys want to join us?" she asks.

"No, thanks, we're exhausted," I say, giving her another hug. "But I'll see you at the shop tomorrow," I add, mustering a smile.

I know I'm being dismissive and awkward with Angela and Darren, but I blame the long flight and my headache, which is close to becoming a migraine.

"Alright, well, get some rest!" Angela says as we exchange goodbyes. James and I jump into my car while Darren and Angela disappear into the house. As we drive off, I let out a deep sigh—I feel like I can finally breathe again.

Chapter Forty

Joe

"I saw Annie yesterday," Darren says as he passes me the basketball.

"Oh, yeah?" I take a jump shot without taking my eyes off the net. "Where at?"

"At *casa* Preston. She was picking up her car with *you know who*—it was just for a few minutes." I chuckle, appreciating that Darren won't say that asshole's name in my presence. I pass him the ball, and he shoots it straight back into the net.

"That's cool," I respond.

"Oh, my bad, bro…" Darren says, "I shouldn't have brought it up."

"It's okay, man, I don't care," I lie.

We continue shooting hoops.

Ever since I found out that Annie was in New York with that prick, I've been pissed. I couldn't believe she was back with him less than forty-eight hours after we slept together. What's worse is that my anxiety has skyrocketed, and my cravings for coke and booze have been at an all-time high since that night.

It got so bad that I contemplated going out a few times to see what people were up to—I even almost called Patrick—

anything to get Annie off my mind. But I did the right thing and ended up at one of those *godawful* AA meetings instead—a horrible experience that I won't be repeating anytime soon.

"Talk to me, Joseph," Darren catches the ball from the net and holds on to it. He gives me that familiar *older brother* concerned look. "Let's take a breather," he says, dribbling the ball toward the benches where we put our stuff down. I follow him and sit on one of the benches under a big, shady tree. I grab my water bottle and take a long gulp.

"What's bothering you, bro?" Darren breaks our silence.

I look into the distance—I don't like it when he gives me that look. "Nothing! Why do you keep asking me if something's wrong?"

"I don't know! You haven't been yourself lately… But look, if you say there's nothing wrong or don't want to talk about it, then no worries. I'm not going to pry. I just want you to know that I'm here if you need to talk, that's all."

I finally look over at Darren and smile, shaking my head at his persistence. "Thanks, D." I relax, leaning back into the bench. "I just… I don't know…. It's Audrey… I think we're pretty much over."

Darren's look turns surprised. "Oh, Audrey… sorry, bro, I had no idea… what's going on?"

"I don't know… she's great, and I like her, but…" I stop myself from saying what I'm thinking… *She's not Annie.*

Darren nods, listening intently.

"I just don't think we're compatible," I add.

"Really? That's not the impression I get seeing you two together. You seem happy with her."

I agree with Darren; Audrey makes me happy. She's beautiful, she's fun, the sex is great, but that's about it. After being with Annie again, it's hard to ignore what a real connection feels like. Annie and I have the same humor, similar interests, and a deep friendship. And the sex—still incredible. I miss that.

My feelings for Audrey had faded when we broke up the first time—before I went to rehab and before I found out she was pregnant. I only got back together with her after we bonded over the fucked-up decision we had to make. We were both a mess and leaned on each other to get through it. I can't believe we almost had a baby together! I didn't want to abandon her after that whole thing—but now, there's not much keeping us together.

"Well, if it's not working, it's not working!" Darren says, giving me a firm slap on the back. "Man up and end it, bro."

I shake my head, "I know that's what I have to do, but I just can't right now. Her sister's getting married this weekend in Hawaii, and I'm going with her. I feel all this pressure… I'm going to meet her whole family…. I can't do it now…."

I look away from Darren's gaze, which has turned concerned again. I can't bring myself to add that I'm scared to break up with Audrey because, at this point, being with her is the only thing helping me stay sober.

"I'm sorry, Joe…." Darren stops mid-sentence as two cute college girls walk by on their way to the tennis court. In true Darren style, he gives them a big smile and a flirty *"hello,"* which makes the girls giggle as they return the greeting.

"See…" Darren says, swatting me on the knee, "That's what I'm talking about right there," he motions toward the girls as we watch them enter the tennis court. "There are plenty of fish in the sea. If you're not happy with the one you got—it's time to find a new one!" We both laugh at his corny advice.

Darren and I return to the court and shoot hoops for another hour. I have to admit, I feel better after our chat. It's hard to talk about my feelings—even with my friends. I prefer to keep it all inside—it's easier that way.

My therapist in rehab said it's probably because *"I'm an only child with success-driven, absentee, Hollywood parents."* It still cracks me up at how accurately he nailed my childhood experience. Since my parents were never around, I had to figure shit out on my own and relied on escapism to cope, *according to my therapist.*

I know there are things I can't escape from anymore, though—like breaking up with Audrey and figuring out a way to move on from Annie. I also have to figure out how to win this fucking battle with addiction that I struggle with every day, especially since it's been harder to fight lately.

Chapter Forty-One

Three days after returning from New York, things start to feel normal again. I've been working at the shop every day, and James and I are in a much better place. I've decided to stuff my guilt deep inside and never look at it again. I want to make peace with Joe, and I know the only way to do that is to talk to him, clear the air, and move on.

There's a lull at the shop, and Hillary is helping the only customer. I pull out my phone from under the counter and search for my last text with Joe. I suddenly remember that I deleted our entire text history. His last message, though, is still fresh in my mind: *Have fun.*

The guilt tries to resurface, but I keep it at bay by making a bold decision—*I'm going to stop being a coward*—*I'm going to call Joe.*

His phone rings a few times and then goes straight to voicemail. "Hey, it's me… Uhh, I just wanted to say hi. Can you call me back? Thanks." I hang up and feel stupid for leaving the message. I wait for Joe to call me back all day, but he doesn't. So, I try again and text him before we close the shop:

> Hello?? Are you around? Can we talk for a
> minute?

No response.

I get home, sure that he would at least return my text, but he doesn't.

THE NEXT DAY, AS SOON AS I GET INTO MY CAR BEFORE heading to the shop, I call Joe again. His phone rings, and to my surprise, he picks up.

"Hello?"

"Hey!" My heart races; I don't know what to say.

"Hey," he doesn't sound particularly excited to hear from me.

"I've been trying to reach you. Did you get my messages?"

"Oh, sorry about that. I'm in Hawaii—I was traveling yesterday, so it's been a little crazy."

"Oh… What are you doing in Hawaii?"

"Audrey's sister is getting married today—in a few hours, actually."

"Oh, I'm sorry to bother you then—I should let you go…." I'm now flustered and want to get off the phone ASAP.

"It's okay. What did you want to talk about?"

"Nothing, I just wanted to say hi and talk… But I don't want to bother you. Let's talk when you get back. I just wanted to say hi mostly," I facepalm myself to stop rambling like an idiot.

"Sure," he says, "I'll call you when I get back."

We say goodbye, and I swiftly hang up.

UGH. I lean on the steering wheel, pressing my forehead against its hard surface, and fold my arms over my head. I cringe at how the call went and feel ridiculous for feeling a twinge of jealousy as I picture Joe and Audrey on a beach in Hawaii. *I feel so stupid.*

TWO WEEKS GO BY, AND JOE NEVER CALLS. I KNOW HE'S BEEN back for over a week because Angela saw him at Darren's the day after he returned from Hawaii. I know I should let Joe reach out whenever he's ready, but I've become obsessed with getting things straightened out between us. His silence feels heavy and punishing. He clearly wants nothing to do with me, but I have to make things right between us. The thought of hurting Joe destroys me, and it feels urgent to repair the horrible rift between us—if only I could talk to him.

I tell Angela how much this situation is stressing me out, and she suggests I go with her to visit Darren at the studio tonight. The guys will be recording with Trent, and I know Joe will be there, so it's the perfect opportunity to talk to him.

ANGELA AND I ARRIVE AT THE STUDIO ON HOLLYWOOD AND Vine at ten p.m. The security guard greets Angela with familiarity because she's a regular at the recording sessions, which makes me feel out of the loop and slightly jealous. We take the elevator to the third floor and emerge in a hallway with doors and signs that say RECORDING in bright red lights.

I follow Angela to one of the studios—the red light isn't on for this door, so we walk right in. This will be the first time I see Joe since *that night* almost a month ago, and my stomach does somersaults. We walk into the studio and are immediately hit with the sweet, pungent scent of marijuana. The guys are talking and working at the soundboard, so they don't immediately notice us.

"Hey, guys!" Angela announces our arrival, and Max,

Darren, and Joe turn around to face us. She heads straight for Darren to greet him with a kiss. I love how cute and affectionate they are now that their relationship is out in the open. Max greets me with a hug, and Joe looks at me and then returns to whatever he's doing on the soundboard. *Ouch.*

Angela notices and gives me a look. "What's up, Joe!" she says, grabbing his shoulder to give him a playful shake.

He looks at her with a tight smile, "What's up, Ang," he responds, refusing to acknowledge me.

I take a deep breath and try to ignore his icy demeanor.

"You guys were *this close* to being locked out—We're about to record the last track," Max tells us. "You ready, man?!" He raises his voice so Trent can hear him behind the transparent partition that separates the studio from the recording booth. Trent nods and gives him a thumbs-up. Joe gives Trent instructions from a mic on the soundboard into Trent's headphones.

"Alright, last one, man," Joe says.

"This track is so dope! You guys will love it!" Darren says, turning to Angela and me. We all gather closer to the booth as Joe starts the track on the soundboard, and Trent begins rapping to the beat. The song is catchy and high-energy, with deep drumbeats and electronic pitches.

Trent does two amazing freestyle rap verses all in one shot and *kills it*. The vibe in the room lifts as Darren lights a joint and passes it around. I need this joint more than everyone here because I've become increasingly anxious in Joe's presence.

Joe, on the other hand, loosens up and starts joking around, making us laugh. I make my move and step closer to hand him the joint. To my surprise, he smiles. He takes it from me, inhales a long drag, and leans back into his chair.

"How are you?" I ask, looking into his eyes, bloodshot from the weed. His skin is golden tan, surely from the Hawaii sun, and he's grown some stubble. His dirty blond hair is pushed back in a messy sort of way, and he looks so damn cute. Bits and pieces from *that night* flash through my mind, making my cheeks hot. I drop my gaze for a moment—I didn't think I would feel this way seeing him again.

"I'm good," he responds in the same breath as he exhales a cloud of smoke. "And you?" He takes another drag.

"Good," I say, meeting his eyes. I'm suddenly at a loss for words.

Darren asks Joe a question, and his attention turns away from me.

"Play the whole thing again, man," Darren requests, so Joe cues up the track Trent just recorded, and the song booms from the speakers.

The joint gets passed around until it's gone, and everyone listens to the other songs Trent recorded tonight. I've always loved seeing Joe in his element—making music is his passion, and I'm so proud of him for all the hard work he's putting into this album.

We hang out for a while, and it's well after midnight when the recording session ends. Our group emerges from the studio and back onto Hollywood Boulevard.

"Hey, can we talk for a minute?" I ask Joe as we walk to our cars.

"Sure," he says with a shrug. Angela takes off with Darren and Max, leaving Joe and me alone in the parking lot.

We reach his car and look at each other in awkward silence. Joe leans back on his car and fidgets with his keys, looking ready to leave. "So, what's up?" he asks, looking blankly at me.

"Why didn't you call me when you got back?"

He looks down at his keys, avoiding my eyes. "Was I supposed to call you?" He sounds annoyed.

"Yeah. You said you'd call me when you got back... I just wanted to talk to make sure that we're okay and that what happened didn't change things between us."

He shakes his head and looks at me with a sigh. "Relax, Annie. It was just sex. It didn't mean anything. Why are you making such a big deal out of it?"

His words sting.

I take a breath, "I'm not making a big deal out of it, but you've been avoiding me for the past month, so I thought you were mad at me or something."

"It's not about you," he says, looking me in the eye. "I've been busy… I have a girlfriend… I have other stuff going on in my life."

I don't know what to say; I'm stunned by his response. "Look," he says, irritated, "I'm just trying to take things one day at a time." His words echo the mantra of recovering addicts, so I decide not to press him further.

"Okay," I say, "I'm sorry I brought it up."

I walk away, and he doesn't stop me. I turn back to look at him, and he's watching me get into my car. I sigh, sinking into the driver's seat. I hear his car door close, and his engine revs up. He drives past me, and I'm left wondering, *What the fuck just happened?*

Chapter Forty-Two

It's two weeks before Thanksgiving, and Three-Two-Three is bustling with customers as holiday shopping is already in full swing. Considering we've only been open for two months and barely know what we're doing, Angela and I are doing better than expected. We're still learning how to run a business, but we're improving every day and finally getting used to the shop's rhythm.

James has been gone for a week on his first official business trip to London to start work on the new club with the Brits, and he won't be back until Thanksgiving. We've been Face-Timing every day, and the sadness I felt when he left has been replaced with happiness, knowing how excited he is about the project.

The only downside is being alone at his house, so I've been spending nights at my parents' house, even though my bedroom holds so many memories that still haunt me.

"Hey, isn't that Audrey?" Angela elbows me as we stand at the counter, helping customers.

I crane my neck toward Angela's gaze and spot Audrey looking through a rack of dresses. She's dressed in jeans, a white T-shirt, and black flats, and her hair is in a ponytail. With all the activity in the shop, I didn't notice her come in.

I finish with my customer and go over to Audrey.

"Hey," I gently tap her on the shoulder.

She turns to me and gives me a tight smile. "Hey, Annie."

"How's it going?" I reach out to properly greet her with a hug. She hugs me back, and a flash of guilt for sleeping with her boyfriend washes over me.

"It's going okay…. I just had a meeting with my agent down the street, so I thought I'd come by and check out the shop. It looks great," she says, perking up.

The last time I saw her was at our opening night party, and I don't think she's here today to shop.

"Cool, I'm glad you're here. I haven't seen you in a while. How have you been?"

She turns away and moves a few dresses on the rack. She shrugs, "Oh, you know, okay, I guess." I'm concerned by her response, and I can tell something is wrong.

"Are you alright?"

She turns to me, her eyes are noticeably misty, "You haven't heard?"

"No, heard what?"

"We broke up—well, Joe broke up with me," she says as tears pool in her eyes.

I can't believe what I'm hearing.

"Audrey… I'm sorry, I hadn't heard…" I reach out to hug her, and she sniffs back tears. "I'm so sorry…" I repeat, trying to comfort her.

She pulls away from me, wiping her tears. "Ugh, I'm so sorry!" Her gaze drops. "I don't know what's wrong with me! I didn't mean to come here and do this."

"It's okay," I say, touching her arm. "Why don't we go get coffee?" She nods, and we step out of the shop together.

Audrey and I walk to the café a few doors down without saying anything to each other. We sit at a table on the patio and order two lattes. I don't know what to say, so I let her talk first.

"You must think I'm totally nuts!" she says, forcing a smile while trying to hold back tears. "I really *am* fine; I guess I'm just extra emotional today," she says, shaking her head.

"No, I don't think that…" I assure her, "I'm so sorry that this happened—what *happened?*" The server delivers our drinks, and I wait for her to continue.

"I don't know, Annie," she says, taking a sip. "Joe's been acting weird for weeks. I can't explain it, but he's been… *different.* Withdrawn or something."

I nod, listening intently.

"I think he's been partying again," she says, looking down at her cup. Tears start rolling down her cheeks again.

Her words land like a punch in the gut, and I'm afraid of what she'll say next.

"He's been hanging out with Trent and his crew *a lot*, and he's at the studio every night. At least, that's where he says he is. There were days when he'd disappear and wouldn't call or text…" She pauses to dab her nose with a napkin.

"Are you sure?"

"He denies it," she says, "And he's never done anything in front of me, but I can tell. He showed up at my place last week at, like, five in the morning, and I think he was high."

I haven't seen Joe in weeks—the last time I saw him was at the studio. I'm surprised Angela hasn't said anything about this, considering she always sees him with Darren.

"What do you mean? You *think* he was high?" I ask as my fear escalates.

"I don't know," she says. "He denied it. He said he had a few beers and smoked a joint. But no, I know it was more than that," she says, looking me in the eye.

The news makes my stomach turn, and I can't drink any more coffee. "How did this happen?"

"I don't know… I guess it just did… I tried talking to him

about it a couple of days ago, and he snapped and told me he was fine and wanted to take a break... We haven't talked... He hasn't called me since," she says as tears roll down her cheeks.

I reach across the table for her hand.

"I know there's nothing I can do, so I thought maybe you or Max or Darren can do something?" The helpless look in her eyes is heartbreaking, and now *I* have to fight the urge to cry.

"Honestly, Audrey, I had no idea this was happening. I haven't seen Joe or talked to him in weeks, and nobody else has said anything, so this is all news to me. But of course, I'll find out what's going on, and hopefully, it's not as bad as you think."

She nods and blows her nose again. "I hope so," she says. "And you're probably right. It's probably not as bad as I think."

We don't touch our coffees again; there's not much more to say. She looks at her phone and says she has to go.

When we leave the café, she's finally calm. "Well, I hope we'll still see each other around," she says as we hug goodbye.

"Yeah, I hope so," I respond, knowing we will probably never see each other again.

I walk into the shop in shock, processing everything Audrey told me. I head straight to the office and plop down on the couch as Angela follows me in, "What's wrong?" she asks.

"Did you know they broke up?"

"Who?"

"Joe and Audrey."

"Again? No, I didn't... Is that what that was all about?"

I nod and close my eyes as it all suddenly hits me.

Angela starts asking questions, and I repeat everything Audrey just told me, including her suspicions that Joe is back on drugs.

"Did you know about this?" I ask, searching her eyes.

"No, I didn't." Angela shakes her head and looks as sad as I feel. "Every time I've seen Joe, he's been fine… I mean, I think I saw him drink a beer once, and he's still smoking weed, of course…" I'm relieved that Angela's account differs from Audrey's and hope that Audrey has it wrong. "I'm sure it's not that bad," Angela says, trying to comfort me.

The possibility of Joe relapsing fills me with deep sadness, and I can no longer hold back my tears. "I'm so scared for him," I cry into my hands.

Angela puts her arm around me. "Annie, we don't know what's going on yet. Why don't you talk to him?"

"I can't," I shake my head, "He doesn't want to have anything to do with me!" The admission makes me cry harder, as saying the words out loud makes them real. I haven't told Angela everything that's happened between Joe and me—like how cold he's been to me after the night we slept together. I never told her about our conversation in the parking lot at the studio, which was the last time we talked. I've buried those feelings deep inside, pretending I don't care. But *I do care.* This is the first time that Joe and I haven't talked for this long— ever. Even when we broke up in the past, we always managed to be cordial and maintained some connection, but it feels different this time—it feels so… final.

"Annie, it's going to be okay," Angela insists, with an arm around my shoulder. I wipe my tears and try to compose myself. Angela doesn't understand that I'm crying because I know Joe's in trouble, and there's nothing I can do to help him.

Chapter Forty-Three

My cousin Matt's thirtieth birthday celebration is tonight, and I've been in bed for hours, trying to figure out a way to skip it. I've been an anxious wreck since my talk with Audrey two days ago, and I feel so emotionally spent that partying is the last thing I want to do. But Matt's been so excited about his milestone birthday, and I can't flake out on him.

I'm also nervous about seeing Joe—unsure of what version of him I'll get tonight and scared to find out if what Audrey told me is true. I'm also annoyed that James and I missed our regular afternoon call because he's been in meetings all day. With the time difference, we won't be able to talk again until tomorrow.

At around five, I finally stop moping and start getting ready for Matt's birthday dinner.

THE HOSTESS AT RALEIGH'S LEADS ME TO THE PRIVATE AREA with the communal table where all our gatherings take place.

Guests mingle, and the mood is lively and warm as the area glows with soft lighting and candlelight.

I spot Matt and walk directly toward him—I feel more at ease seeing his happy smile.

"There she is," Matt extends his arms to welcome me with a hug.

"Happy Birthday!" I say as we embrace.

"Thanks, love. Now that you're here, my night is complete!"

We pull apart, and he inspects my outfit, "You look ah-mazing!" he exclaims, giving me a twirl. I'm wearing a little black leather dress and sexy black heels.

I giggle at his reaction and return the compliment, admiring his dapper suit. "For you," I say, handing him his gift.

"Ooh. *Her-mes*," his eyes light up as he takes the small iconic orange bag with black silk ribbon. He kisses me on the cheek. "Thank you, darling; this will be the first one I open tonight." I got him a beautiful pair of Hermès cufflinks that I know he'll love. We hug again, and he introduces me to a few people nearby.

I spot Angela, Darren, Max, Michelle, and, of course, Joe sitting at the end of the table. I excuse myself from Matt and make my way over to them. As I get closer, Joe and I make eye contact, and it's clear that what Audrey told me is true.

I greet everyone at the table, and when I get to Joe, he gives me a weak *"hello,"* then picks up his phone and ignores me. He's being a dick, but I pretend to be unbothered. I sit between Angela and Michelle, and we start to chat.

I'm having a hard time concentrating on the conversation around me because I'm distracted by Joe openly drinking a beer. I can hear him cracking jokes and bantering with some of the guests who have come to our end of the table.

Joe's demeanor is all too familiar—glassy-eyes, fidgety, and overly talkative—I can tell he's high. I look around the table, trying to see if anyone else is disturbed by this, but nobody seems to care. Everyone is laughing and drinking and having a good old time, engaging with Joe as if there's nothing wrong, as if he didn't get out of rehab just a few months ago. *Am I the only one that cares?*

Matt announces to the group that dinner is about to be served, and everyone sits at the table. Within minutes, servers come around with the first course.

"Are you alright?" Angela asks, "You're being quiet."

I muster a smile and say, "I'm fine." I look over at Joe a few times, and our eyes occasionally meet, but we've yet to say more than two words to each other.

More food arrives, and I notice that Joe's barely eating. He gets up from the table a few times to talk to people and to take trips to the bathroom—all signs that he's probably coked up.

When he returns to the table, he orders another beer from the cocktail server, and according to my count, he's already had two, and who knows how many before I arrived.

Everyone's laughter and chatter around me suddenly feels grating. Seeing Joe like this breaks my heart, and I feel helpless and alone since everyone is either deep in denial about his addiction or just doesn't give a fuck.

I snap out of my thoughts, noticing that the conversation has turned to Trent's album and the video the guys want to shoot for his latest single. Darren throws around ideas for locations while Max looks at me, "Hey, Annie, do you think James would let us shoot a video at Light?"

"Huh?" Max catches me off guard as I barely follow the conversation. "Sorry, what?" I ask, turning my attention to him. He repeats himself, and I have no idea how to answer. "Um, yeah. I think that would be fine." I shrug.

Joe cuts in, ignoring me, and responds to Max, "Nah, we should just do it at Sixteen—it's better," he says, taking a swig of his beer.

I look directly at him, but he avoids my eyes. *Okay, here we go.* Asshole Joe is back with snide comments and shade. I take a deep breath and glance over at Angela. She gives me a knowing look, and I feel her hand on my knee, giving me a supportive squeeze.

"No, Sixteen is too big…" Max says, "I'm thinking… something small and intimate. Something sexy like Light." I don't think Max is intentionally needling Joe, but I can tell the conversation is irritating him.

We're briefly interrupted by the server taking drink orders.

"Where's James tonight?" Michelle asks, turning to me. "Is he meeting up with us later?"

As I answer her, I hear Darren ask the server for another Scotch and soda, and Joe asks her for a gin and tonic.

"Oh, he's in London," I answer.

"What's he doing there?" Michelle looks surprised.

"Oh… He's working with these two British club owners on their new nightclub. They hired him as creative director and consultant on the project." Michelle asks more questions, and I do my best to answer her because, frankly, I don't know much about the project.

The server returns with cocktails, and flashbacks of Joe getting wasted during his darkest moments come flooding back as he takes the first sip of his drink. It's painful to watch him tank his sobriety so carelessly and so audaciously, and it feels like a clear *fuck-you* directed at me. After all, I was the one with him that morning at The Roosevelt, I was the one who figured out how to get him into rehab, and I was the one who drove him there! I've always wanted Joe to succeed and be happy. There's nothing I've wanted more than for him to be healthy and sober—and he knows it. His actions are in direct contrast to all the work he's done on himself, and it's clear that he's deliberately provoking me tonight, trying to hurt me even if it's at his own expense.

The conversation changes to another topic, and everyone talks around me, but my racing thoughts and the pounding in my chest drown out their voices. I look directly at Joe, and our eyes meet—there's so much anger and pain, and I can no longer sit here and watch him fuck up his life.

I turn to Angela, "I'm leaving," I whisper.

"No, why?" she says, "Don't go…"

I stand up, and Michelle asks me where I'm going. My plan for a stealthy escape fails as everyone around me fusses and asks me where I'm going.

"I have to go," I say, trying to step away without much explanation. "You guys have fun. I'll see you later. "

I barely take two steps when I hear Joe's voice, "Hey, Annie!" I pause and turn to look at him. "Do you want some company? I can spend the night with you like the last time your boyfriend was out of town," he says.

I freeze. *Did I hear him correctly?*

He doesn't miss a beat and casually adds, "We can go to my place this time; it's closer." He gives me a smirk, and his words finally register.

"Fuck you," I say, as rage and humiliation flares in my chest.

"Relax, Annie, it's not a secret—they all know! You don't have to be embarrassed!" he says loudly, making sure that I hear him as I walk away.

The room feels like it's spinning, and I want to disappear. *Did I HEAR him correctly?! Did he just out us to a table of people? Did he turn something so special even though it was so wrong—into a reason to hurt and humiliate me?*

I feel a hand on my shoulder, "Annie, Annie, stop!" It's Angela. I turn around to face her as tears start to spill over. "Come here," she says, grabbing me by the hand and leading me into the restroom.

"I can't believe he did this!" I cry while Angela holds me.

"He's such a fucking asshole, Annie, I'm so sorry."

I'm beyond embarrassed that all our friends know what

happened between us, and I'm so angry and hurt by the way Joe just treated me.

"I'm scared James is going to find out," I keep saying through the tears.

"He won't," Angela says, wiping my cheeks. "How would he find out? We won't tell him—no one at that table would ever say anything to him."

Joe's voice echoes in my head, *"They all know—It's not a secret!"*

Anger turns into panic, "Joe might tell him," my stomach plummets at the thought.

Angela shakes her head, trying to convince me, "He won't," she says.

But I know how volatile and impulsive Joe can be, especially when he's wasted. He can be a loose cannon and doesn't care about the damage he causes.

"He might, Angela. He hates me so much right now; I wouldn't be surprised if he says something to James… I have to keep them apart forever!" I know that I'm unraveling and sounding crazy. I cry uncontrollably at the thought of James finding out.

Michelle walks into the restroom. "There you are," she says, coming over to console me. "Annie, I'm sorry about what happened. Are you okay?"

I shake my head and take a deep breath to compose myself. "I'll be fine," I say, trying to pull myself together.

Michelle brushes a lock of hair from my eyes and rubs my arm. "He's gone. He left a few minutes ago," she says.

I search her face, trying to gauge her reaction from the bomb Joe just dropped. "Did you know?"

She shakes her head. "No, I didn't. Is it true?"

Just as I suspected, Joe maliciously betrayed me in the worst way, revealing our secret to people who had no idea it had happened.

My silence is telling, and she gives me a compassionate look, "It's okay, Annie… It's nobody's business."

I turn to Angela, "Does Darren know?"

"Joe told Darren after it happened," she confirms, "But of course he would tell him."

I ask Michelle if Max knows. "I don't know," she says, "He hasn't said anything to me."

I'm mortified that everyone knows about our illicit night together. "Did Joe say anything else?" Angela asks Michelle.

"No, the guys told him he was fucked-up and to chill out. Max got pissed and told him to stop being an asshole and to sober up. Then Joe just got up and left."

I'm calmer now, but I feel numb. "I want to leave," I tell them.

"We love you, Annie; please don't feel like this means anything," Michelle says, trying to comfort me.

Angela accompanies me to the valet until my car arrives. I can't wait to get into bed and forget this night ever happened.

Chapter Forty-Four

"It smells amazing in here!" James enters the kitchen, approaching me for a kiss. I proudly show him the pumpkin pie I just took out of the oven. "Can I try it?" he asks, reaching for it on the cooling rack.

"No!" I swat his hand, "You have to wait until dinner."

He smiles and pulls me into him. "Can I try you instead?" he says, playfully biting my neck and nibbling on my earlobe. James returned from London two days ago, just in time for Thanksgiving.

His nibbles turn into kisses, and before I know it, I'm pinned against the kitchen island, and he's kissing me deep with full lips and tongue. The sweet scent of vanilla and spices wafting through the warm kitchen, combined with his affection, is intoxicating. The last three weeks apart were like a reset for our relationship, and it feels like we're closer than ever.

James continues seducing me, and it's hard to resist him. "Again?" I smile. He picks me up by my hips, and I wrap my legs around his waist. We've been having non-stop sex since he got back, and now he wants more.

"Well, you taste so good, so now I have to have you," he says with a grin.

He carries me into the living room, lays me on the couch, and undresses me. He unzips my jeans, pulling them down slowly past my hips and down my legs. He kisses my legs up from my feet to my thighs as I squirm in anticipation. He stops when he gets to my hip bone, then takes off my shirt, leaving me in only my panties. He takes off his T-shirt, then resumes his kisses—slowly across my belly and up my chest until he reaches my breasts, lightly biting my nipples.

Mini spasms erupt throughout my body as he continues his pleasure torture by fingering me slowly. *I want him so bad.* He pulls down my panties, then positions himself between my thighs, sliding full inside of me.

I gasp at how good he feels.

We make slow, passionate love in the confined space of the couch, which makes our movements tighter and more intense. I close my eyes and hold him close as he rocks deeper and deeper inside of me. His breath quickens as I arch my back and squeeze my thighs around him. "Mmm, you feel so fucking good," he whispers as he cums.

James collapses on top of me, and I wrap my arms tighter around him, enjoying the fuzzy bliss of orgasm. We're expected at my parents' house for Thanksgiving dinner in a few hours, and I already know it will be impossible to get ready and make it out the door.

"Do we have to go?" James whispers sleepily as he squeezes me tighter.

"It's Thanksgiving, James; of course, we have to go!"

"All I'm thankful for is right here," he says, repositioning himself to spoon me. I turn and look into his eyes, running my fingers through his hair. The guilt from *that night* rears its ugly head at the worst moments, and this is one of them.

"I love you," I say, wrapping my arms around him, stuffing the memory back deep inside.

Two hours later, we're in James's Porsche, finally on our way to my parents' house. The pumpkin pie lays gently on my lap, nicely wrapped and ready to be unveiled at dinner.

"What do you think about moving with me to London for a few months?" he asks out of the blue.

I look over at him, "What?"

We're at a red light. "I'm serious, Annie, I have to go back and forth until the club opens, so I was talking with the Brits, and we were thinking it makes more sense if I move out there for a few months to make the project move faster."

I'm taken aback by his news. "Really? How many months?"

"Two or three, four, maybe. The Brits want the club open by the end of March at the latest."

I shake my head, speechless.

"We talked about this, Annie…" he says, reaching for my hand.

"No, we talked about you going back and forth until the club opens, not moving there for four months!" I'm getting heated, and I hate that he dropped this bomb on me on the way to Thanksgiving dinner.

James brings my hand to his lips for a kiss and looks at me with his flirty smile. It's hard to be mad at him when he gives me *that* smile. "Think about it: four months in London. We can get a great flat or a townhouse in Chelsea…" The light turns green, and his eyes are back on the road.

"And leave the shop? We just opened it—Angela would flip!" I cut in.

"Okay, then you can join me in January. Things slow down in the first quarter, so it'll be the perfect time for you to get away. You can use the time in London to source new designers and merchandise for the shop—look at it as a business opportunity!"

I turn away from him and look directly ahead. Everything he's saying makes sense, and a few months in London with him sounds incredible. "I don't know, James; I don't think it'll be fair to Angela."

"Why don't you ask her? Or, better yet, let me talk to her… I'm great at closing deals." He gives me *that* smile again, and I can't help but soften.

"What if I don't go? Are you really going to leave me for four months?" I can't imagine what that would be like.

"I'd prefer it if you came with me, Annie. And if not, then you'll visit… or fuck it, I'll just tell them that I'll keep going back and forth and scratch the move."

I feel like a brat for putting up a fight about this. I know what an incredible opportunity this is for him, and I don't want to spoil it. "No, it's okay…" I concede. "I'm sorry… I just hate the idea of you being gone for so long, but I understand. Do what you think is right; we'll make it work," I say, squeezing his hand.

"Really?"

I nod.

"Thanks for understanding, Annie," he says with a big smile. "Please think about it. I really want you to come with me."

WE ARRIVE AT MY PARENTS' HOUSE FOR DINNER AND everyone's here. Joe usually joins us for Thanksgiving—sometimes alone and sometimes with his parents—but there's no chance of that happening this year.

I don't dare ask if anyone has seen him, and frankly, after the humiliation he put me through at Matt's dinner, I don't care if I ever see him again. After that night, I vowed to stop caring about Joe. I no longer care if he's sober or if he destroys his life. The way he treated me in front of our friends was traumatizing and unforgivable. *Why would I forgive him? He hasn't even apologized?!* I'm convinced that he has no remorse.

Regardless of how angry I am at him right now, I can't help but wonder how he's doing, and it breaks my heart that he's using drugs again.

"Are you okay?" James puts his arm around me. We're well into dinner, and everyone's enjoying the decadent meal, accompanied by laughter and lively conversation.

"Yeah, I'm fine," I nod.

"Are you sure?" he asks, squeezing my shoulder.

"I'm fine," I repeat, kissing him on the cheek.

My pumpkin pie is the hit of the dessert course, and my mood finally lifts from the sugar high and my third glass of wine.

James and I stay until the end of the night, and I'm full and sleepy by the time we get home.

In bed, I think about how great it would be to get away from here for a while, to leave all the bad memories and drama behind. As my thoughts race, I devise a plan to convince Angela to take care of the shop on her own for four months so that I can go to London with James.

Chapter Forty-Five

A week after Thanksgiving, James returns to London. We made the most of his time in LA by having frequent date nights, lazy days at home, and a few social outings with friends. It felt like a whirlwind to make it all happen, but we managed to spend significant quality time together until we reunite in three weeks to spend Christmas and the end of the year together.

That was our compromise after Angela nixed my idea to move to London with him. I even pitched her James's brilliant idea to use my time out there to source stylish new merchandise and discover hot, young British designers for the shop, but she didn't go for it.

As predicted, she freaked out and gave me a major guilt trip. I've had more than enough drama lately, so I had to let go of the plan to avoid more stress and conflict.

Meanwhile, James and I are doing our best to make the long-distance thing work. We text and FaceTime every day, and when I feel sad, I remind myself that it's only for a few months and try to remember how much this project means to him. Besides, I'll be with him soon, and until then, I have plenty to occupy myself with at Three-Two-Three now that the holiday season is here and we're busier than ever.

During a lull at the shop on a hectic Thursday afternoon, I take a breather to check my phone and discover a text from Max:

> Hey. Last chance to put you on the list for Trent's party tonight. Let me know ASAP if you want to go.

I've been struggling to decide whether to attend a holiday party thrown by Trent's record label tonight. It's at The Chateau Marmont, and I know it will be super fun, but the thought of seeing Joe there is what's keeping me on the fence.

After the incident at Matt's birthday dinner, I accepted that my friendship with Joe is over and that I have to move on without an apology from him. That night, it was abundantly clear that he's harboring plenty of animosity toward me and has no desire to continue our friendship. He also has no intention of being sober, which has been most painful for me to accept.

"Did you get Max's text?" Angela asks, approaching me at the counter and interrupting my thoughts.

"Yeah, I don't think I'm going to go," I shrug.

"Come on, Annie. You have to! Since James left, you've returned to hermit mode, and you'll be off to London soon... Why not make the most of your time here with us before you're gone till next year!"

I crack a smile at how dramatic she's being and also at her persuasiveness.

"I know Joe's going to be there, and..." I trail off as my smile fades.

"Ugh. Really? Are you going to let Joe steal your joy like that? He's not worth it, Annie. Fuck him!"

"I'm not... it's just that..."

Angela cuts me off, "You are! I know that's why you've been keeping to yourself. You're avoiding running into him, and I get it! What he did to you was fucked-up, and I'm sorry he hasn't had the *decency* to apologize yet!" She softens her tone as her expression turns sympathetic. "Sis, don't let him win. It's not fair that he's been having the time of his life all over town while you've been stuck at home, stewing in your thoughts."

"I haven't been *stuck at home, stewing in my thoughts*, Angela," I retort, rolling my eyes.

"Okay, whatever! I just mean, it's time for you to get out of the house and have a little fun! Just put on a fucking hot dress tonight, have a few drinks, have a great time with us, and MOVE ON."

Angela makes it sound so easy, but she has a point. "Okay," I concede, without giving it much more thought.

"Yay!" she claps victoriously. "Text Max right now and tell him you're coming!" she demands.

Her enthusiasm makes me giggle, "Yes, ma'am," I reply, smiling back.

Later that night, I arrive with Angela and Darren at The Chateau Marmont, and the party is in full swing. As expected, it is *the* place to be, crawling with starlets and luminaries from the music industry, sipping champagne and mingling to the tunes of an energetic soundtrack.

I had a few drinks at dinner, so I'm still enjoying a happy buzz and looking forward to keeping the fun going. As I step closer into the crowd to make my way toward the bar, I feel Angela squeeze my arm.

"Don't freak out, but he's here," she says, pulling me in and leaning into my ear.

I scan the room until I spot Joe. He's with Trent and a group of people standing by the bar. As usual, he seems to be the life of the party, as everyone around him has their attention fixed on him.

I haven't seen Joe since he humiliated me at Matt's

birthday dinner. I've gone from hating him to feeling sorry and sad for him and then back to hating him again. Now, I'm just exhausted and indifferent.

I watch Darren approach Joe, and he lights up, greeting him with a hug. His hair is a cute mess of waves, and he looks a bit scruffy. He's wearing a fitted black suit with a thin black tie hanging loose around the collar of his white button-down shirt. Joe always exudes charm and confidence, which makes him so sexy.

I stiffen, watching Joe introduce Darren to a tall blonde, grabbing her around the waist.

"Let's get a drink," Angela says, leading me to another bar on the opposite side of the room.

"Sure," I respond, leaning into the indifference I've been feeling toward Joe.

"I know I pressured you to come, but we don't have to stay," Angela says, handing me a glass of champagne at the bar.

I take a sip and shake my head, "No, why would we leave? I'm fine. I want to stay."

Max and Michelle appear through the crowd and join us at the bar. "Well, if it isn't *the life of the party!*" Max quips, nodding towards Joe, rolling his eyes.

I follow his gaze, taking a sip of my drink, refraining from commenting. I've noticed that Max and Joe haven't been hanging out as much lately, and I know it's because he's still pissed at Joe for the way he treated me. I also know Max is disappointed at Joe for relapsing, even though he pretends he doesn't care.

Darren returns to our group, and it feels strange that Joe is on one side of the room with a group of random people and not with us. *How quickly things change.*

I think back to the night we celebrated Trent's number-one single at this very bar. Joe was still sober and, in fact, left early because Patrick was trying to tempt him to party. It saddens me that we're back at square one, and I have no idea what will happen now that he's back to his old ways.

I look down at my phone and notice a missed call from James. I excuse myself and step outside to call him back. The crisp air is a relief from the suffocating atmosphere inside. I stand by the valet stand at the bar's entrance and dial him back.

"Hey, baby," James picks up right away, and it's so good to hear his voice. "Are you all set for your trip?" he asks excitedly.

"Yes! I can't wait to see you!" I smile, unable to contain my excitement.

"Three more days, baby," he reminds me.

James and I chat for a few minutes, and he tells me London is cold and rainy. It's almost midnight here, but he's making coffee because his day is just starting.

"I miss you," I say, feeling a knot in my throat from the distance between us.

"I miss you too, Annie. I can't wait to see you."

I nod into the phone as we start to say our goodbyes.

"I'll call you tomorrow," he says before we hang up.

I take a deep breath and walk back into The Chateau with a heaviness in my heart. I try to shake off the sadness as I reenter the lively party when I suddenly come face to face with Joe.

"Hey, Annie," he says, stopping in his tracks.

I freeze, and it takes me a few seconds to react. "Hi," I respond.

He puts his hands in his pockets. "How are you?"

"Fine." I have nothing to say to him.

Up close, he looks tired, and his voice is raspy from smoking. I can tell he's back to partying hard. As he starts to say something, the tall blonde I saw him with earlier appears out of the restroom and slinks to his side, threading her arm between his. She gives me a blank stare.

"Oh, um… this is Summer," he glances at her, introducing us.

We give each other a cordial greeting and a forced smile.

"So, is everything good?" Joe is trying to be friendly and make this less awkward, but it isn't working.

"Yes, everything's great," I say.

"Cool. Well, we were just leaving." He pauses. "I've been meaning to talk to you… Can we get a coffee or something next week?" he asks as she pulls him away.

I'm shocked that he's acting like he did nothing wrong.

"I can't. I won't be here next week. I'll be in London," I respond dryly.

He opens his mouth like he's about to say something but stops himself. "Okay… have a good trip," he says before turning away with the blonde, still clinging to him tight.

I watch them leave, finally noticing that my heart is beating wildly.

I walk back to the group at the bar and sigh loudly—I feel like the wind was just knocked out of me. *What the fuck just happened?*

"Are you okay?" Angela asks as I take a seat next to her. I nod, grabbing my champagne to take a long sip.

"I just talked to Joe."

Angela turns her attention to me, "What happened?"

It's loud in the bar, so she leans close to hear me.

"He was with *that girl*; we didn't say much. He just asked if we could talk next week, and I told him no, and that was it. They left. She practically dragged him out the door." I'm not in a good mood anymore, and I hate myself for letting him get to me.

"I just found out who she is," Angela says, looking over at Darren and Max, who are talking to some people near our table. "Do you want to know?"

Part of me doesn't care, and I wish I could resist the urge to know. I shrug, and Angela leans in again.

"Well, according to Darren, her name is Summer, and she's a stripper that Joe met at a club in the Valley."

I'm not surprised, considering her cheap and provocative look.

"Apparently, Joe's new BFF is Trent, and you know how much that dude loves the strip clubs," she adds.

I don't want to know anymore and tell her I've heard enough.

"I'm sorry, Annie," she says, reaching for my hand. I grab my drink and take it down, shaking off the anger and hurt from everything that's happened between Joe and me.

Angela looks at me and whispers in my ear, "I think you should stay in London for as long as you want. I'll be fine at the shop. It'll be good for you."

A deep sense of relief comes over me, feeling *so* grateful to have Angela's blessing. "Really?" I look at her in disbelief, unable to hold back tears. However, this time, they're tears of joy. I hug her, "Thank you, sis," I say, squeezing her tight.

"Whoa, what's going on here?" Max gives us a puzzled look as he returns to our table. I'm wiping away tears, and Angela is doing the same.

"Annie's moving to London!" she says.

"What?!" Max exclaims.

I get the same shocked response from Darren and Michelle, who've also joined us. Everyone knows I'm going to London for the holidays, but *moving there* is news.

"It's only for a few months," I tell them. "James will be there until the club opens in the spring, and he asked me to join him." The group gets quiet as the news sinks in.

"Well, James and London Town are lucky to have you. We're gonna miss you, Annie!" Darren says, lifting his glass as everyone else joins in to toast me.

Chapter Forty-Six

James is waiting for me at Heathrow Airport with a big smile. Even though I'm exhausted from the ten-hour direct flight from LAX, I'm elated to see him.

"I missed you so much," I say, throwing my arms tightly around him. His embrace and his kisses feel better than I remember. He also looks more handsome than ever, wearing a smart black coat layered over a chunky cable knit sweater, jeans, and boots. His hair is a little longer, and he's clean-shaven and smells delicious.

"I'm glad you're finally here," he says, holding me close. He grabs my carry-on and suitcase and leads me outside to the crisp London air.

We climb into the waiting chauffeured SUV and head to his place in Chelsea. He holds me the entire time, and I'm finally at peace, resting my head on his shoulder.

James plays tour guide, pointing out the towns we drive through, and enthusiastically tells me about all the places he'll take me. I'm overwhelmed and excited, and I can't believe how lucky I am to be here with him.

"We're taking the scenic route through central London so you can see some of the sights," he says, meeting my eyes with a smile. It's been a few years since I was last here, and I know it will be a much better experience with James by my side.

My excitement escalates as Big Ben comes into view. I beam, taking in the sights and sounds of London, dressed up in holiday cheer—it's a pretty magical sight.

The city sparkles with twinkling lights and elaborate Christmas decorations. Shop windows display winter wonderland scenes, and sidewalks fill with stylish people, integrating into the city's pulsating, unique rhythm.

"This is so fucking cool," I say, turning to James with a big grin.

"You're gonna love it here, Annie. I promise," he says, pulling me into him.

We finally arrive at our destination on Redburn Street. The car pulls up to a gorgeous, sleek townhouse with a split-level exterior—crisp white on the lower level and classic red brick on the top. The house sits on a row of similar homes with stately, jet-black, wrought-iron fences. The driver assists with my luggage and tells James that he'll pick him up in the morning.

I'm giddy as James opens the door to the townhouse. "You ready?" He gives me a teasing smile as I nod with excitement.

I gasp, stepping inside the sexy two-level with dark wood accents and clean, modern furnishings reminiscent of his house in LA.

After a tour through the living room, den, and dining room, we end up in the spacious kitchen, where James pulls out a bottle of champagne from the fridge and pours two glasses.

"How are you feeling?" he asks, handing me a glass.

"Amazing!" I respond. I'm no longer tired, as adrenaline from all the excitement pumps through me.

"Welcome to our new home, baby," he says, raising his glass. We toast and sip on the crisp, bubbly champagne. "Let me show you upstairs," he says, taking my hand and leading me toward the stairs.

The primary suite is spacious and elegant, with a king-size bed and dark wood and leather furniture. James lights a sleek fireplace that separates the bedroom and the bathroom as I turn to the floor-to-ceiling window to admire the view. He comes up behind me and wraps his arms around my waist. "So, what do you think?" he whispers as his lips trace the crook of my neck. It's been two weeks since we saw each other, and I've eagerly anticipated this moment.

I turn to face him and pull him in for a kiss, "I love it." I respond.

James guides me toward the bed, devouring me in kisses. "Fuck me," I whisper, tugging at his belt buckle. I've waited long enough—I *ache* for him.

We undress each other, and he covers my body with more kisses, torturing me by making me wait. He continues to tease me by gently biting my nipples and then kissing my belly and the inside of my thighs. His lips and tongue finally reach the spot between my legs, and I surrender to the pleasure that surges through me.

We make love in front of the roaring fireplace, night falling over London as our reunion passionately unfolds.

Chapter Forty-Seven

Joe

I open my eyes and am immediately disoriented. My mouth feels like cotton, and my head's pounding like a *motherfucker*. I'm sweaty and shivering and getting hit with waves of nausea. I know this feeling—a familiar crash—from last night's coke binge and whatever pill I probably took to help me sleep.

I sit up in bed, and the pounding in my head gets worse. *Where the fuck am I?* I look around the dark room in a haze. I turn on a lamp, finally remembering that I'm at the Four Seasons in LA, as everything starts coming back.

I got back in town two days ago from being on tour with Trent. I had so much anxiety about being back in LA that I couldn't bring myself to go home to my condo. I didn't want to deal with my friends coming around, checking up on me to see how I was doing—asking about the tour. I know I fucked up by falling off the wagon, and I don't need anyone to remind me or tell me how concerned they are. So, the Four Seasons has been the perfect spot to keep a low profile and disappear for a while—I don't think anyone knows I'm here. I just need a few more days to clear my head; then, I'll be ready to return to my place and join the real world again.

The end of Trent's first leg of the tour was a week of non-stop debauchery. We hit five cities on the West Coast—flying private, partying, fucking groupies, and doing an insane amount of drinking and drugging. I had a moment of clarity one night, realizing how lucky I am to be alive after all the crazy shit I've been doing and putting into my body. It's been a hell of a time, and I'm glad I could party in peace since Darren and Max stayed back to handle other projects in the wings.

I look around the room for something to drink and come up short, so I settle for a lone beer submerged in lukewarm water in what was once an icy champagne bucket. I pop it open and take a long sip—It's room temperature and tastes disgusting, but I don't care; I'm starting to feel like myself again.

I draw open the heavy curtains, and by the look of the orange and red streaked sky, I realize that it's dusk—*Fuck, another day gone.* I look for my phone, and when I find it, I have another rude awakening—It's December twenty-fifth. I have several missed calls and texts from people asking where I'm at and what I'm up to. I feel like an asshole for forgetting Christmas, but the last few weeks have been a blur.

My last clear memories from before the tour come into focus. I remember seeing Annie at Trent's label's holiday party. I wasn't expecting to see her there, but as always, she looked beautiful, and her presence overjoyed and destroyed me.

Seeing her made me spiral from guilt from the way I treated her at Matt's birthday dinner, and as much as I've tried to block that horrible night from my mind, it's all I can fucking think about.

I wanted to take it easy at Matt's dinner, but one drink led to another, and once I started to hit the coke to level me out, it was over for me. That's when the demon inside usually takes over, and all self-control goes out the window. If I hadn't been so wasted, I would've never said those awful things to Annie. I was just so fucking angry at her.

It pissed me off that one day she's fucking me, and the next, she's across the country with that asshole. She didn't even tell me she was back with him. I was sure they were over. As much as I tried not to let our night together affect me, it did. It ate me up inside that she went back to him, and the only way I could deal with it was to drink and do drugs.

I sit on the edge of the bed and take down the warm beer. *Fuck being sober. I don't even have a problem!*

My mind starts spiraling again—The only reason I went to rehab was to make Annie happy. Everyone I know drinks and parties—Why can't I?! It's not like my life is unraveling or anything. I co-produced one of the most successful albums of the year! I'm not some loser crackhead—I'm totally fine! And I had been fine at Matt's dinner, but being that close to Annie and so irrationally angry at her proved to be a terrible combination.

I know that I humiliated her in front of our friends, and I know that things between us will never be the same.

And now, she's in London—**LONDON**—with that fucking guy, and I have no choice but to accept that I've lost her forever.

A sinking feeling sets in, and before it turns into a panic attack, I scroll through my phone, looking for Patrick's number. When I find it, I hesitate and call Darren instead.

"Hey, bro!" Darren picks up right away. "Where you at, man, I've been calling you all day!"

"Yeah, my bad. I… uh… couldn't find my phone, but I'm good… Merry Christmas." I hear voices in the background. "Where are you?"

"I'm at the Preston's having Christmas dinner. Come over!"

"Um… I don't know, man. I'm not really in the mood to do the whole *Christmas* thing."

"C'mon, Joe, you're coming over here—I'll come get you —are you home?"

"Naw, man. I'm at my parents'. I'm crashing here for a few days."

"Ahh…" Darren says.

"And I think I'm coming down with the flu or some shit. Probably picked up something on the road…"

Darren is quiet, and I know he knows I'm full of shit.

"It's all good, man. I hope you feel better," he says without pressing me further.

"You're coming to Miami, right?" I ask, changing the subject. Trent's hosting a New Year's Eve party at a new nightclub in South Beach, and we all decided to go down there for New Year's Eve and my birthday, which is on New Year's Day.

"Yeah, man. Of course! We'll all be there!" he says, perking up.

"Cool," I respond, feeling a glimmer of happiness at the thought of reuniting with my friends and celebrating my birthday in Miami.

"We're just hanging out here; it's very chill. Are you sure you don't want me to come get you real quick?" Darren tries one last time to convince me.

"No, I'm cool. I just took some flu medicine—I'm just gonna chill tonight."

"Alright, bro, let's grab lunch when you feel better."

"Sure," I say before we hang up.

There's no way I can go to the Preston's tonight or probably ever again. Annie will never allow it, let alone Max, who I know wants nothing to do with me right now. I also don't know how I'll ever be able to face Dr. Preston again after all he did for me.

My heart sinks at the reminder that I've fucked up and hurt some of the closest people in my life. It's too much to think about, so I turn back to my phone and scroll through my contacts, landing on Patrick's number.

"Yo, yo, yo! My dude!!" he answers.

"What up, man?"

"Chill, baby. Just having a little yuletide celebration at my *casa*—come through, dude!"

"Oh, yeah? Yuletide celebration? You got eggnog and shit?" I laugh, already feeling more relaxed.

"You know it, man, we got eggnog, gingerbread cookies, tinsel and shit—we got it all!" Patrick cracks me up; he's such a clown.

"Damn, that sounds festive."

"Yeah, man, and you know what else is festive? SNOW—we got that shit too—got it shipped fresh from the Alps and shit!"

"Man, it sure 'ain't Christmas without snow. Sounds like you got it covered!" I chuckle, playing along.

"Yeah, man, we got it all covered—it's a BLIZZARD up in here! Grab your parka and come on by man," he says.

I laugh and tell him I'll be right over.

Chapter Forty-Eight

Christmas in London is bittersweet. It's the first time I've been away from my family during the holidays, and it's been hard to stay cheerful with the gloomy weather that doesn't let up, amplifying the acute homesickness that's set in.

Lauren and James's mom, Julia, arrived from New York yesterday, and we had a lovely time catching up and decorating the tree James got for the townhouse. We had a great Christmas Eve dinner at Claridge's, where Lauren and Julia are staying, and then a nightcap back at the house. This morning, we opened presents, and Julia made Christmas Day brunch.

For dinner, we went to Thomas's house for an elaborate feast with his family and the other American expats in town who are also working on the nightclub project. Lauren's boyfriend, Scott, arrived from New York right before dinner, so we were a big group and had a fantastic time.

I look over at the clock on the bedside table, and it's one forty-five in the morning. James and I got home from the dinner party after midnight, and I've been tossing and turning in bed ever since. I'm still adjusting to the time difference, and my head has been racing with thoughts all day. I would've loved to stay up for a little longer—anything to stop thinking about home and everything back there that haunts me. But James was exhausted, so we called it a night and went to bed.

I turn over and place my arm around James, resting my head on his chest. He's sound asleep, and the steady rise and fall of his breathing feels comforting. The sadness I felt earlier returns as I remember my brief call with my family to wish them a Merry Christmas. I'm nostalgic for my parents' Christmas dinner celebration at the house with all our loved ones, and it breaks my heart to have missed it.

I feel tears starting to burn my eyes, but I refuse to cry. I have to focus on how wonderful today was and how lucky I am to be here in beautiful London with James.

I ache to be comforted and yearn for James to make love to me, so I trail a few kisses on his chest, hoping he'll wake up, but he only stirs briefly. I close my eyes and take a deep breath. *It's time to go to sleep, Annie. It'll be better tomorrow.*

JAMES'S MOTHER LEAVES LONDON TWO DAYS AFTER CHRISTMAS to meet with her new beau in Italy to close the year. Lauren and Scott leave for Paris for a few days and plan on returning to spend New Year's Eve with us at a big bash thrown by the Brits at Red Room, the crown jewel of their nightclub portfolio.

The week feels like limbo as the year crawls to an end and anticipation builds for the new one to begin. James continues working long hours to meet the Brits' strict deadline for the club's opening. Meanwhile, I keep myself busy by walking around Chelsea and Kensington, getting familiar with my new neighborhood. I also take up cooking to surprise James with elaborate meals when he gets home from work.

It's cold and gray in London, contrasting the blue skies

and sun I'm used to, which hits me hard. I feel myself slipping into seasonal depression, which I try desperately to hide from James. My funk gets worse on New Year's Eve because it means Joe's birthday is tomorrow. It'll be the first time since we were ten that we've spent a birthday apart. As much as I resent him for everything that happened between us, I still miss our friendship, and it breaks my heart every time I think about how things fell apart. I hate that I still blame myself for being reckless by sleeping with him, and I can't shake the memory of that night even though it happened three months ago.

I talk to Angela almost every day, and she told me the last time we spoke that they're all going to Miami for a New Year's Eve party that Trent's hosting and, of course, to celebrate Joe's birthday. I pretend I'm not jealous of their plans, but I'd rather be in hot and sunny Miami with my friends than in freezing London.

The FOMO over Miami makes me irritable and cranky. I can't stop thinking about what everyone's up to as I do my makeup at the gorgeous vanity James had installed for me, getting ready for our New Year's Eve celebration.

James peeks into the bedroom, "Hey, baby," he says, approaching me. "How's it going in here?" He straddles me from behind on the vanity bench and rests his chin on my shoulder. Our eyes meet in the mirror as he wraps his arms around my waist. "Are you alright?"

I nod and smile at him, "Yeah, I'm great. Why?"

He looks at me closely and shrugs. "You've barely said two words since I got home… you don't seem like yourself."

I look down at the blush brush in my hand, suddenly afraid that he'll see through me if I continue to hold his gaze in the mirror.

"Nothing's wrong," I say, lifting his hand from around my waist for a kiss. "I guess I was just thinking about home, that's all," I say, looking up at his reflection again. It's as honest as I can be without telling him I've been thinking about home, Miami, and Joe all day.

"Are you not having fun? We won't be here forever, Annie. It's just a few months; let's enjoy it." He smiles and kisses my shoulder. I nod and assure him that I'm having a great time.

James continues to pepper my shoulder with kisses, then trails his lips to my neck. His hands slip underneath my silk robe to stroke my thighs, and the gloominess hanging over me starts to dissipate. I close my eyes and lean back into him, wanting more. He unties my robe and slips it down past my shoulders, revealing my breasts.

I guide his hands over my breasts, down my belly, and inside my panties.

I exhale softly, releasing the tension I've held all day as he slips his fingers inside me. I turn to face him and meet his lips and tongue, tasting a trace of Scotch in his kiss.

James gets up from the vanity bench, lifting me with him. He guides me to the bed, barely releasing my lips. We make love, and my mind is finally quiet. The torturous thoughts are gone.

Chapter Forty-Nine

When January finally arrives, and the excitement of the holidays and New Year's wears off, my new life in London feels more settled. James works long days at the club, and I'm back to keeping myself busy. I visit all the hot showrooms and buy a ton of new merchandise for the shop. I keep my spirits up by walking around the city, visiting museums, having long, leisurely lunches, and reading at different cafés around Chelsea.

I arrive home at four in the afternoon after a long day of running around London. I'm excited to FaceTime Angela and tell her about all the incredible merchandise that will soon arrive at the shop.

I turn on the kettle and text Angela to see if she's up—it's eight in the morning in LA. I've become accustomed to tea time, and it's now a part of my daily routine, whether I'm home alone or out and about with James when he's not working.

As the kettle starts whistling, Angela FaceTimes me back.

"Hi!!" I greet her excitedly when she pops up on the screen.

"Hi!!" she says, flashing her beautiful smile. A pang of

sadness hits me—I miss my sister, and all I want to do is give her a big hug.

Angela looks gorgeous, even straight out of bed. Her brown hair falls loosely around her delicate face, framing her glowing complexion.

"How's it going, sis?!" she asks. The last time we talked was after New Year's two weeks ago. It was a brief call because she was still in Miami, so we're finally having a proper catch-up.

"Angela!" I say, inspecting her closely on the screen, "You're so tan!"

"I know! I got major sun in Miami... What are you doing?" She squints her eyes as she watches me prepare my tea.

"It's tea time!" I giggle.

"Oh *gawd*, you're so British now!" she teases.

We laugh, and I pull up a stool at the kitchen island, excited to catch up.

"What are you doing?" I ask. She's in a pretty silk robe, sitting in a sun-drenched room that looks like Darren's dining room.

She yawns, stretching her arms. "I was just reading emails and trying to detox," she says, holding up a glass of thick, green juice.

"Are you at Darren's?"

"Yup." She gives me a coy smile. "He asked me to move in with him... and I said yes!" she beams.

I'm thrilled for her, yet I'm hurt that life is moving forward in LA without me. "That's wonderful... I'm so happy for you!" I sip my tea and ask if Darren's there so I can say hi.

"He's sleeping. He was at the studio until five in the morning, so he'll be out for a few hours," she says, stretching again.

"Cool..." I hesitate, "So... how was Miami?" I've been dying to get the scoop on the trip.

"Ugh, let me tell you, I'm still recovering!"

"Was it nuts?"

"Oh man, Annie, it was insane…"

Angela proceeds to tell me everything from the moment she arrived at Burbank airport to get on the private jet with the whole crew plus Trent, a few of his best friends, and three random girls who were either "strippers or escorts," and of course, Joe. She said Joe was with one of the girls and that they were engaged in full PDA all the way to Miami.

Angela confirms my suspicions about that weekend—Joe was a fucked-up mess.

"How was his birthday?" I can't help asking; I have to know.

"Exactly as you can imagine. He was wasted the whole time, but he looked like he was having the time of his life… Do you really want to hear about it?" she asks.

It doesn't do me any good to know, but curiosity gets the best of me. "Yes, I want to know," I respond.

"Well, he brought you up a few times…" she pauses.

"Okay…?"

"He kept saying things like, 'Your sister hates me,' and 'Your sister hasn't even called me on my birthday.'"

I roll my eyes at his audacity. Like, I'm supposed to call him on his birthday after he's been a total dick to me for months?!

"I tried to humor him, but I mostly ignored him. I don't think he knew what he was saying. He was way gone," Angela adds.

Part of me is heartbroken that Joe's back in that dark place, but another part of me is still angry and hurt at the way he treated me at Matt's birthday dinner.

"Why didn't anyone help him? Why didn't Darren or Max do something? They could've tried." I shake my head, disheartened.

"Annie, there was none of that. You know how Joe gets when he's fucked-up. He's like a hyper teenager—there's no controlling him…" Angela pauses again. "Maybe I said too much… I mean, what's the point of telling you all this?"

I shrug. "It's okay, I don't need to hear anymore." Everything Angela described is typical fucked-up Joe behavior. I've been witness to his antics for years.

"I'm sorry, Annie," Angela gives me a somber look.

I'm quiet, staring at my tea.

"Annie? Hello?" Angela tries to get my attention. "I can see you're upset. I shouldn't have said anything."

"No, no," I snap out of it. "Thank you, I'm glad you told me. It's all good. There's nothing I can do from here, so I have to let it go and let him live his life."

Angela changes the subject and asks me about London. I don't want to tell her how I really feel—homesick and depressed from the dreary weather—so I lie and tell her it's going great. I tell her about my purchases for the shop and the cool new designers I've been meeting at the showrooms.

"That sounds amazing!" she says. "And don't worry about a thing. I have everything under control here. Enjoy London and say hi to James. We miss you both so much!"

I smile, nodding. "We miss you guys, too," I say before we hang up. I'm alone again with my thoughts, staring at a cold cup of tea.

Chapter Fifty

The sun hasn't come out in London for three weeks. It's rained almost every day, and the gloomy and cold weather has taken a serious emotional toll on this LA girl.

It's been getting harder to hide my funk from James, and he's starting to question me about it. I suspect he knows I'm unhappy here because he reminds me I can go home whenever I want. But I refuse to be a baby and leave London because of the weather and the homesickness. I'm committed to staying until James finishes the nightclub project, and that's what I intend to do.

It's Wednesday night, and James surprises me by coming home early. "Annie, you home?!" His voice booms from the foyer.

I'm on my laptop and perk up, "I'm in the kitchen!" I yell back. I hear his footsteps approaching, and my eyes light up when he appears, holding a bouquet of roses. He gives me *that* smile. "Hi," I greet him, grinning.

"I've been dying to see you all day," he says, pulling me in for a kiss. He hands me the roses, and I take in their scent.

"What are these for?" I smile ear to ear.

"I saw them at the flower stand on the way over, and I wanted you to have them," he says, looking into my eyes. I'm touched by his gesture.

"Thank you," I say, throwing my arms around him.

James removes his coat and heads to the bar to pour himself a drink. "Would you like one?" he asks, holding up a bottle of Scotch.

"Sure," I giggle, feeling adventurous. I don't usually drink Scotch. I look for a vase to put the flowers in while he pours the drinks.

"What a nice surprise to have you home early," I smile.

"Yeah, we had a slow day, so I bailed," he says, placing my drink on the counter.

I locate a beautiful crystal vase and arrange the bright red roses. "They're gorgeous," I say, admiring the arrangement.

"You're gorgeous," he says, approaching me for another kiss. I'm giddy from his affection and wonder if he's up to something.

"Okay, what's going on?" I ask, giving him a look.

He smiles big and laughs. "Ah fuck, I'm terrible at being subtle." He walks over to his coat and pulls an envelope from one of the pockets. I'm intrigued.

"I know you haven't had the easiest time here, and I know how much you're giving up to be here with me…"

I drop my eyes, suddenly feeling emotional, and *so* seen. He lifts my chin with his finger, and our eyes meet again. I swallow hard, holding back tears.

"And I know I've been working long hours, and I'm sorry you spend so much time alone."

I refuse to break.

James's eyes soften as he continues. "So… I couldn't wait to get home to give you this…" he says, handing me the envelope.

I take it from him while trying to read his eyes. "Open it," he says.

Inside the envelope, I find two Eurostar tickets. "We're going to Paris?" I gasp.

"We're going to Paris, baby!" he grins. I throw my arms around him again. "I know I promised you this trip when you got here, so I took time off so we can go for your birthday."

My birthday is next week, and I was starting to feel bummed out about it, but this changes everything.

I hold him tighter as tears finally spill over. "Thank you," I say into his ear.

He squeezes me tight. "I'm so happy you're here with me, Annie. I want you to be happy too."

I nod. "As long as you're with me, I'm happy," I say, meeting his eyes again.

"We're going to have an amazing time in Paris, and you're going to have the best birthday ever, I promise."

James and I arrive in the City of Light at the Gare du Nord train station, hand in hand. My eyes take in all the sights and sounds as soon as we step off the train and into the bustling station. James beams, leading me through the crowd as we approach the exit.

We left gloomy London two-and-a-half hours ago, and we've arrived to crystal clear, blue Parisian skies and a blazing afternoon sun. Even though it's winter, it feels warmer here than in London, but I'm sure *anywhere* is warmer than London.

"Let's grab a taxi," James says, raising his hand to flag one down. I can't stop smiling as I hold onto his other hand.

"I'm so happy to be here!" I say, reaching up to kiss him on the cheek.

"I'm glad," he says with a proud smile. "We're going to have a great time."

A black sedan with a little sign on its roof with the words *Taxis Parisiens* pulls up, and we climb in with our two weekender bags. "Le Plaza Athénée, s'il vous plaît," James says to the driver.

"You're so hot when you speak French," I giggle, nuzzling him while gently biting his earlobe. I'm feeling extra frisky in Paris.

James squeezes my knee and rubs my thigh, "You're already making me so hard," he whispers in my ear, moving my hand over the growing bulge in his pants. I blush, darting my eyes toward the driver, whose gaze is firmly on the road as we make our way through traffic.

"*Stop*," I mouth, shaking my head, trying not to laugh.

He grins, pulling me in tighter for a kiss. It seems James is feeling extra frisky in Paris, too.

I glance out the window and gasp, "Look!"

"Ah, there she is, baby." I lean over him to get a better look at the Eiffel Tower, looking so much more beautiful and majestic since the last time I was here, the summer after my first year of college. It takes my breath away.

Our taxi drops us off at the palatial Plaza Athénée, and I bounce out like an excited little girl arriving at Cinderella's castle. *Keep cool, Annie,* I tell myself. But I can't help it—I'm so happy I could burst! It feels so good to be out of London and free from the heavy, lonely feeling I haven't been able to shake for weeks. Right now, I feel like myself again, overjoyed to be in this beautiful city with my boyfriend, whom I can't keep my hands off.

I watch James tip the driver and handle our luggage. He looks so sexy in his black Burberry trench, dark jeans, and white T-shirt combo that he wears so well. He gives me a look as he approaches me at the hotel entrance. "What?" he asks, noticing I've been staring at him.

"What?!" I respond playfully while holding onto his arm as the doorman welcomes us with a friendly "Bonjour."

The interior of the Plaza Athénée is even more breath-taking than I expected. It's elegant, chic, and classically

French, adorned with stately columns, exquisite chandeliers, and beautiful flower arrangements. James holds my hand as we make our way to the concierge desk, where a dapper Frenchman, impeccably dressed, greets us with a smile.

Within minutes, we're given our keys and offered assistance to our room. We only have two bags, so we politely decline and head to the elevators and our suite.

"Here you go," James says, handing me the key as we arrive at the door to our room on the twenty-first floor. I open the door and enter an enormous corner suite with a direct view of the Eiffel Tower.

"Are you fucking kidding me!?" I squeal.

James smiles, looking pleased. "Do you like it?"

I walk around the room in awe. Even though I'm pretty familiar with the extravagances of Beverly Hills, I haven't seen anything like this before. "It's perfect," I say, swinging open the French doors to the balcony and stepping outside.

James joins me, wrapping his arms around me from behind. "Je t'aime, Annie," he whispers in my ear.

I turn around and wrap my arms around him. "I love you, too, James," I whisper.

Later that night, James and I step out into the city streets, aglow and buzzing after enjoying a bottle of champagne, indulging in great sex, followed by a hot shower. My hormones are on overdrive in Paris, and the dopamine from the sex and the champagne have me feeling giddy. I also feel extra sexy in my slinky black Dior slip dress, classic Louboutin pumps, and red lipstick. I threw on a gorgeous vintage leopard coat I found on Portobello Road to complete my look.

James and I explore Avenue Montaigne in search of a dinner spot. He holds me with a protective arm around my shoulder while pointing out little things about the lively neighborhood as we try to find the perfect place to eat. He tells me he came here often when he lived in London with Lauren.

"Ooh, this looks cute," I say as we pass a little bistro on the famed avenue. It's small, candlelit, and not very crowded.

"Let's try it," James says, opening the door.

The restaurant is warm and cozy, with a roaring fireplace. "It's perfect," I say, looking around. The hostess greets us and leads us to a table with a great view of *La Tour d'Eiffel*, twinkling in the distance.

We settle into our chairs as the hostess walks away with our coats. "So…" James says, reaching across the table for my hand. "What do you think so far?" He knows I'm having the time of my life, but I indulge his ego and praise him for his stellar getaway planning.

"Baby, you did amazing. This is the best trip I've ever been on." I lean in to kiss him on the lips.

"Ever, ever?" He's being playful, fishing for more compliments.

"Yes, ever, ever!"

He smiles and kisses my hand. "Good, and it's just the beginning," he says, looking down at his watch—a Rolex that his father gave him for his high school graduation, "And guess what, your official birthday celebration starts in three hours!"

I sigh, unsure how I'm supposed to feel. It hardly *feels* like my birthday. It's not the same without my friends and family, not to mention being a million miles from LA.

"You're not excited about your birthday?" he asks, noticing the dip in my mood.

"No, not at all—I mean, of course I am!" I'm suddenly flustered. I pause and put on a happy face, squeezing his hand. "I am excited. And I'm especially excited to spend it with you in this beautiful, magical city. Thank you," I say, bringing his hand to my lips for a kiss.

The server arrives at our table, speaking rapidly in French, explaining the wine list and the menu. I shake off the sudden gloom that washed over me and summon sexy Annie back. James surprises me with how much French he knows, and I get a little turned on watching him order for us. When she walks away, I give his leg a little nudge with the point of my pump under the table. "That was so hot," I tell him, making him laugh.

We continue our perfect night at the little bistro with excellent food and wine. I guess we can't go wrong—we're in PARIS, after all!

James and I spend dinner talking and laughing and exchanging sweet kisses. It's reminiscent of our first dates when everything we did packed a punch of pure lust and sexual desire. I can't believe we're three months away from our first anniversary, and I can't believe so much has happened since.

I don't want our perfect date to end, but we're among the last patrons at the restaurant. The other remaining couple is putting on their coats and heading out the door.

"Wow, we shut this place down," I say, looking around.

"Are you ready to go back?" James asks, placing his hand on mine. I nod, excited to get back to the hotel.

Our server appears with the check and our coats, and we know it's time to go.

The chilly air feels refreshing after our long, decadent dinner at the cozy restaurant. The walk back to the hotel seems quick, and once inside the splendor of the Plaza Athénée, I notice a subtle scent of roses in the air, arranged beautifully throughout the lobby. Their sweet smell, mixed with the scent of James' pheromones that surely only I can detect—have me completely aroused. I'm also buzzed from the wine and haven't felt this good in a long time.

We're alone in the elevator, riding up to our suite. James kisses me slow and sweet and holds me tight by my hips. The elevator pings when we reach our floor, and we reluctantly pull apart, not wanting to let go. James takes my hand and leads me to our room. He opens the door, and as soon as we walk in, he pins me against the wall and slips off my coat and the slinky Dior, both falling to the floor.

The room is dark, but the Eiffel Tower sparkles brightly in the distance outside our window. I close my eyes and surrender to him. I want him to take me now.

"Happy Birthday, baby," he whispers, covering me with kisses. Our beautiful night continues, making love into the morning.

Chapter Fifty-One

I wake up in Paris on my birthday feeling like the luckiest girl in the world. Last night was pure magic, and despite the dull hangover and throbbing headache, I've never felt better.

James is still sleeping, so I decide to take a bath and enjoy the luxurious tub in our suite, which also has a fantastic view of the city. As I soak in the warm, soft suds and wait for the two Advils to kick in, I think about home and remember my last birthday, which I coincidentally spent at Light. At the time, it was the hot, new club in LA, and it was our new hangout since Max had just started DJing there.

I remember arriving drunk and coked up. Joe had just started to get into his weekends of heavy partying, and I was in complete denial that he was out of control. I thought that if I just partied and did drugs with him, I would never lose him to the habit, which was slowly taking over his life and snatching him away from me. Despite all that, Joe and I managed to keep our relationship going while I ignored his problem and masked my unhappiness by partying alongside him.

I remember seeing James in passing that night as he

chatted with Max and Darren at our table. He even wished me a happy birthday. His cool yet friendly demeanor seemed refreshing compared to Joe's erratic mood swings and recent detached behavior. I was curious about James, the mysterious, handsome owner of the club my brother DJ'd at. But my curiosity was innocent—I was in a deeply committed relationship that I was desperately trying to save.

As I soak in the tub and try to piece together little bits of that night out of pure nostalgia, my mood regresses to a familiar dark feeling that was all too present in those days. But I refuse to let the feeling take over, so I shake off the memories. I'm grateful that those days are over and that I'm in this gorgeous suite overlooking the most beautiful city in the world. *Forget it all, Annie,* I tell myself as I sink deeper into the tub. *It's all in the past.*

It starts to feel more like my birthday as the day unfolds, and I begin receiving texts and phone calls from my friends and family back home. Hearing from them puts me back on my Paris high.

James has a full day planned for us. We start with a lovely room service breakfast while we leisurely get ready. Then, he surprises me with presents delivered to our room. I beam as I unwrap the packages, which reveal a python Givenchy clutch I've been lusting over for weeks and a cocktail dress he saw me admire at the Chanel store in London. Paris was a good enough gift, but the thoughtful and chic presents he picked out for me made my day.

When we finally leave the hotel, we explore the city. We walk along the Champs-Élysée, popping into little boutiques and galleries, then end up at Café de Flore for espressos and pastries. Later that evening, we visit the Eiffel Tower for a lovely night stroll. Afterward, we head to what James calls my "official birthday dinner" at L'Avenue, where we have a romantic dinner with birthday cake and lots of champagne. We cap the night with one last cocktail at Le Bar back at the Plaza Athénée, followed by lots of hot sex. I fall asleep feeling just as I did this morning—like the luckiest girl in the world.

JAMES AND I SPEND TWO MORE AMAZING DAYS IN PARIS. WE continue our city tour, visiting more magical places like the Louvre and Versailles. On Monday, the final full day of our getaway, James takes a last-minute meeting with the Brits in town to look at a potential space for a new Parisian nightclub. James promises not to be gone too long and tells me he's going as a favor to the Brits to "put in his two cents" about the space. He makes arrangements with the concierge to secure a car to take me wherever I want before he leaves, and we agree to meet back at the hotel before dinner.

I use the afternoon to visit a few showrooms to place orders for Three-Two-Three. I love discovering new designers and brands, and I can't wait for our shop to be the only one in LA carrying them. Angela told me the things I sent her from my London buying trips were doing phenomenally well, which eased my guilt from being away from the shop.

On my way back to the hotel, I impulsively ask the driver to stop at Cartier. I'm in the mood to get something special for James. As I peruse the cases of breathtaking jewels and fight the urge to buy something for myself, I finally decide on a handsome watch for him. It's sleek, elegant, and sexy—just like him. I smile as the salesman wraps my purchase, imagining James's reaction. I can't wait to give it to him.

James and I meet back at the suite around dinner time as planned. He's having a glass of wine while looking over some papers when I arrive.

"Hi, baby," he greets me as I rest my shopping bags on the floor before joining him on the couch.

"Hi," I say, squeezing him tight. He chuckles at my affectionate greeting.

"Mmmm, did you miss me?" He looks me in the eye, smiling.

I nod. "Did you miss me?"

"Very much," he responds, leaning in for a kiss. We chat about our day, and I help myself to a glass of wine. I ask him about the meeting with the Brits, and he excitedly shares that they looked at a space for their first Paris nightclub. He mentions the concept: "A high-end, burlesque theater like the legendary *Le Can Can*, but with a sexy 21st-century vibe." I tune out most of what he's saying as I plot in my head how and when to give him the watch.

"It sounds very cool, babe," I say, barely paying attention.

"How did it go at the showrooms?"

"Great!" I respond, recounting my day.

"It looks like you did some shopping for yourself?" he questions, eyeing the shopping bags on the floor.

"I did! I had time to kill between showroom appointments, so I got a few things for myself and little gifts for everyone back home," I say, walking to the bags. I recognize that this is the perfect time to give him the watch.

I pick out the small, crimson bag from one of the big shopping bags and turn to him. "I got something for you, too," I say, pausing to wait for his reaction.

He flashes a smile and a surprised look. I join him on the couch again and hand him the bag.

"Really? You got me something?"

"Yes, open it!" I nod.

"Annie…What did you do?" He looks touched.

Thus far, James has given me quite a few beautiful gifts from Cartier, like the key ring he gave me when he asked me to move in with him and the chic pair of solitaire earrings he gave me for Christmas. So, I wanted to give him something with the same sentiment.

"I wanted to get you something special so you can remember this trip," I say, meeting his eyes.

He shakes his head as he opens the bag, pulling out the signature red box with gold detail. He gives me another look before opening the box, then smiles bigger when he sees what's inside.

"Wow… This is… Wow," he's speechless as he admires the watch. "Annie, this is… gorgeous!" He reaches over to kiss me. "Thank you," he says, inspecting the watch closer.

"It reminded me of you," I say.

"I don't know what to say… I love it, thank you." He pulls me in for a deep kiss and wastes no time putting it on.

Our last night in Paris is busy and social. We meet the Brits for a decadent dinner and then continue the fun by drinking and dancing at one of the city's hottest nightclubs. James wears the watch, and it looks so good with his sleek black suit. I'm proud of my purchase and love catching the Brits discreetly admiring it on him.

The night turns toward the wild side when the Brits break out party favors. James and I share a tab of Molly and have an incredible time dancing and making out in dark corners of the loud and smoky nightclub. Since I've stopped DJing at Light, my party nights have been few and far between, and I miss them. James and I have become somewhat of a boring couple lately, especially in London, since he works all day and I have zero social life. I'm glad tonight feels like our old party days, and I'm thrilled to relive them.

On the taxi ride back to our hotel, as dawn breaks, I nuzzle into James while he holds me close. "I wish we could stay here forever," I whisper, looking out into Paris's empty, quiet streets. I'm still high, hoping that this feeling never ends.

Chapter Fifty-Two

The doorbell rings just as I'm about to start a bath before meeting James for dinner. "Ugh, coming!" I yell out as the ringing continues. I sprint out of the bedroom and down the stairs. "Coming!" I repeat, landing in the foyer. I open the door and find a semi-soaked delivery man with a big, beat-up FedEx box.

"Delivery for Annie Preston," he says in an annoyed, brash tone.

"Yes, that's me," I answer, breathless.

He pushes an electronic device toward me and tells me to "sign." It's pouring outside, and I feel bad for the poor guy.

I give him back the device, and he hands me the box. Then, without saying another word, he turns on his heel.

It's finally here! I grin, inspecting the box before closing the door. Angela told me she sent me a birthday surprise when we talked while I was in Paris. But when the package didn't arrive a week after James and I returned to London, she tracked it and found it stuck in customs. I feared it was lost and waited every day for it. Now, I'm relieved that it's finally in my hands.

I shake the box, grinning as I head back upstairs. The box is damp from the rain, and I have to use scissors to open it. I clap with excitement at the sight of the beautifully wrapped packages inside. I sit on the bed and pull them out one by one. There are five packages in the box—each with a handwritten note. There's also one thick, square, white envelope.

I am immediately drawn to a package wrapped in black paper with shimmery silver stars and a big silver bow. I pick it up and read the card:

Happy Birthday to our beautiful Annie. We love and miss you very much! - Mom and Dad.

A knot forms in my throat, and I have to swallow it back before I start crying. I unwrap the gift and find a Hermès orange box with a beautiful pair of buttery soft, hunter-green leather gloves inside. I hold them up to my cheek, tearing up. I can picture my mom shopping for them at her favorite store, and all I want to do is give her a hug. I put the gloves on the bed and unwrap the rest of the packages. I receive a Chanel silk scarf from Max and Michelle, a cashmere cardigan from Angela and Darren, and a delicate gold chain bracelet from Matt and Daniel. I wipe the tears from my eyes, admiring the gifts on the bed and the sweet notes as a pang of homesickness comes over me.

As I gather the torn wrapping paper to dispose of it, the white envelope catches my eye, almost blending into the comforter. Inside, I find promotional material for Trent's new album. A smile spreads across my face as I admire the sleek design of the old-school CD and the booklet showcasing minimalist black-and-white photos of Trent. The album's self-titled name is elegantly written in a black font on the cover, and he looks handsome in all the photos.

Two cards and a folded, lined sheet of paper are also enclosed. I read the card on top first:

Annie, there's so much I want to say to you and apologize for, and I hope you'll give me a chance to do so someday—hopefully in person. For now, please know that I'm aware that I ruined everything between us, and I'm sorry that I hurt you so many times. I want you to know that I dedicate my work on this album to you, as you inspired it. You always bring out the best in me, Ace. I wrote song #4 for you. I love you, and I miss you. —Joe

My hands tremble as I read the note two more times. I flip through the booklet and read the tracklist. Song number four is called "Home." I'm so stunned by Joe's note that my happy tears from a minute ago have suddenly stopped. I never expected to receive anything like this from him.

I read the second card. It's an announcement from Trent's record label congratulating Joe, Max, Darren, and Trent for his first album going platinum. There are details for a ceremony taking place next month at The Beverly Hilton.

OMG. I shake my head, shocked and simultaneously swelling with pride over their monumental accomplishment. I unfold the lined sheet of paper and find scribbled lyrics for the song "Home." At the top, it says, *For Annie.*

The booklet has a scannable link to stream the album, but I prefer to play the CD after happily discovering that the stereo in the bedroom has a CD player. I insert the disc, skip to track four, and press play.

An up-tempo ballad starts to play as the speakers boom, Trent's soulful voice oozing with ease and emotion. The lyrics are about a couple finding their way home: "*In the darkness girl, I lost you, but now we're finding our way home.*"

The song is beautiful and sexy, and it sounds like the type of song you want to drive to and dance to and make love to.

I listen to the lyrics closer, and the tears return, this time unrelenting. I sob as an avalanche of emotions takes me under as memories start flooding back. Flashbacks of my relationship with Joe run through my head: childhood birthday pool parties and trips to Disneyland, our first kiss when we were fourteen years old in the parking lot after the school dance, losing my virginity to him a year later in the bedroom overlooking the ocean at his parents' old beach house in Malibu. The laughter, the sweet moments, the intimacy, the explosive fights, the tears, breaking up and making up, and then losing him, which now feels so permanent.

I bury my face in my hands. The song ends, and the next one begins. I listen to Trent sing about partying and smoking and women and fucking—rap songs full of bravado and ego, a façade for raw emotion and hurt. I take a deep breath and wipe my tears, reaching for the booklet. I flip through the pages containing moody, black-and-white photos of Trent, lyrics for each track, and the production credits. I skim the lyrics and credits and notice that all of the songs were written or co-written by Joe. I remember him saying he spent most of his time in rehab writing songs, and I'm sure these are them.

Pride swells in my chest, seeing Max and Darren's names in the credits as co-producers as well.

I snap back to the present, glancing at the clock. It's almost five. I'm supposed to meet James at eight for a dinner party at a new restaurant on Kings Road, and it's the last thing I want to do right now.

My eyes are bloodshot and puffy when I inspect myself in the mirror. *Fuck.* I take a deep breath to compose myself—I'm emotionally spent. The CD continues to play, and my eyes fill with tears again. I can't show up to dinner three hours from now with a swollen face from crying! So, I pour a vodka on the rocks and get in the bath. I light up a joint to calm my nerves, all the while clutching the remote to the stereo in my hand, playing track number four over and over again.

Chapter Fifty-Three

James

My meeting ends early, so I head home to surprise Annie. I step out into the damp, foggy evening and into my waiting car. I'm glad we're getting a break from all the fucking rain we had all day.

"I'm heading home, George, thanks," I say to my driver, courtesy of the Brits. The streets are alive with honking cars and smiling people ready to hit the town for their Friday night plans. The short ride from the club in Kensington to the townhouse in Chelsea is one of my favorite parts of the day—People-watching in London never gets old.

"I'll see you Monday morning, sir," George says as I step out of the car back on Redburn Street.

"Have a nice weekend, George," I respond.

I open the door, and the house is dark except for a dim light in the hallway leading to the kitchen. I hear music upstairs, "Annie?!" I call out, heading up. The music gets louder as I get closer to the bedroom.

I step into the room expecting to see her, but instead, I find torn wrapping paper strewn about the bed and on the floor. There are also various things scattered on the bed. I get closer, scanning the objects—a Hermès box, a sweater, a scarf… My eyes dart to a handwritten note. I tense up reading it as the words start to sink in slowly. *No way. No fucking way.*

I read the second card—details of some record ceremony, and skim the words on a lined sheet of paper. *That fucking asshole.*

Anger rises, hot in my chest, as I scan the room, noticing the door to the bathroom slightly ajar. I place the items back on the bed just as I found them.

I swing the door open, finding the source of the music booming from the bathroom speakers. Annie is soaking in the tub, covered in frothy bubbles, her eyes are closed.

"Uh, hmm," I clear my throat. She opens her eyes and sits up, splashing water around as she steadies herself in the tub.

"Oh my God!" she says, holding her chest. I fume inside as the words on the note from that prick come rushing back.

"James! You fucking scared me!" She presses her hand on her chest as if keeping her heart from shooting out.

I can't help but smile at her reaction, "I'm sorry, I didn't mean to startle you."

Annie reaches for the remote on the edge of the tub, but she knocks it over, crashing loudly on the marble floor.

I reach for it, turn down the volume a few notches, and sit on the edge of the tub. The sight of her big brown eyes and glistening skin cools my rage.

"What are you doing here?" She looks at me, reaching for the remote in my hand.

I hold it back from her, "What are you listening to?"

"Trent's new album," she says softly as she tries to reach for the remote again.

My impulse is to throw the remote across the room, but I stop myself. *I know it's Trent's fucking album.* I settle for making her squirm, raising the remote above my head, teasing her. "No, I want to hear it," I smile, being playful.

Annie sinks back into the tub. The suds around her body thin into the water, exposing her full breasts and flat stomach.

"You almost gave me a heart attack," she says, shooting me a look.

My dick gets hard, admiring her perky nipples peeking out of the sudsy water that smells like roses. "I'm sorry," I repeat, reaching over to kiss her forehead. Our eyes meet, and I notice that hers are bloodshot. I scan around the tub and spot a half-smoked joint in an ashtray and a glass with melting ice sitting on the other edge.

"What have you been up to?" I ask, trying to read her.

"Nothing," she says, avoiding my eyes. "I was getting ready to meet you at the restaurant—I thought that was the plan." She looks up at me again.

"Yeah, my meeting wrapped early, so I thought we could go together. What's all that stuff on the bed?"

Her eyes dart back down to the water as she fidgets with her hands. "They're birthday gifts from home." She pauses and looks up at me; a hint of panic flashes in her eyes. "I should get out," she says, rising abruptly as water and suds drip down her body. She looks around the tub and teeters, almost losing her balance. I reach out to steady her, grabbing her by the hip—her skin is warm and damp.

"You, alright?"

"Yeah, I just forgot a towel. Can you grab one for me?"

I get up from the tub's edge as she carefully climbs out, immediately reaching for the remote and turning off the music. I grab a towel from the cabinet and hand it to her. We're silent as she towels off—she's still avoiding my eyes.

"Have you been crying?" I ask, looking at her closer.

"No," she shakes her head and gives me a nervous giggle, "I'm just stoned."

I follow her out of the bathroom. She heads straight to the bed, collects the torn wrapping paper, and stuffs it into the box along with the other objects.

"Show me your presents," I say, stepping closer. She fixes the towel around her body as it starts slipping and shows me the gifts, omitting the notes from that prick, which she's already stuffed in the box.

"Who sent you Trent's album?"

"Max," she says softly. "It's a promo CD."

The heat in my chest returns. *I can't believe she's fucking lying to me.* I walk to the wet bar and reach for the bottle of Macallan. "Do you want another?" I hold up the uncapped bottle of Belvedere sitting on the bar. She nods and looks away. I pour my drink, take it down in a shot, and pour her a vodka.

"It sounded good. Why did you turn it off?" I ask, turning on the stereo and switching the audio to the bedroom speakers. The CD starts again as I hand her the drink. Pulsating beats begin to boom, and Annie looks uncomfortable as she takes a sip.

"I heard the whole thing already," she shrugs.

"Are you still upset because I startled you?" I soften my posture as I approach. "Don't be mad, Annie," I say, grabbing her by the hips, giving her a little sway, trying to break the tension. I tilt her chin with my finger, and our eyes meet again.

"I'm not mad…" she says, smiling, "I told you, I'm just really stoned."

I catch pieces of the song lyrics, inflaming my hatred for Joe more than ever. How dare that fucking prick try to fuck with my relationship again? I brought Annie to another continent, and that asshole still won't leave her alone! He has some nerve, trying to win her back.

"I think the gifts made me homesick, that's all," she says as her eyes get misty. I hate knowing that she's lying. I pull her into my chest and refrain from calling her out.

Annie squirms in my arms as she tries to adjust her towel.

"Relax, baby," I whisper, kissing her neck.

Chapter Fifty-Four

There's no way he saw the notes. He would've said something by now! My mind races as paranoia sets in. I try to block out the music while James pulls me closer, peppering my neck with kisses. I have a sudden impulse to push him off —*but this feels so good.*

His hands move slowly down my arms, then unwrap the towel around me, and it falls to the floor. His lips move down my neck to my breasts, stopping to lick my nipples, biting them gently. I'm dizzy from the vodka and the weed and his seduction. I become even more aroused as he slides his hand between my legs and slips his fingers inside of me. "Ahhh," I exhale, feeling my knees weaken. I open my eyes when James stops abruptly to take the drink from my hand and place it on the nightstand.

I'm wet and aching for him to continue. He guides me to the bed, pushing the FedEx box to the side. The song ends, and another starts, resurfacing emotions from earlier as Joe's note flashes through my mind.

James climbs on top of me and licks my nipples, biting them with a little more force this time, making me flinch and hitch my breath. He fingers me slowly as our lips meet again, and I wrap my arms around him.

The song continues to play, and I become increasingly uncomfortable. I want James to stop because I want to turn off the music, but everything he's doing feels *so fucking good*. I'm breathless as he kisses my breasts, trailing his lips to my belly. He pushes me further back on the bed and parts my legs. Tingles surge through my body as he kisses the inside of my thighs until I feel his lips and tongue tasting me. "Mmmmm," I moan; he knows exactly what spot to linger on.

I clutch a handful of his hair and arch my back in response to the slow and deliberate movements of his tongue. "I'm gonna cum," I whisper. He pauses, taking off his shirt and pants. Track number three comes on, and the freestyle rap I heard Trent record the night I dropped by the studio with Angela booms through the speakers. I close my eyes as James enters me with force, almost knocking the wind out of me.

Fragmented pieces of that night in the studio flash through my mind: the thin veil of marijuana smoke in the room, Joe's tan skin, the look in his eye, and him telling me that it was *"just sex"* and that *"it didn't mean anything"* in the parking lot of the studio under the dull yellow lights.

James thrusts into me harder, "MMMM," I moan louder and tell him to slow down. He responds, fucking me more gently. He buries his head in the crook of my neck and pins my hands firmly on the bed as his thrusts turn sharp and deep again. He rocks into me hard, then suddenly stops, pulling out and finishing with his hand, exploding semen all over my breasts and stomach.

He collapses next to me, breathless. He runs his fingers through his hair, exhaling loudly. I didn't cum, and I don't care. I'm glad he stopped because the room is spinning as track number four comes on, and I can't bear listening to *that song* right now.

I sit up abruptly and get off the bed, trying to catch my breath. I stumble over to the stereo—my legs shaking, my vagina throbbing, and James's cum sliding down my chest. I turn off the stereo, and the room is finally silent, except for the soft hissing of James's breath as it steadies.

The room spins again, and I feel the vodka slowly making its way up my throat. I run to the bathroom and slam the door behind me, making it just in time to throw up uncontrollably into the toilet.

I EMERGE FROM THE BATHROOM A FEW MINUTES LATER, FEELING better after puking my guts out and freshening up. James is sitting at the desk smoking a cigarette and cutting lines of coke on a mirror. "Are you alright?" he asks without looking up from the rolled-up fifty-pound note in his hand.

He bends his head down and does two lines, one into each nostril. A distant hum of passing cars and the chatter of people outside drift in through the open window, along with a welcoming cool breeze. The heaviness from before has lifted.

I get under the comforter in my robe. James looks at me with a blank stare, waiting for me to answer. "Yeah, I'm fine," I say.

He takes a long drag from his cigarette. "We have to be at dinner in thirty minutes."

"I don't feel like going."

"Why?" He takes another drag and cuts another line.

"I drank too much already. I don't feel well."

"Come on, Annie," he cracks a flirty smile. "We haven't gone out since we got back from Paris. Come over here and do one of these; you'll feel better."

The thought of doing coke right now makes my stomach turn, and I feel like I might throw up again. "Can you just get me some club soda with ice?" I ask. He obliges, making the drink and bringing it over to me. I'm still too stoned and rattled to ask him why he just fucked me so aggressively.

He sits on the edge of the bed and takes another drag from his cigarette, watching me sip my drink. "We'll just go for a little while. Aren't you hungry?" he asks, blowing out a cloud of smoke.

I don't want to fight. *Maybe it'll be good to get out of the house.*

"Okay," I say, taking down the club soda. I get out of bed, and he returns to the desk to do another line. I walk into the closet and look around without wanting to get dressed. Music comes on again, and I'm relieved it's not Trent's CD. I grab a little black dress with a plunging neckline from its hanger and put it on without bothering to put on any underwear—my vagina is still sore. I slip on my black Louboutin pumps, and I'm done getting dressed.

I hear the water running in the bathroom as I emerge from the closet and sit at the vanity to do my makeup. I look at myself in the mirror and feel like shit. I'm emotionally drained.

I glance at the little mound of coke on the desk through the reflection in the mirror with disgust. I hate when James gets like this—it's almost like he goes overboard with the coke to piss me off.

"Oh, good. I'm glad you're getting ready!" James says, emerging from the bathroom. I give him a weak smile. He's dressed in a sleek gray suit, crisp white shirt, and no tie. His hair is tamed and slicked, and he looks so damn sexy.

I watch him from the mirror at the vanity as he makes two drinks. He hands me one, placing a kiss on top of my head. I take a long sip and feel a little better. I take my hair down from the messy top knot it's been in and let it fall in soft waves around my face. I watch James do another line at the desk through the mirror.

"You gonna be ready soon?" he asks, lighting another cigarette.

"Um, hmm," I say, taking another sip of my drink and continue doing my makeup.

Chapter Fifty-Five

P*andora's box* arrived last week, and I'm still recovering from the havoc it caused on my mental and emotional state. I'm still processing Joe's apology, his declaration of love, and the song lyrics—all of it haunts me.

I haven't touched the CD since that night. I put it in the back of one of my dresser drawers and everything that came with it back inside the envelope, pretending it doesn't exist. It's too bad that every word on Joe's note is permanently seared in my mind, and I don't have to touch the CD to feel its presence.

"Hey, sis!" Angela greets me cheerfully on FaceTime. We've been missing each other's calls for days, and I'm glad to connect with her finally.

"I got the box," I say.

She lights up, clapping excitedly. "Yay! Did you like everything?!"

I nod, feeling another wave of homesickness coming on. "Yes, everything is perfect, thank you." I fall silent, and Angela gives me a look.

"What? Is something wrong?"

"Do you know what Joe sent me?"

"Um, Trent's new album, right? He came by the shop with the promo package and asked me to send it to you. Did you listen to it?!"

"Yes, I heard it… It's great…" My eyes become blurry with tears. "That's not all he sent."

I tell Angela about the note, the handwritten lyrics, and the Platinum Record ceremony announcement.

"Wow, I had no idea that was in the envelope," she says. I hold back the tears, but she knows I'm upset. "I'm sorry, Annie. I wish I had known what he was sending; I would've given you a heads-up."

I shake my head, "It's fine… I'm just confused… Part of me wants to call him, but… what good would that do…?" I hesitate but can't help myself and ask, "Have you seen him lately? How is he?" The look on her face says it all.

"It's the same, Annie. I wish I had something better to tell you."

I nod, heartbroken that he's still in that dark place.

"But!" Angela says, perking up. "The Platinum Record is a huge accomplishment; I know he's excited about that. Darren and Max, too! You should see them. Trent is flipping out!"

I break into a smile, still incredulous over their monumental accomplishment.

"And guess what?! I'm going to the ceremony with Darren, and Max is taking Michelle, of course. It's going to be a huge event with dinner and special performances. Trent's even performing!"

My mood dips again as serious FOMO sets in. "That sounds fun," I respond, forcing a smile.

"You'll have to help me pick out my dress. I'll text you pics of my options!"

"Sure, that sounds good."

"Oh, and it's going to be live-streamed so you can watch it from London… if you want." Angela trails off. "Shit, I'm sorry, Annie. You probably don't want to hear about all this… or do you?"

I nod to reassure her, "Of course, I want to hear about it. It's great news. I'm really proud of them."

Another call comes in, and it's James. I tell Angela I have to go. "Okay, let's talk tomorrow!" she says before we hang up.

I miss James's call, so I dial him back.

"Hey, babe," he answers. I can picture his smile on the other end.

"Hi," I respond, happy to hear from him. Things were chilly between us last week. I confronted him about being aggressive with me in bed, and he swore he didn't know what I was talking about. He said he was just "really turned on" and apologized. Maybe I imagined it. I was pretty fucked-up, after all.

"What are you doing?" he asks.

"Nothing, waiting for you to come home so we can decide what to do for dinner."

"Well, why don't you come meet me?"

"Yeah? Where?"

"How about Nobu?"

I love the sound of that and accept. I'm excited to leave the house—I've been so bored all day.

"Great, I'll send a car over, be ready in twenty minutes," he says.

I ARRIVE AT NOBU, THE ICONIC JAPANESE RESTAURANT, WHICH is almost as good as their Malibu outpost. The hostess walks me to a table where James is having a beer. He perks up when he sees me and gets up to greet me with a kiss. We sit back down, and he reaches for my hand across the table.

"You're in a good mood," I reflect.

"I am? I'm just happy to see you," he says, leaning in to plant another kiss on my lips.

The server comes to the table, and James orders a bottle of sake. "Are you hungry?" He looks at me as I skim the menu.

"Starving. It's all too good to decide. Can you order for us?"

"Sure," he says, glancing at his menu. Our server returns to take our order and pours our sake. "To us," James says, raising his cup.

"To us," I repeat, meeting his eyes as we toast.

Since our talk about the aggressive sex, James has been extra attentive and sweet. He's been coming home early most nights and surprising me with flowers and impromptu dinners like this. On an even better note, he's been telling me the project is going well, and he seems less stressed.

An array of sushi rolls and sashimi arrive at our table. Our dinner is delicious, and our conversation is even better as we catch up on each other's day, enjoying our usual fun banter.

"So, the Brits offered to make me a partner of their new club in Paris," he says casually.

"What?" A sinking feeling creeps in.

"Yeah," he says, grinning. "They want me to lead the project for their Paris nightclub—The whole thing: concept, design, music, menu, everything… Basically, everything I'm doing here," he trails off, waiting for my reaction.

I stare at him blankly, "And what did you say?"

"I told them I'd think about it."

His casual tone irritates me. "You're going to think about it?" I shake my head, stunned that he would even consider such an offer, especially since we're both eager to go home.

"Yeah, they brought it up while we were in Paris, and I told them I would think about it. It's a big deal, Annie. It's an incredible offer. I'd be part owner of a nightclub in Paris!"

"They asked you while we were in Paris, and this is the

first time you're telling me?" The sinking feeling morphs into anger.

"Relax," he reaches across the table for my hand. "I haven't decided yet, but it is worth considering."

I'm stunned and unsure how to respond. "Well, I can't go with you if you decide to take it," I blurt out. His expression turns serious, then softens as his lips curl into a smile.

"Babe…" he says, gently rubbing my hand with his thumb. "It's not like it's going to happen tomorrow. The project won't start until summer."

"So, you've made up your mind?"

"No, no, Annie. That's not what I'm saying. I haven't decided, and of course, I want us to make this decision together… Will you think about it… please?" He lifts my hand to his lips for a kiss.

I don't know what to say. I thought James was ready to return to LA, so I can't imagine why he would commit to another long-term project in another country. And this time, it sounds more permanent if he's going to be a partner!

My mood sours, and he notices.

"Annie… Like I said, I haven't decided yet, but if you could think about it for a second, imagine how cool it would be. We could get an amazing flat in Paris, maybe in Le Marais, that neighborhood you liked so much…" He's smiling big, and his eyes sparkle with excitement, but I can't muster emotion. All I can think about is being far from everyone and everything I care about back home.

"You said it yourself—that you wished we could stay there forever," he says.

"What?" I pull my hand back from his. "When did I say that?"

"You said it. That morning, on the way back to the hotel after our night at the club. You loved it… And now's our chance to make it happen."

The conversation makes me lose my appetite, and I push

my plate aside. "I was on *Molly*, remember? I was high as fuck!" I look him in the eye, vaguely remembering the taxi ride back to the hotel that morning in Paris.

He sighs and leans back in his chair. "This is a once-in-a-lifetime opportunity, Annie. I don't understand why you're being so closed-minded."

"I'm not being *closed-minded*... I dropped my life, my friends, my family, my business to be here—with you!" My voice escalates and he leans in to grab my hand again, telling me to calm down.

I take a deep breath and continue, "Can't you see I'm miserable here?" I finally admit what I've been hiding from him for so long. "I don't know anyone; I don't have a life here. I'm here only because I love you and don't want to be away from you!" I pull my hand back to hide my face as tears pool in my eyes.

"Annie... I'm sorry... Please don't be upset... We should go... We can talk about this at home."

"No," I take a deep breath to compose myself. "I'm sorry; I didn't mean to snap at you." I look up at him, meeting his blank expression.

"Baby, I know it hasn't been easy here, and if you want to go back to LA, that's fine. You don't have to stay any longer..."

"No..." I cut him off, "I don't mean to be ungrateful. Being here has been great... I don't want to go home without you. I just can't imagine doing this again and moving to Paris..." I trail off, trying to imagine spending more time miserable and alone in a foreign country.

"Listen, the last thing I'll say is that it would be different in Paris. I could find you an amazing little spot on Avenue Montaigne or Rue Saint-Honoré where you can open a boutique—a Paris outpost of Three-Two-Three. Maybe Angela could help you open it. Think how great that could be for you—for both of you! I would be happy to take care of it

—all of it. You wouldn't have to worry about a thing," he says, softening his expression.

I appreciate his offer and don't want to be an ungrateful brat. I remind myself that he hasn't decided, so I relax and hope he'll turn the Brits down and go back to LA with me. "Thank you for being so thoughtful. I'll think about it," I say, knowing full well that there's *no fucking way* I'm moving to Paris.

Chapter Fifty-Six

The sun has finally come out in London. It's the second week of February, and the city has been blessed with a few consecutive days of sunshine and unusually spring-like temperatures. The weather has done wonders for my mood, and now I have no doubt that seasonal depression is real. Like the perpetual fog that lingered over the city for weeks, my funk has also lifted, and I finally feel like myself again.

The club project is running smoothly and on time, so James has been working less and spending more time with me.

It's Saturday night, and we're cooking dinner after spending a fun day in the city. We bopped around town and ended up at a farmer's market in Notting Hill, where we picked up fresh ingredients for dinner.

The doors to the back terrace are open, and a balmy breeze fills the kitchen. Old-school jams play in the background as we enjoy a bottle of wine while preparing a salad and fresh gnocchi with meat sauce.

James and I have had a few lovely days together, enjoying the weather and exploring the city. Our talk at Nobu has been on my mind, but neither of us has brought up Paris again. I know I'd feel better knowing his answer, and I could ask him, but I chicken out every time I think about bringing it up. I don't want to ruin the fun we've been having.

"Taste this," James says, bringing a wooden spoon with sauce to my lips.

"Mmmm, it's perfect," I nod, savoring the rich and flavorful red sauce.

"You think it's ready?" He tastes a little bit himself.

"Yes," I nod reassuringly.

"Well, we just have to cook the gnocchi, and then we can eat!" he says, putting the spoon down and pulling me in for a kiss.

I wrap my arms around him as he holds me close. "Dance with me?" he says, looking into my eyes with a playful, cute smile that makes me giggle. He holds me close as we sway in the kitchen to Al Green's "Let's Stay Together." I rest my head on his chest as he leads me to the music, softly singing the lyrics in my ear. When the song ends, he gives me a twirl and a dip. We laugh, and he pulls me in for a long, lingering kiss.

"Stay right here. I'll be right back," he says, bouncing out of the kitchen. "Be right back!" he yells from the hallway.

I giggle and top off our glasses with wine. After taking a sip, I step onto the terrace to enjoy the fresh air. It's a beautiful night, reminiscent of the evenings back home, having dinner by the pool at my parents' house with the whole gang.

I admire the backyard, realizing that this is the first time I've been out here since arriving two months ago. I hadn't noticed how pretty and perfectly manicured it is, even after our harsh winter. Today, James and I discovered string lights on the trellises around the yard. We found the light switch, and when we turned it on, I gasped at how beautifully the lights made the backyard twinkle in the dark.

I hear James's footsteps, so I turn around as he approaches me. "Watcha' doing?" he asks, joining me.

"It's so nice out here. I bet it's beautiful when all those

trees and rose bushes bloom in the spring." I say, gazing out into the yard.

James wraps his arms around me from behind and kisses my cheek. "Yeah, I'm sure it is," he says.

"Should we finish up dinner?" I turn around to face him.

"Um, in a little…" he says, looking at me closely. "I want to ask you something first."

I stare at him, waiting.

He takes a deep breath and steps back. "I wasn't planning on doing this tonight, so I have no idea what to say, but…" he says, reaching into his pocket.

My heart stops when he pulls out a little red box with gold detail—everything else happens in slow motion. He clears his throat and takes my hand, and my heart starts pounding. *Is this really happening?*

"Annie… You've made me the happiest man since the moment I met you. You've made me look at life differently, and I've never had more fun. I want to spend the rest of it with you…" He takes a deep breath and gets on one knee. "Will you marry me, Annie?" he says, opening the Cartier box to reveal the most exquisite cushion-cut diamond ring, twinkling bright even in the darkness on the terrace.

I'm in shock and can't get the words out, so I stare at him blankly—one hand covering my mouth while he holds my trembling left hand.

"Annie?" He smiles, waiting for an answer.

"Yes," the word finally makes it out, "YES!"

He takes the ring out of the box and slips it on my finger. I stare at it and at him in awe as he gets up from his knee. I take his face in my hands and give him a long, deep kiss. I'm still speechless as I look at the ring on my finger.

"Do you like it?" he beams, holding my hand to his eyeline to proudly inspect it.

"It's the most beautiful thing I've ever seen," I say, "I can't believe this is happening."

"Believe it, baby, from now on, it's me and you forever," he says, pulling me in for another kiss.

As soon as I open my eyes, I look at my hand to make sure I wasn't dreaming. Sure enough, the five-carat Cartier sparkler is still on my finger, shining brighter than ever in the morning light. "Good morning," James throws his arm around me, nuzzling into the back of my neck.

"Good morning," I smile, turning to face him. "I still can't believe you did this," I say, holding out my hand, admiring my engagement ring.

"Why not? Isn't this what you do when you love someone?"

The whole thing is so surreal, and now that my thoughts are clearer since the emotional whirlwind of last night, I'm suddenly full of questions. "I didn't think you wanted to get married anytime soon."

"Well, what can I say? I'm ready now," he says, kissing me on the cheek.

"Oh! I have to call my parents!" I blurt out, abruptly sitting up, "I have to call Angela!"

James sits up and holds me back as I grab my phone from the nightstand. "Wait… wait a minute," he says, taking the phone from my hand. He laughs, meeting my eyes. "First of all, it's like one in the morning in LA right now, and second, I have a better idea." He reaches over to his nightstand and pulls an envelope from the drawer. "Happy Valentine's Day," he says, handing me the envelope.

I look down at it and feel stupid because, with all the excitement of last night, I forgot today was Valentine's Day. I open the envelope and find a printout of two first-class flight reservations to LA.

My eyes light up, "We're going home?!"

"Well, just for a few days," he says with a chuckle. "I mean… I can't leave London yet, but if you want to stay home, I'll understand…" he says, trailing off as his smile fades.

"No, no," I sit up straighter, grabbing his hand. I don't want to ruin the moment. "No, this is great… Thank you… You know I don't want to go home without you." I say, gently cupping his cheek.

"Well, we leave Thursday, and I thought we could tell everyone in person instead of over the phone." He looks into my eyes, waiting for a reaction.

"Oh, so you don't want me to tell anyone yet?"

"Well, I didn't ask for your father's blessing, and, um… I think I was supposed to… so…" he says, turning quiet.

"James, my dad isn't traditional like that. I think it's sweet that you thought about it, but I don't think it's a big deal."

He pauses briefly before continuing, "No, it's a big deal to me. I want us to tell everyone in person," he insists. "Please promise me you'll wait and won't tell anyone yet. It would mean a lot to me." His eyes turn serious. "Let's enjoy these next few days… I want to enjoy this with you before we tell everyone…" He pulls me in closer and rubs my thighs under the sheets. "It's just four days, Annie," he says, climbing on top of me.

His hands move up my thighs, slowly making their way between my legs. We're both naked and as he positions himself on top of me, I feel his hardness rubbing up against me. I'm rendered speechless as he kisses my neck, my breasts, and my belly.

"You promise you won't say anything?" he whispers in my ear as he parts my legs wider with his knee and slips his fingers inside of me.

"I promise," I whisper back, closing my eyes and giving in to the delicious, full feeling as he rocks inside of me.

Chapter Fifty-Seven

"*Please secure your seatbelts and return your seats to an upright position.*" The announcement gives me goosebumps. I peek out the window, admiring Los Angeles stretching below us. The sky is bright blue and crystal clear, and warm, golden sunshine filters into the cabin. I've never been happier to see traffic on the 405 Freeway and palm trees —so many palm trees!

James leans over to catch a glimpse, "Welcome home, baby," he says, nuzzling my ear. I nod, afraid to utter a word because I'm so emotional I could cry.

The plane slowly descends toward LAX, and as we get closer, everything on land becomes clearer—big box stores, fast food restaurants, houses, buildings, people! Within minutes, we touch ground, and as we taxi to the gate, there's another announcement, "*Welcome to Los Angeles. The local time is one-twenty p.m., and the current temperature is eighty-eight degrees Fahrenheit, twenty-five degrees Celsius.*" I squeeze James's hand and look at him wide-eyed. *Eighty-eight!* I mouth. God, how I've missed winter in LA.

"I know we don't have much time here, but we have to go to the beach before we go back!" I demand.

He laughs, "You got it."

A driver is waiting for us at baggage claim, and he helps us with our luggage to the car. I've been in my head the whole ride, anxious since James surprised me with this trip. It was hard keeping our engagement a secret, even if it was only for a few days, but I'm glad James caved yesterday and let me share the news.

We FaceTimed my parents together, then Angela and Max. They all had the same reaction—stunned and speechless at first but then excited, especially when we told them about our visit. My mom wasn't thrilled that we gave her such short notice because she wanted to throw us an engagement party right away. She had to settle for a small gathering at the house just for family and close friends and leave the official engagement party for when James and I return home in a few weeks after the nightclub in London opens.

My body tenses as we enter Hollywood, as good and bad memories come flooding back. The excitement of our arrival starts wearing off as I remember the thorn in my side of this trip. Angela texted me after our FaceTime and pointed out that the Platinum Record ceremony is happening this weekend, which means I'll probably have to see Joe. I hate having to tell him my news during such an important moment in his life.

After Angela's text, I tried to get James to change the date of our trip, but he insisted that it was the only time he could take a break. I tried so hard to convince him that he became suspicious of my persistence. There was no way I could tell him that it had anything to do with Joe, so I dropped it.

It's also eating me up inside that I let so much time pass without contacting Joe. I should've acknowledged the CD and congratulated him on his accomplishment.

I sigh, staring out the window. We're on Sunset, passing The Chateau Marmont. I look over at James, and he's on the phone with Oliver, laughing. I can tell he's happy to be home too.

"Alright, man, we're almost home. We'll see you at Annie's parents' tonight," he says before hanging up.

When we get to James's house, I'm more relaxed. We leave our luggage in the foyer and plop on the couch to catch our breath. It's been a long journey from London. "Home, sweet fucking, home!" James says, getting up to open the pocket doors to the backyard.

Chapter Fifty-Eight

The last forty-eight hours in LA have been jam-packed with things to do and people to see. Our welcome home/engagement dinner at my parents' house was lovely. After everyone's lingering shock over the news finally wore off, we all had a great time catching up and celebrating.

I haven't slept well since we arrived, but my excitement for being home cancels out my jet lag. We only have five precious days in sunny Los Angeles, so I have to make the most of them. I make use of my limited time and jump back into my old routine, attempting to feel normal again. I take a Pilates class, hit Erewhon for my favorite smoothie and snacks, and spend as much time as possible at Three-Two-Three, trying to be productive. James does the same, seeing his friends and taking care of business at Light.

It's Saturday afternoon, and I'm happy to be working at the shop again. The whole city is buzzing with parties this week as we're in the middle of awards season. Three-Two-Three has been packed all day with customers shopping for party dresses for all the events.

I'm in the middle of merchandising newly arrived dresses

when Max shows up. I'm surprised to see him because he hardly ever comes to the shop.

"What's up, girls?" he says, approaching Angela and me. He takes off his sunglasses, and his eyes light up. Angela gives him a casual hello, but I greet him with a tight hug. My time in LA is already ticking down, so I want to appreciate everyone as much as possible.

"What are you guys doing?" Max drapes his arm around my shoulder as he surveys the clothes hanging from the two metal racks we're rearranging at the back of the shop.

"*Working,*" Angela responds, rolling her eyes.

"Oh, excuse me," he says, mirroring her expression. "I've been working all morning, too!"

I giggle, happy to be in the middle of Max and Angela's childish bickering, which I've missed so much.

"What are *you* doing here?" I ask him.

"Oh, I'm just passing through…" he pauses momentarily. "Actually, I wanted to talk to you about something."

"Talk to *me?*"

"Yeah, it's not a big deal…" he says, shrugging.

"Okay…" I wait for him to continue. Angela's quiet as she fusses with the clothes on the racks.

"Let's get coffee," Max offers, motioning toward the door. I have a weird feeling about this, but I'm also curious.

Angela finally looks up at me, "Go ahead, Annie, I'll finish up."

"You want to sit in or out?" Max asks as we arrive at our go-to café a few doors down from the shop.

"Out," I nod, happy to enjoy the warm sun and gorgeous weather. We settle at one of the corner patio tables.

"So!" Max says, leaning back into his chair, "How's London?!"

"It's good, but it's cold, and it hasn't stopped raining since I got there, so that part sucks."

The server appears and takes our order.

"So, cold and rainy, huh?" he says, returning to our conversation when she leaves.

"Yeah… Other than that, it's amazing," I exaggerate.

"Wow, let me look at this rock again!" Max says, leaning in to grab my hand for a closer look. "Annie, this is crazy. I can't believe you're getting married." He shakes his head while admiring my ring, sparkling in the sunlight. I smile, admiring it with him.

"Yeah, I can't believe it either!"

Max quietly inspects my face, "So, James, huh? I swear I never saw this coming."

I giggle, realizing that if I hadn't gotten the DJ gig at Light, I would've never dated James and wouldn't be engaged right now. And it was all because Max injured his knee and gave me his DJ gig—almost a year ago! I remind him of the sequence of events, and we have a good laugh.

"You've known James longer than I have. You know he's great," I say.

The server returns with our iced lattes.

"Yeah, I know he's a cool guy, but he's not like *my boy* or anything. We're not really friends, so…" Max pauses to sip his drink.

"Well, he's great, and I'm happy," I firmly reply.

"Cool, that's all that matters. That's all I care about," he says.

I change the subject and ask Max to fill me in on what he's been up to.

"Oh, you know, working hard, we've been promoting Trent's new album—the first single's coming out next week. The tour's been good. Trent's coming back to town tonight for tomorrow's ceremony. He'll be here for a few days and then back on the road. Can you fucking believe it? He sold out the tour!" Max shakes his head in disbelief. I can't believe it either —Trent is a superstar!

"The tour ends next month, so…" he trails off. I recall Angela's stories about the wild tour and Joe's antics. I sip my latte as Max looks closely at me again.

"Have you heard the new album?" he asks.

I drop my gaze as flashbacks from the day I heard it for the first time return. I nod without saying anything. I look back up at him, and his eyes are fixed on me.

"What did you think?"

I want to tell him that the album is beautiful and brilliant and cool. And that it broke my heart for so many reasons, and I haven't been able to get it or Joe out of my head for weeks.

"It's amazing," I muster, "You guys did an amazing job."

"Thanks," he says, breaking his serious expression with a smile. "You know, Joe had a lot to do with how it turned out." His smile fades.

I sigh, knowing we're about to discuss something I've been avoiding for weeks. I'm silent as Max continues.

"Have you talked to him lately?"

I shake my head, "No, how is he?"

Max leans back in his chair, searching for his words. "I'm not gonna lie to you, Annie… We're all really worried about him."

The words feel like a punch in the gut. The fact that Max —who's avoided acknowledging Joe's problems—is now finally voicing concern is unnerving. I'm afraid to hear more, yet I can't help but ask him to continue.

Max shakes his head and leans forward, resting his arms on the table. "I don't know how else to say it, Annie—he's fucked up. He's been on the road with Trent for weeks now— partying non-stop, disappearing sometimes—completely out of control."

I swallow hard as he continues.

"Darren and I went on the road for a couple of shows,

and it was nuts. Lots of drugs, groupies, shady individuals, chaos! We tried to get him to return with us, but he refused. He's like Trent's *BFF* now—they're inseparable, and they're both having the time of their lives." He shakes his head. "I mean, it's scary because Joe has so much talent and so much going for him, but he doesn't realize that he could lose it all... Trent doesn't have a choice. He has to be on the road doing shows, being *a star*..."

I have so much to say and have so many questions, but I don't know where to start. "Trent's just enabling him..." I cut in, "You have to get Joe off the tour!"

"Trent's not the problem. Joe's out of control and doesn't want to acknowledge that *he's* the problem."

I sigh. "So, now what?"

"I'm not sure... We've talked about doing an intervention..."

My heart races and I'm suddenly afraid that Max is about to ask me to be a part of it, something I don't think I could do, even if it's to help Joe. I know I wouldn't be able to get through it—it would break my heart. I look at Max with fear in my eyes.

"Please don't ask me to be a part of that," I say, grabbing his hand.

"No, no, relax. I'm not asking you to do that. I don't even know how or when we would do it," he says.

I'm slightly relieved but still in knots about everything he's saying.

"So, why are you telling me this?" I feel helpless.

"Annie, I'm sorry to have to ask you this, and I really thought about it long and hard, so please don't think that I'm just being an asshole for what I'm about to say..."

Max's tone and directness scare me. "What...?"

He takes a deep breath. "I think—we all think—that it's probably best if Joe doesn't see you until after the Platinum Record ceremony..." He pauses to gauge my reaction.

I'm confused, trying to process what he's saying. "Who's *'we all'?*" I ask, shocked that this is somehow a group decision rather than just his request.

"Darren and I—even Angela… *Especially now,*" he says, glancing at the ring on my finger. "Look, Annie, we both know how Joe is… He doesn't know how to handle things, and I think he won't take it well when he finds out about you and James."

I stare at Max blankly, my eyes blurry with tears.

"I'm sorry, Annie, I don't know what else to say… I know your engagement is great news, and we want to celebrate it— no doubt—but the timing is just…. We're afraid that if Joe finds out before the ceremony, he may disappear. It's as simple and as fucked up as that," he says flatly.

"So, do you want me to leave town or pretend I'm not here?" I'm confused and suddenly angry at how unfair this all is. I feel unwelcome in my own home!

"No, just until the ceremony is over tomorrow. This is a big deal—we made a Platinum Record! Joe has to be there— we've worked so hard for this—*he's* worked so hard for this, you have no idea! He deserves to enjoy the night and be there with us… But we're afraid that if he finds out about you before the ceremony, it'll make him act out and go on a bender or something." Max looks me directly in the eye.

I can't tell if I feel sad, angry, or guilty, but I feel like being here is a huge inconvenience for everyone.

"So, now I have to sacrifice something and pretend I'm not here just so Joe's feelings *don't get hurt?*" I'm stunned at Max's request.

"Yeah, that sounds shitty. Forget it," he says, dropping his gaze while shaking his head. "I know it's unfair to you and a lot to ask. If he loses it and fucks up this once-in-a-lifetime experience, then that's on him."

Max looks as defeated as I feel.

"Are you sure he'll even care…? He has no reason to act

out… I mean, he's been with lots of women—I know he has! Maybe it won't matter, maybe he's moved on…"

"He's gonna care. You know he will—he's gonna care…" Max meets my eyes again. I bite my lower lip and fight back tears. "Annie…" Max softens his tone and takes my hand. "I'm sorry I asked… I'm not telling you what to do… If you think I'm out of line, do what you think is right."

I take a deep breath to ease the tightness in my chest. I understand what he's saying, but it doesn't change the fact that his request feels crushing. "So, James and I can't go to dinner or Trent's party with you guys tonight?" I ask, making sure that I'm understanding.

"Joe's going to be there tonight. If you don't come, we won't tell him you're in town. He can find out tomorrow after the ceremony. He'll probably lose his shit then, but we'll handle it from there. At least he'll get to be at the ceremony. I mean, this may be the only time we make a Platinum Record!" he says, being dramatic.

I know Max is in a tough position, and I understand what he's saying. I manage to force a smile, hoping that my tears won't spill over. "It's okay, I understand, and I don't want to ruin this for you… for you guys."

"No, no…" he cuts me off, but I don't let him finish.

"It's okay, Max. It's the truth. You guys worked hard for this accomplishment, and I know how much this means to you —to all of you… I know you had no choice but to ask me to do this." I grab his hand, trying to be stoic as I accept his request.

We leave the café, and Max walks me back to the shop. We stop at the door, and he hugs me. "I'm so sorry I had to ask you to do this, sis. I really am. And I meant it when I said you don't have to do this if you don't want to. If you decide to come tonight, I'll be happy to see you," he says with a smile. "No matter what happens, everything's going to be fine," he adds, unable to hide the uncertainty in his tone.

"It's okay, Max. I know it's for the best. It's not a big deal," I lie. We hug again and say goodbye.

I don't feel like being at the shop anymore, so I walk straight to the office to get my things. I find Angela on the computer—she knew exactly what Max came here to talk to me about. She was in on it, and I'm pissed.

Angela gives me her explanation and reiterates all the points Max made. I tell her I understand and don't want to talk about it anymore. She tries to keep me from leaving and even offers to accompany me, but I tell her I want to be alone.

"Annie, call me if you don't go to the party tonight. I won't go either. We can hang out together. I don't need to be at another one of Trent's parties," she says. I appreciate her offer because I know how excited she's been about this weekend and how much Darren wants her there by his side.

"It's okay, Angela. It's not a big deal, really," I lie again. "I need to clear my head. I'm going for a drive."

She finally stops insisting that I stay.

I DRIVE AROUND FOR A WHILE, AIMLESS. I DON'T WANT TO GO back to James's house or my parents'—I want to be alone. My thoughts are still racing after my conversation with Max, and I need somewhere quiet to think so I can process it all.

After driving around West Hollywood without a destination, I head west and end up in Santa Monica. I find a parking spot and walk straight to the beach. I take off my shoes; the sand is warm under my bare feet, and I break down in tears as soon as I touch the surf's edge. This trip, the engagement—everything that should be joyful and exciting feels like a burden. Home doesn't even feel like home anymore.

I plop down on the sand, feeling crushed. I replay my conversation with Max and realize that whatever Joe is going through must be serious enough for Max to disinvite me from tonight's celebrations that he knows I've been looking forward to.

The surf is rough today, and I feel uneasy as I look out into the ocean. *Why did James want to keep our engagement a secret until we arrived? Why did he insist that we tell everyone in person? Why did he plan this trip for this particular weekend?* Thoughts run wild in my head—and no matter how much I try to rationalize everything, I can't shake a nagging feeling that something isn't right. *But what?* I can't pin down the feeling. There's no reason I should doubt James or this trip—He wanted us to celebrate our engagement at home with my family! He had no idea about the Platinum Record ceremony until he found out at our welcome-home dinner; it's not something he would care about!

When I think about how fucked up it is that our good news could sour Joe's night, the nagging feeling in the pit of my stomach intensifies. The thought of seeing Joe for the first time after everything that's happened between us and telling him that I'm engaged—on a night he's been dreaming of for as long as I can remember, feels wrong. What a horrible coincidence, and like Max said, what terrible timing.

I start crying again, thinking about how terrible this is. I also realize Max is *one hundred percent* right to ask me to stay away from Joe. I almost want to go back to London tomorrow so I don't have to see Joe at all.

Chapter Fifty-Nine

"James, are you home?!" I call out as soon as I walk through the door. I feel better after my beach breakdown.

"In the den!" he responds. I find him sprawled out on the couch on his phone. "Where have you been, baby?" he smiles.

"At the shop…" I can't possibly tell him where I've been.

"I texted you a couple of times…" He looks at me closely and motions for me to join him.

"We were swamped… Sorry."

"Come here," he says, making room on the couch. I sit next to him, and he leans in to kiss me. "Are you okay?"

I nod, "The jet lag is killing me."

He's quiet as he inspects my eyes, and I'm suddenly uncomfortable. "Well, we're going to Trent's party for that record thing later, right?" He looks at his watch, "Why don't I make us some drinks before we start getting ready."

I drop my gaze, "I don't want to go anymore."

"What? Really? You've been so excited about tonight—to be with your friends again and to celebrate Trent and your brother…"

"I'm too tired," I cut him off, "I don't want to go." I get up from the couch and walk out of the den. James follows me.

"Annie, what's wrong? Did something happen?"

"No," I say.

He follows me up the stairs and into the bedroom, insisting I tell him what's wrong.

"Nothing," I repeat, kicking off my shoes and climbing into bed.

He stops and stares at me, "There's something wrong… I know you… you should tell me," he says firmly.

"James, I'm exhausted. I don't want to go. I want to take a pill and go to sleep so I don't feel like shit for the rest of this trip," I say, looking directly at him.

"I don't get it. You've been looking forward to this—to be with your friends—you've been complaining about not having a life in London, and we're here, and now you don't want to go out? I just don't get it," he says.

I stare back at him without responding.

"Come on," he says, sitting on the edge of the bed and taking my hand. "It'll be fun," his tone softens, and a smile crosses his lips. "If you're tired, I can make you an espresso or maybe cut you a line or something…" he says, smiling bigger.

"Why did you want to keep our engagement a secret until we got here?" I blurt out, looking him in the eye.

He furrows his brow, "What?"

I repeat myself, and he looks at me, pausing before responding, "I told you—I thought it would be more special that way."

"Why did you want to come here *this weekend?*" I can't help the accusatory tone in my voice.

"Why are you asking me this?" He looks at me closely, waiting for my answer. "Annie…" he sighs, "I told you, it was the only time I could get away. What's the big deal about this weekend anyway? Aren't you glad you can celebrate your brother's record *thing*? I think it's pretty good timing if you ask me."

I realize how crazy I'm being. "I'm sorry, I'm not thinking straight…" I scoot closer to him, and we're both silent.

"So, does that mean we're going to Trent's party as planned?"

I shake my head. "No… I don't want to go. We can go to the party after the ceremony tomorrow. Tonight, I just want to sleep."

He pulls away and stares at me blankly. "Well, I'm going out tonight," he scoffs, hastily getting up from the bed. "I'll be at the club if you change your mind," he says, leaving the room. A few minutes later, I hear the front door slam downstairs.

THE NEXT MORNING, JAMES IS IN BED WITH ME WHEN I WAKE up. The sleeping pill I took knocked me out, and I didn't feel him get home. I'm glad I slept through the night, so I didn't have to deal with the FOMO over Trent's party and the thoughts of all the fun everyone was having without me.

I'm emotionally hungover from everything that happened yesterday, and the residual anger and sadness still feel heavy in my chest. I wish it had all been a nightmare, but there's no denying it's all very real.

I look over at James, and his back is to me. I feel bad for letting him down and not having a fun night together like we had planned. But there's no way I could've told him about my talk with Max and his request for me to stay away from Joe. James would've lost his shit! He would've told me I was catering to Joe again, and he would've hated that Joe was the reason I denied us having a good time, celebrating with our friends. I feel guilty that we fought, and I don't want yesterday to ruin the rest of our trip—we only have a few days left in LA.

I move closer to James and put my arm around him. I brush my lips on his bare back, planting soft kisses, hoping he'll wake up and make love to me. I want us to move past what happened yesterday.

My touch and my kisses work because he starts to stir. I trace my fingers down his chest, and our hands meet, fingers interlocking under the sheets.

"James…" I whisper.

"Mmhmm…" he responds.

"I'm sorry about yesterday…"

He stirs again and turns to face me. He squints his eyes open, and I smile at his cute, tousled morning hair.

"I'm sorry that I ruined our night…" I continue.

He pulls me into his chest and kisses the top of my head. "Tonight will be different… I want us to enjoy each other and have a good time… like the old days…"

James releases me from his grip and looks me in the eye. "You didn't ruin anything. I'm sorry, too… I was a dick," he says, brushing a lock of hair from my face.

I lean in to kiss him, and he pulls me on top of him. I straddle his hips, sinking into him for a delicious stretch of morning sex. I finally release the tension from the past twenty-four hours when I climax.

Chapter Sixty

I leave James in bed, sound asleep after making love, and head to my parents' house, where Angela, Michelle, and I are getting glammed and ready for the night's events.

My parents are throwing a small party at the house to watch the livestream of the ceremony before we all go together to The Roosevelt Hotel, *of all fucking places,* for the afterparty.

When I get to the house, I find my parents in the kitchen making breakfast, which instantly lifts my mood. The three of us have a great time catching up over my dad's specialty—French Toast with berries.

They grill me about London and the engagement, and I notice a hint of concern in their tone. I know the engagement is a shock to them, and I understand why—they barely know James.

I'm relieved when Angela arrives just as they start asking specific questions about the wedding and our plans for the future—I'm not ready to think about any of that yet.

Angela fills the room with her humor and airy disposition. She bounces around the kitchen, talking animatedly about tonight. She tells us that Darren is *so* excited that he hardly slept and went for a run at five in the morning to calm his nerves.

Max and Michelle also join us and share more stories about last night's party, which only makes me feel like shit. I nod and listen, pretending I don't care that I was disinvited.

Our glam squad arrives at noon to get us dolled up for the big night. We set up in the den and get glammed in two shifts —Angela and Michelle go first since they're going to the ceremony with Max and Darren, and my mom and I go after since we're staying behind for the livestream watch party.

My nerves skyrocket when I remember I'm going to see Joe tonight. I have no idea what I'm going to say about my engagement, and I have no idea how he'll take it. I text Max to see if he has any weed to help take the edge off, and he invites me to join him in the pool house for a smoke.

Soon enough, I'm happy and stoned, lounging with Max by the pool under the big umbrellas, enjoying a beautiful, sunny afternoon. The sky is cloudless and bright blue, and I love watching the tall palm trees in the yard sway lazily in the balmy winter breeze.

I look over at Max in the lounge chair next to mine, "Do you know what a big fucking deal it is to have a *Platinum Record?*" I ask, breaking our silence.

He meets my eyes and shakes his head. "I know. It's wild. I have no idea how it happened."

"I do. You guys busted your ass on that album. I know how much work went into it. I'm so proud of you," I say, reaching for his hand.

"Thanks, sis, that means a lot," he says with a smile.

My curiosity gets the best of me, and I ask him if he saw Joe last night.

"Yep," he responds without elaborating. I have to pry and ask more questions. "It's just like I told you. He was wasted as usual... nothing new."

I don't ask any more questions and try to push thoughts of Joe out of my head.

AT PRECISELY FIVE P.M., DARREN ARRIVES IN A CHAUFFEURED SUV, and suddenly, everyone's in a frenzy, taking photos and talking excitedly—It feels like prom night. Angela and Michelle look amazing in their slinky cocktail dresses, and Max and Darren look dapper in their suits. My mom innocently asks where Joe is, and Darren tells her he's riding with Trent. I didn't expect him to show up here, and I'm sure Max and Darren arranged the whole thing so I wouldn't ruin Joe's big night.

My parents give a lovely speech, and we all have a glass of champagne to toast Darren and Max before they leave for the ceremony.

Matt arrives with one of the chefs from Raleigh's, who is catering our watch party. Just before the livestream starts at six, the rest of the guests arrive.

James shows up just as the show gets underway. "You look gorgeous," he whispers in my ear, admiring my silky white mini dress. I return the compliment, straightening the tie of his handsome, slim, black suit.

My parents welcome him warmly, and James seems comfortable, mingling with all the guests present: Aunt Gia, Aaron, Matt, Daniel, and a few of my parents' closest friends.

Meanwhile, I'm a nervous wreck, watching the ceremony for glimpses of the guys. About thirty minutes in, just as I'm pouring myself another drink at the bar, I hear the show's host announce a performance by Trent from his *"newly released sophomore album."*

My heart stops as I hear the first few beats, immediately recognizing *track number four.*

The room goes quiet as everyone focuses on the livestream

playing on the TV screen. My hands shake as I cap the Grey Goose bottle. Daniel comments on how hot the song is and how good Trent looks on stage. I have to act cool to hide the nerves rattling inside me, so I take a deep breath and walk back to the group. Everyone's eyes are glued on Trent, except James, who stares at me as I approach him.

"I love this song! Have you heard it before, Annie?" Aunt Gia asks, directing her attention to me.

"Uh, yeah," I respond softly. I clear my throat and agree that it's a great song.

"It's gonna be a huge hit!" Matt says, bopping to the beat. "It's so *sexy*," he adds emphatically.

I want to crawl into a hole, feeling embarrassed, guilty, and uncomfortable as I listen to the song Joe wrote for me—the lined paper with the lyrics in his handwriting flashes in my head—*for Annie*.

I stand next to James, and he pulls me in by the waist, wrapping his arms around me from behind. I keep my cool and watch Trent move on stage, full of confidence and sex appeal, belting out, "Home."

As he hits the last note, the crowd on screen and around me erupts in cheers as Trent proudly grins. I'm relieved the song is over, and I clap with everyone, trying my hardest to keep it together.

After the performance, I continue to self-soothe with champagne, and sneak a few cigarettes here and there by the pool with James, even though my dad shoots me disapproving looks. But I don't care—I'm wrecked with anxiety, knowing that the worst is yet to come as I prepare to face Joe in a few hours.

"They're up! They're about to present their plaque!" Matt announces as everyone gathers again in front of the TV.

"Let's go," James says, leading me back into the house by the hand.

Newly minted pop princess Monica Jones and R&B crooner Travis Richie do a corny and scripted bit as they introduce a short video package capturing Trent's rise to fame. The video features snippets of Trent on stage, on the road, and in the recording studio.

"Oh, look!" My mom says, pointing at the screen as a snippet of Max, Darren, and Joe in the studio with Trent flashes on the screen. The room suddenly feels like a sauna.

The video package ends and the crowd claps. Monica and Travis call Trent and the guys by name to the stage to receive their plaques. The camera cuts to a shot of the table where they're sitting, and my eyes immediately land on Joe and a gorgeous brunette by his side. The guys get up and share a cute group hug before climbing the steps to the stage to collect their accolades.

I hold my breath as my parents and everyone else in the room cheer. It is surreal to watch the guys receive such an incredible honor.

"This is so fucking cool!" Matt exclaims as everyone erupts in more cheers while I remain frozen. Monica and Travis hand out the plaques, and Trent takes center stage to give a speech as the guys stand behind him, looking proud and amused.

I haven't seen Joe in months, and I've had no idea what to expect since he looked a bit worse for wear the last time I saw him at the party where he showed up with a stripper. Max also painted such a somber picture of his current state that I've been preparing to see Joe at his worst. But to my surprise, he looks great. He's wearing a sharp, dark blue suit that brings out the blue in his eyes. He's clean-shaven, and his wavy hair is perfectly tamed. He looks nothing like I imagined, and I start to wonder if Max was exaggerating about everything.

Trent continues his speech, and I can't hear it over the chatter in the room. Darren takes the podium next and says a few words. The room finally goes silent when Max takes the mic and gives his speech.

"I want to thank our families… Mom and Dad watching from home, thank you for always believing in my dream, and to these guys, my brothers, for life…"

I look over at my mother, who's dabbing her eyes, and my father, who looks prouder than ever.

Joe takes the mic last, thanking Trent, the label, and Darren and Max. "And, uh, thanks to the muses that inspired this album," he says with a smile, holding up the iconic Platinum Record plaque while looking at the camera. The guys are ushered off the stage by Monica and Travis, and two new presenters appear on stage to award the next plaque.

Everyone in the room talks excitedly, but it's just noise as my heart pounds in my ears, drowning everything out. I look up at James, who meets my gaze with intense eyes. "Pretty cool," he says, trying to sound excited.

"Yeah," I say, barely able to formulate a sentence. My throat goes dry, and my hands feel trembly. "I'll be right back," I say, excusing myself. I'm suffocating, and it feels like the room is closing in on me. I ignore the look James shoots me as I hurry toward the hallway.

I'm shaking as I head to the powder room. I close the door, finally able to exhale. I hold onto the wall with one hand and clutch my stomach with the other—I can't tell if I'm going to throw up or pass out—the anxiety has escalated into a mini panic attack.

Relax, Annie, relax, I tell myself as I breathe in and out rhythmically, trying to steady my breath and heart rate. I run a hand towel under cold water and press it to my neck and chest. I look at my reflection in the mirror and firmly tell myself to *chill the fuck out.*

I compose myself and return to the party, where everyone is preparing to leave. "Are we leaving?" I ask James.

"Yeah, the ceremony's ending soon, so we should get to The Roosevelt before it gets crazy," he says.

My mom announces that the cars are here, and everyone makes their way toward the front door. James looks at me closely and asks, "Are you okay?"

"Yeah, I didn't eat much today, and the champagne just got to me." I'm trying my best to be calm and collected despite the frenzy I feel inside.

He smiles and pulls me in for a hug. "Well, grab something to eat, and let's go," he says, motioning toward the door. His mood is upbeat, and he seems anxious to leave.

I hesitate and consider pulling out. *Maybe I can pretend like I'm too sick to go?*

"Come on, baby," he says, "Don't you want to congratulate your brother and see your friends?" I know there's no way I can pull out now, so I take a deep breath and take his hand as we head out the door.

THE SCENE AT THE ROOSEVELT IS INSANE. WE ARRIVE AT THE perfect time, just as a long car line forms behind us in the VIP valet line. James and I arrive in his Porsche, while my parents and the rest of the group arrive in the black SUVs.

As we approach the entrance to the Tropicana Bar, a handsome man greets James with a big hug and a handshake. "James *fuckin'* Hunter! Where have you been hiding, my man —it's been a minute!" he says.

James greets him with equal enthusiasm and then introduces me as his *fiancé*, a word I cannot get used to. The man, Sean, is one of the hotel managers, and from what I gather from their conversation, they're old friends from the LA club scene. James tells him we've been living in London, and Sean appears shocked to hear that we're getting married. "Wow, and I thought this man would be the eternal bachelor!" he says to me with a laugh.

Inside, the party is in full swing. I'm starstruck by all the music artists, beautiful starlets, and models milling about. There are also lots of industry types, schmoozing. The iconic Hockney pool, the crown jewel of the bar, is lit up brightly and decorated beautifully with floating disco balls and votive candles. James leads me through the crowd, greeting a few people along the way. I'm still anxious as fuck, but I do my best to keep it inside and pretend that I'm having a great time.

Everyone from my parents' party is here, and we've gathered again to wait for the guys to arrive. A noticeable buzz erupts at the entrance as photographers start firing their flashbulbs. The DJ cuts to Trent's first number-one single, announcing his arrival.

My stomach flutters as I look toward the commotion. Through the crowd, I catch a glimpse of Trent and his date posing for the photographers. Then Max, Michelle, Angela, and Darren couple up for the cameras. I can't help but chuckle; this is all so strange and surreal!

Angela comes over to us excitedly. She greets everyone with a hug and looks like she's on cloud nine. "Oh my God, did you guys watch?" she asks, beaming.

Max, Michelle, and Darren also join us, and there are more hugs and congratulations as excitement fills the air. I notice that Joe and his date are photographed more often, and she's photographed alone a few times.

"Isn't that Nicky Chambers?" James whispers in my ear as he catches me staring at her. I realize why she looks familiar. Nicky is an actress on a series with a cult-like following. I'm shocked that he knows who she is and embarrassed that he caught me staring.

I shrug, ignoring his smirk, and pretend I don't know what he's talking about.

Joe glances over at our group, then looks away. He grabs

Nicky's hand and leads her through the crowd to the other side of the bar. His actions speak louder than words, and I feel terrible for not responding to his note or addressing the huge rift between us. I try pushing away these thoughts and turn my attention back to James, quietly sipping his drink and listening to Darren talk about the ceremony.

Trent and his date come by after they work the crowd, and more hugs and congratulations go around. Amidst the commotion, Angela pulls me aside and asks how I'm doing.

"Fine," I say, giving her my best smile.

"I have to tell you something," she says, turning serious.

"What?"

"He knows," she says, leaning into my ear.

I give her a puzzled look, "What are you talking about?"

"Darren told Joe—that *you know*… that you're engaged."

I nod as I take in the news, "When? What did he say?"

"After the ceremony at some point… You know how Joe is; he just… shrugged it off. I couldn't tell how he took it," she says.

I look toward the crowd, where I saw Joe disappear, but he's nowhere in sight. I know that the time has come, and I have to be the one to go to him.

After wandering around the lively poolside party, I find Joe at one of the bars. "Hey," I say, poking him in the arm. He looks surprised to see me.

"Hey," he says, pausing for a second.

"Congratulations!" I smile and reach out to hug him. He hugs me back, but his touch feels cold and awkward. He stares at me for a second after we pull apart and leans back on the bar, waiting for me to continue. I have to admit, he looks as great in person as he did on screen.

"I'm really proud of you," I say.

"Thanks…" he pauses. "When did you get into town?" There's a chill in his tone, and I'm surprised at his directness.

"A few days ago. It wasn't planned—kinda last minute…"

"Any particular reason?" he asks, glancing at my hand. I know that he knows, but he wants me to say it.

"Well, actually…"

He tenses, looking directly at me. I look away from his piercing blue eyes and can't bear to say it. "Um…" I try again, "Joe, I've wanted to talk to you for a while now, and…" I look back up at him. My thoughts are swimming as I try to choose my words carefully. "I got your note and Trent's album—"

He cuts me off. "Forget about that. I don't want to talk about that…" He looks annoyed all of a sudden. Just then, I feel a hand on my back.

"There you are," James says, pulling me in. "Congratulations, man!" James says, extending his hand to Joe as if he were happy to see him.

Joe shakes his hand and thanks him tepidly.

"Trent is everywhere in Europe," James continues as he puts his arm around me. "His first album is huge in London, and Annie and I were in Paris for her birthday and it was all over the radio and the clubs." James is drunk and being obnoxious.

Joe nods and says, "Cool."

"And I'm sure the new album will be a hit too. Annie played it for me when Max sent it, and I gotta say—it's really good."

Joe stares blankly at him and then at me.

I wish I could disappear.

"Did you tell him?" James asks, turning to me. I hate that it's happening like this, and I regret being here. I regret this night, and I regret *so much* that I approached Joe.

I look down, forming the words in my head, when Joe cuts in, "I already heard—congratulations," he says flatly.

I look up at him, recognizing heartbreak in his eyes.

"Thanks," James says, grinning as he pulls me closer.

Joe turns around and grabs the two drinks the bartender left on the bar top while we've been talking. "Take care, Annie," he says, excusing himself abruptly, then disappears into the crowd.

Chapter Sixty-One

Joe

One Month Later

I've been waiting for my big moment in the music industry my entire life. I never imagined the first album I produced would go platinum, nor did I ever imagine that the accomplishment would forever be remembered as the best and worst night of my life.

The night of the Platinum Record ceremony, I felt untouchable. I was being honored alongside my best friends and had the hottest actress on my arm as my date. Even though I had been partying non-stop for months, I vowed to myself that I wasn't going to fuck up that night. I wanted to be lucid, I wanted to be present, I wanted to soak it all in—I wanted to be *sober.*

So, instead of my usual cocktail and cocaine breakfast, I decided to fight the demons head-on that day and pushed through the cravings. It wasn't even that hard—I was too excited and pumped with adrenaline—a natural high that drugs couldn't match.

The night of the ceremony was supposed to be perfect—and it was. Arriving at the Beverly Hilton, I felt the crowd's energy and the heightened anticipation of receiving the coveted honor. It was a feeling better than drugs—I was literally high on life! I was among some of my idols and now my peers and I felt a sense of belonging that I hadn't felt before—it was incredible.

The most important moment of my career thus far happened when I held that iconic plaque in my hands. But my world stopped spinning on its axis and went back to spinning off kilter when Darren pulled me aside for a talk as we waited for our car in the valet line after the ceremony.

By the look on his face, I wondered what I had done wrong—I only had one drink at the event, and I hadn't touched blow or popped a pill all day. I had no idea what the problem was, but I could tell it wasn't good. I'll never forget that moment…

"Bro," Darren said in that protective and stern tone he gets with me sometimes, "I gotta tell you something." He pulled out a pack of cigarettes and handed me one without even asking if I wanted it. I lit it and took a long drag, waiting for him to continue. "There's something I have to tell you, and I've been trying to figure out how to say it without sounding fucked up…"

"Spit it out, D!" I laughed, "Are you fucking with me?"

Darren looked directly into my eyes, placing his hand on my shoulder. "Annie's in town…"

The sound of her name was so sharp and sweet. *Annie.* I hadn't heard it or said it out loud in so long.

"Okay…" I said as his words sank in.

Darren then said something that I didn't understand, "What?" I asked him to repeat himself.

"She's in town with James… and they're engaged," he said. This time, I heard him clearly, and it felt like he had punched me in the stomach.

I was silent as he squeezed my shoulder, telling me he was sorry. "You're fucking with me," I said again.

"No, I'm not. I'm sorry," he said.

At that precise moment, I felt my world crumble.

Darren kept talking, apologizing for not telling me sooner, telling me he wanted me to enjoy the night. He was going on and on, and I was only hearing bits and pieces as I tried to understand what it all meant. When our car arrived, Darren dropped another bomb—that Annie would probably be at the afterparty. That's when the worst night of my life began.

The memory of that night plays over and over again in my head as I lay in this cold hospital room.

I look at the clock, and it's two a.m. Everything is silent except for the beeping of the machines I'm hooked up to and the low whispers from the nurses in the hallway. I've been going in and out of sleep from the meds and the painkillers for the past twenty-four hours since the accident. Whenever I wake up, the night of the ceremony replays in my head like a nightmare I can't shake, even though it happened a month ago.

The memory of seeing Annie that night, seeing that ring on her finger, and feeling the warmth of her touch when we hugged is more unbearable than the pounding in my head from the concussion and the searing pain in my hand from crushing it so badly that I almost lost a finger. I would even take the misery of having two broken ribs for the rest of my life if I could erase that night from my head or from it ever happening.

If I could go back in time, I would change the course of my life and take back all the moments that drove Annie and me apart and drove her to him. There are so many things I wish I could take back. I wish I hadn't let my addiction win. I wish I hadn't been so weak that I had to drown my mistakes and my problems in booze and numb out on drugs. And I wish I hadn't been stupid and reckless, driving completely wasted yesterday, almost losing my life.

Thank God I was alone and not with the hot model I was

making out with all night at the club. Thank God I crashed into a tree and not into some innocent person. *What have I become?* I have never felt so low in my life.

I look down at my bandaged hand, realizing how lucky I am to be alive. The mangled hand, the concussion, the broken ribs, and the cuts and bruises on my face will heal. I don't know if what I'm feeling inside ever will.

And still, the worst part is that I haven't been able to stop thinking about Annie. She was the only thought in my head as I was going in and out of consciousness when they pulled me out of the car wreck. I could've let go—I was so tired and weak; it would've been so easy. But I didn't. I couldn't—*Annie.* Through the lights, the sirens, the chaos, and the pain, she was all I could think about.

Thinking back on it now, I know that I was in denial about her engagement for weeks, but when it finally hit me—it hit me hard. I was back on tour with Trent, and we stopped somewhere on the road on our way to Chicago. I stepped off the tour bus at a gas station and saw a woman who resembled Annie comforting a crying baby. The man she was with took the baby into his arms in a fatherly way and tried to soothe him. I stared at them, sharing such an intimate moment, and it hit me then—she will have that with James. They will be a family; they'll probably have kids together.

I had been smoking weed, drinking, and doing coke on the bus for hours. I was so fucked up that seeing that family messed with my head so badly that it caused a physical reaction, and I had to find a bathroom to throw up. The drugs and the partying were getting to me; they were messing with my head. I should've realized then that I was a mess—I should've come back to LA to fix my life right then and there. But instead, I shook it off and buried those feelings deep inside, and kept partying.

I didn't want to deal with reality on the road. Shit, I didn't deal with reality even after the tour ended, and I had no choice but to come home. Reality didn't hit me until yesterday when I came out of the anesthesia from the emergency surgery on my hand. It was a hell of a rude awakening.

Another rude awakening was seeing my parents when I woke up after the surgery. It killed me to feel the distance between us. I hadn't seen them in months and hated that we had to reunite under such terrible circumstances. Even so, it felt good to have them here, strained relationship and all.

A smile manages to cross my lips, recalling the visit from Darren and Max today. I missed them so much—I hadn't seen them since the night of the ceremony when I decided for some crazy reason that I had to push away the closest people in my life. I abandoned my brothers and had so much to apologize for, but they wouldn't let me. Instead, they were encouraging and tried to lift my spirits.

Despite the haze I've been in from the meds and the shock of the accident, I'm glad I had a moment of clarity when Angela stopped by, and I asked her not to tell Annie about the accident. I'm embarrassed, and I don't want her to worry. I've put her through enough. Angela promised she wouldn't tell Annie, and I made Max and Darren also promise that they wouldn't tell her.

"Oh, you're awake!" A nurse enters my room and turns on the blaring overhead lights, interrupting my spiraling thoughts. "How are you feeling?" she asks as she checks my vitals.

"Like shit," I reply.

Her eyes convey pity, and she tells me how sorry she is that she can't give me anything stronger for the pain. All the shit I've been putting in my body showed up in the blood tests—cocaine, THC, alcohol and Xanax. Now I'm under mandatory detox and considered "high risk" for addiction, so they aren't giving me the good stuff. *Imagine that.*

The nurse is gentle as she takes my temperature. "I can

give you a sleeping pill if you like," she says, straightening my pillows and adjusting my bed.

"Sure," I respond. I've been sleeping most of the day, but now I'm wired and can't stop the racing thoughts.

"Okay," she says, patting me lightly on the shoulder. "I'll be right back with that."

As soon as I'm alone again, my thoughts return to everything that happened today. The best defense attorney and close personal friend of my father's, Bill Warner, a man I've known since I was a kid, also came by, and they explained the charges against me from the accident and the repercussions of my monumental fuck-up.

The cops found coke and Xanax on me and charged me with possession, DUI, reckless driving, endangerment, and destruction of public property. The cops were not fucking around and wanted to fry my ass. I'm lucky that a superstar lawyer like Bill is taking my case, and he assured me that since these are my first offenses, there's a high probability I can avoid jail if I go to rehab and do community service. I'll still have to go to court and go through all that bullshit, but at least I have a chance at avoiding jail. After talking to my dad and Bill, I've come to terms with the fact that I have to change my life—I have no choice.

The nurse returns and hands me a pill and a cup of water. It feels like my insides are ripping apart as I try to sit up. I grimace, and she pats me gently on the arm.

"Try to relax," she says, "This will help you sleep."

I take the pill and thank her.

"Get some rest," she says as she turns off the lights and exits the room. I try getting comfortable again in the most uncomfortable bed I've ever slept on and close my eyes, hoping the thoughts will stop, waiting for everything to fade to black.

Chapter Sixty-Two

Joe

"Here, I brought you some clothes to wear home," my dad says, handing me a shopping bag. Inside, I find a pair of sneakers, gray sweatpants, a white T-shirt, and new underwear and socks.

"These aren't mine," I say, inspecting the items.

"They're mine. Mom's been at some press thing all day, and I was in court until thirty minutes ago, so neither of us could make it to your place to get your stuff. I'm sorry." He gives me a lukewarm smile, patting my leg. "They're spare gym clothes I had at the office. Don't worry—*they're clean.* I had Helen shop for the other things," he says.

"Did they say when I can leave?" I sink back into the bed, tired from waiting all day to be discharged. I've been in the hospital for five days, and the thought of spending one more night here is unbearable.

"They said soon," he sighs loudly, taking a seat in a chair across from me.

"So, what happens next?" I ask, trying to calm the anxiety that's kept me in knots all day.

"Well, it's like we talked about. We'll fly out to Utah

tomorrow. You'll be there for as long as they think you need to stay, and when you get out, we'll deal with the court."

"Tomorrow?" I can't believe it's all happening so fast.

"You're lucky you're getting this chance," he says. "If you didn't have me or Bill on your side, you'd be booked into jail tomorrow." My dad crosses his arms and gives me a stern look. I drop my gaze as the disappointment in his eyes burns through me.

"What about this?" I ask, holding up the bandaged lump encasing my left hand.

"Dr. Stephens will refer you to a specialist in Utah. He said you'll need another surgery soon."

We're silent for a moment.

"How are you feeling today?" He relaxes his posture, softening his tone.

"Like shit. But at least I'm getting used to the pain," I say, looking back up at him.

"Mr. Montgomery!" A commanding voice interrupts us. Dr. Stephens finally shows up with the nice nurse who's been caring for me during the evening shift. "You ready to get out of here?" he asks, turning to me.

My dad stands up to greet Dr. Stephens with a handshake. Dr. Stephens is the best reconstructive surgeon at Cedars-Sinai, and I'm lucky he was the doctor who performed the emergency surgery on my hand when I arrived at the hospital. He was the first person I saw when I came out of the anesthesia haze after the surgery, and he was the person who explained what had happened. I can't remember what he said, but he made me feel like everything would be okay despite all the chaos and confusion.

Dr. Stephens speaks with my dad, then turns his attention to me.

"I'm ready to go," I say, excited to leave the hospital even though I know that my hell is just beginning.

"Well, Alice will take your vitals one more time, and then

you'll need to sign some papers, and you'll be good to go," he says.

"Um, Dr. Stephens, you do know that Joe is being admitted into a facility in Utah tomorrow…" my dad says, trying to find the right words without mentioning the dreaded one—*rehab*.

"Oh, yes. I do know," Dr. Stephens says, looking at the computer screen and pulling up my chart. "Yes, The Lodge," he says, eyes fixed on the screen. "It's an excellent facility. You'll get the care you need there." He turns to me with a reassuring look.

"And, uh, what about his medical treatment? You mentioned the other day he was going to need a few more surgeries?" my dad asks.

"That's right. I want to review Joe's X-rays from this morning and tell you what will happen next." Dr. Stephens wheels the portable computer unit closer to us and pulls up my X-rays, which appear crystal clear on the screen.

I sit up, bracing myself for what he's about to say.

"Joe, as I explained to you already, you suffered a serious injury." He turns to the screen and points with a pen at the skeletal image of my hand that even I can tell looks pretty fucked up. "You fractured the bone in your ring finger. This is the screw we put in your knuckle to hold the bone together," Dr. Stephens explains, motioning in circles with the pen over the screen.

I look at my dad, who has his arms crossed and brow furrowed, concentrating on what Dr. Stephens is saying.

"You also needed a small bone graft to support this part," he says, circling another part of my bone on the X-ray. "From the looks of this, your hand is taking to the graft nicely. The fact that you haven't had an infection or any side effects is a good sign," he says, looking at me. "We'll need to give the hand a few weeks to heal, but you'll probably need another screw and a plate put in next to ensure the finger straightens out properly."

"How will I do that if I'm going to be in rehab for God knows how long?" I can't hide the frustration in my voice.

"Well, that can wait until you get back," he says. "I'll make sure you're seen by one of the best specialists in Utah for a follow-up in two weeks. We can do the rest of the procedures when you return home."

I sigh, "How many more surgeries am I going to need?"

"It depends. It could be two or three. It's hard to tell right now," he says.

"And the recovery time?" my dad interjects.

"Well, if you're diligent with physical therapy and follow medical advice, you might be good in six months, assuming there are no complications," he adds.

My dad and I look at each other, and I wonder if he can sense my panic.

"Will I be able to use my hand again?" I ask, even though it sounds like a ridiculous question.

"Yes, you will. But I have to be honest; you may not have complete mobility on that finger after all is said and done. I've seen close to full recoveries in similar cases. We'll do the best we can," he says, giving me another reassuring look.

Dr. Stephens gives me some final words on how to take care of my hand and the other injuries I've suffered, then goes over the prescriptions he's writing for me before wishing me well. My dad thanks him and walks with him out of the room.

"You're all set!" Alice says as she finishes recording my vitals on the computer.

I look at the shopping bag sitting on the bedside table. "Hey, Alice, any idea where my stuff is?" I have no idea where the clothes I wore when I got here ended up.

"Oh," she says, giving me a hesitant look. She opens the closet door and pulls out a white plastic bag with the words

"Patient Belongings" in big blue letters across it. As she hands it to me, my dad re-enters the room.

"It was noted in your chart that the shirt and jacket you were wearing had to be cut off and disposed of… sorry," she says. "The rest should be in there."

I open the bag and find my favorite sneakers and new Paul Smith plaid pants crusted and covered with blood. My stomach turns at the sight and smell of them. I see my wallet at the bottom of the bag, and it's in a similar condition—crusted with blood and covered in dirt.

My dad catches me staring at the stuff. "You'll have to get a new car when you come back—and sorry, I asked the police about your phone, and it never turned up," he says.

I close the bag, leaving the pants and shoes inside. "This can go in the trash," I say, handing him the bag.

An hour later, my dad and I arrive at my condo so I can pack for rehab. When I walk in, I'm shocked and embarrassed at the condition my place is in. In the harsh light of sobriety, it becomes clear what a mess my life has become—literally. I never bothered unpacking from the tour, so my suitcases are still scattered on the floor, spilling over with clothes.

Empty beer bottles and dirty ashtrays clutter almost every surface, and dirty carryout boxes are stacked on the dining room table. I watch my dad survey the place without saying a word.

"I won't be long," I say, quickly scanning the room for forgotten drugs or paraphernalia. The only thing that stands out is some dried weed in a plastic baggie among the random debris on the kitchen island, but I can't do anything about it now. "Check the fridge if you want something to drink," I say, unsure if there's anything in there.

"I'm fine," he says.

When I walk into my room, I find it in a similar state of chaos. I don't know where to begin.

I can hear my dad moving around in the kitchen, and it makes me nervous. "Do you have any trash bags?" he yells out loud.

"Um, under the sink—maybe?" I yell back as I look in my closet, trying to figure out what to pack. I hear him opening drawers and cabinets, but he doesn't say anything.

I find my Tumi duffle bag in the back of my closet and start filling it with random T-shirts and pants from my drawers and the wayward suitcases on the floor in my room.

I hear my dad's voice, but I can't make out what he's saying this time.

"What?!" I yell out, but I still can't understand him when he repeats himself. I come out of the room and find him in the kitchen holding my Platinum Record plaque.

"What did you say?"

"I was just saying that I can't believe you have one of these," he says, examining it. He looks at me, waiting for an answer, but I can only shrug—I don't know what to say.

"Why is it here, among all this junk?" he asks, motioning at the trash and dirty dishes on the kitchen island. "It was just sitting here in a box with trash." He waits for me to respond.

I can't ignore the sadness and concern in his eyes, and it guts me.

"Don't you want to put it somewhere special? Aren't you proud of this?" he shakes his head.

I still don't know what to say because I don't know how to feel about it. Every time I look at the damn thing, it only brings back bad memories of that night.

"You don't have to clean up," I say, turning around and walking back to my bedroom.

"Joseph, we're really proud of you for this!" he says loudly.

My parents were in Italy on the night of the ceremony, and I was back on the road when they returned to LA. We texted a few times, and they congratulated me. But this is the first time he's saying out loud that he's proud of me for it.

I try to ignore the tightness in my chest as anxiety escalates inside of me. So, I pack as best as I can with my bandaged hand in a sling, going as fast as possible. When I'm finally done, I find my dad knotting up a trash bag with all the bottles and crap he picked up from all over the condo.

"I'll have Amelia come by and clean this place tomorrow," he says while washing his hands.

I stare at him, not knowing what to say. I have never felt this helpless or this low in my life.

I look down and realize I'm still wearing his gym clothes— I don't even know who the hell I am anymore.

He dries his hands and takes the duffle bag from me.

"Thank you," I say, meeting his eyes, which my mom swears are identical to mine.

"You got everything?" he asks.

I glance around the kitchen and living room, noticing the Platinum Record plaque hanging above the custom Steinway my parents gave me for my eighteenth birthday, replacing the painting that usually occupies that spot.

"Yeah," I say, turning off the lights as we walk out the door.

My dad and I drive to Holmby Hills in silence. I'm spending the night at my parents' so they can drop my ass off at rehab bright and early tomorrow—in UTAH, no less. My head is swimming with thoughts as I try to come to terms with the events of the last few days, which still feel surreal. I feel like I've been living a nightmare.

I look down at my fucked-up hand, trying to ignore the

throbbing pain radiating from it and every bone in my body. I still can't believe I'm alive. Fuck it, maybe I needed this wake-up call. Otherwise, who knows how long I would have survived with my reckless behavior.

We pull up to my childhood home, and I finally snap out of my thoughts. My mom greets us at the door. She looks put together as always, in a sharp red dress, heels, and lots of jewelry. Her blonde hair is in a sleek bob, which is a new look since I last saw her.

"I'm sorry I wasn't able to go to the hospital today," she says, giving me a gentle hug. She flashes me a smile, but she can't hide the worried expression on her face.

"It's fine," I say, ready to head upstairs to call it a night.

"How about some dinner?" she asks before I turn away.

"Joe, you should eat," my dad says, giving me a stern look.

I sigh, giving in. "Fine," I say, following them into the kitchen.

To my surprise, my mom's hot assistant, Sasha, is plating food from carry-out containers in the kitchen. I'm suddenly self-conscious and embarrassed about the state I'm in.

"Sasha was a sweetheart and picked up La Scala for us," my mom says, smiling at her.

Sasha isn't able to hide the shock in her eyes from seeing my fucked-up state. "Hi, Joe…" she says, trying to sound chipper, "How are you feeling?"

I give her a weak smile and tell her I'm fine.

Sasha finishes plating the food and then chats with my mom, making work arrangements for when she'll be out of town and settling me into rehab.

"I'll be on my phone if you need me for anything— anything at all," my mom tells Sasha as she walks her out.

"Take care, Joe," Sasha says, waving at me.

I give her a wave and a nod back.

When my mom returns, it's just the three of us in the minimalist, stark-white kitchen she spent months remodeling.

"Did you reserve the plane?" she asks my dad as she sets plates on the table.

"Yup, nine a.m., Burbank," he says, reaching for a bottle of white from the wine fridge.

"Great!" she says, "The food's getting cold—let's eat!"

Chapter Sixty-Three

In London, James and I are back to our old routine. He works long hours, and I keep myself busy with yoga, Pilates, and shopping. It would be a really fun life if I wasn't so miserable.

James tries to make up for his absence by ensuring I have a driver at my disposal, and even though I can handle my own expenses, he always leaves his black card behind and insists I use it.

To get into wedding planning mode and to make the most of my free time, I make appointments at a few couture ateliers to look at dresses, but the visits do little to excite me. I feel lonelier than ever in London, and I wish my mom and sister were with me as I look at exquisite dress after exquisite dress and sip champagne with the lovely atelier directors.

I leave my third appointment of the day without trying on a single dress and with a knot in my stomach because, frankly, I'm having a hard time getting excited about the wedding. After being engaged for almost two months, I thought I would be used to the idea of commitment and *forever,* but so far… it's not happening. Everything feels so rushed!

James, on the other hand, is very excited. He's asked me a

few times about eloping. *"Let's hop on a jet, fly to Bali, and get married on the beach,"* he says in all seriousness. I had to put the brakes on the idea, reminding him that we have all the time in the world. When we return home, we'll have our perfect wedding in LA with our friends and families.

I make it back to the townhouse just before it starts pouring again and decide to make a cup of tea. It's four in the afternoon, and James will be home in a few hours, so we can decide what to do for dinner. I can't wait to hear his latest update on the project's progress, especially with the club's opening date fast approaching. Last night, he shared that they're in the final stage: adding the last decorating touches, receiving liquor deliveries, and training the newly hired staff.

The idea of returning home in a matter of weeks makes my mind wander back to my trip to LA as I settle on the couch with my steaming cup of Earl Grey.

I still can't shake the unsettling feeling from the visit. I hated the distance I felt from Angela and Max, and I hated telling Joe about my engagement on his special night—the memory of that moment has been torturing me. I know there's nothing I could've done given the circumstances, but the whole situation is still painful, and I can't believe how much it still bothers me.

It's time to move on, Annie. Leave it in the past. I repeat in my head, hoping the racing thoughts will stop amidst the house's silence, broken only by the soft patter of rain on the window.

Chapter Sixty-Four

Two weeks later, opening night finally arrives. I can't contain my excitement because James and I will be back in LA soon, and I'll be back to my normal life.

James comes home at six sharp in a mad rush to shower and change. He's already had a few drinks, and he's happy and chatty, bouncing around the townhouse, barely able to contain his excitement. We get dressed and have a drink, and an hour later, we're in a car heading to the private dinner party at the club before the doors officially open for a VIP soft launch at ten p.m.

I'm all smiles, full of nervous excitement, in my sexy new Versace dress, ready for a fun night celebrating James, the Brits, and their new club.

The car drops us off in front of Sunset, the chosen name for the nightclub in chic South Kensington. The name is a nod to LA, its inspiration.

I stand before a commanding set of gilded doors at the main entrance. James escorts me in, holding my hand. My jaw drops as I admire live palm trees and elegant beachy, cabana-esque tables surrounding the dance floor. Beautiful murals of sunsets and beaches cover the walls, and sexy cocktail servers and bartenders mill about. The women wear nineteen-fifties style hot pants and halter-tops—Old Hollywood Style, and the men wear Polos and linen pants. I can barely speak as I look around in awe at the gorgeous club.

"Do you like it?!" James looks at me, beaming.

"It's amazing. You captured LA so beautifully!"

I stopped by the club a few times throughout its construction, and up until two weeks ago, it was still sawdust and crates, exposed wires, and unfinished walls.

"It's incredible, I'm so proud of you!" I say, giving him a hug and a lingering kiss in the middle of the dance floor.

People mill about the space, and some sit at the bar for cocktails before the sit-down dinner begins. I spot an elegant table bathed in candlelight, set up in a roped-off area overlooking the dance floor.

"That's the VIP terrace," James says, pointing to the area where a few people mingle around the table.

"It looks beautiful," I say, unable to stop smiling.

James points out a few more notable spots in the nightclub, then leads me to the bar, where he introduces me to the bartenders. Henry and Thomas join us, greeting me with hugs and brimming enthusiasm. I can tell they've been celebrating all day.

"This fucking guy right here!" Thomas says in his thick British accent as he grabs James by the arm and slaps him playfully on the shoulder. "The mastermind behind this fucking place! Look at it!" he says in awe, motioning around as James tries to contain his pride.

"Annie, in all seriousness…" Thomas continues, looking me directly in the eye, "We've got to thank you for letting us take up so much of your *fiancé's* time…" he stresses the word. "But look at this fucking place!" he exclaims, smiling big and raising his voice with excitement. We all laugh, and I realize how important this project was for James. I'm grateful to have been by his side throughout its development.

The four of us continue chatting until we're interrupted by a statuesque blonde who greets James and the Brits with a coquettish smile. She introduces herself to me as Annabelle, the Executive Hostess.

"We're ready to sit for dinner," she says in a more refined British accent than Thomas's.

"Well, I guess we should sit," Thomas says, exchanging a flirty look with her.

We make our way across the dance floor and up to the VIP terrace to join the rest of the guests at the long table. The club emotes a warm and beautiful LA vibe, and I take it all in as my heart swells with pride. "It's stunning," I say, leaning into James's ear as he sits beside me.

The dinner guests include the club's architects, interior decorators, investors, and London socialites.

Thomas's wife, Gigi, greets me with an air kiss on each cheek. "You look fabulous, as always," she says with her signature contained smile as she sits on my other side. She's one of the ring leaders of the posh socialites, and I've always found her quite intimidating, even though she's been nothing but sweet to me. I thank her and return the compliment, admiring her couture dress and the impressive diamonds around her neck.

"Isn't the club fabulous?" Gigi asks, scanning the space before landing her piercing blue eyes on me. Her sleek, jet-black bob shines even in the dim glow of candlelight.

"It's gorgeous," I say.

Gigi sips her champagne, purses her plump lips, and turns to me, "Your man is quite talented," she says while looking around me toward James. She exudes a *desperate housewife* vibe in need of a good fuck. I doubt middle-aged party boy Thomas is satisfying her needs.

"Yes, he is," I say, reaching for my champagne flute while flashing the rock on my finger in her face as I bring the glass to my lips. She stares at me, sipping her champagne, refraining from further comment.

Servers present the first course, and I watch as everyone pushes their food around their plates, sipping cocktails instead. I'm mostly sober and famished, so I dig into the meal, feeling happier than I have in a long time. Dinner is perfect, and I'm enjoying the conversation, the food, the drinks, and James's affectionate and loving demeanor.

Sometime around nine-thirty, Henry stands at the head of the table and clinks his glass with a knife, demanding everyone's attention. The chatter at the table fades as we all fix our eyes on him.

"We are about thirty minutes away from the official opening of Sunset and a journey that began almost a year ago in a magical *la la land* about five thousand miles from our fair city…" He begins his speech as everyone laughs. "Tonight is very special, and Thomas and I are quite grateful to share it with all of you, gorgeous people…" More laughs and cheers erupt around the table.

"I'm going to keep this short and sweet, but there are a few people I'd like to thank for making Sunset possible…" he says. "The first person I want to thank is a handsome lad we kidnapped from that magical place I spoke of earlier…" He looks directly at James. "Come up here, mate!" he says as everyone claps and cheers.

James looks at me, embarrassed, shaking his head yet flashing his gorgeous smile. I clap along with everyone, giving him a wink as he reluctantly gets up from his chair to join Henry. Henry greets him with a hug and a hearty pat on the back. James relaxes and stands confidently beside him and Thomas, who has joined them.

Thomas starts his speech, but I'm distracted by Gigi whispering in my ear, "I can't wait to see what James does with the club in Paris…"

"What?" I turn in my chair to give her my full attention.

"Darling, the club in Paris, aren't you excited to see what James does with the place?" she whispers again. I hear her clearly this time, but her words don't make sense. I look back at James, smiling next to Henry and Thomas as they continue their speech.

My mind scrambles as I try to make sense of Gigi's words. "There must be some misunderstanding…" I say, looking her in the eye, "James isn't involved with the club in Paris. We're going home next week."

Gigi laughs, throwing her head back like it's the funniest thing she's ever heard. She looks back at me with wide eyes. "Darling, I was there when he signed the contract! Your beloved is officially in partnership with those two bastards," she says with a big grin, motioning toward Thomas and Henry. "How do you not know?!"

My blood runs cold as I struggle to catch my breath. She looks at me, and her smile fades, "Oh fuck. Oh fuck! You didn't know…. Annie, I'm sorry. I'm afraid I may have spoiled some kind of surprise." She gently places her hand on my arm, and her lips move, but I've tuned her out.

I look over at James, and he's finishing his speech, and everyone's clapping. Music comes on, thumping through the speakers, and the servers return to clear the plates and deliver more champagne to everyone at the table.

"To Sunset!" Thomas exclaims loudly over the music, raising his glass. Everyone raises a glass, but me; I'm in shock.

James looks over at me, and I watch his smile crumble when our eyes meet. People start getting up from the table as the soft, glowing house lights are dimmed lower, and the flashing club lights come on, spinning in dizzying colors. There's so much commotion around me, but I'm frozen. *Partner in the nightclub in Paris? How could he do this to me?*

James returns to his seat.

"When were you going to tell me?" I stare at him blankly.

The music is now at full volume, and the chatter of the

people around us makes it hard to talk. He leans into me, opening his mouth to say something, but I push him away and get up from the table. I make my way hastily through the club and the thickening crowd now that the VIP party has officially started.

This cannot be happening, I keep saying in my head as I make my way through the club until I'm finally outside. I take a deep breath, but my thoughts are still racing, and I don't know what to do.

I walk a few steps, then feel a hand grab me by the arm and pull me back. "Annie, stop, please," James says as he tries to hold me back. I'm furious and unable to face him.

"You're an asshole," I say, trying to wrangle out of his grip.

He pulls me into him again with force, restraining me with his arm tightly around my waist. "Relax for a second," he whispers in my ear, "You're making a scene." A few people are in line outside the club, and some stare at us. I don't care, I'm livid.

"Let me go, or I'll really make a fucking scene," I say, pushing him off. He releases me, and I run down the street, my heels clicking on the pavement, and hail the first taxi I see.

Chapter Sixty-Five

I storm into the house in a rage. *How could he do this to me?* I run up the stairs and head straight to the bedroom. I'm not moving to *fucking* Paris. I'm getting the fuck out of London as soon as possible—I've had enough! I'm not thinking straight, but I manage to find my suitcase and start emptying my drawers, dumping clothes into it.

"Annie!" I hear the front door slam, then footsteps running up the stairs. James enters the room, but I ignore him as I frantically throw my belongings into the suitcase. "What are you doing?" he asks calmly.

I finally look at him, "You fucking signed a contract to be a partner in the PARIS club, and you didn't fucking tell me?! You fucking lied to me, you completely disregarded how I felt about Paris, and you expect me to be fine with it?!" I stare at him, shaking my head, waiting for an answer.

He inches toward me, extending his hand.

"Don't fucking touch me, James! I am so fucking mad right now," I say, pushing him away.

"Let me explain," he says, trying to calm me.

"Yes, fucking explain why don't you?!" I raise my voice again.

"I wanted to surprise you! I've been looking for flats for us and spaces for you for a boutique, and I wanted to make this perfect for you—for us!"

"You're insane," I respond, blood boiling from his weak explanation. "Please understand…" I look him straight in the eye, "I Don't. Want. To. Fucking. Go. To. Paris! I don't want to move there. I don't want to live there—ever! The only place I want to go is home, and I want to go now!"

James stares at me, anger flashing in his eyes. "LA. *Fucking* LA!" he says, raising his voice. "What the fuck is so special about LA?! Don't you want to live a little? Explore the world and have these amazing experiences that I'm giving you?! You want to go back to fucking *Los Angeles* and hang around your parents' pool with the same fucking people and go to the same fucking places you've been going to since high school? The *fucking* Ivy? The Chateau Marmont? Rodeo Drive? Fuck, Annie, I'm asking you to move to Paris, not some fucking place in the middle of nowhere!"

I'm stunned as he continues.

"Grow the fuck up! Life is bigger than fucking Beverly Hills, you know! Live a little!"

"Don't try to turn this around on me! You fucked up! You went behind my back and made this HUGE life decision for us without involving me?! How can we get married? I can't trust you!"

"Oh, so now you don't want to get married? Is that what you're saying? I want to give you an amazing life, give you the fucking world—literally! Haven't I treated you better than your last boyfriend?! And you can't trust me? You don't think I would be a good husband to you? I don't fucking get you! What, you want me to be an emotionally abusive drug addict? Is that the perfect man for you, Annie?!"

His words knock the wind out of me.

"You know what you are? You're a fucking spoiled brat," he says, turning around and walking out of the room,

"Grow the fuck up!" he yells back at me. I hear him run down the stairs and slam the front door so hard the house shakes.

I sink into the bed, defeated. I can't even cry. James's words ring loudly in my head, and I start questioning everything. *Am I overreacting? Am I being a spoiled brat?* I soon realize that that's not the point. James MADE this decision without me. He made plans for our lives that I had no say in—it's not fair!

It dawns on me that he's been lying to me this whole time. I've been making plans for our return home while he's been *secretly* making plans for us to move to Paris! I think back to my birthday trip and remember that he met with the Brits while we were there. It breaks my heart to think that the trip was probably a ruse so he could secure his partnership with them. I hate feeling like I can't trust him.

Tears finally break as I look around the room, surveying the explosion of my belongings. I push my suitcase off the bed and throw my clothes on the floor. I cry face down on the comforter until the tears run out.

When I manage to peel myself from the bed, I wander into the bathroom. My eyes are puffy, and my makeup is smeared. I wash my face and brush my teeth—I'm on autopilot. I take off my dress and throw on a T-shirt. I come out of the bathroom, back to ground zero, and get in bed. It's past midnight, and I don't know if or when James will return—and I don't care.

"Annie, Annie…" I open my eyes and barely make out James's silhouette in the dark as he sits on the edge of the bed, looking down at me.

"What?" He startles me. I glance at the clock on the nightstand; it's four-forty a.m.

"I'm sorry…" he says in a whisper. "Can we talk… I'm sorry about tonight…"

"James, it's four in the morning, and you're drunk; this isn't the time to talk."

He sighs and tries again, "I just want to talk for a minute… Please?"

"I don't want to talk right now," I say, turning my back to him. I feel him get up from the bed and go into the bathroom. A few minutes later, he emerges, and I watch him move around the room through the dim light coming in through the window. I watch him undress, and then he gets in bed with me. I close my eyes and turn over again. I can't face him.

He pulls me in close and buries his face in my hair. "I'm sorry," he whispers.

I don't want to fight anymore, so I don't respond and let him hold me.

After a few restless hours of sleep, I get out of bed and from under James's tight grip and realize that my nightmare is real. He's sound asleep and barely stirs. It's gray outside, and now the clock says six a.m.

I walk through the explosion of my clothes scattered around the floor, pick up a pair of jeans and a sweatshirt, and put them on. I can't believe what happened only a few hours ago.

I go downstairs and sit on the front steps of the townhouse to get some air, watching our lovely Chelsea neighborhood come alive on this quiet, drizzly Sunday morning. It's after ten at night in LA, so I call Angela and tell her everything. She comforts me as I cry and reassures me that everything will be fine. She then begs me to come home. I know it's time to leave London, and I tell her I'll book a flight out tomorrow.

"I'm here for you, Annie, we all are!" she says before we hang up.

Even after talking to Angela, I'm still restless and need to clear my head. I can't shake the ugly feelings from last night's fight. I continue questioning everything and start to blame myself for it. Before I spiral further, I throw on a coat, put on my rain boots, and go for a walk. The gray clouds suddenly give way to a light shower, but I keep going. As I walk past the perfectly manicured rows of townhouses with their stately, jet-black iron fences, my thoughts become clearer, and I know what I have to do.

———

JAMES IS SITTING ON THE COUCH WHEN I RETURN. "WHERE have you been?" he asks with worry in his eyes.

"I went for a walk," I shrug. I'm numb and emotionally spent.

"Can I make you breakfast?"

"Okay," I nod.

I head upstairs to get out of my damp clothes and take a hot shower. When I join James in the kitchen, I feel slightly better. He's made eggs, toast, and tea. We sit at the kitchen island just as we always do when we cook at home and try to have a normal breakfast, but it's awkward and far from normal.

"I don't want to fight, but I need to explain everything," he blurts out.

"You explained it perfectly last night, James."

"Then why can't you see that it was meant to be something good for us?"

I don't want to look up at him because I'm on the brink of tears again. I shake my head slowly. "You lied to me."

He touches my hand and pauses for a moment.

"I did, and I'm sorry... I fucked up, I'm sorry. I swear, Annie, I thought it would be an amazing surprise; please try to understand that."

I can't hold back the tears anymore, and they spill over, plopping on the table, barely missing my plate. I wipe them from my cheeks and swallow back the knot in my throat that makes it hard to talk. "I think we want different things," I whisper.

He takes a deep breath and sinks into his seat. After a few seconds of silence, I finally look up at him and see his heart breaking like mine.

"We wanted the same things yesterday," he says.

I shrug and shake my head slowly. "I don't think we have for a while now."

"I know that I want *you…*" he says as his eyes meet mine.

"Then come to LA and forget Paris. Forget the Brits, and let's go home," I plead. I can't hide the desperation in my tone.

He tenses, and his eyes turn cold, "I can't do that," he says without hesitating.

"Why not?"

He's quiet for a moment, "I don't think LA is right for us," he says cryptically.

I look at him, confused and too exhausted to try to understand. "Then we want different things," I say flatly. He takes my hand, raises it to his cheek, and closes his eyes. We're back at square one, and he knows it's true. James shakes his head as he holds my hand to his cheek, and the reality of the situation hits him. I get up from my stool and wrap my arms around him as we shed tears together.

The morning is brutal. After James and I pull ourselves together, we have a serious talk. He doesn't want to go back to LA, apparently *ever again*, and I don't want to go to Paris *at all*. We're at an impasse—a lose-lose situation. James suggests we try the long-distance thing for a while, but it's a reaching thought.

I look down at my engagement ring and remove it from my finger. He shakes his head and pushes my hand away when I try to give it to him.

"No, Annie… It's yours, I want you to have it… You don't

have to wear it. Think about us. Think about me when you're back home; maybe you'll decide to join me in Paris after all." He cracks a smile, hoping to hit me at my weak spot.

It works, and I return his smile. It's a light moment that we both need.

"I'm serious, Annie," he says as his smile fades, "Keep the ring, even if you never want to see me or be with me again. I love you, and I want you to remember that forever."

His words gut me. All that's left is to accept that we've reached the end of our relationship.

We're both emotionally drained, but we agree to spend one last night in London together. As the realization that we're over sinks in, it takes every bit of strength in me not to fall apart.

James leaves the house after our talk because he says he can't stand being here while I start to pack. "I'll be back to pick you up at eight for dinner," he says, kissing me on the forehead before leaving me alone in the kitchen.

Chapter Sixty-Six

"Miss, we'll be departing in a few minutes. Can you please put on your seatbelt?"

I'm lost in thought as I look out the window at the foggy tarmac at Heathrow Airport. I'm barely functioning after the most emotional and intense twenty-four hours of my life. I look up at the stewardess. Her kind face and bright eyes patiently wait for me to follow her instructions.

"Oh, sure," I say, snapping out of my haze to fasten my seatbelt. She must've noticed that I'm going through something because she offers to bring me a drink and I gratefully accept.

A man's voice in a British accent comes through the intercom, "*Thank you for your patience and apologies for the delay. We've been cleared for takeoff, and we'll be on our way to Los Angeles shortly. Sit back and relax, and thank you for flying with us this evening.*"

I sink into the plush leather seat, closing my eyes. James's face flashes through my mind. I can't stop thinking about him or last night.

Our final night together was incredible. James picked me up at eight, just as he said he would. We dressed up, and I had butterflies as if it were our first date. We went to a lovely little restaurant in Primrose Hill for a candlelit dinner, where we laughed and talked, avoiding any stressful topics.

After dinner, we had drinks at a rooftop bar on Boundary Street. By the time we got home, we were tipsy and all over each other. We made out as soon as we walked in and barely paused as we made our way to the bedroom. We made love and held each other all night, barely sleeping.

In the morning, we talked and shed tears in each other's arms until the last possible moment. I refused to let him take me to the airport and asked him to leave before I had to go. I was trying to make the goodbye less painful. When it happened, it was a blur. We hugged at the door, and he gave me one last kiss. "I love you, Annie," he said. That's all I remember.

"Here you go," the stewardess returns. Her voice pulls me out of my thoughts again as she hands me a glass of champagne.

"Thank you," I say, forcing a smile.

The plane suddenly starts to move as it taxis from the gate, making its way to the runway, which feels endless. It finally stops, and the pilot's voice comes through the intercom, "*Clear for takeoff,*" he says.

Within seconds, the plane accelerates, bumping, jolting, and speeding at full throttle until we're finally airborne. As it climbs higher and higher in the sky, I look out the window at the grayness of London below one last time.

Chapter Sixty-Seven

Stepping through the sliding glass doors at LAX into the dry Los Angeles evening feels like a rebirth. I take a deep breath and savor the non-pressurized air. It feels delicious despite the faint smell of cigarette smoke and the trace of lingering rush-hour smog. It's been almost twelve hours since I left London, and surprisingly, it already feels like a distant memory.

Angela's Range Rover pulls up to the curb, and I smile, my heart swelling with genuine joy. She grins ear to ear as she jumps out of the car and runs to give me the tightest, warmest hug ever.

"Ah!! I'm so happy you're here!!" she says, looking at me closely, cupping my face with her hands. A security guard walks by and gives us a menacing look.

"Pick up and loading only. Let's keep it moving!" he says loudly, waving his hands and motioning for us to hurry. We giggle and quickly put my luggage into the trunk of her car.

"Is that all your stuff?" Angela asks as we pull out from the curb and into thick airport traffic.

"Yeah, I'm shipping the rest," I say, momentarily remembering another snippet from my last conversation with James when I reminded him that FedEx would pick up the rest of my boxed-up belongings tomorrow.

Angela puts her hand on my knee and gives me a concerned look, "How are you feeling?"

I shrug and tell her I'm fine. I don't want to talk about London or James or my feelings. I just want to enjoy being back home on this beautiful spring evening; otherwise, I'll break.

Angela reads me loud and clear and doesn't ask any more questions. As we head west, the sunset paints the sky with streaks of pink, orange, and violet pastel clouds. I roll down my window and admire the beautiful sight, which I'm sure only exists in the skies above Los Angeles. I put my hand out the window and feel the air cutting through my fingers, relishing the familiar feeling of home.

I can barely contain my excitement as we pull up to our childhood home. I bounce out of the car, hurry toward the back door, and enter through the kitchen. I find my parents at the kitchen island, and they look up as I swing open the door.

"Annie!" they greet me as I rush toward them. I hug my mom, and when I hug my dad, I break down in tears.

"It's okay, sweetheart. You're home now. Everything's going to be fine." He tries to look me in the eye, but I can't bear to look at him. I'm unable to articulate that, despite all the pain I'm feeling, I'm also crying tears of joy.

"I missed you guys so much," I say.

My parents hug me again, overcome with emotion. "We missed you, too, Annie," my mom says, wiping tears from my cheeks.

I've finally reached the end of an exhausting and emotionally draining journey, and the moment is overwhelming. "We are celebrating tonight!" my dad says, "So, no more tears!"

I smile, taking a deep breath to compose myself.

"How about we pop this open?" he grins, pulling out a bottle of Dom Pérignon from the wine fridge.

I look around the kitchen and notice a beautiful flower arrangement on the table, a bouquet of colorful balloons, and a big sign that says: "Welcome Home, Annie!!"

"This is great, guys. Thank you," I say, smiling at the decorations.

Max enters the kitchen, "Oh, fuck! Did I miss the big *welcome home* part?!" He approaches me with open arms for a hug.

"Yes, but you sure have perfect timing for champagne," Angela teases him.

"Welcome home, sis," Max says, hugging me tightly and planting a kiss on my head. My mom hands out champagne flutes, and my dad pours us each a glass.

"What do you know…" my dad says, "We're finally together under one roof again, just as it should be!" We hold our glasses up to toast, and he continues, "To our beautiful family and to finally being whole again!"

"Here, here!" We respond in unison, clinking our glasses to toast.

As I enjoy a delicious dinner, talking and laughing with my family by the pool on this perfect night, I flashback to the horrible fight James and I had two nights ago.

"You want to go back to fucking Los Angeles to hang around your parents' pool with the same fucking people and go to the same fucking places you've been going to since high school…?"

I can't believe he was so cruel. Reflecting on it now, with a clear head and a lot of distance between us, I'm sure I made the right decision.

"Darren's on his way," Angela says, looking up from her phone.

"Oh, good. I hope he's hungry," my mom says, because, per usual, they've overdone it with the food.

Within fifteen minutes, Darren arrives, and I jump up from my seat to greet him with a hug. "Welcome home, Annie!" he says with a tight embrace.

"I missed you so much, D!" I reply, squeezing him back.

After dinner and a long catch-up, my parents head to bed, and Angela, Max, Darren, and I hang out by the pool and smoke a joint. Max looks at his phone and tells us Michelle is stuck at work, prepping to style a new client for an event, and won't be *home* until later.

To my surprise, she recently moved into the pool house with him, and I couldn't be happier for them.

I lean back in the lounge chair, staring into the hazy night sky. I soak in the moment, surrounded once again by the most important people in my life.

"So, where's Joe tonight?" I ask, noticing his absence. I wait for their response, but they exchange glances without answering.

"What...?" I say, sitting up, questioning their silence.

"You haven't told her yet?" Max says, looking at Angela.

"Tell me what?" I ask.

"Um, Annie..." Angela says, moving to sit with me on the edge of my lounge chair.

"Did something happen?" I'm alarmed by her tone and the suspicious way they're acting. My heart beats faster as I look at Max and Darren, who are now sitting across from us on the other lounge chair—their somber expressions concern me.

"Listen..." Angela continues in her serious voice that annoys me, "Yes, something happened, but he's fine..." I brace myself for what she's about to say. "Joe was in a car accident about a month ago. He was driving, wasted from a party, and crashed into a tree on Doheny."

"What?!" Her words stun me.

"He's *fine*," she stresses, grabbing my hand and looking me in the eye.

"A car accident?!" I shake my head, trying to process her words.

"He's lucky to be alive," Max chimes in, "It was pretty serious, he fucked up his hand… broke a couple of ribs…"

"It was legit a miracle…" Darren adds, "He was at the hospital for a few days, and now… he's in rehab… that's all that matters."

"A month ago?! Why didn't anyone tell me?!" My voice escalates as shock turns into anger.

"Let me finish…" Angela continues as she motions for me to calm down. "When we saw him at the hospital, he begged us not to tell you. He made us all promise that we wouldn't say anything." Her voice softens as she drops her gaze, "He didn't want you to worry or cause you any problems with James."

My stomach sinks as the gravity of the news hits me. I struggle to catch my breath as my heart continues to pound.

"Annie," Angela pleads, "I'm sorry we didn't tell you, but we also didn't want you to worry or freak out!" She goes quiet again as I break into tears, sinking back into the lounge chair.

Angela wraps an arm around me, and Max goes into the pool house, returning with a box of tissues. Darren sits beside me, rubbing my arm to comfort me.

"He's fine, Annie. I swear," he says.

"You guys have to tell me everything right now," I demand, reaching for the tissues to dry my tears.

Darren obliges and continues, "He was wasted. We lost him after the night of the Platinum Record ceremony. He was partying non-stop. He went back on the road with Trent for the final shows of the tour; then he came home. He was here for about a week when it happened."

He pauses, gauging my reaction, and I tell him to continue.

"The night of the accident, he was partying… he was, you know, doing the usual… The cops found coke and pills in his pockets after the crash. He'll probably get off on probation and a fine, but right now, he's at mandatory rehab, at some fancy facility in Utah. He's going to be there for another month."

I shake my head, numb. Max was right—my news the night of the ceremony probably affected him, and now I feel so guilty and responsible for what happened.

Angela squeezes my hand, "What's important is that he's alive and getting the help he's needed for so long. Sometimes bad things happen so that things can get better." Her words comfort me slightly, helping me to calm down.

"Yeah, Annie," Max says, "What happened was awful, but we have to focus on the positive and just help him through it when he gets back."

"What about the intervention?" I ask, looking at him.

"We tried. He knew it was coming. He avoided us like the plague. Refused to come around or hang out. We didn't even see him when he got back from the tour. He was getting way out of control when this happened. We have to look at this as a blessing in disguise."

I take a deep breath; the tears have finally stopped. "Have you guys seen him or talked to him?"

They shake their heads. "Not since the hospital," Angela says, "The doctors at the facility don't want him to have any distractions right now. He can only see or talk to his parents, but they say he's doing well."

I don't know what else to say. Within the last forty-eight hours, I broke my engagement, flew intercontinental for half a day, and now I'm finding out that my best friend and the other man I've ever loved almost died and is in rehab… in another state! It's all too much to bear.

"I need a sleeping pill or something to knock me out," I

say out loud to no one in particular. I'm emotionally spent and desperate for the night to be over.

"I got you," Max says, going back into the pool house and returning with a pill.

Angela stands up and extends her hand to me. "Let's get you some water, and I'll walk you to bed," she says.

Chapter Sixty-Eight

The next few weeks are a rollercoaster. I'm happy to be home and to my old life, but I'm still mourning the end of my relationship with James and still processing the news that Joe is back in rehab. My emotions are everywhere, and my anxiety is through the roof. Nevertheless, I push through.

I'm at Three-Two-Three every day, which is a welcome distraction, but the nights are lonely and hard. I retreat and become anti-social, which sucks because I wanted to be back in LA with my friends and family so bad when I was in London.

I think about James all the time, and on particularly emotional and lonely nights, I wonder if I made a mistake. I still can't believe that instead of celebrating our one-year anniversary, we were breaking up and ending our engagement.

Surprisingly, we maintain some communication, texting here and there. We both try to get over our breakup by ironically staying in touch. Sometimes, just hearing his voice is enough, and I know it's the same for him, so I answer whenever he calls.

During one of our calls, James mentioned that he had moved out of the townhouse and into a suite at Claridge's. He said he couldn't bear to stay at the townhouse by himself. I know what he meant because when he suggested that I continue living at his house while he's in London, there was no way I could do it. I couldn't be in the house we lived in for almost a year without him. There are too many memories there, and it would be torture.

As the weeks go on, James and I talk less and less. It's too hard to continue, and we both know it's for the best to end all contact. On our final call, he shared that he's going on holiday in the South of France, and I know it's only a matter of time before he's with someone new. I'm okay with it because it alleviates the guilt I've been carrying over ending our relationship, even though I know we both played a part in its demise.

On a positive note, and thanks to serendipitous timing, Max is moving out of the pool house, which means I can move in. Living at my parents' house in my childhood bedroom after everything I've been through is humbling and depressing. Even though the pool house is still technically *home*, having my own separate space is exciting and exactly what I need to help me get back on my feet while I figure out what the fuck I'm going to do with my life.

THE DAY OF THE MOVE FINALLY ARRIVES, AND I STAY BACK AT the pool house, overseeing all of the action while Max and Michelle set up their new home—a condo Max purchased in the Sierra Towers—the same building where Darren and Joe also live.

The movers are fast and efficient, and after they clear out the last of Max's belongings, I'm left alone in the empty pool house. I walk through the vacant space feeling genuinely happy for the first time in weeks. It feels like a new chapter of my life is beginning, and I can't wait for what happens next. I smile ear to ear, imagining a complete remodel, and fantasize about what it will be like to have the pool house all to myself. Once I have my fill of daydreaming, I head to Max's new place to help him and Michelle unpack.

Max's condo is breathtaking. He has a corner unit on the thirty-fifth floor with sweeping views of the city, the mountains, and the ocean. It's a two-bedroom with high ceilings and abundant natural light. The place is bigger than Joe's and Darren's and perfect for him and Michelle.

I arrive to a lot of activity. Delivery people come in and out with furniture and boxes while technicians set up Max's recording equipment and other electronics. Michelle and I aren't much help, so we sprawl out on the floor of the gorgeous, sun-drenched living room, talking and browsing decorating magazines. Max paces around, taking phone calls and directing the delivery people.

The doorbell rings, and Max greets whoever has arrived enthusiastically. Michelle and I can't see who it is, but as the voice at the door gets clearer, I freeze, realizing it's Joe. Michelle glances at me, wide-eyed, just as shocked. I didn't know he was back from rehab.

"Bro, this place is sick!" Joe's voice booms as he walks into the living room with Max close behind. He stops in his tracks when his eyes land on me.

Michelle jumps up from the floor, excited to greet him. "Joe! You're home!" she exclaims with open arms. "When did you get back?"

I need a minute to catch my breath—the butterflies in my stomach appear out of nowhere.

I get up from the floor and stare at Joe as he greets Michelle with a hug. "Like an hour ago," he responds.

I'm relieved that he looks healthy and happy. I notice that his left hand is bandaged and remember the story of the car accident. He lets go of Michelle and turns to me. I'm speech-less. His blue eyes are clear and bright as they meet mine.

"Hi, Ace," he says.

"Hi, Joe," I respond.

He steps forward to hug me, and I close my eyes as we embrace. His arms warmly envelop me, and I take in his familiar scent, which can only be his pheromones, immediately clicking with something inside me. We release each other, and I notice Max and Michelle staring at us.

"Babe, can you help me with something in the kitchen?" Max says to Michelle, leaving Joe and me alone in the living room.

"I wasn't expecting to see you here," Joe says with surprise in his eyes.

"Yeah, I wasn't expecting to see you either."

"I'm sure you heard…" he says, cracking an uncomfortable smile and lifting his bandaged hand.

I nod. "Yes, how are you?"

"Better…" he says, "I'm a lot better. My hand is still fucked up, but it'll be fine." He looks down at it. "What about you? Are you visiting…?"

It dawns on me that he doesn't know I broke up with James. "No, I'm back now," I say, holding up my hand to show him the ring is gone. It's too painful to say the words out loud.

"Oh," he says as it registers. "I'm sorry, I didn't know…"

"Yeah, it's a long story… Everything's fine, though. I'm just glad to be home." He has no idea that everything has *not* been fine, but I do my best to seem cheerful and unaffected. We hold each other's gaze, and he smiles.

"Yeah, I'm glad to be home too."

The last of Max's furniture is delivered, and the technicians wrap up their job. The condo fills with crimson and gold light pouring through the massive windows as the sun begins to set. Max, Michelle, Joe, and I sit around the kitchen island, catching up while we wait for dinner to arrive.

Joe shares stories about rehab and Utah, turning a dark situation into a laughing matter with his usual wit. I watch him closely, relieved that the Joe I've known and loved since childhood has returned. He's sharper and funnier than ever, and his warm demeanor brightens the room more than the sun. I'm happy and grateful we didn't lose him—the thought is unbearable.

Darren and Angela finally arrive with takeout from Nobu. Joe wanted to surprise them, and they're shocked to find him here. Darren chokes up as he hugs Joe, making me misty-eyed. The mood is joyous and loving, and we have so much to celebrate.

"Um, I'd like to make a toast," Max says as we gather around the kitchen island to eat. We give him our attention as he stands up, raising his glass of water and looking at each of us.

"I want to thank you guys for being here at our new place..." He glances at Michelle and smiles. "We had a good run at the pool house, but I'm passing the baton to Annie now, and I'm sure she will not disappoint us as the new mistress of the manor..."

We laugh, and he continues, "And, um, this is also a special night because our man Joe is back!" He looks at Joe, and his voice cracks, "Brother, welcome home. We missed you and are so glad to have you back with us again." Joe nods, for once speechless.

"Annie, you too. It wasn't the same without you, sis," Max continues, turning to me. He clears his throat. "And, in the words of the wise Dr. Preston, who said the other day..." He pauses and smiles, "Here's to finally being together under one roof, as it should be. To our beautiful family and to finally being whole again."

We all raise our glasses, "Hear, hear!" Toasting to our reunion.

Epilogue

As soon as Max moved out, I started remodeling the pool house, and with Aunt Gia's help, the place turned out even more beautiful than I imagined. It got a fresh coat of paint, new appliances, fixtures, and furniture, and when it was done, it looked lighter and more spacious than Max's dark bachelor pad.

After moving in, I felt more stable, and my life slowly returned to normal. I felt like myself again—running Three-Two-Three with Angela and finally enjoying a social life.

Joe and I started spending more time together, too. Since getting out of rehab, his focus was back on music, producing an album for a hot new artist and supporting Max and Darren from the sidelines on Trent's third album. Joe spent long hours at the studio, and when he wasn't working, he was usually with me. We leaned on each other, trying to figure out how to start over after our lives separately fell apart in the spring.

It's hard to describe what our relationship became because it wasn't romantic or sexual. Neither of us wanted to *go there* out of fear that we'd ruin our friendship, which was top priority after we practically destroyed it.

From time to time, Joe dated random girls, and I went

on a few dates myself after much convincing from Angela and my cousin Matt. Nothing good came out of my dating life, and apparently, Joe's dating life wasn't any better, as we often ended up at Max's or Darren's condos with the crew, playing video games or watching movies at the end of the night.

However, everything changed at the end of the summer, right before Labor Day Weekend, when James came back into my life. He returned to LA to sell his house before moving to Paris permanently. We hadn't seen each other in almost five months, and it didn't take long to be under his spell again.

James and I spent an exhilarating two weeks of fun-filled days and passionate nights. We were back to reliving our lusty past—incredible sex and all. It felt *so good* to be back on his arm and in his bed again. Even though so much happened between us, it felt like nothing had changed.

James mentioned Paris almost every day and tried to convince me to move with him, but I always turned him down. He even offered to break the Paris contract with the Brits and stay in LA if I gave him another chance.

"I won't go to Paris, and I won't sell the house if you say yes," he said. I considered it, but I couldn't let him give up his dream, and I couldn't imagine leaving LA again. So, I told him that if we were meant to be, life would find a way to bring us back together.

The Following Summer...

THERE'S A KNOCK AT THE DOOR, AND I HEAR MY DAD'S VOICE, "Are you ready, sweetheart?"

I take a deep breath as Michelle secures the last bobby pin to the veil in my hair. "There, it's perfect," she says with a proud smile.

"Thank you," I say, hugging her. I look over at Angela as she hurries to get the door.

"Yes, we're ready, Dad!" she says.

I look at myself in the mirror again and can't believe I'm about to get married. I take in my reflection, admiring the ethereal yet chic Valentino wedding dress of my dreams and the slight roundness of my expanding baby bump poking out.

"You look beautiful," my dad says as he stands in the doorway, misty-eyed.

"Pull it together, Dad," Angela says, playfully slapping his arm. I turn to face him and almost fall apart, overcome with emotion. "You too, Annie," Angela says, giving me a disapproving look. "Your makeup is perfect! Don't ruin it!"

I swallow back tears and look down. "Are you sure I look okay?" I cup my belly, suddenly self-conscious.

"You look perfect," my dad says, wrapping me in a delicate embrace. Angela falls silent, teary-eyed and nodding in agreement.

"It's showtime!" A warm voice breaks the silence, and I look up to see Carlos, my wedding coordinator, beaming in the doorway. "Oh, my *Gawd*," he says with his signature dramatic flair, which I've come to love. "You are a vision!" he exclaims, wide-eyed and mouth agape. "Stunning!" He flails his hands in the air.

We laugh, and I'm glad he showed up before the tears could break.

"So, are we ready?!" he asks, turning serious.

I nod. Then he turns to Angela and Michelle and instructs them on how to pace their walk down the aisle. He then takes my dad's arm and shows him how to hold it out for me.

"Okay, let's do this, honey! There is a *very* handsome man waiting for you at the end of that aisle," he says, giving me a wink.

My stomach flutters, and I can't tell if it's butterflies or the baby kicking. I'm five months pregnant and can attest that both feel about the same.

Carlos leads the way from my bridal bungalow through the pristine lawns of The Beverly Hills Hotel down a lush, tree-lined path to the Polo Garden. We reach the end of the path, which opens into the garden just past a canopy of palm and magnolia trees. Carlos positions Michelle first, then Angela behind her. They both look back at me, smiling in nervous anticipation as we wait for him to give us the signal.

"You both look beautiful," I say, finally finding my voice to admire my sister and Michelle, who's newly engaged to Max. They look radiant and chic in the slinky, dusty pink dresses we picked out together. I hold on to my dad's arm and exhale loudly.

"You, alright?" He narrows his eyes on me. I nod, meeting his gaze. "I love you, Annie. Your mother and I are so happy and excited for this new chapter of your life," he says, placing a delicate kiss on my forehead. I nod again, afraid that speaking will lead to tears.

The string quartet starts playing, signaling that it's *go time*. Carlos looks at us and gives Michelle the nod to walk. She disappears through the canopy of trees, and Angela follows after he gives her the same cue. Carlos holds my father and me back a few beats, then gives me a wink, "Go get 'em," he says, gently nudging us toward the aisle.

What follows happens in blurry, slow motion. I'm surrounded by my family and closest friends, but the only person I focus on is him. Smiling big, standing tall and proud, and so handsome at the end of the aisle. His blue eyes brighter than ever. My first love, my best friend, and the father of the baby boy kicking wildly in my belly.

I float down the aisle, happiness in my sails. When I reach him, our eyes lock, and I know that this is the moment I've been waiting for since we first met as kids.

My father kisses me on the cheek and gives Joe a firm hug.

A warm July breeze rustles through the trees, carrying the sweet scent of jasmine and roses through the garden.

The officiant begins the ceremony as our guests take their seats. I hand Angela my bouquet of dusty pink peonies and ivory teacup roses, and then Joe holds my hands, and we look into each other's eyes the entire time.

When we take our vows, we pledge our love for each other and the baby we're bringing into the world. The exchanging of the rings happens in a blur, but the last moment is crystal clear.

"By the power of God and the great state of California, I now pronounce you husband and wife. You may kiss the bride!" The officiant says as our friends and family clap and cheer.

I cup Joe's face with my hands, and he pulls me in tight. His arms wrap around me, and my belly presses into him as we kiss.

We're lost in the moment, the cheers, and the love surrounding us. When we pull apart, I finally come back to earth. I see my mom and dad dabbing their eyes in the first row. Joe's parents are also shedding tears of joy. Everyone's here—Matt, Daniel, Aunt Gia, Aaron, Trent, and all our friends, beaming. I finally notice Max and Darren, clapping and smiling wide in their dapper suits, proudly standing behind Joe, sharing best man duties. I take a deep breath and take in every detail of this moment, hoping I'll never forget it.

After the beautiful ceremony, our party moves into the Rodeo Room of the hotel for a magical night of eating, dancing, and celebrating. Not only is this the happiest night of my life for obvious reasons, but I'm also relieved to be free from the morning sickness and exhaustion that plagued the first trimester of my pregnancy. I'm relaxed and on cloud nine, enjoying every minute of the festivities—mingling and laughing with all our guests and savoring the first glimpses of married life.

The party continues for hours, with Max taking on DJ duties for a fun dance party to close the night as everyone lets loose and has a blast.

"Alright, alright…" Max says into the microphone as he slowly fades the volume on the upbeat song he's playing. "The newlyweds have requested this absolute *classic jam* as the last song of the night, and they'd like to invite everyone to join them on the dance floor. So, let's *do this!*"

I giggle at Max's perfect delivery as Joe takes my hand, leading me to the dance floor. Sade's "By Your Side" fades in as Joe takes me in his arms, slow dancing to the beautiful ballad. I rest my head on his shoulder, savoring the moment and imprinting the core memory into my mind forever. We're joined by all the people we love on the dance floor, and I can't help but think back to all the things Joe and I went through and overcame to bring us to this moment.

When we found ourselves back in LA last spring, we fought the impulse to get back together for fear of destroying our friendship again. That only lasted a few months—our reconciliation was inevitable. Our love for each other was stronger, no matter who or what got in our way.

I think of James for a split second and recall the incident last summer that finally severed our connection. *We weren't meant to be.*

I look up, meeting Joe's eyes as we sway to the music. He mouths a few lyrics, singing to me. I smile and pull him close, flashing back to the group trip we took to Cabo San Lucas earlier this year to celebrate Trent's first Grammy win and how I carelessly forgot my birth control pills, which led to the shocking realization a few weeks later that I was pregnant.

Joe and I always knew we'd get married—we talked about it since we were teenagers in the throes of first love. We knew we'd have a family someday but never imagined it would be like this. But it doesn't matter; we wouldn't have it any other way. It's life or destiny or whatever you want to call it. It's our own love story—our own little LA love story.

About the Author

L.M. Skye fell in love with books at a young age, which sparked her passion for writing. This love for storytelling eventually led her to write emotionally gripping stories that explore themes of love, loss, and friendship.

When she's not writing, Skye enjoys immersing herself in art, catching live music shows, and traveling to new places. After living in Los Angeles and New York City for over a decade, she now resides in Northern California.

FALLING: An LA Love Story is her debut novel.

Thank you for reading! If you enjoyed this story, please consider leaving a review on your favorite platform.

instagram.com/l.m.skye_author

pinterest.com/fallinglalovestory

Immerse yourself in the world of

Falling

An LA Love Story

Curated Playlists on Spotify

Inspirational Images on Pinterest

Let's Connect on Instagram

www.fallinglalovestory.com

If you or someone you know is struggling with drug or alcohol addiction, help is available. Below are a few resources where you can find support and information:

- **Substance Abuse and Mental Health Services Administration (SAMHSA)**
- National Helpline: 1-800-662-HELP (4357)
- Website: www.samhsa.gov
- A free, confidential 24/7 helpline providing treatment referrals and information for drug and alcohol addiction.
- **National Institute on Drug Abuse (NIDA)**
- Website: www.drugabuse.gov
- Offers research-based information and resources on both drug and alcohol addiction.